About the Author

Patrick started his working career as a cabinet maker and spent many successful years working on high-end projects including the restoration at Windsor Castle following the fire there in the early nineties.

He had his own business for several years designing and making one-off pieces of furniture and, having now left the trade, he uses his creative talents writing. He currently lives in Suffolk with his wife Rachel and their Miniature Schnauzer, Ralphie.

Swallowed by the Sea

P. H. Spurgeon

Swallowed by the Sea

Olympia Publishers
London

www.olympiapublishers.com

OLYMPIA PAPERBACK EDITION

A CIP catalogue record for this title is
available from the British Library.

ISBN: 978-1-78830-855-7

First Published in 2021

Olympia Publishers
Tallis House
2 Tallis Street
London
EC4Y 0AB

Printed in Great Britain

Dedication

To my beloved wife Rachel. My rock and soulmate.

Acknowledgements

During the writing of this book, I have talked to quite a few people 'off the record' as it were, about various subject matters. For those of you concerned: if you recognise anything in the book from one of those conversations, thank you. I would also like to thank my wife, Rachel, who has supported me fully in this venture and has provided me with a sounding board to bounce ideas off when my brain turns to treacle.

Finally, I would like to thank Tim Berners-Lee, whose little invention called the Internet, has made writing a book such as this so much easier.

1

It was five thirty in the evening when Jim Jackson finally escaped the confines of his office and made his way into the moonlit half-light of a winter's evening in Suffolk. Although it was mid-December, the weather had been unseasonably warm and with a scarf wrapped around his neck and his trench coat flapping lightly as he walked, he headed towards the centre of town to do some late-night Christmas shopping.

Jim, James, or JJ were just three of the titles given to him over the years and being an easy-going sort of guy, he didn't really care what people called him as long as it was polite and NOT Jimbo.

Jimbo he hated. It made him sound like the James Garner character in the 70s American TV show *The Rockford Files,* a situation that wasn't helped by his occupation, which involved investigating possible fraudulent insurance claims.

He had worked in the insurance business since leaving school and, following many years in general household insurance in a similar role, he was persuaded by a friend to move into the marine market.

That was six years ago and following several successful cases in which many hundreds of thousands of pounds had been recovered, Jim was now head of the Moore's & Thackeray Marine Fraud Investigation department (MFI) or Flatpack as his colleagues liked to call it, in reference to the now defunct DIY furniture manufacturer.

His office was in a converted grain store on Neptune Quay in Ipswich and the success of this first conversion from derelict building to swanky offices had started the ball rolling on the old dock front.

A second suite of offices was just about to come 'online' and with a seafood restaurant and bar already opened a little further along the quay, the area was quickly becoming a very pleasant part of town in which to work and socialise, but to Jim's dismay this was about to change.

Next to Moore's & Thackeray's offices was the old Custom House, and just beyond that were several storage sheds, maltings and flourmills all of which were now pretty much unused and just ripe for the redevelopers' magic wand.

The plans for this project had already been submitted and included more offices, restaurants, bars and hundreds of new apartments, from which the new tenants could gawk at their swanky boats in the new marina below.

Jim was not impressed. He had spent years working his way up the insurance ladder to a point where he had a nice office, with a pleasant outlook and a good income and it seemed to him that if the developers had their way, in a few months' time he would be working in the middle of the biggest building sites in Ipswich.

'Progress' he thought 'thanks a bunch.'

As he walked along the waterfront the small waves in the dock lapped gently against the brick wall of the quay. He glanced at his reflection in the dock and gave himself a metaphoric pat on the back. Not bad for a forty-something he thought as he turned up Wherry Lane towards Fore Street and the town centre.

The old cobbles in the lane were slightly slippery under his feet and it was only now that Jim recognised a slight dampness in the air. He tied the belt on his coat and continued up the narrow old lane with its old timber-framed buildings reaching over towards each other as if in some sort of long-standing embrace, towards Sunshine Corner.

Sunshine Corner does not appear on any map of Ipswich either as part of the legend or as a locally recognised feature. It was so named by Jim, following a very dark period in his life and only a handful of other people in Ipswich knew it by that name.

He and his wife Catherine had met at a party on board the *Shannon,* an old Thames sailing barge two years earlier which offered evening trips down the River Orwell.

These old vessels, many of which were built in the local shipyards, were the lifeblood of not only the River Thames but also many other small ports up and down the east coast. Although most were quite large, carrying anything up to 250 tons of cargo they were surprisingly easy to sail and would very often have a crew of only two. The crew of the *Shannon* stretched to nine, four to sail the barge and the remainder to keep the guests well fed and watered.

At the time he had only recently joined Moore's & Thackeray and the invitation had come via his manager, Nigel, who thought this corporate get-together would be a useful place to network with people within the industry. Jim wasn't so sure he wanted to spend the evening trapped on a boat, talking to people about a business that he had only just joined, but knew that he wouldn't get many brownie points from his new boss if he turned the invitation down.

As was his way, Jim arrived five minutes early and was standing with his back leant against the Old Custom House, enjoying the ambience of the night and trying to imagine how the dock would have looked in years gone by when Ipswich was a thriving east coast port. His thoughts were broken when a bright yellow Mazda MX-5 rolled up beside him. Feeling like he was in the wrong place at the wrong time, he moved along the quay slightly and then turned back to see who was driving the little sports car.

The decision to move away was a good one, because as he turned, he was greeted with a beautifully formed denim backside, the owner of which was bending over to retrieve her cardigan from the passenger seat. As she extricated herself fully from the car and turned towards the barge, she smiled at Jim and asked if he was going on the cruise.

'Yes,' he said, 'I'm just waiting for a colleague; he shouldn't be long.'

'Don't miss the boat,' she said and gave him a knowing sort of smile before heading for the gangplank.

Jim watched as she boarded the barge. With her dark shoulder-length hair and slim body clad in those tight jeans and a white T-shirt that overemphasised her small but perfectly formed breasts, she made quite an impact and he had to concede that suddenly an evening trip down the river seemed a great deal more appetising.

'That's Catherine Taylor,' said Nigel from over Jim's shoulder. 'She works for Anglian Shipping, in Felixstowe, something to do with disbursements I think.'

'What are disbursements?' asked Jim.

'Disbursements are the costs that a ship incurs when it's in port. Could be pilot fees, mooring charges, agency fees *et cetera et cetera et cetera,* Catherine's job is to make sure they all get paid, I'll introduce you later if you like.'

'Thanks, I'll look forward to that.'

As they walked towards the barge Jim pointed to the huge fin-like appendage running down its side.

'What are they?' he asked Nigel, somehow sensing that he knew more about these old vessels than he did.

'They're called leeboards,' said Nigel, 'and they serve several purposes. Because the barge has a flat bottom and can operate in only six feet of water, they tend to be lacking in the old directional stability department, especially when empty. The leeboards, there's one on the other side as well, act as a keel. They usually only use one at a time, the one on the leeward side of the barge, hence leeboard. They also help when tacking, helping the boat to pivot quickly and because they extend below the hull, they give the crew an early warning of shallow water.'

Jim was mildly surprised by Nigel's knowledge, as a director of a company that dealt with shipping insurance it was to be expected that he would have some knowledge of things nautical, but Jim had already realised that this went far deeper.

'See the sails?' he continued. 'Ever wondered why they are that brown colour when all other sailing vessels of the period had white sails?'

'I thought it was just a different material they used.'

'No, it's down to the "dressing". To make the sail more efficient and to prolong its life they used to "dress" the sail with a mixture of fish oil and horse urine. Trouble was this made the sail a dirty grey colour, so to get over this, they would add a little red ochre to the mixture.'

'Horse urine and fish oil, I bet that smelt good.'

'Horse urine wasn't always available in large enough quantities so they often watered it down with sea water, which probably helped lessen the smell as well.'

'You seem to know a lot about these old barges,' said Jim as they went on board.

'It's a family interest, my grandfather used to own five barges that worked the Thames up until the early sixties. They used to come up here occasionally and when they did, we would have a family get-together on board, so it's sort of in my blood.'

'What happened to your grandfather's barges, are they still sailing?'

'One, *The Oyster* has been converted into a houseboat and is moored up at Pin Mill just down the river from here and the other three are rotting away in creeks near Malden in Essex.'

'Wait a minute,' said Jim, 'that only makes four, what about the fifth one?'

'Oh, she's still sailing, or at least she will be in about twenty minutes once we get through the dock gates and onto the open river.'

'You mean…?'

'Yep. *The Shannon* was once owned by my grandfather.'

'That's fantastic, is she still owned by your family?'

'No afraid not, but we do keep in very close contact with the present, Nick Edwards, that's him over there, with the checked shirt, coiling the rope. Come on, I'll introduce you.'

Nick Edwards was a huge bear of a man with a big shaggy dark beard and wild, shoulder-length hair. As Jim and Nigel approached, he finished coiling his rope and turned around right into their path.

'Nigel!' he roared. 'So pleased you could make it, how

the hell are you?'

'Very well, yourself?'

'Never been better, took a bit of a beating last week though, did you see it?'

'No afraid not my friend, I must have been out, who was it this time?'

'Wild Wally again, still it pays the bills.'

Nigel turned to Jim.

'Nick. this is Jim. he has just joined Moore's & Thackeray as part of the fraud team, so you two could be working together before too long.'

'A pleasure,' said Nick and reached out a huge hand for Jim to shake.

He took the big man's hand and was relieved that the handshake was nowhere as hard as it either could have been, or should have been for that matter.

At just over six feet tall, Jim seldom had to look up to anyone, but Nick was in a different league. Standing at least six feet six inches tall and tipping the scales at what Jim estimated must be eighteen stones plus, Nick was not the sort of chap you would want to meet in a dark alley late at night.

'How does she look?' asked Nick

'Fantastic,' enthused Nigel, 'you've had the paintbrush out again by the looks of things?'

'Thought I'd better, seeing as your party was coming on board this week. Why don't you show Jim here around, while I get us underway?'

'Good idea,' said Nigel and led the way towards what was the hold area of the barge from which most of the noise now seemed to be emanating. The entrance was down a steep set of wooden stairs, at the bottom of which was a large room set out with tables and chairs.

'This was originally the cargo hold,' said Nigel, 'I can remember when this was filled with grain or animal feed, but when Nick converted it for cruising, he created this bar and seating area, did a pretty good job I reckon. Fancy a drink?'

Nigel moved down the length of the hold greeting people as he went.

'What's your poison?' he asked Jim as they reached the bar.

'Have they got any Irish whiskey?'

'Should have, two Irish whiskeys, please?' he said to the young girl behind the bar.

'Would you like to take a seat?' she said pointing at an empty table, 'I'll bring your drinks straight over.'

'Thank you very much,' said Nigel and moved across to a small round table surrounded by four chairs.

'This is very nice,' said Jim

'You wait till we get under way, then you really will be impressed. When this baby starts moving it's like being on board a living breathing creature.'

At that moment, Catherine Taylor snuck up behind Nigel, threw her arms around his neck and gave him a peck on the cheek, before ruffling his hair and retiring three feet out of harm's way.

'Let me guess,' he said thoughtfully without turning around, 'Catherine I presume?'

'How did you guess?' she said as she moved swiftly around the table to the chair opposite Nigel.

'Just a hunch,' said Nigel as he smiled at Catherine, whilst straightening his hair and then gently kicking her with the side of his foot under the table.

'So, aren't you going to introduce us?' she said ignoring Nigel's kick.

'Oh, the young are so fickle,' said Nigel. 'You bored with me already then?' he continued light-heartedly.

'A little,' she said dipping her head and looking up at him from under her eyebrows. 'It's ages since you last bought me anything other than a drink.'

'That not true,' cut in Nigel. 'What about that cheese ploughman's sandwich I bought you last November?'

At that moment the barmaid arrived with the two whiskeys.

'Can I have an orange juice please?' asked Catherine as the girl placed the two whiskeys on the table.

'No problem, coming right up.'

'I take it you two know each other?' said Jim as the barmaid headed back to the bar.

'It's not something I would admit to, except under extreme duress,' said Nigel.

'Actually, we are related,' said Catherine. 'Nigel is married to an aunt of mine, which makes us… related.'

'Anyway,' said Nigel, 'let me introduce you my dear, this is Jim Jackson who has recently joined the company and will be working with me in Flatpack.'

'Pleased to meet you,' said Catherine offering Jim a slender well-manicured hand.

'You too,' said Jim.

'So what did you do before joining Flatpack,' asked Catherine.

'Same sort of thing really, but I investigated fraud on the more mundane household and motor policies, so this is all quite new to me.'

'What, boats or marine insurance?'

'Both,' he replied. 'In fact, if you disregard cross-channel ferries this is the first proper boat I have been on and certainly the first with sails and masts and things.'

'Well, I hope you've got a good set of sea legs on you,' said Nigel, 'because that is going to change a lot over the coming months.'

'You mean I will have to do my investigations at sea, instead of on dry land?' said Jim, a little surprised.

'Sometimes,' said Nigel

'You didn't tell me that at the interview!'

'Didn't want to scare you too much.'

'So, what was the best scam you came across?' asked Catherine trying to steer the conversation away from Nigel.

'Ooh, there were so many,' said Jim, giving the question some deep thought, 'but I think my favourite involved a couple from Dagenham who tried to claim £10,000 for a set of jewellery that wasn't even theirs.'

'Sounds interesting, tell me more?' said Catherine leaning forward slightly in her chair. 'Well,' said Jim, 'they were invited to a really posh dinner dance through the husband's connections at the local golf club. Nothing unusual in that, I'm sure it happens up and down the country every weekend, but they came up with a plan that almost netted them 10k.

'His wife had been cleaning house for a fairly well-off family for several years and was very well respected and trusted and, on telling the lady of the house about the dinner dance, was offered the use of this particular jewellery set which consisted of a very distinctive necklace, bracelet and watch all encrusted with rubies.

'On the Saturday morning she went and picked up the set

of jewellery, but then took it into town and had it valued in her name. That night she made sure that she was photographed several times, so that she had the photographic proof for later on. The jewellery was then returned the following day and her boss was none the wiser. It was four months later that the claim came in following a "burglary" at their home.' Jim put the word *burglary* in air quotes by way of emphasis.

'The couple claimed that they had all the usual stuff nicked, telly, DVD, camcorder and the set of jewellery.'

'They provided the valuation certificate for the jewellery and several photos of it being worn at the party, all very convincing, except for the fact that he worked for Ford Motor Company as a manager on the production line and she had the cleaning job, not the sort of people who you would expect to be spending vast sums of money on high-class jewellery.'

'All sounds a bit dodgy to me as well,' said Catherine, swilling her newly arrived orange juice with a cocktail stirrer, the ice clinking against the side of the glass as she did so.

'Ah, but it gets better. The police had their doubts straight away, but couldn't find any evidence to suggest that the break-in was a hoax, so it was left to me to investigate. When I spoke to her about spending a large amount of money on the set, she said that they had been left some money and had decided to invest it in the jewellery.

'The next stop was the jeweller who carried out the valuation and it was here that I had an incredible piece of luck. As I explained earlier the jewellery was quite distinctive, and this was because all three pieces were crescent shaped. When I took the photos into the jeweller, he recognised the lady and the items straight away and explained that it is rare to do a valuation straight away, the usual practice being to leave the item with the jeweller for a few hours or even a day or so.

'The lady in the picture however was most insistent that the valuation was done there and then, and even gave the party as the reason for the urgency; apparently she was worried about losing a stone or worse still a whole item at the party without having the correct paperwork in place, so he agreed to do it straight away as requested.'

'Seems pretty cut and dry to me,' said Nigel.

'Yes, as I walked out of the shop, I was thinking the same thing,' said Jim, taking a sip of his whiskey, 'but then I had this stroke of luck that turned the whole claim on its head. As I was walking back to where my car was parked, I took a wrong turn and ended up in a completely different street. There right in front of me was another jeweller's shop and what should be in the window but a very similar piece of ruby encrusted crescent-shaped jewellery.

'When I showed the photos to the proprietor, he told me that he had only ever sold two complete sets and better still he kept records of all his major sales. With a little persuasion he gave me the addresses of the couples that had purchased them. The first couple drew a blank but when I questioned the second couple the whole story came out, plus of course the fact that the set of jewellery was still intact in their safe.'

'Wow,' said Catherine, 'so they nearly got away with it?'

'Yes indeed, if I hadn't had that extraordinary stroke of luck they may well have done. Since this case, insurance companies across the board have tightened up on the procedures around high-value jewellery, I suppose it was a bit of a wake-up call for them.'

'So what happened to the couple?' asked Nigel

'Once I reported my findings to the police, they arrested

the couple and then did a complete search of the house where they not only found the TV, DVD player and camcorder that they claimed had been stolen, but also about £16,000 of other stolen goods, everything from saucepans to leather jackets.

'It turned out that while to the outside world they were just Mr and Mrs Average, behind that veneer was a couple who were always up for fencing some hooky gear. The police managed to trace some of the gear back to lorry thefts and strongly suspected that the £16,000 worth was just the tip of the iceberg and that their raid had taken place at a fairly quiet moment in their activities. Needless to say, they both lost their jobs and ended up in prison. Their house was repossessed, the car went the same way and basically they lost just about everything, a definite case of crime not paying.'

At that moment there were shouts from the deck above and the dull throb of a diesel engine started to chug slowly into life.

'Looks like we are under way,' said Nigel. 'Come on let's go and take a look.'

The three of them rose from the table and followed the other guests up the steep steps back onto the deck.

Nigel led the way towards the stern of the barge to where Nick was standing behind the helm and Jim watched with wonder as Nick guided the old vessel deftly through the gates of the inner harbour and out into the main channel of the river. To their right was what was left of the port activities which now dealt mostly with container traffic from the near continent. To their left the old Cliff Quay came into view, a large rectangular storage shed now standing where a huge coal-fired power station, that supplied Ipswich and the surrounding area up until the mid-eighties, had once dominated the riverside.

With open water now in front of them a shout went up and moments later, the huge brown sails were unfurled and the whole feel of the barge changed quite dramatically.

Suddenly she felt taught and poised, ready for some action, and as Nigel predicted as the wind filled the sails, she started to take on the persona of a living creature. The rigging started to creak under the strain of the wind, and once the sails had given up their initial excitement at being unfurled and free once again, they too could be heard straining against the wind. The woodwork was also having its say and creaked and groaned along with the ropes and sails as if some avant garde orchestra was trying to tune up.

'Close your eyes and tell me what you hear?' said Nigel to both Catherine and Jim.

They both did as they were told.

'I can hear a lot of things,' said Jim. 'The rigging, the mast, the sails, the water, the wind, even the helm here; they are all making their own noise.'

'No, it's deeper than that,' said Catherine. 'Describe the noise, is it alarming?'

'No,' said Jim, and then fell silent for a moment.

'It's sort of sensual, like she's actually enjoying the experience.'

'Yes.' said Catherine, 'the moans and groans are not those of pain or discomfort, they are of pleasure, satisfaction, and contentment.'

'Like she's being made love to by the wind and currents,' said Jim out of nowhere.

'Brilliant! You've got it,' proclaimed Nigel, 'that's it exactly, we will make barge enthusiasts out of you two yet, what do you think Nick?'

'No doubt about it, I can see me and Jim getting along just fine.'

Jim opened his eyes to find Catherine staring at him.

'Where did that come from?' she asked with a quizzical look.

'Don't know,' he said, 'I hope I didn't embarrass you?'

'Not at all,' said Catherine.

Catherine turned towards the bow, the wind billowing her hair into Jim's face. He could smell the faint traces of her apple-scented conditioner.

'Look there's Ben,' she said to Nigel. 'Must go, he lost five boxes in the Atlantic last week, see you later.'

'She likes you,' said Nigel when she was out of earshot.

'She's very nice,' said Jim, 'what did you say she did?'

'Disbursements I think,' said Nigel. 'Trouble is she is quite ambitious and I keep losing track of exactly what role she is in.'

Nigel moved down the barge slightly and stood looking up at the sails.

'What did she mean about Ben losing boxes in the Atlantic?' asked Jim as he caught up with Nigel.

'Boxes are another term for containers,' said Nigel leaning back against the gunwale.

'In heavy weather it is not uncommon for the containers to break loose from their mountings and fall over the side of the ship. Trouble is, if they're in good condition and stay structurally sound after their fall from sixty feet plus, they will often float, sometimes for several months and then they become a serious risk to other shipping, especially smaller craft.'

'Crikey! I had no idea.'

'You've got a lot to learn about this business,' said Nigel, 'but one of the reasons we took you on was because you are not afraid to ask questions, so whenever you want to know something, ask away.'

'Thanks, I will,' said Jim pleased that his curiosity was not getting on his boss's nerves.

'The bridge looks even more impressive from the river than it does from the shore,' said Jim looking up at the huge concrete structure that towered above them taking the A14 across the River Orwell.

'Yes, even more remarkable when you remember it was built from both sides and had to meet in the middle millimetre perfect.'

Both men were stood looking up at the huge span when the girl from behind the bar arrived carrying a large wicker basket supported on a leather strap around her neck and shoulders. In the basket were lots of small pots containing shelled seafood and small wooden forks.

'Can I interest anyone in some seafood?' she asked. 'I've got mussels, whelks, shrimps, winkles and cockles, all nicely shelled for you so they won't put up a fight.'

'I'll have some whelks,' said Nigel, 'what about you Jim?'

'Not a great lover of seafood, but I should be able to cope with some shrimps.'

As they were served with the little pots and a chunk of French stick, they passed Pin Mill where Nigel pointed out the only other floating barge once owned by his grandfather.

'That's the *Hermes,* second one from the left,' said Nick pointing to a row of old barges in a small inlet beside the Butt and Oyster public house. 'She's been converted to a sort of houseboat now and I don't think she will ever sail again,' he said with a tinge of sadness, 'but at least she's being well looked after.'

For the next five minutes they both fell silent as they ate the freshly potted seafood and enjoyed the river as it passed effortlessly under them. Jim was surprised by how much he had tuned into the old vessel, already recognising the different sounds created by the trimming of the sails.

Nigel seemed to be in a different world and stood next to him with a permanent grin on his face.

'What's the story with Nick then?' asked Jim, rousing Nigel out of his trance.

'You don't recognise him, do you?' said Nigel with a smile.

'Should I?' said Jim a little puzzled. 'And what's that about him getting a bit beaten up last week? Who the hell beats up a man that size? And why should you have seen it? And who's Wild Wally?'

'So many questions, I take it you've never heard of The Caveman?' said Nigel nodding towards Nick.

Jim swung round to find Nick giving him a wink.

'You mean…'

'Yep,' cut in Nigel. 'Say hello to Nick "The Caveman" Edwards, part-time professional wrestler and all-round bad guy.'

'Bloody hell,' stumbled Jim as he suddenly realised the big man from the publicity shots was now standing eight feet away from him at the helm of the old Thames barge.

Nick was smiling like a Cheshire cat. 'There are three

ways people react to me,' he said from behind the ship's wheel.

'The first is when they recognise me as the bad guy wrestler and seem to think I'm going to beat them to a pulp and eat them for breakfast. The second is when they know I'm just an ordinary guy doing a job and come up to me for an autograph or something, but by far the best is those who react like you just have, it just kills me every time; the look on your face.' Nick gave out a roar of laughter and then returned his gaze to the ship's compass to recheck his heading.

Jim turned back to Nigel who was also wearing a sizeable grin.

'I'm not doing it,' he said now leaving Nigel with a slightly puzzled look.

'Not doing what?' said Nigel.

'Earlier when you introduced me to Nick you said something about us working together. Now if you think I'm getting into a wrestling ring with him think again, 'cause it isn't gonna happen!'

He looked at Nigel with a defiant look on his face, Nigel turned to Nick and the two of them erupted once again into howls of laughter.

'I think I had better do a bit of explaining,' said Nigel and turned back to look at the river.

'Yes please,' replied Jim. 'I'm more than a little confused at the moment.'

'Nick is a somewhat unusual package,' said Nigel turning back towards him. 'Let's take a walk up to the bow and I'll do some of that explaining.'

As they walked up to the front of the barge, they passed Catherine who was now enjoying some light-hearted banter with another group of people Jim had never met before. On the way past Catherine landed a slap on Jim's buttock, the loud smack it produced taking them both by surprise.

'I told you she liked you,' said Nigel over his shoulder. 'She only hits people she likes, I should know, I've still got the bruises to prove it.'

As they neared the bow a group that were sitting on what was the front hatch cover got up and headed for a top-up at the bar.

'This will do nicely,' said Nigel and sat down on the hatch looking down the river before them. 'Now let me tell you a bit more about our friend Nick who basically leads three very different lives.

'A couple of nights a week during the winter and spring he is "The Caveman" a bad-tempered wrestler who seemingly pummels the crap out of his opponents. The housewives hate him especially when he beats up one of the good-looking young wrestlers. However, this is wrestling and as a general rule he gets hurt more by well-aimed handbags during the trip from the ring to his dressing room at the end of the bout, than he does in the previous twenty minutes in the ring.

'The summer months are spent with the *Shannon,* sailing up and down the river once or twice a week giving the likes of you and I a night to remember.

'Now it doesn't take a genius to realise that this is not going to bring in enough money to keep this old lady in the water. Owning a vessel like this has been compared to standing under the shower tearing up twenty-pound notes, such are the costs involved.

'Luckily for Nick there is a third very profitable string to his bow and this is where you come in.

'Many years ago, Nick's family were trawlermen in Hull, so like me he has been associated with the sea most of his life. As with my family, his family were forced to sell up their fleet in the early seventies and maybe that is part of the reason he has become so passionate about these old barges, at least with these old vessels he can preserve part of the past and still make an income from them. I guess that's just not possible with a smelly old trawler.

'Anyway, in the mid-eighties when wrestling was providing him with a good income, he struck up a partnership with a family friend and between them they started up a small marine salvage business. They bought back one of the old trawlers added a crane or two to it and recovered smallish vessels that had sunk in fairly shallow water. It took them several years to get established but they soon had a good reputation for being able to successfully raise large pleasure boats and yachts with minimal fuss and damage.'

'How do you raise a large boat from the seabed without damaging it still further?' asked Jim.

'Nick employed divers to dive onto the vessel and then wrap large straps around it. Attached to these were huge airbags. When these were inflated, they gently prised the wreck from the seabed and from there they either used the cranes on board to do the rest of the lifting or brought in a salvage barge to finish the job.'

'I wouldn't have thought there was much call for that sort of thing; after all I'm guessing the costs of the salvage must have been quite high.'

'In many cases yes,' continued Nigel. 'But the clever bit of the business is where they were operating from... Southampton.

'The Solent is full of idiots all year round, with lots of money and little or no boating experience, and many of these find it very easy to get into trouble in relatively shallow water.

'In the eighties especially, the yuppies would think nothing of spending a couple of hundred thousand on a large sports boat and then accidentally ground it on a sandbank where it was at the mercy of the tide.

'Nick and his crew would rescue said boat, take it to a dry-dock where it could be dried out and repaired or refitted and then resold to another idiot. Very profitable.'

'So you want me to move to Southampton and help recover pleasure boats from the Solent?' said a puzzled Jim.

'Not exactly, continued Nigel. Things have moved on a bit since then. By the end of the eighties Nick and his partner realised that the economy was slowing down and sold up the business as a going concern, making a nice profit along the way.

'In 1990 he bought the *Shannon*. She had been through a couple of owners since my family sold her and neither had spent much money on her, so when I got news that she was in a dry dock being restored I hotfooted it down to Southampton.

'That was the first time I met Nick and we have been firm friends ever since. It took five years for Nick and his girlfriend Sandie to restore her to roughly what you see today. Nearly cost me my marriage, because every weekend Karen hadn't got anything booked, I was down in Southampton helping Nick and Sandie.'

'Which one is Sandie?' said Jim looking around the deck.

'She's not here,' said Nigel lowering his voice slightly.

'Once the *Shannon* was back in the water, Nick decided that he and Sandie deserved a holiday, so off they went to

Antigua for three weeks of R & R. On the third day of the holiday, they were out snorkelling when Sandie was hit by a jet ski and killed instantly.

'Nick took it very badly and was holed up here, on board, for the best part of nine months. Rather surprisingly to me, Karen was an absolute brick through it all, and would very often come down to Southampton with me at the weekends to try and support the big man. It was well over a year before he got back into the wrestling ring and even now, he very rarely talks about what happened, so my advice to you is "don't go there".'

Jim turned to look at Nick, but a short stocky chap wearing a baseball cap now manned the helm and Nick was nowhere in sight.

Nigel stood up and walked to the bow rail and stood facing up the river for a minute or so before turning to face Jim once again. When he did Jim noticed he had tears in his eyes. 'I'm sorry,' he said, 'it's just, well, she was one hell of a lady and we both owe her so much in so many different ways.'

Nigel looked up into the sails and then all around the deck as if trying to catch a glimpse of Sandie somewhere.

'Anyway,' he said, regaining his composure, 'a year after the accident Nick bought an old survey ship that he renamed the *Sandie Watson* and this is now his main source of income.

'She's forty metres long with a permanent crew of six and can operate anywhere in the world. She's now equipped with all the latest gizmos and gadgets for searching the seabed and regularly works for us when we need to investigate a suspicious sinking, loss of cargo, or some other maritime malady, something that happens far more often than you would think.

'This is what I meant when I referred to you and Nick working together and, as you can now see, it doesn't involve going anywhere near a wrestling ring.

'We as a company are often asked to investigate unusual losses by the marine insurance industry as a whole and this is largely due to our association with a certain Mr Nick Edwards, who is widely recognised as being one of the best in this field.

'Lloyds of London regularly send us files that they need investigating and if the price is right, which it always is, we are more than happy to oblige.

'As the newest member of Flatpack I need your expertise at sniffing out a fraud, but I also need someone to work closely with Nick and liaise between him and us on a one-to-one basis. This used to be part of my job, but my role within the company has changed a great deal over the last year or so and with two daughters in the mix as well now, I just can't go gallivanting around like I used to.

'So what do you think? You said in your interview you liked a challenge.'

'I do, but this is like a bolt out of the blue, can I have a little time to think about it?'

'Of course you can,' said Nigel with a slightly pensive look on his face.

Jim leaned back on the hatch cover with a deep thoughtful look on his face, letting the wind blow through his hair.

'Okay' said Jim. 'I've thought about it and I'll do it.'

'Good man,' said Nigel with a grin on his face from ear to ear, 'I thought you would, but you had me going there for a minute.'

'So what happens next?'

'Well, you know how I have insisted you read all those

case files over the last couple of weeks.'

'Yes, I thought it was just a sort of insight into the business.'

'Well, it was and it wasn't, it was also done to give you an introduction into the terminology within our business and to introduce you to some of the equipment you will be using.'

'What like a "side-scan sonar" and a "remotely operated vehicle,"?' said Jim. 'I've been meaning to ask you about those two.'

'Exactly,' said Nigel, 'but don't ask me, have a chat with Nick about those; he will fill you in fully on the technical stuff.'

'Oh right,' said Jim looking around once again for the big man.

'No need to worry about that now,' said Nigel, 'you've got most of next week to chat, you, Nick and the *Sandie Watson* are off to Cowes on the Isle of Wight to investigate the unexpected sinking of a twenty-metre luxury yacht. But there is one thing I do need you to do now.'

'Okay what's that?' said Jim

'Go and talk to Catherine, she's been trying to catch your eye for the last ten minutes. No wonder you're still single!'

Jim smiled at Nigel and moved back towards the stern of the barge where Catherine was now standing with Nick who had retaken his position at the helm. As he approached, Catherine turned and gave Nick a quick peck on the cheek before moving towards Jim. They met about amidships and stood silently side by side enjoying the breeze and river scenery.

'So what do you think?' said Catherine.

'It's magical,' he replied, instinctively knowing what the

question referred to. 'The sound of the rigging creaking as it strains against the sails, the different smells of the river, the feeling of the breeze rushing through my hair, it all seems so effortless and yet you can feel there is great power being harnessed here. It reminds me of an experience I had a few years ago when I swam with some dolphins in Florida. I was very conscious that they could do me a great deal of harm if they wanted to, but I felt no fear because, like Nick and his crew, they seemed totally tuned into their surroundings and the effects their actions would have on us.'

Catherine looked into Jim's eyes and a shiver ran down her spine, she didn't know what it was but there was something going on between them, a sort of sixth sense at work. Unbeknown to Catherine, he was feeling something very similar.

'How about another drink?' said Jim realising they were both holding empty glasses.

'Why not?' said Catherine and grabbed him by the hand. 'It's about time you brought me one!'

Over the next few weeks Jim and Catherine became almost inseparable, spending every minute they could together. Friendships elsewhere were put on hold and weekends were often spent living in Jim's king-sized bed, making love until totally exhausted, then sleeping for a couple of hours before making a snack and then continuing to satisfy their carnal desires all over again.

A year later they announced their engagement and nine months after that in the spring of 1998 they were married on board the *Shannon* as she passed under Tower Bridge on the Thames.

The following summer they bought a slightly run-down house that overlooked Alexandra Park in Ipswich. It was the unusual design that caught their eye, with a full-length wooden balcony stretching across the front of the house at first floor level. Their lovemaking was still a joining of souls experience, but now they could retire onto the balcony with their snack and enjoy the park spread out before them before returning to bed.

Jim was now heavily involved with Nick and the two of them had an excellent working relationship which was proving very profitable to both Nick and Moore's & Thackeray. Nick had now retired from the wrestling game and was focussing all his energies on the *Shannon* and the *Sandie Watson*. The *Sandie* was now equipped with the latest computer-controlled remotely operated vehicle (ROV) and Nick was building up quite a reputation as a pilot for these little craft which with their tiny cameras and robotic arms could film and pick up samples, from depths not accessible to divers. He had also invested in a miniature two-man submarine that due to a combination of his size and the internals of the sub he was not able to operate, so his second in command, Mark Peters, was put in charge of this particular craft. The work would often take him away from home for several days at a time, but although the parting was always difficult, the welcome home always made it all worthwhile.

Catherine had moved to a shipping company based in Ipswich and from their new home it was only a short walk across the park to the dock area of Ipswich where she and Jim now both worked.

To say life was good was a major understatement, Jim and Catherine were on a real high with everything seeming to fall into place the way life does from time to time. Their happiness was completed in early November 1999 when Catherine discovered she was pregnant, and the next few months were spent getting the rest of the house refurbished and a nursery created for the baby due in July.

The first few weeks of pregnancy proved to be very unpleasant for Catherine with acute morning sickness, but as the weeks went by this passed and a new blooming Catherine appeared. Her skin had seemed to take on a different complexion and she positively glowed with new life.

Jim couldn't keep his hands off her. With this new radiance he found her even sexier than before and their lovemaking continued unabated. When they had finished Jim would gently run his hand back and forth over her tummy, caressing their unborn child until they all slipped into a peaceful sleep.

At the beginning of June 2000, Catherine started her maternity leave. By now she was quite large, her condition being overemphasised by her small frame and several friends were convinced she was carrying twins such was the extent of "the Bump".

Midsummer's Day that year fell on a Wednesday and with the birth about three weeks away Catherine decided to plan a secret picnic tea in the park for her and Jim that evening. She spent the day making homemade snacks that they could enjoy and packed them all into a small orange rucksack that had hung on the back of the bedroom door untouched for nearly a year.

At four thirty that afternoon she set out from home to surprise Jim by meeting him from work. Her route was a familiar one that took her past her office and she had already spoken to one of her colleagues explaining that if she had enough time she would call in for a quick catch-up.

At the corner where Fore Street turns into Key Street, the road is part of a two-lane one-way system that extends around the dock area. At this point there is a pelican crossing controlled by lights and, as Catherine approached, the lights began to change to red. The youth who had activated the lights quickly crossed in front of the stationary lorry on Catherine's side of the street and, checking that the driver had seen her, Catherine followed him across.

It was all over in a split second. The car driver had seen the youth cross the road as he approached the red lights and made the massive mistake of assuming there was no one following him. As he accelerated through the still red lights a small but heavily pregnant woman appeared briefly in front of him, before being catapulted high over the roof of his car.

Catherine landed face down in the road with a sickening thud, an impact that broke her neck and killed the unborn child in one cruel blow. As she lay there, passers-by rushed to her aid and the truck driver who witnessed the car starting to accelerate through the crossing, but was unable to warn Catherine, immediately dialled the emergency services on his mobile.

Catherine was now totally at the mercy of the emergency services, and with the one-way system now gridlocked behind the accident the only way through for the ambulance crew was to drive the wrong way down Key Street. Not only did this add extra minutes to their journey, it also alerted the employees at Moore's & Thackeray that something was very wrong.

Cruelly Jim was at the tea station at the time making himself his final cup of coffee for the day and was one of the first to notice the sudden lack of traffic on the street below. Even stranger was an ambulance travelling the wrong way along it.

It was five minutes later that word came back from a tearful receptionist that she thought it was Catherine lying in the road surrounded by paramedics.

For a moment Jim froze trying to comprehend what had just been said to him and was shocked out of his stupor by Nigel who shouted from the other side of the office 'GO!'

With tears welling up in his eyes Jim half ran and half fell down the three flights of stairs finally losing his footing at the top of the final flight. He tumbled down into the reception area just as the managing director was seeing off an important client, before crashing out through the glass entrance doors and heading towards Fore Street. Nigel who appeared in reception ten seconds later, tried to quickly explain the situation and then set off after Jim who was now arriving at Catherine's side.

Jim knew it was Catherine when he saw the small orange rucksack lying beside the kerb and as he fought his way through the onlookers, he cried out her name. A lady paramedic moved quickly towards Jim as if trying to protect him from the scene. Jim wasn't interested and pushed her roughly to one side, before moving into the only space available at Catherine's head.

He didn't need to have any medical training to know that her injuries were very serious, and with both legs now housed in bright orange inflatable splints and her neck in a brace he guessed the paramedics would soon be able to move her. Her face was also a bloody mess, with a large gash across her forehead and her pretty little nose pushed across to one side. With tears filling his eyes he bent forward and whispered her name in her ear. Her eyes flickered open briefly and she tried to give him a smile before slipping back into unconsciousness.

The lady medic, who he had roughly pushed aside, gently touched him on the shoulder and asked him to move back a little so they could get a board under her back to protect her spine from any further damage. He tried to stand but his legs wouldn't take his weight and he half fell backwards into the arms of Nigel who was now standing behind him. Nigel pulled him back to his feet and they now embraced each other in a desperate attempt for some mutual comfort.

Four minutes later Catherine was in the ambulance and on her way to the hospital on the east side of town. Because of the seriousness of the injuries one of the police units volunteered to escort them through the rush-hour traffic and Nigel was now sat in the back of this vehicle frantically making phone calls to Catherine and Jim's family.

In the ambulance Jim could tell from the concerned looks on the medics' faces that things were not good. Her blood pressure was dropping to a dangerous level and her pulse rate was rising, both signs of heavy internal bleeding and massive trauma. One of the medics moved a stethoscope around Catherine's tummy and then, looking up at Jim's questioning face, shook her head.

'I'm sorry,' was all she said before returning to monitor the drips that were pumping fluids into Catherine's arm.

When they arrived at the hospital a full trauma team at the front of A&E greeted them and seconds later, she was being hooked up to various machines so that they could monitor her condition more accurately.

Jim and Nigel were asked to wait in a small anteroom, and as Jim paced up and down the ten-foot-long room trying to make sense of what had just happened Nigel continued to try and contact immediate family. Between the calls Jim threw unanswerable questions at him which Nigel did his best to field, but they both knew deep down that Catherine's chances were being measured in single figures.

The minutes seemed to pass like hours. Yet ten minutes later a doctor entered and asked which one was the next of kin. As Jim stepped forward a surging pain stabbed through his heart and he nearly collapsed onto the floor.

'We have to get her into theatre now to try and stop the internal bleeding, if you like you can walk down with her.'

He didn't need asking twice and followed the doctor to Catherine's side.

She was deathly pale now. Her skin almost grey in colour but, as Jim took hold of her hand, she once again opened her eyes.

'I love you,' she whispered, so faintly that the words were almost lost in the hubbub that accompanied them along the corridor.

'I love you too,' burbled Jim through the tears, 'we're going to get through this, hang in there, sweetheart.'

Catherine closed her eyes once again and somehow Jim knew that those were the last words they would exchange. He kissed her lightly on the lips as she entered the operating theatre and then retired to the relatives' room to wait with Nigel.

It was only fifteen minutes later that the doctor returned and explained there was nothing they could do, and that Catherine and their unborn daughter had passed away as a result of their injuries.

Jim stood still, staring at the doctor as his body went into shock. He was faintly aware that the sounds of the hospital around him were fading into a blur of muffled noise and then two otherworldly hands reached into his body and grabbed hold of his heart. He let out a cry and then as the hands squeezed tighter and tighter the cry became a wail and then a tormented scream. His vision turned to white and then started to fade to black and the only sound he could hear was a muffled scream inside his head. Seconds later he slipped into unconsciousness.

It was four months before Jim even considered getting back on the world, such was his devastation at losing his unborn child, wife and soulmate. In the weeks following the accident he would often go for long walks around the streets of Ipswich crying uncontrollably as he went. He didn't know where he was going or where he had been, all he knew was that it was better than being at home with its freshly decorated nursery and no Catherine.

It took three weeks for Nick to finally track him down and the two of them then went on a two-week bender in Amsterdam. Jim's loss had brought a mountain of metaphorical skeletons out of Nick's cupboard and following a brawl outside an Amsterdam club, they became blood brothers, merging their blood in defiance to their situation, swearing to look out for each other from that point onwards.

On their return it was Nigel who once again came up trumps, taking them both into his home, while Karen and the girls, Hannah and Georgia had a 'holiday' at Uncle Jim's house.

After forty-eight hours of almost non-stop talking and a good deal of whiskey, Nigel persuaded them both to seek expert help with a psychiatrist called Sarah that he had known for some years.

This turned out to be a real turning point in both of their lives and over the following weeks she slowly put them both back on the straight and narrow. Strangely it was Jim who seemed to be making the best progress, the reasoning being that he had "let go" of his grief while Nick had bottled it all up until the trip to Holland. That was the upside if there was such a thing; the downside however was that Jim had effectively lost two loved ones, whereas Nick had just lost the one.

Early on in the sessions it became clear to Sarah that both men were harbouring a huge amount of anger over the loss of their partners. She suggested to Nick that it might be an idea for him to take Jim to his wrestling trainer and for the two of them to work off some of the anger either on each other, or at least within a controlled environment.

This proved to be an extremely successful idea, and over the following months Nick and Jim let loose some of the angst they were feeling and with it some of the pain they were both harbouring so deeply inside. Nick also taught Jim a good deal about the wrestling game and, although he was no match for Nick, he came out of the experience a much better fighter than when he went in and a lot fitter.

It was about four months into the sessions with Sarah that Jim reached a point where he was ready to confront his two greatest demons; giving a name to his unborn daughter and dealing with the accident site which he had to pass each day in order to get to work.

He had spent months trying to decide whether or not to name the daughter he never met, but in the end, it proved to be a deceptively easy process.

It was a bright crisp February morning and as Jim walked

towards Sarah's practice in Park Road, the frost covered pavement crunching under his feet. His route took him up through Christchurch Park, one of Ipswich's biggest and best parks and he marvelled at the beauty of Mother Nature's frosty grip on the trees. The rain the previous evening had left the trees dripping wet and this drenching was now frozen on the underside of each branch in a mass of little stalactites. The grass was full of frost and was now sticking up stiffly. Here and there were the clearly marked paths of various animals as they made their way around in the endless search for food. It was a good morning to be alive, he thought.

Ten seconds later his loss once again hit him like a lorry loaded with molasses, dragging him down into a sticky goo that he felt totally unable to escape from. He stumbled to a park bench, put his head in his hands and wept uncontrollably. It was a full five minutes before he could pull himself together enough to continue to Sarah's and his steps were now very slow, deliberate and heavy when compared to those he had taken ten minutes earlier.

As he plodded up the driveway to Sarah's front door he came to a complete halt and a hundred questions started tumbling through his head. Did he need to go through this again? Was it doing him any good? What if he just turned around and walked away? Could he cope?

At that moment Sarah, who had been watching him closely from the waiting room at the front of the house, opened the front door and called out his name.

Jim slowly came out of his trance-like state and stood looking in Sarah's direction. She moved towards him and took him by the arm.

'Come on you,' she said calmly, 'you look like you could

do with a cuppa tea' and gently escorted him inside.

Once inside she sat Jim down in the empty waiting room and then asked her secretary to make them some tea.

'Bad morning hey?'

Jim explained what had just happened in the park and how he wished his wife and daughter could have enjoyed the winter's morning as he just had.

'You've spoken a lot about your daughter in recent weeks,' Sarah continued, 'have you thought about giving her a name?'

'Wouldn't know where to start with that one,' said Jim.

'How about using something natural like the Red Indian tribes of North America, Snowflake, Maple, or maybe something longer like Rabbit Droppings?'

Jim looked at Sarah with a look of bemuscment on his face and, for the first time that day, smiled.

'That's terrible,' he said, 'but I see where you are coming from.'

At that moment there was a knock on the door and the middle-aged receptionist silently brought in a tray with the tea and biscuits.

As Sarah poured the tea into two large mugs Jim sat quietly thinking.

'Sunshine,' he whispered, 'that's what I'm going to call her, Sunshine, it fits perfectly' and then without any warning he once again broke down in to howls of tears.

Over the coming weeks Jim continued to build on this positive step by naming the corner where the accident happened Sunshine Corner as a sort of tribute to his wife and unborn daughter. For the first time in many months, he began to feel that life was once again worth living.

He re-joined the gym where he used to work out and slowly weaned himself off the sessions with Sarah. He and Nick also no longer felt the need to work out their aggression at the wrestling gym and slowly their lives began to get back to 'normal' whatever that was!

With some of the money from Catherine's insurance policies he and Nick bought a Norfolk wherry, a craft not too dissimilar to the *Shannon*. The *Poacher* as she was called had been well maintained and was in good shape, just needing a bit of TLC to bring her back up to scratch. It was good therapy for both men and with the evenings and weekends now being spent on board the *Poacher* the black holes of grief started to close up and begin to disappear.

2

High in the hills above Kaliningrad, Sergei Petrov stood at his bedroom window looking down on the port below. It was a cold morning even by Baltic standards and the docks were already busy handling the many cargo ships that supplied the region and Russia beyond.

Although part of the Russian Federation, Kaliningrad is surrounded by Lithuania and Poland which makes it impossible to transport goods from this Russian annex to the motherland without crossing at least one EU member state.

It was this situation that had made Sergei his vast fortune and although a great part of this wealth was made from legal imports and exports, there was also a large amount of it that came from smuggling goods across either Lithuania or Poland for the Russian mafia.

In 1993 Kaliningrad was designated a Special Economic Zone with any companies based there getting tax and customs duty breaks on goods sent back to Russia. It was these tax breaks that attracted the likes of BMW and Hummer to build car plants in the country and, once again, Sergei was in at the sharp end supplying the raw materials to the factories.

In 1996 Sergei took this a step further and set up a dismantling plant for BMWs on the dockside. Here the cars were brought in from all over Europe to be stripped down and the materials sold back to BMW effectively recycling old for new. His plant was now the biggest of its kind in Europe and had been expanded to dismantle up to date crash-damaged models, and with the growth of the Internet in the late nineties these parts were now resold worldwide via hundreds of websites.

Now in his mid-forties Sergei was your Mr Average. Medium build, medium height, with medium brown hair. His only distinguishing feature was a small neatly trimmed moustache covering his top lip and he was the sort of person who had no trouble blending into the crowd when the need arose. Despite his somewhat dubious background he was well educated and good with languages, speaking Dutch and English alongside his native Russian. It was his business empire that always came first however, and his restless nature was always looking for the next big deal, the next opportunity to screw someone over. Where business was concerned, he was totally ruthless and with a close-knit rank of professional mercenaries dressed in business suits at his side, it was not uncommon for his competitors to unexpectedly "disappear".

'What's the matter sweetheart? You seem a little pensive.'

Sergei turned and looked at his wife sitting up in bed, her nipples still pert from their lovemaking a few minutes earlier.

'I've got to go away on business again next week, another big BMW deal. I was just running through a few things in my head, nothing for you to worry about.'

'How long will you be away? It's the sixteenth today, you will be home for Christmas, won't you? I couldn't bear us being apart on Christmas Day.'

'Of course, I will, should be back on Christmas Eve morning, lunchtime at the latest.'

His wife Anouska was far from average and although

Sergei tried to keep some of his more unscrupulous dealings hidden from her, she was no dumb blonde and was more than aware that some of his transactions crossed into Mafia-type territory.

Twenty years earlier she had been crowned Miss Kaliningrad and her beauty had not deserted her in the intervening years. Standing at a slim six feet tall and with long naturally blonde hair she was easily recognisable in a crowd and despite the fact that she had been unable to produce any heirs for Sergei, he loved her more than anything else in the world.

'I suppose I had better get going,' he said heading for the en-suite. 'We've got another delivery of cars coming in on the *Baltic Carrier* today and I don't want to miss that. Bloody ship has cost me a small fortune to repaint in the last few months.'

'I sometimes feel you think more of that ship than you do of me,' pouted Anouska.

He turned and returned to the bed giving his wife a big kiss.

'Now you know that's not true,' he said cupping her face in his hands and kissing her once again before turning back towards the bathroom.

'You have both been excellent investments.'

Just before reaching the threshold a pillow hit him on the back, and as he ducked inside the door grinning to himself a book followed him in making a loud smacking sound as it landed on the marble floor.

The *Baltic Carrier* as Sergei renamed her was one of a pair of identical ferries built in the mid-nineties for service in the Greek Islands. Although especially commissioned, her and her sister ship proved to be a tight fit in some of the smaller ports and following several collisions and expensive repair bills, both ships were sold and replaced with smaller but faster hydrofoils.

Ironically the *Baltic Carrier's* sister ship, the *Tricolor* as she was renamed, was now Norwegian registered, so once again both vessels were plying their trade in the same part of the world's seas.

The *Baltic Carrier* was transporting 2,000 crash-damaged vehicles to Kaliningrad from Hamburg where they had been stockpiled for several weeks. Sergei had estimated the cargo to be worth about three million US dollars as scrap, but that was a drop in the ocean compared with what he hoped to make from this cargo.

As he stood in the shower washing the shampoo from his hair, he felt a blast of cold air around his backside as the cubicle door was opened and then silently closed again.

Seconds later a pair of hands slipped around his midriff and as he turned Anouska's lips met his.

Down on the dockside Sergei's right-hand man Viktor Demidov was supervising the preparations for the *Baltic Carrier's* arrival. A big thickset man, Viktor had been working with Sergei for nearly ten years following a period in the Russian Secret Service. He was fiercely loyal to Sergei, trusted no one, had a reputation for being totally ruthless to anyone who crossed him and behind his neatly trimmed salt and pepper beard was a face heavily scarred by the lifestyle and company he kept.

It was while he was on the other side of this metaphorical fence that he had crossed swords with a good number of the Russian mafia with whom he and Sergei now did business and, although his no-compromise attitude had caused a few problems along the way, he was an excellent judge of character and could usually smell a rat or a deal going sour long before he and Sergei were in too deep. For this reason, Sergei treated him like a brother and Viktor and his wife Martina were frequent visitors to Sergei's home.

As he walked back towards the huge storage sheds where the cars were stored prior to being dismantled he noticed a small figure skirting around the back of Shed Three clutching something to his chest.

Viktor recognised the man as Yuri Beketov, a small wiry little man with eyes that never stopped moving. Viktor had caught him a few months previously behind a scam at the dismantling plant that involved sending out spare parts to non-existent customers. At least that was the conclusion that Viktor came to, in truth the only proof he had was that parts were being sent to an address in Moscow that didn't exist and no payments could be traced for the goods, hence Yuri who was a good worker, had been given a second chance and was allowed to continue working at the plant.

As Viktor watched on, Yuri disappeared behind the shed still clutching his chest. This area of the site was strictly out of bounds to the workers, the only people allowed there being Sergei, Viktor and personnel who had been cleared to work on Sergei's eight-foot Ferretti motor yacht that was moored there during the summer. In previous years the yacht had been moved to Spain for the winter months but this year it had been left in situ, just in case it was required.

Viktor quickly ran along the side of the shed and peered around the corner, to find Yuri lying on his stomach at the edge of the quay passing the item down to a waiting boat below.

Quietly he walked up behind Yuri and waited for him to get back to his feet. Because of the deep dock sides Yuri's accomplices were unable to see Viktor on the dockside above and as they puttered off down the dock, they were completely unaware of the predicament their friend Yuri was just about to find himself in.

Yuri was fully to his feet before he realised, he had company.

'So Yuri what is it this time, selling my parts a little closer to home now eh?' said Viktor taking a step forward.

'No,' said Yuri. 'I was just coming around here to have a smoke.'

'Right,' said Viktor. 'So I don't suppose you have any idea who that is heading out of the dock in the inflatable.'

Yuri stood frozen to the spot but as usual his eyes were darting around looking for some way out of the situation.

Without warning Yuri bent down on one knee as if to tie his shoelace and then launched himself at Viktor's midriff head first.

Although surprised Viktor was fleet-footed enough to sidestep Yuri, and as he sped past, Viktor grabbed his arm and swung him round and back where he came from.

As Yuri caught his balance, Viktor moved forward and mule kicked him in the stomach sending him flying through the air and over the side of the quay.

Yuri hit the water just behind Sergei's motor yacht with a huge splash and seconds later let out an ear-piercing scream as the near-freezing water quickly permeated his heavy winter clothing.

Knowing that Yuri only had minutes to live, Viktor moved rapidly towards the rear of the Ferretti and leapt down onto the rear deck. Once on board he quickly located the six-foot-long gaff that he and Sergei used when fishing off the Spanish coast and caught Yuri under the arm with the fearsome-looking hook.

Yuri was now screaming like a two-year-old and as Viktor pulled him over the side of the boat with the gaff, a security detail arrived to help get him on board.

'Hold him still,' shouted Viktor to the security men and then pushed hard on the gaff to release it from under Yuri's arm.

'Now get him off the boat and up to the hospital,' said Viktor to the security men and then leaned forward so that his face was only inches away from Yuri's.

'And if I ever see you around here again, I will put you in a freezer and Sergei and I will use you as shark bait on our next fishing trip, do you understand?'

Yuri nodded his head a little, although even Viktor wasn't sure if it was a nod of understanding, the effects of the cold water, or the gaff wound.

Forty minutes later as Viktor finished hosing away Yuri's blood from the deck Sergei arrived on the quayside.

'Word has it you're some sort of hero,' said Sergei. 'Rescued that weasel Beketov from the dock after he accidentally fell in. At least that's what security are telling me.'

'Something like that,' answered Viktor. 'Guess I was just in the right place at the right time.'

'C'mon my friend you can tell me all about it later, right now we have a ship to greet and some more BMWs to prep for their final voyage.'

Victor turned off the hose and coiled it up on the rear deck before climbing up the ladder to the top of the quay.

'How many cars have we got in Shed Two ready to go?' said Sergei as Viktor fell into step beside him.

'At the last count about seventeen hundred,' said Viktor.

'And they are all clean?'

'As clean as we can make them,' said Viktor. Number plates, insurance or tax discs holders, and dealer stickers have all been removed. We have also cleaned out the interiors; you would be amazed what some people leave in their crashed cars, we even found a laptop in one of the 7 Series.'

'Anything useful on it?' asked Sergei.

'No, just the usual mix of emails, letters, spreadsheets and porn. I've looked closely at the spreadsheets but they are not titled so I don't think we can do anything with them. There was an email from a company in Munich that makes ironmongery but again nothing we can work with.'

'Give it to Boris,' said Sergei. 'There must be something on there somewhere that we can turn a profit from.'

'Already done that,' said Viktor. 'Says he will get back to us in a couple of days.'

'Good, now what about the crews?' asked Sergei. 'Are they all assembled and ready for tonight's meetings?'

'Yes, they are all here in Kaliningrad but I thought it wise to split them up. I've put one team in the old house near the football ground, and the IT crew are housed in my mother and father's old villa on the main road.'

'Excellent, that will give us three days to rehearse,' said Sergei, 'although I'm sure once they have spent a few hours exploring the *Baltic Carrier* it will all go like clockwork.'

On board the *Baltic Carrier,* Captain Leif Anderson was slowly bringing the ship into the port of Kaliningrad. Sergei's quays and sheds were furthest from the port entrance and the mouth of the river Pregolya, a position that made the unscrupulous side of his operation considerably easier to manage.

Following the necessary clearances from the port authorities Leif and his crew began to spin the ship round using the bow and stern thrusters so that she could be berthed stern first alongside Sergei's quay. Leif Anderson had been carrying out this manoeuvre for nearly five years and, with his fine touch on the helm, the ship spun gently around with all the grace and finesse of a ballerina on a stage. Just as the stern looked like it was about to get away from him the stern port thrusters came to the rescue and two minutes later, the ship gently nudged up to the quay.

Leif Anderson stood over six feet tall with a mane of nearly white hair that cascaded over his shoulders. Although the consummate professional whilst at the helm of a ship, Leif was not one to follow the well-trodden path of most sea captains as far as any dress codes were concerned and his hair was a prime example of his dislike of the establishmentarianism that existed elsewhere is his profession. Dressed in a pair of fur-lined chino trousers, tan cowboy boots and a sheepskin flying jacket he walked out onto the flying bridge and threw a loose salute to Sergei and Viktor, standing on the quayside.

'Give me ten minutes to secure the ship!' he shouted down to the men standing forty feet below him.

'I'll meet you on the main car deck once you've boarded.'

As he turned and re-entered the bridge a gangplank was

lowered from the side of the ship landing just in front of where Sergei and Victor were standing.

Sergei was first on board and quickly headed below to view his latest cargo of BMWs.

'Isn't that a wonderful sight?' he said turning to Viktor.

'Magnificent,' replied Viktor as they started to walk down between the written-off cars.

The cars on this deck were all medium-sized 5 Series models and the damaged they sustained varied from heavy rear-end collisions, to cars that looked as if they had taken part in a full demolition derby somewhere. For the most part they were all structurally okay, with only the occasional one missing a windscreen or boot lid.

As the two men made their way between the cars, Leif appeared from a doorway just in front of them.

'Happy boss?' he said as he approached Sergei.

'Very good,' said Sergei. 'What about the other decks? Are they all up to this standard?'

'The top deck is even better, come take a look.'

Sergei and Viktor followed Leif through the door and up some stairs to the top deck where they were greeted with a deck of pristine cars.

Sergei walked down between the 3 Series looking closely for any damage.

'I don't understand,' he said turning back to Leif. 'These are all undamaged. What are they doing here?'

Leif smiled. 'Open the door.'

Sergei looked puzzled.

'What, this one?' said Sergei pointing at the blue 318 he stood nearest to.

'Any one you wish,' grinned Leif, enjoying the fact that

he had one over on his boss.

Sergei moved forward and tugged on the door handle of the Beamer. The door opened effortlessly and as it opened fully Sergei recoiled backwards into the car behind him.

'Bloody hell, what's that smell?'

'Allow me to tell you a little story,' said Leif, moving forward and opening the door of a 323i next to Viktor.

'Jesus!' he cried moving swiftly towards the back of the car. 'That's awful.'

'Tony found these quite by chance in Utrecht about eight weeks ago and I thought they were too good to pass up.'

Tony Groen was Sergei's Dutch contact who bought up written-off BMWs from all over Holland, Belgium and northern Germany.

'Apparently he was staying in Arnhem when the local news channel ran some footage of a fire at a chemical plant on the outskirts of Utrecht. As the cameraman pulled away from the main fire Tony noticed a compound full of Beamers behind a local dealership. The following day he went to investigate and discovered that the dealership had just taken delivery of fifty brand-new cars, which were stored in the compound awaiting preparation for sale. It turned out that these cars were directly in line with the fumes and smoke from the chemical plant and that's what you can smell. See that 320 convertible over there?' Leif pointed to a cherry red 3 Series towards the front of the column of cars.

'According to Tony the dealership spent ten days and about one thousand euros valeting that car's interior, and it's still they couldn't get it anywhere near a saleable condition. Following a visit by several insurance assessors the dealership was paid in full for the fifty cars and Tony did a deal with them to take the whole lot off their hands for a cool 100k.'

'Viktor remind me when this is all over to send Tony a bonus for his endeavours,' said Sergei. 'This is a superb result and just what we have been looking for, unmarked cars with absolutely no history.'

Viktor nodded his head and pointed to further thirty or so cars behind the main batch.

'What about those?' he asked Leif.

'Those,' said Leif, 'are the remainder of the cars at the dealership that night. They were either in the service area, customer compound, or showroom and they all stink as bad as the others.'

Sergei was stood to one side of the deck thinking.

'Viktor,' he said, 'I think we need a change of plan here. Get up to your mother and father's villa and get the IT crew down here pronto. I want the computer IDs stripped off these cars as soon as possible; we'll have to reschedule their meeting for tomorrow afternoon; and I want the other team in the boardroom at seven p.m., sharp.'

'Okay Boss.'

'Oh, and I need a crew down here from the plant, swapping all these wheels, we can't do anything about the rest of these vehicles they're all too contaminated, but we can put some shitty old alloys on these cars and flog the originals, should get most of that 100k back on the wheels and tyres alone.'

'Yes Boss.'

Viktor turned and headed back towards the door they had come through five minutes earlier.

Sergei turned to Leif and patted him across the shoulder. 'Well done, losing a couple of thousand cars was a price I was willing to pay in the short term, but you and Tony have just effectively saved me nearly a hundred cars.'

'I thought you'd be pleased,' said Leif. 'Time for a drink I think, I've got a bottle of 98% proof Russian Imperial Vodka hidden in my cabin; for medicinal purposes only of course, I'm sure I can find a couple of glasses.'

'Good,' said Sergei, 'it will give me a chance for another run-through with you before we set sail, nothing must go wrong you understand, there's too much at stake.'

That evening at seven o'clock the first of Sergei's two teams was briefed on the operation. At eight thirty p.m. they were sent on board the *Baltic Carrier* where they meticulously walked every corridor and examined all the cabins and ancillary rooms. Stripped of anything of value over the previous weeks, the ship was now nothing more than a shell. The only complete areas of the whole ship were the bridge and engine room and even the radio room was down to the bare essentials.

At nine p.m. two members of Sergei's IT crew arrived on board carrying a large wooden crate between them. They were greeted by Leif at the top of the gangplank who then directed them towards what was left of the radio room.

'So, this is the jammer?' said Leif to one of the men.

'Yep, where do you want it put?'

'Doesn't really matter,' said Leif, 'as you can see there's plenty of room so put it wherever you think best.' He watched as the men manoeuvred the crate onto a table stood against one of the walls.

'Will it do what we want it to do?' Leif asked.

'Of course,' said his colleague. 'It basically jams any radar signal, probably wouldn't be enough to fool a warship because they are trained to spot this sort of thing, but it should be enough to hide you from the coastguards.'

'Excellent,' said Leif. 'I'll leave you to it, if you need anything, you'll find me on the bridge.'

Over the following two days the ship was a hive of activity with various personnel all of whom had been carefully vetted by Viktor and his security team, carrying out their tasks without complaint. Each man had been promised a large Christmas bonus for their endeavours and the loss of various extremities if they so much as breathed a word of their work to anyone else. After seeing what had happened to Yuri Beketov only days earlier it seemed sensible to keep their mouths shut and take the money.

It was on the car decks that most of the action was taking place. The IT crew had worked through the first night downloading all the eighty-five cars details from their on-board computers onto laptops.

Following them was a specialised team responsible for removing the vehicle identification plates without damaging them and these plates, when married up to the on-board computer ID, would enable a completely different car to be given a full new identification.

Finally came the pit lane crew as they were jokingly called, who replaced all the wheels and tyres on the new cars Tony Groen had purchased for scuffed and damaged items from the recycling plant.

At last, the other seventeen hundred cars that had already been prepared in the same way could be taken from Shed Two and swapped with the remainder of those on board.

After two days of frenetic activity the ship fell silent once again and one of the biggest frauds ever attempted was ready to set sail.

3

The small town of Zeebrugge on the North Sea coast of Belgium has very little to shout about other than being one of the busiest ports in northern Europe, supplying goods from all over the continent to marketplaces in the UK and beyond. It is also Belgium's biggest fishing port and has one of the largest fish markets anywhere in Europe. Sadly, its biggest claim to fame was the capsizing of the car ferry *Herald of Free Enterprise* in 1987 when 193 people lost their lives just outside the harbour walls. A memorial service is held each year on March sixth to remember those lost and in 2012 Ed Collins had been one of those present at the ceremony.

Nine months later Ed stood against the harbour wall looking out over the North Sea thinking about what it must have been like on that night. It was a dull overcast day with a cold wind blowing in from the north, not unlike the night the *Herald* capsized. The North Sea was never very attractive, with its grey water and near constant swell, but on that fateful night even Ed couldn't begin to imagine the horror of the situation those poor souls found themselves in. An involuntary shiver pulsed down his back as he turned and headed back towards the main port, thanking God that in all his years at sea he had always remained on it, rather than in it.

Ed pulled the zip on his seaman's coat up to his chin as the wind freshened and pulled his woolly hat down over his ears. Up until the last couple of days the weather had been quite mild for the time of year, but it now appeared that Mother Nature had finally got a wintery grip on the North Sea and the temperatures were falling fast.

March the sixth was going to live with him for a long time also, not because he had known anyone on the doomed ship but because his own life had slipped into meltdown two days after the service.

A merchant seaman for nearly thirty years, he had advanced his way through the ranks to his current position of captain of the Norwegian-registered *Tricolor*. A tall thickset rugged man with a heavily pockmarked face, neatly trimmed grey goatee beard and grey crew cut hair, he was a man who despite playing life by the rules, had recently seemed to get more than his fair share of shitty stick ends.

His personal winter had started earlier that year when he was promoted to the rank of captain. His wife Margaret had organised a big party in a local hotel on the evening of March eighth to celebrate his promotion and Ed was surprised and deeply touched by how many of his seafaring colleagues had managed to engineer that particular night in port and he could only guess at the numbers of favours being owed by those around him. The night was great success and as most of the guests left for home Ed and some of his closest friends headed for the hotel bar. Margaret had grown accustomed to these occasional late-night drinking sessions and bade them all goodnight.

It was half an hour later that Ed hit the drinking wall, whereby he knew that if he drank any more, he was going to be seriously ill and much to the surprise of his mates he bade them farewell and headed back to his room. It was as he stumbled drunkenly into his room that his whole life went pear-shaped with a capital P.

Drunk he may have been, but as he fell through the door, he wasn't so intoxicated that he didn't recognise his wife of twenty-five years being vigorously screwed over the sofa by the man who had been one of his best friends since his youth.

He couldn't explain what happened next, maybe it was the booze, or maybe it was just the shock of finding his wife and best friend at it right under his nose. The result however was way beyond dispute, a night in the local police cells, his ex-best friend in hospital with cuts and bruises to his back after Edward smashed a chair across it and a soon to be ex-wife nursing a black eye.

Ed had never considered himself capable of hitting a woman, but that night had changed him forever and his memories of what happened were like a loop of video tape in his head going round and round, always there, ready to bound forward into the front of his thoughts whenever his guard was down.

It was an agonising two weeks before his wife would agree to meet him in a local pub and then it was only with her brother sitting two tables away as a chaperone. She explained that she and Tom had been "friends" for several years and that in some ways she was quite glad that it was all out in the open. She explained that they were going to set up home together and that she never wanted to see Ed again. Then she left without even a backward glance.

It was two hours later that a call of nature finally stirred him from his seat and over the following weeks he had had to come to terms with losing his best friend, his wife, his house, and ultimately his two grown-up daughters who took their mother's side and now refused to have anything to do with their "ex-father" as they now insisted on calling him.

The police didn't press charges so at least his career was still in one piece, but he now found himself almost totally broke except for a small rented flat and his classic 1972 Mercedes-Benz 350SL. It was a devastating experience and the only morsel of consolation he could take from it, was that if that was the sort of woman his wife was, he was better off without her.

It was June when he was approached out of the blue by a Russian called Viktor who he later found out worked for a multimillionaire called Sergei Petrov and following several meetings was offered a small fortune if he helped out in a scam to relieve BMW of some of its cars. With seemingly nothing left to lose Ed agreed, and with thoughts of a new start in Brazil on the horizon, his life seemed to be on the up once again.

It was now a week before Christmas and as Ed was making his way back to the *Tricolor* when his mobile phone began to vibrate in his pocket.

'Ed Collins,' he answered.

'Ah Mr Collins, its Viktor,' came the reply. 'How are you doing my friend?'

'I'm good, yourself?'

'Ya, very well,' answered the Russian. 'I just need to confirm the schedule with you regarding our rendezvous on the twenty-second, has anything changed at your end?'

'No nothing, the ship is being loaded as we speak and we will leave port as planned. The meteorological reports look good, so no issues there either.'

'Excellent, excellent, if anything changes be sure to let us know.'

'Of course,' said Ed. 'No problem.'

'Okay I'll see you on the twenty-second then, Goodbye and good luck.'

The phone went dead and Ed slipped it back in his pocket, boy was this going to be a Christmas to remember, he thought.

As he rounded one of the large storage sheds on the quay the *Tricolor* appeared in front of him resplendent in her new coat of paint. Ed stopped and looked up at his ship. He had spent many years getting to the rank of captain and now he was going to kiss it all goodbye.

The butterflies returned to his stomach, was he doing the right thing by getting involved with the Russians? Could they be trusted? Yes of course they could. He thought back to that morning's conversation with his bank in Brazil who confirmed that $100,000 dollars had been deposited in his account as agreed, and Sergei had promised another $400,000 to be added to that in two days' time. Anyway, what had the sea given him; a hard and often lonely life and a wife at home screwing his best mate? Of course it was the right decision.

He flashed his pass at the security personnel and bounded up the gangplank in a very uncaptain like way, of course it was the right decision what could possibly go wrong?

4

It was a cold, damp, and grey December morning that greeted Sergei and the rest of the crew as Leif inched the *Baltic Carrier* out of Kaliningrad. The night before had left a heavy blanket of snow, which somehow seemed to make the day brighter than it actually was and the temperature was well below freezing, making the warmth of the ship a very welcoming place to be.

'December the twenty-first,' said Sergei to the men gathered around the bridge of the ship, 'the shortest day.'

'Not for everybody,' said Viktor, 'looks like it's going to be a very long one to me.'

'Well let's not waste it then,' Sergei said. 'I want a full run-through again at noon in the mess and then a weapons check, nothing must go wrong, there's too much riding on it.'

'Consider it done,' said Viktor nodding to the man on his right.

'I think that's your department,' said Viktor with a grin.

The man stood beside Viktor was Michael Duggan and it was he who was in charge of one of the teams. Standing a slim, muscular six feet tall, with close-cropped dark hair and dark eyes that gave nothing away, he was an enviable man to have on your side if things got tough, and when Duggan was around, trouble wasn't usually far behind.

Born in Southern Ireland to English parents he spent his

early years at boarding school in England and on leaving, joined first the regular army and then the SAS. Following several tours of duty in Northern Ireland he was then seconded to infiltrate the provisional IRA on behalf of the British government.

This was to take him deep undercover and over the next few years he worked his way up the organisation, always making sure that on the few occasions he had to shoot at British troops he left behind only flesh wounds.

In 1985, totally exasperated by his seeming ineptitude with any sort of firearm his IRA commander sent him and five other members to a farm in Roscommon, for some weapons training. It was while he was there that he discovered by chance that the farm was also the site of a huge weapons dump, containing everything from grenades and AK-47 assault rifles, through to rocket launchers.

On his return to Belfast, he passed on all he had learned to the British intelligence agent he was working with and thought little more of it. Three weeks later the dump was hit by a crack team of Duggan's colleagues from the SAS and blown sky high. This completely compromised his cover and it wasn't long before the IRA came knocking. He and the five other men were rounded up and taken to a small isolated farmhouse in County Clare.

After four days of sleep deprivation and heavy beatings he was released, but the other five men were not so fortunate. Although completely innocent his five comrades were all compromised one by one by the constant questioning, lack of sleep and beatings, before being executed in front of the remaining prisoners.

Being the IRA, these were not your standard one bullet

through the head executions. Each man was stripped naked and then nailed through the hands to a board crucifixion style. They were then kneecapped with a shotgun before being castrated and left to bleed to death. The cries of those men were to haunt Duggan from that day to this and, despite the fact that they were "the enemy", he struggled with his conscience over the next few weeks knowing that he had sent five men to agonising deaths.

Sensing the turmoil he was in, the British government started making threats of their own if he pulled out, but this proved to be the final straw and two months later he fled Northern Ireland and joined a band of mercenaries heading for Africa.

Since then, he had seen action in Bosnia and Afghanistan where his exploits as a cold-blooded killer became almost legendary. He was now sought after all over the world as an assassin and had returned to Ireland on two occasions to take out two of the execution squad present at County Clare. There were two men left and yet, nearly twenty years on and with the troubles at an end, these men were now the walking dead, and he made sure they knew it.

It was while he was in Afghanistan that he met Viktor's brother Dimitri who then held the rank of *Polkovnik* or colonel in the Russian army. Following a bloody encounter with some Afghan rebels high in the mountains above Kabul in which Duggan's recognisance had saved a high percentage of Dimitri's regiment from ambush he was asked to work alongside the Russians. Over the next few months, he helped train over fifty Russian troops, showing them how to scout and live undetected in the harsh landscape that surrounded Kabul.

In late 1987 while still unofficially serving with the

Russian forces Duggan and the five men he was training were ambushed by twenty mujahedin near to Kandahar in the south of the country. Following a fierce firefight in which half of the rebels were killed or wounded, he and the Russians eventually had to retreat and, in so doing, two of the Russians were killed and Duggan himself badly wounded.

The three remaining men managed to get him to a field hospital, just in the nick of time and, following several blood transfusions and a four-hour operation to remove shrapnel and bullets from his stomach and legs, he was able to look forward to fighting another day.

The field hospital was only a very temporary billet and a decision had to be made as to where to send him to recuperate. He couldn't go back to the UK as the British army would court martial him on any number of charges for leaving Northern Ireland in a hurry.

Although his parents still lived in Eire, he would never consider compromising their safety by going back there, in fact the only time he ever met up with them was when they were on holiday, usually in Spain or Portugal.

The third option was to send him to a Russian forces' hospital, but Dimitri was at a loss as to how to explain about the Englishman who spoke fairly good Russian and was wounded in southern Afghanistan while training Russian soldiers, especially when he had no papers. In a field hospital these details don't matter, their job is to save soldiers' lives and the circumstances surrounding the wounds were not of their concern, but higher up the chain of command there were questions waiting that Dimitri didn't have answers for.

It was while talking to Duggan one evening about their respective families that the answer to this conundrum became clear and, a few days later, he was on his way to Moscow to stay with Dimitri's brother Viktor and his wife Martina.

His recuperation went well, with Martina making an excellent nurse, seemingly oblivious to the horror of the wounds on Duggan's abdomen and legs, which she redressed for him every day. As the days turned into weeks, they began to go out for walks together and Martina showed him the parts of Moscow that the tourists rarely see. Meanwhile Viktor was making sure that Duggan's exploits in Afghanistan didn't go totally unrewarded and six weeks after his arrival he was presented with a full set of papers that would allow him entry and exit in and out of Russia whenever he liked, something that was going to prove invaluable to him in the future.

As his wounds healed Viktor realised that he may be useful to the secret services and offered him the opportunity to eliminate a particularly troublesome member of the local mafia.

Duggan accepted the job and carried out the assassination without fuss and so began his new career as a hit man for the Russian Secret Service. Over the coming years he took out several key underworld figures both in Russia and its neighbouring states and, when Viktor teamed up with Sergei, Duggan found a whole new lucrative avenue of crime in which to ply his trade.

From Kaliningrad the sailing to the North Sea was far from simple. On leaving the port the ship entered a long man-made canal before emerging into a large area of inland sea, which was only separated from the Baltic by a thin peninsular of land. This long, drawn-out spit of land emanated from Poland in the south and heads north to where there was a small opening before the land re-emerged and continued north to Lithuania.

As the *Baltic Carrier* passed through the canal Leif stood on the bridge plotting the next part of his course that would take them out into the Baltic proper and then round the southern tip of Sweden. They would then follow a northerly heading up between Sweden's west coast and Denmark's most easterly island called Sjaelland, before rounding the north of Denmark and entering the North Sea.

'How long before we reach the North Sea?' asked Sergei as he watched Leif doing his calculations at the chart table.

'We've got a few hours to go yet,' said Leif turning to face Sergei. 'It all depends on the weather conditions of course, but I'm guessing it will be about ten a.m. tomorrow.'

'And then we are going to sail north, right?' said Sergei asking for confirmation to a question that he already knew the answer to.

'Yep, that's right boss,' answered Leif. 'We can afford to sail north for two or three hours before switching on the radar jammer and then turning around and heading back to where we are going to meet up with the *Tricolor.*'

'Excellent, excellent,' said Sergei thoughtfully. 'Keep me posted, I'm off to what's left of the mess to get some lunch.'

'No problem, boss,' said Leif, turning back to his charts.

5

As predicted the *Baltic Carrier* reached the North Sea at about ten a.m. the following morning.

The sea was remarkably calm for the time of year and the sun was bright, but low in the sky. On the bridge, Leif took over once more from his second in command Oleg Peterson who had been on duty since three a.m. that morning.

'Everything okay?' Leif asked.

'Yes, nothing much to report,' said his colleague. 'We did get buzzed by what looked like a fisheries protection plane about two hours ago, but he made one pass, realised we weren't a trawler and then went on his way.'

'How's the fuel looking?' asked Leif, moving over to a bank of gauges at the rear of the bridge.

'Should be okay' said Oleg. 'By my reckoning we've got about a day and a half's worth left; should be more than enough even if something was to go disastrously wrong with our schedule.'

At that moment Sergei arrived on the bridge closely followed by Viktor with a tray of steaming hot coffee.

'Lovely day for it,' smiled Sergei whilst handing out the mugs of coffee.

'Yes, it looks like we are going to be extremely lucky with the weather,' said Leif hugging his hot mug. 'According to the shipping forecast this is about as rough as it's going to get, we just need to get a bit of cloud cover tonight and it will be perfect.'

'I can't wait,' said Viktor, with an evil glint in his eye.

The rest of the day went smoothly on board the *Baltic Carrier.* Leif followed a northerly course until midday as if heading for the Norwegian port of Bergen, before the radar jammer was activated and the ship swung round 180 degrees and headed south towards a point off the Humberside coast where they were due to meet up with Captain Ed Collins.

They were now in a part of the North Sea that saw little traffic and Leif took great care to avoid being spotted by the few ships in the vicinity. As the light started to fade a boson's chair was dangled in turn over each side of the bow and then the stern and, with the aid of a cowling to block out the welding arc, the *Baltic Carrier* became the *Tricolor.*

With a radio silence enforced on both ships, communication was left to the signal lamp, a high-powered lantern with the ability to transmit Morse code in pulses of light by opening and closing a shutter on its lens.

The night was dark, cold, and as Leif had requested there was good cloud cover to hide their activities. It wasn't until ten thirty that the ships finally made contact, and over the next half an hour they started edging their way towards each other using the signal lamps to relay their messages. As they drew closer Leif shouted instructions to Ed Collins through a megaphone and shortly afterwards the two vessels sat side by side, locked in position by their GPS, the port and bow thrusters maintaining an uneasy forty-foot gap between them.

Sergei was by now leaning against the port gunwale, gazing across at an identical ship to his own. As his eyes moved along the vessel, he saw Ed Collins looking at him with a bemused smile on his face.

'Lower your rear loading ramp!' shouted Sergei. 'I'll send a boat to bring you on board'

Ed Put his thumb up to acknowledge the instruction and then moved towards the stern of his ship to lower the ramp. As he did so a Zodiac inflatable appeared from the rear of Sergei's ship and quickly sped across the short gap between the two ships.

Ed leapt into the boat like only an experienced seaman is able to do, closely followed by his chief officer and in less than a minute they were being welcomed aboard by Sergei and Viktor.

With the introductions dealt with Sergei put his arm across Ed's shoulders and together they walked along the lower car deck to a staircase that would take them up to the bridge several levels above.

'How are you then my friend?' asked Sergei.

'I am very well, thank you,' said Ed, 'although I have to confess, I never expected to be greeted by a vessel like this! I thought you said you were going to steal the BMWs on my ship and tie up my crew and me to make it look like an act of piracy. I think I expected a crane and a large barge of some sort not a vessel identical to the *Tricolor*... and what's with all these damaged cars in here?'

'So many questions,' replied Sergei, 'let's go up to the bridge and everything will become clear.'

Unbeknown to Ed, as he and his chief officer were being taken up the stairs to the bridge, Duggan and his six comrades were heading to the *Tricolor* in the Zodiac armed to the teeth and ready for action.

As they landed on the ramp Duggan split his men into two groups of three, before they slid seamlessly into their prearranged plan. With their soft-soled desert combat boots they padded swiftly and silently along the car deck between the rows of brand new 5 Series BMWs, taking care to move on the balls of their feet and using only hand signals to communicate.

On reaching the stairs the group that included Duggan headed up towards the bridge and crew quarters, while the second team headed along a service corridor towards the engine room.

He and his men quickly climbed up the first flight of stairs. At the top there was a long corridor identical to the one below and to their right another car deck packed with more brand-new BMWs. On one side of the corridor there was a series of storerooms and the team now split again and systematically searched each room in turn for any crew members. This was where the extensive training exercises on the *Baltic Carrier* paid dividends, with each man supremely confident of where he was going and what to expect behind each of the doors.

With the deck secured, they returned to the stairwell and on reaching the next level repeated the search pattern.

This deck housed the crew quarters and as Duggan crept along the corridor it wasn't long before he heard voices from one of the cabins. As he and his two comrades approached, the cabin door was suddenly flung open and a small middle-aged oriental man stepped out right into his path. On seeing Duggan and his men the man immediately froze and a second later a karate chop to the neck had rendered him unconscious. Surprised at seeing his colleague suddenly and inexplicably hit the floor outside his cabin, the second crewman rushed forward to help, but before he could do anything he too was also struck and fell to the floor with a dull thump.

They quickly gagged and tied the two men together with gaffer tape and industrial cable ties before continuing down the corridor. They only found one other crew member in his quarters and he was in his bunk fast asleep. Like his colleagues he was gagged and bound and then quickly tied to his bunk.

Duggan had hoped he would find more of the crew in their quarters, as this would have made the job of securing the ship a good deal easier. Ed Collins had told Viktor a few days earlier that he was going to hire a crew of twenty-two all from the Philippines, so working on the assumption that his second crew would find the three that manned the engine room in situ, that now left sixteen to find.

As they made their way up the next flight of stairs, they could hear laughter and the smell of food wafting down towards them.

This floor contained the mess hall and by the sound of it this was where many of their remaining quarry were to be found.

Duggan moved swiftly along the corridor to where the entrance to the mess was, while his two comrades quickly swept the corridor for any other crewmen.

Still using nothing but hand signals Duggan instructed his men to throw in a pair of XM84 stun grenades in five… four… three… two… one. Five seconds later there was a loud thump as the grenades exploded in the mess.

The XM84 is known as a "Flashbang" stun grenade and is designed to be a non-lethal way of disorientating and confusing an enemy force. Lobbing two of these devices into a relatively small area with steel walls, floors and ceilings was a sure-fire way of getting people's attention. When they entered the mess room the scene was one of total confusion with ten grown men staggering around like drunken schoolboys, each man clutching his head, hands over the ears like they were about to fall off their shoulders. The chef who at the time of the explosions was towards the rear of the galley was now standing behind a serving area with small drops of blood oozing from his ears and, as Duggan's men burst in clothed in full combat gear, he reached for a couple of large knives on the counter behind him.

Duggan spotted the danger immediately and pulled a throwing knife from the shoulder of his tunic and sent it hurtling towards the chef. The man didn't stand a chance and, as the knife buried itself up to the hilt in his right shoulder, the knives he was holding fell to the floor with a metallic crash.

Duggan rushed forward and frogmarched the chef out from behind the serving counter before shoving him backwards onto the floor. As he started on his downward trajectory Duggan grabbed hold of his knife and with a little help from gravity the knife swiftly exited the chef's shoulder. The man let out an ear-piercing scream before rolling onto his damaged shoulder and curling up in a ball.

It took them no more than three minutes to gag and tie up the crew members and just as they turned to leave the second team arrived having completed their mission in the engine room. With a man stationed at the door, Duggan for the first time since arriving on the ship spoke to his men. As he was confirming the numbers already seized and planning how to capture the remaining five crew members, a series of gunshots rang out from the *Baltic Carrier*.

Instantly recognising that there was a good chance the remaining crew had also heard the gunfire and were now probably moving out on deck to see what was happening on the sister vessel, Duggan ordered his men into full assault mode.

The team moved swiftly up through the ship and as predicted they found the first officer, the ships medic, and the radio operator standing on the wing bridge trying to ascertain what was happening on the identical ship sitting next to them.

The surprise attack from behind quickly had the men subdued and as they were being tied up a shout came from a cabin behind the bridge and the remaining two crewmen appeared still holding their playing cards closely followed by one of Duggan's men pointing an AK-47 at the back of their heads.

With the crew of twenty-two now all accounted for Duggan moved up to the bridge and flashed a signal to the *Baltic Carrier* with his torch, before rejoining his men to help secure the crew in the recreation room on board where they were to be kept under guard for the next couple of weeks. Mobile phones were confiscated and the computers in the room from which the crew would normally be able to send emails to their families or just surf the Net were removed. Duggan had been told by Viktor that the men would be released when the ship docked in China with a bonus to keep their mouths shut. Unbeknown to him, however, Sergei had other plans.

With the operation to secure the *Tricolor* underway Sergei had taken an unsuspecting Ed Collins up to his cabin while his second officer accompanied Viktor to the bridge.

'I take it this is the *Tricolor's* sister ship' said Ed as they walked along the corridor towards the bow end of the ship. 'I knew there was a second vessel built, but I must admit I had no idea what happened to her after she was sold by the Greeks.'

'Yes, it's quite ironic isn't it?' said Sergei. 'Both vessels spending their first few years sailing around each other at the eastern end of the Mediterranean and now here they are again both working the North Sea.'

Sergei came to an abrupt halt, pushed a door open and then stood to one side to allow Ed to enter. Ed immediately noticed how sparsely the cabin was furnished: two chairs stood by a table and along one wall was a bed and that was pretty much it, no comfy chairs, no drinks cabinet, not even a picture on the wall, or a lampshade on the light bulb overhead.

Ed turned and looked at Sergei with a very puzzled look on his face.

'I'm afraid I don't understand,' said Ed apologetically.

'Why should you?' said Sergei. 'This operation has taken years and years of planning and has cost me hundreds of thousands of roubles to get this far, why should I tell you anything before today and risk jeopardising my investment?'

'Fair point,' conceded Ed, 'but I find this all very intriguing. You meet me in the middle of the North Sea in a vessel identical in every way to my own, it even has the same colour scheme! My ship is full of unregistered brand-new BMWs and yours with crashed used versions. You lead me to your cabin through deserted corridors and then when we get here you have nothing more than a bed, two chairs and a table, it doesn't make a lot of sense at the moment.'

'You forgot to mention the bottle of vodka and the two glasses,' grinned Sergei obviously enjoying the game he was playing with Ed.

'Sit down and I will explain everything.'

Sergei moved across to the table and poured a large shot of the clear liquid into each glass and then handed one to Ed, who had now seated himself in the right hand of the two chairs.

Sergei started by telling Ed all about his past, running "goods" for the Russian mafia and how, fifteen years later, he had built up a vast fortune dismantling old BMWs and recycling the parts.

'Five years ago,' he continued, 'I was on the lookout for a new ship that could transport my "raw materials" in far greater numbers. I employ agents throughout Europe to track down the best cars, those that are written off but are still able to offer up a wealth of second-hand parts, which I now sell to spares dealers and on the Internet. Quite by chance I came across the *Baltic Carrier,* as she is now called, and all my transportation problems were solved overnight.

'It was about three months later that I discovered that she had a sister ship owned by your employees West Coast Shipping and when I found out that she too was transporting cars around the North Sea, I started to hatch a plan, a plan that has taken nearly four year to bear fruit.'

Sergei moved across the cabin and sat on the bed with his back up against the wall and his glass of vodka resting on his outstretched legs.

'So, what's with the scrap cars on board your ship? How are they going to help?' asked Ed intrigued by Sergei's plan.

Sergei got up and poured them both another vodka and then returned to the bed.

'As we speak, I have a crack team of commandoes moving through your ship effectively arresting your crew.

'Once we have accounted for them all, they will be taken to the recreation room and held under guard.

'If you had looked up when you came on board you would have noticed that the *Baltic Carrier* is already carrying the name *Tricolor* and over the next three hours every item on the ship that has any reference on it that can link it to that ship will be transferred to this ship and vice versa. We will be swapping everything from the ship's compass and lifebelts to the salt and pepper pots and ashtrays that on your ship bear the insignia W.C.S.'

'Ooookay,' said Ed hesitantly trying to work out the reasoning behind all the effort to swap the ships' identities.

'So, you end up with a ship full of brand-new BMWs and I end up with a ship full of trashed cars.'

'Sort of,' said Sergei. 'Over the last seven or eight months I have been stockpiling any cars that are less than two years old because that was when the last facelift was carried out by BMW.

'Like this ship these cars have had all their identities removed. On the outside there is little to do, mainly just license plates and dealership stickers. The clever bit is the on-board computers.

'The technology these days has moved on so far that each car now has its own signature when plugged into a diagnostic computer. This can tell the operator everything about the vehicle, from the chassis and engine numbers, to the dealership at which the car was last serviced and what was done to it.

'All the information about the cars on board this vessel is now held on several laptops and when the *Tricolor* is secure,' Sergei looked down at his watch, 'which should be in about eight minutes, my team of computer engineers will begin to give the cars on board your ship their new identities. Obviously, any data referring to servicing etc. will not be downloaded, but with the help of the vehicle identification plates which my team have managed to perfect a way of replacing without any visible signs of tampering, all the new cars' will have the old cars identities and will therefore appear perfectly legitimate when sold on.'

'Very clever,' said Ed, 'but there are over two thousand cars on board my ship, it will take you years to sell on that many cars without raising a few suspicions, especially on BMW's doorstep!'

Sergei smiled as he remembered his own concerns about how he was going to make a profit out of all these new cars.

'China,' he said getting up and heading towards the table for another refill.

'China?' said Ed

'Yes,' said Sergei offering Ed another shot of vodka, which he refused, 'China. As you may have noticed, over the last few years the Chinese economy has gone from strength to strength and with a thriving economy comes wealth. The Chinese at the moment are crying out for luxury cars and BMWs are particularly sought after.

'As you are now aware, over the years I have built up very close relationships with the Russian mafia. The people I deal with are some of the most important underworld figures in the whole of Russia and much like the head of Sony or Ford they make it their business to find out what their competitors are up to. Unlike Sony or Ford however, instead of trying to beat their competitors to the next big seller they work out ways of maximising the profits by exploiting whatever is on offer. That's why the drug barons in Columbia have a marketplace for their goods in the USA. They effectively sell the drugs to the Mafia in America who then look after the distribution side of things.'

'So, you are selling the cars to the Chinese mafia?'

'Indirectly yes,' continued Sergei. 'I am actually going to sell them to my Russian mafia friends who in turn are going to sell them on to the most powerful Triad group in China.'

'So what happens to this vessel with all your damaged vehicles on board?' asked Ed his mind still trying to come to terms with the complexities of the plan. 'It's not like I'm going to be able to sail her into port without someone noticing a rather large change in the particulars of the cargo.'

Sergei took another gulp of his vodka.

'There are several very good reasons why we asked you to meet us at this point in the North Sea,' continued Sergei. 'Firstly, we are far enough out not to be noticed by any coastguards or excise patrols. Secondly this is not on a recognised shipping lane and therefore again we won't be seen, and thirdly and most importantly we are now located over the Liberman Trench, a mile-wide gouge across the sea floor that extends almost ten miles from end to end.'

'You're going to sink her?' said Ed looking around him at the spartan cabin.

'Got it in one,' smiled Sergei

'But why?'

'No choice I'm afraid,' said Sergei. 'Following a SOS message that we will be sending out on your behalf when the time is right, the minimum the authorities will expect to find is a wreck on the seabed.

'We have calculated that with the Liberman Trench at this point 150 metres deep, it will keep all but a handful of divers away, however there is a possibility that a more determined salvage company might try to raise her, or send down a diving bell or minisub to take a look. If that turns out to be the case, we need them to be able to find the right ship with the right cargo.

'Unfortunately, as the ship sinks the cargo is going to get pretty roughed up so all they will find, is the ship they are expecting to find; the *Tricolor* and its cargo decks full of smashed up BMWs.'

'That's all pretty impressive, but I think you've forgotten one very important thing,' said Ed. 'There's a crew of twenty-two men aboard my ship, what are you going to do about them?'

Sergei had given this a good deal of thought and although the temptation was to let them go down with the *Baltic Carrier,* he was very aware that the crew Leif had, was both small and relatively inexperienced outside the North Sea. This time of year, was renowned for unpredictable weather and with a trip of the scale they had planned and a cargo valued in the millions he had decided it would be prudent to keep the crew alive and available if the going got tough.

'They will be practising their swimming skills from somewhere in the South China Sea,' said Sergei in a matter-of-fact sort of way.

'You're going to kill them?' spluttered Ed hardly believing what he had just been told. 'In cold blood?'

'Once again I have no choice,' said Sergei calmly. 'I cannot risk them going to the authorities and telling them all about what they have witnessed. Think about it what would you do under the circumstances?'

'Well, I err... I err... don't know,' stuttered Ed, his mouth dry at the thought of what was going to happen to his crew. 'But I wouldn't kill them, you can't!'

'Oh, but I can,' said Sergei, with a cold smile.

Ed stood up from his chair and took a step towards Sergei.

In one fluid movement Sergei rolled off the bed and pulled a Stechkin APS pistol from the small of his back and aimed it right between Ed's eyes.

Ed froze momentarily and then lunged at Sergei like a crazed animal, screaming like a banshee as he charged across the cabin.

'Noooooooo!'

Sergei was fully prepared for the onslaught and swiftly clicked off the safety before adjusting his aim and shooting Ed at close range.

Over the years Sergei had shot many men, after all he was in a business where people couldn't always be trusted, but the impact of shooting someone at close range in a confined space would live with him for some time. Ed's head exploded under the impact of the bullet sending blood, bone and tissue everywhere and a split second later he hit the cabin floor with a heavy thud.

As the gun smoke began to dissipate and the ringing in Sergei's ears turned into a hum, the cabin door behind him flew open and Viktor appeared, a Colt 45 sweeping the area in front of him.

'You okay?' said Viktor peering at Sergei's blood-splattered face for any sign of injury.

'Yes, I think so,' said Sergei bending down to pick up a bed sheet. 'Ed was not impressed with certain parts of my plan so I thought it better to "let him go".'

Viktor looked down at the crumpled body lying in front of

them, the top of the skull completely missing.

'You need to get a smaller pistol my friend,' said Viktor, 'that Stechkin is far too powerful for close-range work, look at the state of this cabin, you've even put a bullet through the porthole.'

Sergei looked up at the porthole from behind his bloodied bed sheet.

'I only made one shot,' said Sergei almost apologetically.

'Well, it must have been a good one, because not only did it nearly take his head off, it then continued through glass to freedom.'

Sergei stepped over Ed's body and took a closer look at the porthole, which had a small but perfectly round hole in it just above centre.

'You're right,' he said shakily and then turned and vomited into the corner of the room.

It was five minutes and a change of clothes later, when they both returned to the bridge. Shortly after arriving the signal from the sister ship told them that all was secure and it was now that the real work began. Sergei had by now regained his composure and, as Viktor started barking out orders to the various teams on board the *Baltic Carrier,* Sergei looked across at his new ship.

Although the two ships were handed over to their new Greek owners on the same day in 1996 Sergei's ship was in fact completed one month earlier than the ship facing him and for the last year, he had studied this vessel in great detail to make sure that it was totally identical to his own in every way. He had even had photographs taken when she was in port so he could compare any changes that may have been made in the intervening years, and as he looked on now, he was trying to see if even at this late stage in proceedings there was anything out of place. Fortunately for him because both vessels were commissioned and built side by side, there was no time for any upgrades to be incorporated into either ship and the only differences he could find were very minor indeed.

It was about Easter time that Sergei got word that the *Tricolor* was being repainted and despite the fact that he had plans to send the *Baltic Carrier* to the bottom of the Liberman Trench in a few months, he had it repainted in identical colours.

As he looked out from the bridge it was like looking into a gigantic mirror and he was now confident that when they returned to Kaliningrad nobody would realise that it was a different ship to the one that left port five days earlier.

Despite their lengthy preparations it still took thirty men two and a half hours to completely swap the two ships' identities.

It took a further thirty minutes to transfer all the personnel from the *Baltic Carrier* to the *Tricolor* in the two Zodiacs and with the exception of Duggan and two of his men, the only other crew member still aboard was Captain Leif Anderson who was supervising the opening of the seacocks, allowing thousands of gallons of freezing water to start to flood into the ship.

As Duggan, Leif and his remaining men left the doomed ship towards their escape dingy they could feel the ship starting to list slightly to port.

As the four men jumped into the Zodiac and started to power away from the doomed ship Duggan reached into his backpack and pulled out a remote-control firing mechanism.

When he depressed the firing button a huge explosion boomed out as a limpet mine exploded at the bow of the ship. The blast blew a ten-foot-wide hole in the port side and its effect was almost immediate with thousands of gallons of water flooding through the ship without any bulkheads to slow it down.

It only took five minutes for the Zodiac to catch up with the "new" *Baltic Carrier* but by the time they were aboard and everything was stowed away the *"Tricolor"* was starting to look very low in the water. As Sergei, Viktor and the rest of the crew watched on, the ship started to list heavily to port and in the calm night air the first murmurings of a ship in trouble started to waft across the water. By now the *Baltic Carrier* was over a mile away and to the people looking on the sounds that emanated from the ship sounded muffled and suppressed. To Sergei the guttural moans and shrieks of the ship beginning to break up reminded him of whales communicating with one another in the depths of the ocean and, following another explosion from deep within the ship, she gracefully keeled over onto her port side as if preparing herself for the final act. A few seconds later all the lights went out leaving nothing but the darkness and the haunting sounds of a ship in her final throes.

She sank ten minutes later, the flat calm sea becoming a vortex of water, and air, all fighting their way to the surface, where they bubbled and spat at each other like the contents of a witches' caldron, before calming to form a frothy stain on the surface.

Two hours later an SOS message was sent giving the rough position of the sinking, but despite a massive operation by Norwegian, Dutch, German, Belgian and British search and rescue personnel that lasted three full days, no sign of the ship or her crew were found.

6

Christmas 2013 saw Christmas Day falling in the middle of the week, leaving companies like Moore's & Thackeray having to bring in a skeleton staff team on Friday the twenty-seventh.

The Flatpack team only consisted of a handful of people at full complement and today this was whittled down to just two staff members, Jim and the unfortunately named Richard Balls.

Jim had been trapped in the office for the previous couple of weeks by a backlog of paperwork and was starting to get a bit stir crazy. When he first joined Flatpack his office was like a comfort blanket to him and he was always happy to return to its rhythmic goings-on, but over the last few years this had turned full circle and he was now much happier on board the *Sandie Watson* with Nick, getting to the bottom of some seafaring misdemeanour.

As he sat at his desk throwing screwed-up balls of paper at the wastepaper recycling bin, Richard appeared carrying two cups of coffee. In his usual deliberate manner, he put one of the cups down beside Jim and then moved across to his own desk that sat at right angles to his boss's.

Jim had first met Richard nearly three years earlier when he was recruiting for a PA-cum-dogsbody in the department and, right from the outset, he had tried to alleviate the problem with his name by calling him RB rather than addressing him by his given name.

Jim's idea had slowly taken hold and now everyone from the cleaners to the directors addressed him and introduced him as RB. This had done wonders for his overall confidence and self-esteem and Jim often wondered whether his life would have taken a different path if he had just been plain old Dave Smith instead of Dick Balls.

RB was working for a local cruise company before joining Flatpack and spent his week selling expensive tours around the Norwegian fjords and other off the beaten track destinations.

It was his skill with languages however that the really set RB apart from the other candidates at interview, and although he didn't understand it himself, he freely admitted, that he found learning new languages very easy.

It was these language skills that Jim and Nigel were looking for in the successful candidate, as Jim and Nick's work often took them inside international waters and having someone on hand who could explain what was happening and make requests of the closest countries was invaluable.

Part of RB's role also involved sorting out the logistical side of things, booking flights, hotels, car hire etc. and dealing with the locals in the event that a piece of equipment failed or needed replacing. With most of their work concentrated around Europe, nearly all of which have English as a second language this was not always a major problem for Jim and Nick to sort out, but it was very useful to have RB's skills a phone call away when required.

'You need a haircut, you scruffy individual,' goaded Jim looking at RB's shoulder-length curly mop of dark blond hair.

'And you need to put some polish on those shoes,' RB

countered looking down at Jim's boat shoes that hadn't seen any polish in several weeks of wear.

'Fifteen all,' said Jim in his best umpire's voice, knowing full well that his shoes desperately needed some attention.

They fell silent for a moment each thinking of the next shot in their verbal tennis match.

At that moment the telephone on Jim's desk murmured into life. The phone system in their office was an all singing and dancing affair and in one of his quieter moments RB had found a way to alter the volume of the ring tone on incoming calls. Now when each call came through the ringing would start at a very low volume and with each successive ring the volume would get louder and louder and seemingly more urgent, until just when you thought it couldn't go any higher the voicemail would kick in.

Jim took the call on the second ring.

'Good morning, Moore's & Thackeray, Jim Jackson speaking how can I help?'

'Morning Jim it's Mark at Lloyds, I was hoping you would be in the office today.'

'Mark, how are you? How was your Christmas?'

Mark Roper was their main contact at Lloyds of London and over the years he and Jim had become good friends as well as work colleagues.'

'I'm very well thank you and we had a great Christmas with Vanessa's parents just north of Paris, very relaxing, just the way it should be.'

Mark's wife Vanessa was French and whenever they met up, she would take great delight in throwing in the odd sentence in French and then mercilessly take the mickey out of Jim as he tried to decipher what she had said.

'And how is Mademoiselle Vanessa?' said Jim with his tongue placed firmly in his cheek.

'Miss Vanessa is as beautiful, funny and vivacious as ever,' said Mark subtly putting Jim right on his misuse of the word *Mademoiselle.*

'In fact, we were only saying the other day that we need to get together before too long, it must be three or four months since we last met up for the weekend.'

'Yes, it was the end of September if I remember correctly,' said Jim. 'I'll email you some dates when I'm free and hopefully we can put something together.'

'Look forward to it, how was your festive celebrations?'

'Oh, the usual stuff, Nick and I landed on Nigel and Karen's front doorstep on Christmas Eve and I came to work from there this morning, in fact it's just as well this isn't a video phone link because as RB has already pointed out, I'm looking very second hand this morning. Actually, I'm glad you phoned this morning because I wanted to run something past you and Vanessa.

'As you know since I lost Catherine and Nick lost Sandie, we have been very dependent on Nigel, Karen and the girls for our Christmas cheer. Last night when everyone else had gone to bed Nick and I were thinking of ways to show our appreciation of all their hospitality over the years.'

'Sounds a nice idea,' said Mark. 'So what did you come up with?'

'A chateau.'

'A chateau?' repeated Mark

'Yes,' said Jim.

'What we came up with, was next year we thought we would like to hire a chateau somewhere in eastern France so there is some snow, for a week over Christmas. We would only tell Nigel, Karen and the girls a week in advance and hopefully give them a Christmas to remember. Better still we would invite in secret some of Nigel and Karen's closest friends and family to join us along with yourself and Vanessa.'

'I like the sound of that and I'm sure Vanessa would be up for it.'

'I'm going to need your help with this though,' continued Jim. 'You see I was hoping Vanessa would be able to point us in the right direction as far as finding somewhere that is both in the snowline and able to accommodate maybe twenty-five people.'

'No problem at all, in fact thinking back I'm sure she has an aunt and uncle who run a ski lodge near Annecy and if that's not suitable they are sure to know of something that is, leave it with me, I'll have a word with Vanessa tonight.'

'Thanks that would be great,' said Jim, 'now how can I help you this morning?'

'Have you been reading about the *Tricolor* over the last few days?' asked Mark

'That's the cargo ship that sunk without trace on the twenty-third isn't it?' said Jim. 'Wasn't it carrying a belly full of BMWs.

'Yeah, just one or two, I think the whole cargo has a value of about forty to fifty million pounds and that's without the cost of the *Tricolor* herself. It's all a bit strange though. She left Zeebrugge on schedule heading for Hull where she was due to make a drop of two hundred cars before heading across the Atlantic to visit the good old US of A. Everything seemed fine and the first thing anyone knew about her being in trouble was at four a.m. when a mayday message was picked up giving her position as being about fifty miles north of where she should have been at that time. What is really strange though is that there was only one mayday message sent and when the coastguard answered the message all he got was static, it was as if the ship had gone under in about thirty seconds flat. What's more, as you are probably aware, no survivors or sizeable chunks of wreckage have been found by any one of nearly twenty vessels that rushed to the scene. Even more puzzling, is that rather unusually for this time of year, the sea was flat calm that night.'

'It does sound a little odd,' said Jim

'It's more than a little odd,' said Mark. 'Look, what I'm going to do is send you what we've got at the moment, which to be honest, isn't a lot. How are you and Nick fixed at the moment; got anything on-going?'

'No, your timing is perfect,' confessed Jim. 'I literally finished writing the report on the Fitzgerald sinking last week so we are ready when you are.'

'Okay, that's good,' said Mark excitedly. 'I think the first thing we need to do on this one is find her, as quickly as possible, it must have been the worst Christmas possible for the families of those crewmen.

'At the moment all we have are the co-ordinates given to us very hastily in that single mayday message, but the search parties have found nothing at that point, so we are not 100% sure that those are the right figures.

'I will email across to you what we have and once you've had a flick through it and spoken to Nick can you ring me back with an ETA for the co-ordinates we've been given?'

'Sure thing,' answered Jim who, as with every new case, was already feeling the excitement starting to build in his stomach.

'Just one more thing,' said Mark. 'Can you ask RB to liaise fully with Mike at this end? Because of the Christmas holidays we have been having big problems getting through to people that might be able to answer some of our questions and give us the information we require. Hopefully with these two liaising with each other and working as a team we won't end up phoning the same people twice.'

'All sounds good to me; I'll get RB to call Mike once we've been through your email.'

'Good, speak to you later then.'

Mark hung up and Jim reached forward and gently put the receiver back on its cradle.

'That sounded interesting,' said RB. 'Wouldn't be anything to do with the *Tricolor* would it?'

Jim filled him in on what was said and they then read the email that Mark had sent them. Mark was correct, they had very little information to work with but hopefully with RB and Mike on the case the information would start to flow.

Jim instructed RB to phone Mike and co-ordinate their work and then headed out the door to find Nick.

Despite owning a ship crammed full of the latest gizmos and gadgets, Nick hated mobile phones and when he was 'off duty' so was his mobile. Luckily for Jim they had discussed the previous night a problem they had with part of the rigging on the *Poacher*, which was currently moored at Woodbridge ten miles away, so that was where Jim now headed.

7

Woodbridge lies on the river Deben in Suffolk and a more pleasant little country town you will struggle to find. It's an old-fashioned sort of town with old-fashioned values and winding little streets and back lanes that in parts are totally unable to cope with modern day conveniences like the motorcar. The high street meanders its way through the town centre, and most of the shops open and close at specific times. Some Sunday and Bank Holiday opening has crept in over the years, but you will go hungry if you are hoping to find any of the major fast-food outlets for a quick burger or piece of seasoned chicken.

It's a wealthy but staid sort of town and as long as the well-offs remain in charge, it should stay that way, with the nightlife nothing more riotous than a few posh restaurants. It is these values and attributes that make it so unique and most visitors seem to find it totally charming.

December the twenty-seventh was predictably busy and as Jim made his way down to the quay where the *Poacher* was moored, he found himself thinking about how he and Catherine would often go down to Woodbridge on a Sunday lunchtime, have a couple of pints in The Cherry Tree with a packet of crisps and then walk along the river front watching the wildlife as they went.

The Deben at Woodbridge is still very tidal and when at

low tide the river takes on a whole new look with a single narrow channel running down its middle and wide muddy flanks on either side. With the tide out there would be an influx of waders and it would always amaze Catherine how many footprints a small number of birds could create in the mud between tides. It was like a pattern on a carpet with hardly a square inch untouched by a myriad of small trident-like indentations.

Jim's mind was quickly brought back into focus by the crossing gates he was approaching starting to alert people of an oncoming train. As he pulled up to the barrier, he caught a glimpse of Nick in the distance about ten feet up the mast of the *Poacher,* tugging heavily on a piece of the rigging.

The train was only two carriages, but once it had slowly passed and come to a halt in the riverside station Nick had vanished.

Initially Jim sat patiently waiting for the barriers to lift back up to their open position, but although this only took a few seconds with still no sign of Nick, starting to panic a little, he accelerated across the crossing and down to where the *Poacher* was moored. Climbing out of the car he was relieved at last to see Nick pop up from the far side of the boat still hanging onto his piece of rope.

'Bloody hell!' Jim shouted, 'you just scared the shit out of me, one minute you were halfway up the mast the next gone!'

'Bit of a shock to me as well,' said the big man dusting himself down. 'Luckily it didn't let go altogether and I hit the deck at a reduced rate of fall than I might have done, bloody thing!'

'What were you doing up there anyway?' asked Jim. 'you

don't even like heights!'

'It's that pulley block,' said Nick pointing up to a mahogany-coloured oval-shaped assembly with two little wheels in it around which the rope was threaded.

'One of the pulley wheels has split and the rope keeps jamming up. I was trying to free it up again when it suddenly let go and caught me off balance, the rest you sort of know. It'll have to be replaced; we've got some spares in the forward locker I believe; can you get one for me?'

'Yes, no problem,' Jim said moving towards the bow of the old ship and opening a big wooden trunk-like locker placed behind the front hatch.

'What are you doing here anyway? I thought you were at the office this morning.'

'I was, but we had a call from Mark in London, he's got a job for us. Tell you what, let's have a brew and I'll tell you all about it… here, is this the correct pulley block?'

'Looks like it will do the job. C'mon, I'll put the kettle on, after an experience like I've just had, I might need to add something a little stronger as well.'

Over the next twenty minutes Jim explained to Nick his phone call with Mark and the need to get under way as soon as possible.

'Well, we can leave tomorrow morning, depending on the tides,' said Nick. 'There is one big problem though.'

'Which is?'

'No crew,' said Nick throwing his hands up in the air. 'There's only Alfie on board at the moment and we are going to need at least four of us even if we are only on a search; at the moment our crew compliment is two, you and me.'

Alfie was an old sea dog that Nick had met many years

ago in the Seaman's Mission in Harwich when he first started using the port for the *Sandie Watson*. Like many old sailors who had spent their whole lives at sea, Alfie didn't have anywhere to call home and would earn a few extra pounds here and there by playing caretaker for Nick and one or two others in the port.

'Why, have you stood them all down? You never stand them all down at the same time.'

Nick could tell that Jim wasn't happy with the situation and walked over to the gunwale.

'Look I'm sorry,' he said looking across the river. 'This year has been the busiest we've ever had and I just thought they guys needed some downtime with their families. Guess I'm getting soft in my old age.'

There was a brief silence and Nick turned around to find Jim leaning against the mast with a broad grin on his face.

'What's so funny?' he asked

'I'm just picturing the headlines in the newspapers tomorrow, "Caveman gone soft" they would say.'

Nick laughed. 'Yeah, wouldn't do a lot for my tough guy image would it? C'mon we need to make a few phone calls and see how many crew we can muster.'

By the following morning they had rounded up four of the crew, which would be enough to launch a search mission with the side-scan sonar. Alfie was duly paid off and, following the loading of a few essential fresh supplies, they started to make preparations to leave port. The *Sandie Watson* measured thirty-two metres long and was a proud vessel with her upswept bow painted in dark navy blue. About three feet down from her gunwales was a six-inch-deep white stripe that ran the length of her hull. Her superstructure was all painted white and her most notable feature was a huge communications mast that stood erect behind the bridge. Towards the stern were two substantial cranes that could lift the submersibles in and out of the water and a huge steel cradle that supported a small minisub.

She had started out life as a survey vessel and spent her first ten years working in the Gulf of Mexico with a research crew from Florida's Grassy Key College, studying dolphins. After ten years' service she was replaced with an all-new vessel, and that was when Nick came across her in the small ads of the imaginatively named ship brokering company, Ships R Us.

Powered by a Lister Blackstone 700BHP engine she had a cruising speed of nine knots and a top speed of about eleven and a half knots flat out. Her party trick however was the stern and bow thrusters which when combined with the GPS meant that she could keep herself perfectly positioned over a wreck without any intervention from Nick and the crew. Since taking delivery Nick had added hundreds of thousands of pounds' worth of search equipment and the engine had been upgraded to give her a top speed of nearly fifteen knots.

On all but a handful of previous trips Jim and Nick knew where they were going, knew what to expect when they got there, and had a pretty good idea of the outcome of the voyage, before they even left port. This however was a completely different scenario for them, due partly to the Christmas break and partly to the simple fact that no one had actually come up with a positive position for the wreck site. As they sailed out of the shelter of the port Nick entered the last recorded position of the *Tricolor* into the GPS, set the throttles and headed them in the general direction of Norway.

It took them about six hours sailing to reach the co-ordinates they had been given, by which time the weak winter sun was sinking into the North Sea. The sea was slight and the sky was clear, so apart from the temperature that was likely to plummet to well below zero during the long night-time period, conditions were ideal for the kind of work they had planned.

One of the crew members that Nick had managed to persuade to come on board was Ewan, a thirty-eight-year-old engineer with an amazing ability to be able to fix anything from a fouled propeller to a malfunctioning ROV (remotely operated vehicle). His talents were such that, if he had not made himself available, Nick would have had to find at least three other people to cover the bases left vacant. Despite his obvious skills, Ewan was just "one of the crew" and rarely complained about his multifaceted role aboard the *Sandie Watson*. He was just one of life's 'busy' people, and the old saying "if you want something done in a hurry give it to a busy person" applied fully to the lanky Yorkshireman.

As the sun disappeared below the horizon, it left behind a stunning crimson sky, streaked with the criss-cross vapour trails of aircraft heading to and from mainland Europe to the UK. Ewan's shift in the engine room was complete and as he surfaced from the depths of the ship onto the open rear deck, he reached into his top pocket for a cigarette. It was one of those rare but extremely enjoyable moments when a shift, a cigarette, and a spectacular sunset unexpectedly collided together and he spent the next five minutes quietly enjoying his Marlboro whilst marvelling at the beauty of Mother Nature's handiwork.

The stern of the *Sandie Watson* was very much the business end of the ship and as well as two huge cranes that were used for lifting the ROVs, minisub and some of the smaller salvage on board, there was also a large box room that housed all the dive equipment and the tackle that went with it.

It was here that Ewan felt most at home and the robots that surrounded him were like his children, there to be looked after and fettled and occasionally chastised when they didn't behave themselves. As he sat down at his makeshift desk, which began life as a mess room table, Nick appeared in the doorway.

'How are you doing down here then?' he asked, unaware that Ewan had only just arrived himself.

'Yes, I'm good,' replied Ewan. 'Just got down here myself, so I'm just going to plug in the towfish and while it's doing its diagnostic run-through, which will take about twenty minutes, then I'm going to head for the mess and get an early supper.'

'You could be out of luck there, remember we've got no Roly on this trip, so Jim is doing the cooking and I have to admit I haven't got a clue what he's got planned or how long it will take to prepare.'

Ewan moved across to the on-board intercom.

'JJ it's Ewan, can you give me an ETA for dinner please?'

'Gonna be about 1800 hours, chilli con carne okay for you?'

'Sounds great, thanks, have we got any of those jalapeño peppers on board?'

'I'll see what I can find.'

Ewan turned to Nick.

'Looks like I'm going to have time to check the cabling as well, which with all the bending over involved is probably a job better done before one of JJ's chillis than after, if you know what I mean.'

Both men chuckled at the schoolboy humour as only grown men can and then headed for the rear deck of the ship to check the umbilical cord that supplied the towfish with its power and data link with the *Sandie Watson*.

Nick moved across to a large electrical switch box and threw the lever. Instantly the rear deck was flooded with light and the dusk around them blinked to black.

It took them nearly forty-five minutes to visually check the 150 metres of cable and then another ten to hook it up to the laptop and perform the necessary diagnostics. With the blackness around them now impenetrable and the temperature dropping like the proverbial stone, the men quickly stowed away their gear and headed for the warmth of belowdecks.

'Smells good,' said Ewan as they entered the mess and sat down with the rest of the crew.

'ETA still 1800 hours?' he shouted across to Jim who was half obscured in the galley by the steam rising from a huge saucepan of rice.

'Give or take a few minutes,' he replied, 'does anyone want some bread with this?'

'I will,' piped up Sarah. 'I've had one of your chillis before, remember? Everyone laughed at the memory of Sarah's first encounter with one of Jim's creations, which had been laced with extra jalapeño's as a sort of initiation ceremony. Sarah tilted her head slightly to one side and stuck her tongue out to all and sundry.

Sarah was one of the newer members of the team on board the *Sandie Watson* but had taken to it like a duck to water and after less than six months was already a valued and respected member of the crew.

With her long dark hair, big brown eyes and long legs that appeared to finish somewhere near her armpits, she was not unattractive, but to avoid any on-board complications had made it known from the start that she didn't mix work with pleasure. Nick and Jim were quite pleased with this stance as it kept the harmony of the ship nicely balanced, and with most members of the crew either married or in some sort of relationship, problems were few and far between, but that didn't stop her from sparring with her male colleagues and had a good repertoire of one-liners ready for when they stepped out of line.

As a young girl growing up with two older brothers, she had had to decide at an early age whether to follow the girlie route through childhood with dolls, prams and frilly party frocks, or to try and keep up with her brothers and build go-carts, play football, climb trees and live in T-shirts and jeans all summer.

For Sarah this was a no-brainer and it was during these formative years that she learnt how to deal with, put down and coerce the supposedly stronger members of the species, to the extent that all the men on board now treated her as an equal; which was just how she liked it.

With a degree in oceanography from Southampton University she had been in love with the sea since her first encounter with a rock pool on the beach at Bexhill-on-Sea aged about six. Her ambition was to study in America, preferably on the West Coast but openings over there were very limited, so for now she would have to make do with studying the North Sea and its many river estuaries, rather than the Pacific Ocean. Despite her slightly butch, square-shouldered appearance, like many of the fairer sex Sarah had a very gentle touch and following the near loss of one of the ROVs whilst under Ewan's command, she was now the number two to Nick where the little high-tech submersibles were concerned. This for Sarah was a real honour and in her quieter moments she would sometimes smile to herself when considering her desire to be treated as an equal. As one of her favourite authors George Orwell pointed out in his book *Animal Farm*, some animals were *definitely* more equal than others.

The final member of the depleted crew on this voyage was Duncan Randall a good-natured forty-five-year-old Scotsman who kept the crew on their toes with his constant practical jokes and crazy stories. His favourite trick however was to use his laptop to create bogus letters, messages and official-looking forms that he would then periodically distribute around the ship in the dead of night. He would then be awoken in the morning by complete pandemonium, usually closely followed by Nick bursting into his quarters waving the offending pieces of paper and threatening to have him keel hauled.

His most recent offering was a letter supposedly signed by Nick attached to the mess room door stating that as part of a cost-cutting exercise, he (Nick) had secured a bulk buy of corned beef that would now be imaginatively worked into the menu for the forthcoming trip. This was further fuelled by the fact that Nick had indeed made some savings by buying a cheaper brand of coffee, a brand that the previous day had brought in complaints from almost every member of the crew. Beneath the statement was the menu for the coming week, the first day of which included corned beef fritters instead of sausages and bacon for breakfast, corned beef sandwiches for lunch and corned beef lasagne for supper, which was described as being a combination of fresh pasta sheets, creamy cheese sauce and succulent corned beef all layered together in an unforgettable culinary experience. Other delights on Duncan's menu included corned beef meatballs in onion gravy, corned beef pie and, as a special treat, a dessert of corned beef pavlova.

It was a full half hour before the bedlam died down and by the time Roly the chef served up his usual good helpings of "full English" without a corned beef fritter in sight, everyone was laughing and joking about other additions that could be added to the corned beef menu.

Duncan's main role was that of radio operator, come general dogsbody and his skills with a laptop would often prove invaluable, but like the rest of the crew he was able to perform a variety of other tasks as well, and as they all sat around the table that evening enjoying Jim's chilli they discussed who would be responsible for what, when the search for the *Tricolor* began in earnest the following morning.

8

Sunday 29 December 2013 dawned clear bright and very cold with a bitter northerly wind doing its best to permeate every crack and crevice on board the *Sandie Watson*. Wispy clouds dotted the sky and the occasional seabird circled the ship looking for any fishing activity. Everyone was up early and following a hearty breakfast supplied by their captain, they got to work on what in all probability was going to be a very long and tedious day.

As Ewan carried out some final checks on the side scan sonar, Nick programmed into the GPS system a series of sweeps across where the final co-ordinates of the *Tricolor* had been reported.

As he stood on the bridge his sea nose told him that this was not right. The ship had been lost only a few days earlier and since then the sea had remained quite calm for the time of year. The surface currents here were not that strong, but as he looked around his vessel there was absolutely nothing to indicate any sort of loss. No debris, no life rafts, no buoyancy rings, but most importantly no air bubbles or oil on the surface.

Many years earlier he and Sandie had visited Pearl Harbour where the American Pacific Fleet was almost felled in a single attack in December 1941. Their guide had pointed out to them the fuel oil still escaping the vessels some sixty years after the attack and Nick was reminded of this fact as he looked out over a clear blue sea all around them. Things did not bode well.

With Ewan's last-minute checks complete Duncan climbed up into the cab of one of the cranes and seconds later its diesel engine spluttered into life. Although the sonar was not a particularly heavy piece of gear it was much simpler to winch it into the sea than try and manhandle it and, with Jim manning the umbilical that connected it to the ship and Sarah sitting in the control room the device, was gently lowered into the sea.

The sonar they were using was typical of the sort used for deep-water assignments and its torpedo-shaped body measured no more than eight feet in length. The towfish, as it is called, is dropped to a certain depth and then as the name implies, towed behind the mother vessel at the given depth. With the course logged into the GPS system the boat automatically sweeps backwards and forwards across a given search grid like a man mowing a lawn, each run slightly overlapping the previous one. As it travels along it sends out sound waves and the echoes from these are then sent up the cable to the ship where they are converted into a pictorial map of the seabed. Dense objects like rock and metal bounce back good strong signals whilst a muddy or fauna-covered seabed will send back a much weaker response.

The trick was to know what depth to tow at, as the closer to the sea floor the better the images. However, this also narrowed down the amount that could be scanned in one pass, and then there was the danger of getting snagged on an unexpected outcrop or a sunken ship's mast.

The night before Sarah and Nick had studied detailed maps of the seabed below them and knew that there were very few obstacles in their path other than those manmade. They decided that fifty metres off the bottom was a safe depth and as the *Sandie Watson* set off on the first pass the cabling was played out until the towfish levelled out at exactly that depth.

In the control room the crew huddled together to look at the images being produced on a large monitor mounted on the wall, while Nick stayed on the bridge keeping one eye on the ship's radar for other shipping and the other on the GPS which would tell him when he needed to make a turn.

The GPS system Nick had inherited with the ship was one of the most advanced in the world and by triangulating its course with the twenty-four satellites thousands of miles above, it was able to stay exactly on any given course without any intervention from the helm. The monitor that Nick was looking at showed him the longitude, latitude and even local currents, along with the course he had plotted and the depth to the sea floor. Being wired into the ship's computer and helm meant that ship could have been left completely to its own devices and allowed to make its own turns at the end of each run, but Nick hated not being involved, so when the plotted course was completed and the buzzer sounded, Nick leapt to his feet, switched the system to manual and swung the ship round in a wide 180-degree turn.

His job done he then settled back into his elevated chair and once again took up the role of assistant to the computers.

The first few hours produced very little, the occasional outcrop, but mainly a screen full of gently undulating seabed. After three hours Ewan took over from Sarah as the chief watch, and three hours after that Jim took over from Ewan. This was the worst part of searching for a wreck site with no firm co-ordinates to work from and they all knew there could be several days of this before the *Tricolor* was found.

At two p.m. Sarah volunteered to do a second shift and was just starting to relax into her chair when the seabed started to drop away quite sharply on the port side.

'Hello, hello,' said Jim who was standing looking over Sarah's shoulder, 'what's going on here then?'

'Don't get too excited now,' said Sarah sensing his anticipation building, 'it's called the Liberman Trench, and it was discovered in 1974 by a French survey team led by, wait for it... a chap called Gustav Liberman.'

'Not Gustav Liberman!' said Jim in mock surprise, 'tell me more.'

Sarah, who could sense that he was in one of his less than serious moods, continued.

'Are we sitting comfortably?' Jim moved across to a desk on the far wall of the cabin, cleared himself a space and sat down swinging his legs back and forth like a small child.

'I'm ready,' he said in a squeaky childlike voice.

'Then I'll begin,' said Sarah in her best teacher's voice.

'Gustav Liberman was working for Shell Oil in 1974 when he was asked to survey to the south of the main oilfields in the hope that he would come across some more reserves that could be easily reached.

'As you know, where the North Sea is now, was once a land bridge that linked the UK to Europe and consequently the sea is relatively shallow until you get up towards Norway, between fifty and a hundred metres deep at this point, or at least that's what everyone thought until 1974.

'In July 1974 he was surveying about twenty miles north of here when his readings suddenly went completely haywire. It took him three days of zigzagging backward and forwards

110

to plot this huge gouge in the sea floor which he estimated to be nearly one hundred and fifty metres deep at its deepest point. The rest as they say is history.'

'So what caused it?'

During the Ice Age the ice fields stretched down as far as north Norfolk, which is south of where we are here. It therefore seems likely that it's the result of a large glacier, but to be fair the jury is still out on that one. It's just a shame that "our" Grand Canyon is buried under fifty metres of water and will only ever be seen on a topographical map.'

'You say it stretches north for twenty miles?'

'Yes, and for the most part it's only a hundred metres deep, but as I said in places this increases to nearly one hundred and fifty metres. If the *Tricolor* is in there we're screwed.'

Jim jumped down from the desk and moved over to the monitor to take a closer look at the picture.

'So how wide is Mr Liberman's trench?'

'On average about three quarters of a mile, but at this end it's a little wider, as I said it's still a bit of an anomaly really. Although people have been aware of its existence for nearly thirty years, no one has been able to make a hard-core study of exactly how big it is and precisely how it happened to be here, in the middle of what is now the North Sea.

'As you know Ice Age Glaciers ravaged places like Norway. The steep-sided valleys with the fjords at their base are a similar shape to the Liberman Trench and because glaciers transport a huge amount of debris with them on their journey, which is then distributed at the face edge, many of the fjords are actually deeper than the surrounding sea. It's the same with Mr Liberman's trench, its deepest point is in the middle, Southampton Uni are trying to raise funds to explore it properly, that's how come I know so much about it.'

'I can't believe I've never come across it before,' said Jim.

'Why should you?' said Sarah. 'This is one of the least used pieces of the North Sea, insomuch as there are few shipping lanes that cross here, so if you hadn't studied it like I did, there would be no reason to know of its existence.'

'Yeah, guess so,' said Jim.

At that moment Nick's voice echoed round the ship on the intercom system.

'That's about it boys and girl we've run out of time today, prepare to bring up the fish on my signal.'

'Looks like I'm needed elsewhere,' said Jim pulling on his coat, 'by the way it's your turn to cook tonight, what's for dinner?'

'Have we got any corned beef? I can do a mean corned beef risotto,' said Sarah with a big grin on her face.

Jim laughed and headed out into the gathering dark.

Later that evening as the five of them sat looking at an empty dish of macaroni cheese they discussed how to continue the search.

'I vote we carry on northwards,' said Sarah.

'That's fine,' said Jim, 'but only if the *Tricolor* is north of the co-ordinates we were given. If she's south we are just getting further and further away from her with every sweep, besides which you've got extra motive for going north,' he continued, smiling at Sarah.

'Sarah?' said Nick with a puzzled look on his face.

'It's the Liberman Trench,' said Sarah, 'I studied it at uni and as I explained to Jim earlier it has never been properly mapped by modern surveying equipment. Our priority is obviously to find the *Tricolor* but if we are going to keep traversing the Trench, I could send the data back to Southampton University, they've been wanting to study this for years.'

'Oooookay,' said Nick. 'What about you, Duncan?'

'I'm for continuing north,' said Duncan, 'if we go south, we run into the main shipping lanes out of Humberside. I can't believe that if the ship went down there on a relatively calm night no one would have spotted it, however quickly she sank.'

'Good point,' said Nick. 'Ewan, Jim?'

'I would go along with what Duncan has just said to a point,' said Jim, 'but, don't forget she *was* heading for Humberside herself, so she can't be that far off her plotted course.'

'Ewan?' said Nick

'It's a toughie, but I feel we should try one more day north,' said Ewan. 'If we don't find her then we head south and try our luck.'

Nick sat at the head of the table massaging the corners of his mouth with the thumb and forefinger of his right hand.

'Okay' he said, 'this is what we will do. As we've already ascertained there are very good arguments for searching both north and south, but on balance I'm inclined to go with Duncan on this one. This is a good-sized vessel, 55,000 tons and a ship that size doesn't just disappear in a main shipping channel without someone seeing something, even if it's only debris. On the other hand, why would it be north of Humberside unless maybe that has something to do with her loss?

'So tomorrow we will continue searching to the north and yes Sarah, each time we pass over the Liberman Trench you can record all the data and pass it on to Southampton

University, you never know we may even get a mention in dispatches somewhere.

'Whatever happens tomorrow, the good news is that we will be back in port for New Year's Eve. If we find the *Tricolor* tomorrow we are going to need a few more crew members to do a full post-mortem, and if we don't, we are going to have to move the search into the main shipping lane and I'm not going there without a full complement either. So, I suggest we all get an early night tonight, it's going to be a long day tomorrow.'

As Sarah, Duncan and Ewan moved into the galley to wash up the dishes, Jim looked across the table at Nick.

'You think there's something wrong here, don't you?'

Nick dragged his hands down his face and then, with his elbows on the table, tented his fingers under his bearded chin.

'Do you remember that case about five years ago when we went looking for that sixty-foot Fairline Squadron motor yacht off Southampton?'

'Yes, the owner sank it deliberately to get the insurance money after he discovered the engines were knackered and they were going to cost him the thick end of £20,000 to replace.'

'That's right,' said Nick, 'but do you also remember why we took so long to find her.'

'Now you mention it, yes I do, he "mistakenly" gave the coastguard the wrong co-ordinates, didn't he?'

'Not quite, it was his friend if you remember who gave the coastguard the longitude and latitude, which as we later found out was three nautical miles from where the boat actually went down.'

'That's right,' said Jim, the investigation suddenly

coming into sharp focus in his head. 'They concocted some story about them both independently deciding to take advantage of the excellent late autumn weather, for a final thrash around the Isle of Wight before laying the boats up for the winter.'

'That's the one,' said Nick. 'The story was that his friend just happened to come across him and his wife in the life raft after he had hit some sort of debris in the water off Portsmouth. The truth however was that they had sunk the boat off Ryde on the Isle of Wight and then the three of them fed the coastguard a load of bullshit to cover up the trail.'

'Yes, that's right; but I'm afraid I don't see the link,' Jim said looking slightly puzzled.

'I'm not even sure there is one, BUT I had the same feeling this morning as I did on the first day of that search. I don't know why, but I feel there is more to this than a straightforward sinking. You know how you always bang on about not liking coincidences? Well, with this one there are too many parts that just don't add up and its putting me on edge.'

'I know what you mean,' said Jim. 'I must admit I have a similar feeling, but at least when we find her we can start putting some answers in the boxes. That's what we're good at, right?'

'That's assuming we find her,' said Nick.

Monday 30 December was another early start for the crew of the *Sandie Watson* and once again the weather was very kind to them, with a slight swell and a light drizzle, which in turn had brought the temperature up by a few degrees.

Duncan had provided them with a corned beef free breakfast at six o'clock and the towfish was in the water as the dawn broke at about seven a.m.

With the GPS fed with the necessary data, they once again set off across their invisible grid in search of the *Tricolor*.

They were barely half an hour into the search and on the first run over the Liberman Trench when the pointed shape of a ship's bow emerged from the top edge of the screen. Sarah quickly grabbed the intercom and called up to the bridge where Nick and Jim were looking at the shipping forecast.

'We've got something,' she said excitedly, 'but it's only the very tip of the bow.'

'Did it look like a large vessel? asked Jim

'Difficult to say,' said Sarah. 'It could have been, but then again... I don't know, how long before we get back to the Trench?'

Nick took the microphone.

'It's going to be about another half an hour, did you record the data?'

'Yes of course I did,' Said Sarah almost indignantly. 'I'll send it up.'

The ship had a network of computers on board each one linked to a central server. Seconds later Nick and Jim were looking at a replay of the run across the wreck on a screen at the rear of the bridge.

'Not much to go on there,' said Nick to Sarah over the intercom.

'What do you reckon then?' asked Sarah.

'Don't know,' replied Nick, 'but it's not worth breaking away from the grid for, anyway we'll be back over her in half an hour, keep me posted.'

The "grid" was what they called the criss-cross sets of intersecting lines that made up their search pattern and as each

116

run was completed, the relevant boxes were either crossed off or marked at the point where something had been found.

For Sarah the next half-hour seemed to fly by with first Duncan and then Ewan insisting on seeing a replay of the video. Jim then appeared with a tray of steaming coffee and, before they knew it, they were back over the Liberman Trench all peering intently at the screen on the wall.

'Here we go again,' said Sarah as the sea floor dived away into the Trench.

The cabin went silent, but for the dull throb of the engines two decks below.

'There!' said Ewan.

Everyone moved another inch or two closer to the screen.

As the sonar crossed over the wreck Sarah tapped on the keys of the computer to sharpen up the image.

'It's not big enough,' said Ewan. 'Look there's the bridge... it's just a lousy fishing boat... shit.'

The disappointment was tangible and almost simultaneously they all reached for their respective mugs of coffee.

At that moment Nick radioed down from the bridge.

'Got anything?'

Jim picked up the intercom, 'Not really it's just a fishing trawler or something a similar size.'

'I've got a vessel marked on the map,' said Nick, 'but it's supposed to be about half a mile north of our position.'

'Okay we'll log it and I'll get RB to check it out,' said Jim.

Whenever they found something that was either unexpected or out of place, the procedure was to check it out. This was nearly always done by RB in the office who had now become an expert at sifting through records and details of maritime losses.

Once RB had drawn his conclusions, he would forward on the details to the authorities that would decide if any further investigation needed to be done and make sure that the companies who supply the GPS information update their records to show the obstacle in its correct location.

This information is particularly important to fishermen. To them a wreck is a double-edged sword, often attracting a huge number of fish on the one hand, but also on the other hand able to relieve a trawler of several thousands of pounds worth of gear if snagged.

As Jim sent the details of the find to RB the search continued unabated.

Ewan took over for the second two hours, followed by Jim who monitored the screen up to lunchtime.

At twelve thirty p.m. Duncan sat down in the chair for the first time that trip and was just about to tuck into a cheese and pickle sandwich when something large began to appear on the screen.

'Whoa, I think we've just hit paydirt,' he said turning to Jim and Sarah who were standing behind him.

Sarah reached for the intercom.

'Nick, we've just found something big down here, what's your GPS and charts showing?'

'Nothing on either, tell me more,' replied Nick, the excitement rising in his voice.

'She's in the Trench lying on her port side. The bow section that we've got on the sonar looks intact, can't see any debris, which suggests the stern is still attached to what we can see.'

'Jim, you down there?'

'Yeah, I'm here Nick.'

'What do you think? Should I abandon the grid?'

'If it's not her Nick someone else has lost one pretty big ship without telling anyone. I'm sending up the images, have a look for yourself.'

Thirty seconds later the crew in the control cabin were aware that the throttles had been gunned and that the *Sandie Watson* had turned sharply to port.

As Jim peered out of the small porthole window, he realised that Nick had thrown them into a huge looping arc that would take them lengthways up the Trench.

It was ten long minutes before they were positioned back over the Trench, in which time Ewan had rigged up a live feed up to the bridge for Nick to watch.

'Just coming up on it now,' said Sarah on the intercom.

Nick instinctively reduced the throttles and the *Sandie Watson* settled into the water and then after a second or two's pause continued her forward momentum at little more than two knots. The line to the towfish was fed out a little so that they could benefit from the best possible clarity and in the cabin, everyone huddled around the screen in a deathly silence. As they neared the wreck Sarah gave a whispered countdown and right on cue as she reached zero the bow of a ship started to appear.

They all watched in total silence as the ethereal image developed on the screen. The silence was broken a minute later by Nick's voice on the intercom.

'That's her boys and girl, I'd bet the *Sandie* on it, but she's a bloody long way from where she should be, I really don't understand what she's doing here.'

'What do you want to do?' asked Jim.

'Not much we can do,' answered Nick, 'as I said last night, we are going to need a full complement of crew, so we will finish this run, mark the wreck with a buoy and head back to port.'

The mood in the control cabin had now turned very sombre. They had found what they were looking for but they also knew that it was very likely that below them trapped in the vessel lay the crew of the *Tricolor*.

As the towfish crossed the stern of the ship Ewan, Jim and Duncan silently left the cabin to start retrieving it, leaving Sarah to examine the data in more detail.

With the aid of the powerful computer on board she was able to sharpen up the images and, on rerunning the footage, made a startling discovery.

'Nick are you still on the bridge?' she asked on the intercom.

'Certainly am,' came the reply, 'just about to plot a course back to Harwich. We've got the towfish on board so it's full steam ahead any minute. What's the problem?'

'Well… I've just run the scan through the McIver software suite to sharpen it up and it's come up with two pieces of information that you may like to take a look at.'

'Okay I'm on my way.'

Nick had come to know and trust Sarah's professional judgement very well since she had joined the crew and it was with a certain amount of trepidation that he headed to the control room to find out what she had discovered that was so intriguing.

On entering the cabin, he was greeted by Ewan, Duncan and Jim who were all standing around the blank monitor screen.

'Okay we're all poised,' said Nick trying to lift the mood slightly.

'Right,' said Sarah, 'what do you make of this?'

She hit a key on the computer and a beige-coloured image appeared on the screen. It took them all a second or two to work out what they were looking at and then almost in unison a cry of "bloody hell!" swept through the cabin.

The image they were looking at was of the bow section of the ship lying on its side and clearly visible at the top of the picture was the name *Tricolor*. Below it at roughly waterline level was a huge hole, possibly as much as ten feet across and all around that was a mass of distorted metal.

'I don't know what she hit, but whatever it was it must have been pretty big and heavy to do that sort of damage,' said Duncan leaning forward to get a closer look.

'That's no impact,' said Sarah, 'look a bit closer.' She clicked the mouse over the centre of the image and the hole immediately doubled in size on the screen.

'See what I mean? The hole is far too regular to be an impact wound and all the damage looks to be from the outside in. If I didn't know better, I'd say that was caused by some sort of explosion.'

'What do you think Nick?' asked Jim. 'You've had more years at this game than the rest of us put together.'

'I've never seen anything like it,' said Nick, 'but I have to agree with Sarah it certainly looks like an explosion to me as well.'

'What about an old mine?' said Ewan.

'Possible but not very probable,' said Nick. 'They do occasionally get picked up by trawlers and the like, but I can't ever remember one exploding without some help from the Ministry of Defence.'

'So, what else could cause that sort of damage?' asked Jim.

'I really don't know,' replied Nick. 'We need to get a closer look with the ROV and confirm what we are looking at in more detail and then we can make a judgement. In the meantime, this discovery doesn't go outside these four walls, understood?

Everyone nodded in the affirmative and then, one by one, left the control room to prepare the ship for the trip back to port.

9

Christmas in Kaliningrad had been a fairly quiet affair for Sergei and Anouska and with the exception of a local businessman's ball on Christmas Eve they had managed to share some quality time together for the first time since their late summer vacation to Hurghada on the Egyptian Red Sea coast.

As Sergei looked down on the snow-covered port below him, the warm clear waters of the Red Sea seemed to be a whole world away, but although he loved the warmth of the sun on his back, he had to concede that the snow-covered mountains all around him were as stunning as the view they had enjoyed from their hotel, watching the sun come up over the Red Sea.

Down in the harbour the *Baltic Carrier* lay silently against the quay, the only movement being the patrolling of security personnel guarding the ship's valuable cargo.

Behind the ship was Sergei's huge recycling plant. Normally there would be plumes of steam escaping from the vents in the building and the flash of welding torches as they cut through metal, but today from his high vantage point at the villa nearly two miles away, Sergei could instantly tell that the whole site was silent and still.

As he turned towards the kitchen to make some coffee his mobile started to vibrate in his pocket. Sergei quickly glanced at the number and detoured into his office, quietly closing the door behind him.

'Hello?' said Sergei.

'Sergei my friend, how are you? And how's our cargo?'

The caller was Alexei Nikitin, a Russian mafia boss who controlled large swathes of Moscow and the surrounding countryside. He and Sergei had first met in 1987 when Sergei was trying to offload a forty-foot container full of Western rock music on the then new, compact disc format. Following their initial meeting they then worked closely together for many years smuggling all manner of goods into Moscow from where Alexei's huge network of contacts would then distribute them throughout Western Russia.

Alexei's contacts now extended around the world but when Sergei was trying to work out how to redistribute upwards of two thousand new BMWs there was only one man he needed to call.

'We are both very well,' said Sergei, 'and, how are you?'

'I'm fine, although things are getting a bit heated here in Moscow at the moment, too many entrepreneurs trying to muscle in on my patch, so much for a free economy, I preferred the good old days of hard-line communism, at least we all knew where we stood.'

'You're beginning to sound like an old man,' said Sergei, 'maybe you should let Vladimir and Vasyl take over and retire to the Baltic Coast and fish all day.'

'Maybe you're right Sergei but I'm not sure my boys are ready just yet, it's a lot of responsibility you know.'

'Yes, but none of us are going to live forever, not even you, you old dog, you've got to let go sometime, might as well be now while you can still enjoy your retirement.'

'You're probably right and I must admit, I have given it some thought recently.

'Anyway, back to business. I had a call from my contact in China last night confirming the final arrangements for the cargo.

'He has asked that you take them to a small port called Shantou, which is located about one hundred and fifty kilometres up the coast from Hong Kong. It sounds as if he has a similar set-up to the one you have in Kaliningrad, all very secure. From there he intends to sell them to wealthy businessmen in Hong Kong and even ship some to Taiwan which is about the same distance due west across the South China Sea.'

'Can I trust him?' asked Sergei.

'I've dealt with him on several occasions and have never had any problems. As far as he's concerned this is my operation not yours, so I think you should be okay, but don't let your guard down for one minute. He has told me that there are some pirates operating in that part of the world and a ship such as yours with Northern European markings may attract some unwanted attention, so be on your guard.'

'When does he want the delivery?' asked Sergei.

'He has asked me to make sure the cargo arrives with him no later than the middle of February and I have assured him that this is achievable. Is there anything likely to jeopardise that from your perspective?'

'No not at all,' replied Sergei. 'In fact, the cargo will all be ready to ship by the end of next week, so I could have them with him by the end of January if required.'

'No February will be just fine,' said Alexei, 'just make sure you have the correct documentation in place for each piece of the cargo, so they can be quickly processed.'

'No problem, as I said everything will be in place by the end of next week.'

'Good, good, I'll send you all the details by email tomorrow, and if you need to contact me, ring me on this coded phone okay?'

'Okay,' reiterated Sergei, 'I'll contact you when we leave port, oh and give my regards to the boys.'

'Thanks, I will.'

The phone went dead and Sergei leant back in his big leather executive office chair and interlocked his fingers over his stomach. He wasn't exactly home and dry and there were still plenty of things that could happen to put the whole operation at risk, but at this moment things were looking very promising.

The sound of Anouska opening the office door suddenly interrupted his thoughts.

'Sergei darling, I thought you were getting some breakfast.'

'I'm sorry my dear, I was just about to make some coffee when Alexei called to wish us happy New Year,' lied Sergei.

'That was nice of him,' said Anouska. 'And how are Anna and the boys?'

'They are all very well,' said Sergei continuing to lie through his teeth. 'C'mon let's make us some breakfast and go sit by the pool with the newspapers and see if there is any more news on the *Tricolor*, such a tragedy.'

10

The weather in the North Sea following the New Year was extremely unsettled and stormy and the *Sandie Watson* didn't leave the shelter of port until the 5th January, at which point all the crew were quite keen to get back to work and discover what had happened to the *Tricolor.*

Earlier that week Jim and Nick had visited the office and found out more about the wreck that they had found a few days before.

It had taken RB all day to ascertain that the vessel was in fact the *Lucytania,* a small fishing vessel out of Great Yarmouth that was lost with all hands nearly two years previously.

It turned out that the original position on the chart was correct and that the strong currents that flowed through the Liberman Trench had moved the small vessel nearly half a mile in the intervening years.

Further investigation found out that the crew had consisted of four men all of whom had families, the captain and owner being a Des Wright who left behind two daughters aged six and eight called Lucy and Tania.

This sort of result was not uncommon and for the Flatpack team had resulted in a slightly unusual ritual that had started almost by accident.

The catalyst for this had been one of the first cases the

three of them had dealt with soon after RB joined the team, which resulted in RB having to inform the authorities that the family of five on board the forty-foot sailing yacht *Proactor* had been found in the sunken vessel eight miles off the north Kent coast.

On their return to the office three days later, Nick and Jim had found RB still very distraught at having to be the bearer of such bad news and, when Nick offered to buy him a drink, he was in his coat and standing by the door before Jim was out of his seat.

The Maltings bar was a very popular waterfront venue with its patronage usually spilling out onto the now redundant dockside. Strangely however on this occasion it was completely deserted and Nick was able to walk straight up to the bar and place an order for three Irish whiskeys. The three men all stood at the bar and in quiet unison picked up their glasses. RB said quietly, *'The Proactor'* and then each of them swallowed their drink in one gulp and stood in complete silence for the best part of a minute as a mark of remembrance for those lost.

The unrehearsed moment was not lost on the three men who all seemed to take some solace from the act and from that moment on if they found a missing crew or a vessel from which to their knowledge no one had survived, the same near silent ritual was observed whenever the three of them next convened at the office.

As they left port, the storms of the previous few days were still winding down and the *Sandie Watson* was pitched and rolled about like a model boat on a breezy boating lake.

Once beyond the tight confines of the port and estuary

however Nick was able to point her into the wind a little, which eliminated some of the pitching and rolling, something for which even the most hardened of the crew were very grateful.

Once again, they were sailing without a full complement of crew with Nick's number two at the helm Mark Peters, having to miss the sailing following an emergency appendicitis operation on his wife two days earlier. Everything had gone well but, as Mark put it, she was going to need a few "duvet days" before he could leave her to fend for herself.

As before it took them the best part of a day to reach the wreck site of the *Tricolor* and following one of Roly's special suet pudding suppers, Jim called a meeting to discuss in some depth the plan of action for the following day.

Monday 6th January dawned overcast but dry, with a moderate swell that would not stop the launch of the remotely operated vehicle (ROV) but would keep the crew on their toes for most of the day ahead.

They had all agreed the previous evening that their first target would be the hull area where the sonar had discovered the large hole, and from there they would survey down the starboard side of the ship and see if there was anything else that hadn't been spotted by the sonar.

As Ewan ran a final check through on the ROV, Nick checked the systems that would keep the *Sandie Watson* stationed over the wreck. Satisfied that everything was okay he moved down to the control room and sat down in front of the monitors, the joystick for the ROV cupped lightly in his right hand.

The ROV they were using was about the size of a large suitcase and although not particularly fast with a maximum running speed of two knots, with its forward thrusters it was extremely manoeuvrable and very well suited to the salvage environment in which it earned its keep. At its front end were a bank of powerful spotlights that could illuminate even the darkest depths of the ocean, and a pair of high-resolution cameras that would send back to the mother ship high quality images of the wreck site. Also attached to the front of the craft was a powerful hydraulic manipulator that could pick up small samples if necessary and deposit them in a basket for analysis later on the *Sandie Watson*.

As Duncan lowered the ROV into the water with the crane, the TV monitors went from dark foreboding water to sky in quick succession as it bobbed about alongside the ship.

Happy that everything was in order, Nick radioed Duncan to free the line and seconds later the screen returned permanently to darkness as the little craft sank below the surface and began its decent to the wreck of the *Tricolor*.

It took the ROV fifteen minutes to reach the wreck, coming down at its stern end.

'I thought you said we would look at the hole in the bow first,' said Jim.

'Yes, that was the original plan,' said Nick, 'but after I went to bed, I got to thinking that if we look at the damage up front first, we may miss a vital clue somewhere else because we'll try to fit it to the damage on the bow. Better to see if there are any anomalies elsewhere first and then work forward and see what happened at the pointy end.

'Let's start by having a good look at the stern, usual rules of engagement apply everyone; shout if you see anything out of place.'

Nick expertly manoeuvred the ROV around to the stern of

the ship as the crew crowded around the rear of the control room and intently studied the monitor screen. Following several runs checking the propellers and steering gear, he then proceeded to sweep up and down the side of the ship from the keel to the upper decks and back again looking for any clues as to what had caused her to sink so unexpectedly.

The storms of the previous few days had stirred up a good deal of sediment and silt and Nick was having to fly the craft in very tight lines barely two metres above the stricken vessel in order to get the pictures he wanted.

Despite the spotlights, the images were poorer than the crew had hoped and the propellers and thrusters did nothing to improve the situation, each adjustment causing another cloud of sediment to waft across the screen.

'I've never seen such a build-up in such a short time,' said Jim, gazing at the monitor.

'Yes, it's pretty bad considering she's only been down here a couple of weeks,' agreed Nick. 'Might have something to do with the fact she's lying in the Trench as well. All the currents are passing overhead and the sediment is falling out of those currents and falling like snow onto the wreck.'

'I thought the currents ran up and down the trench' continued Jim. 'After all look what happened to the *Lucytania*, and she's less than half a mile further down the Trench.'

'A wreck of this size will sometimes create its own currents,' said Sarah, 'in fact we may find other parts of the ship are clean as a whistle, depends.'

As Nick brought the ROV down past the rear door Sarah shouted out 'Stop!'

'What is it?' asked Nick, peering at the foggy picture on the screen.

'Back off a bit and aim for the top of the door,' said Sarah.

Nick did as he was asked without question and took the ROV back towards the top of the huge door that formed a loading ramp when the ship was in port.

'I thought so, look,' said Sarah, 'the door isn't fully closed, that's a bit odd don't you think?'

'A little bit,' agreed Nick taking the little robot in for a closer look.

With the ship lying on its side, it was relatively easy for Nick to hover the ROV in a horizontal position, giving the team an excellent view of the top of the door.

'What do you reckon?' asked Jim. 'Three foot?'

'Could be a little more than that,' concluded Nick. 'Let's take a closer look.'

With a deft touch Nick slowly manoeuvred the ROV to the opening and they peered inside.

'Can't see anything,' said Duncan, the disappointment clear in his voice.

'Lights aren't powerful enough,' said Ewan. 'It's like trying to light a football stadium with half a dozen flashlights.'

Nick gently moved the ROV away from the opening. 'Sorry guys, maybe another day, let's see what else we can find first.'

'Do you think that may have been the cause of the sinking?' asked Sarah.

'Very much doubt it,' replied Nick. 'In a heavy sea it may be a factor but it was almost flat calm on the night she went missing. Besides I would lay good money that the breach happened when the ship hit the seabed.'

After a further forty-five minutes in which they found nothing further of any note, Nick passed the joystick to Sarah so he could take a break from the mind-numbing concentration required to fly the ROV in such conditions.

'Just be careful not to snag the umbilical when you make the turn over the deck superstructure,' he reminded Sarah. 'I'll be back in a mo. Anyone want a coffee?'

Four hands were eagerly raised into the air and Nick left the control room and headed for the galley, rubbing his already weary eyes as he went.

On reaching the galley he found Roly cutting up some part-boiled potatoes for a potato, cheese and onion bake, quietly hissing to himself each time the heat from the potatoes got too much for his fingers to stand.

'How's it going down there?' he asked as Nick settled a full kettle of water on the stove.

'Nothing much yet,' replied Nick, 'we've had a good look at the stern and nothing seems amiss, the storms have stirred it up a bit down there, though.'

'What, even though she's lying in the Trench?'

'Yeah, it's a bit of a pea souper at the moment.'

'Who's flying the ROV?' asked Roly.

'I've let Sarah take over while I make some coffee, do you want one?'

'No thanks just finished one,' replied Roly, adding some onions to the dish.

I could do with something a little stronger if you've got it,' said Nick, scanning the shelf where the coffee and tea was kept.

'It's in locker under the sink,' said Roly, without even looking up from his slicing. 'I put it there so no one would find it and so far, it's worked a treat.'

Nick moved across the small galley, opened the locker and smacked his lips as he took out his bottle of Camp coffee.

'Good thinking,' said Nick, 'although I reckon most of the crew would try and clean something with it, even if they did find it.'

'You're probably right there,' agreed Roly, 'although you've got to admit, it is a bit of an acquired taste.'

'Don't knock it,' smiled Nick, 'it's what keeps me going on those long night watches.'

By the time Nick had dispensed the correct ingredients into the five mugs that stood before him, and added milk and sugar in various quantities, the kettle had begun the spit and gurgle on the stove. He quickly poured the boiling water into the mugs, gave each one a cursory stir with a spoon and placed them on an old green and white Carlsberg Lager tray that he and Jim had "borrowed" from a bar in Amsterdam many years previously.

'Would you mind coming to the control room in about half an hour, Roly? I've got something I'd like you to do,' said Nick as he headed for the door.

'Now why would you want me to come along there?' asked Roly with a puzzled look on his face.

'To pick up the empties of course,' said Nick, ducking through the door just in time to miss a greasy wet screwed-up dishcloth, as it whizzed past his shoulder and thudded against the wall of the corridor.

'I'll take that as a no then!' he shouted back to Roly, before hurrying along the corridor to a left-right dogleg that would take him out of the firing range.

As Nick approached the control room, he could hear excited voices from within.

'What's happening then?' he asked as he went through the door.

'Look at this,' said Sarah as she reversed the ROV backwards down the side of the ship. A huge cloud of sediment momentarily fogged the vision before settling back onto the surface of the hull.

'There; what do you make of that?'

Nick leaned forward towards the monitor. On the screen was a round portal about twelve inches across and at its centre was a small round hole about three eighths of an inch in diameter.

'Okay,' said Nick. 'What do you guys think?'

'We all think it's a bullet hole,' said Jim.

'Possible,' said Nick, 'or it could be a hole from a rivet. When ships sink there is always a great deal of trauma to the superstructure, sometimes a rivet will pop at a huge velocity under the pressure and woe betide anything or anyone in its path.'

'The hole's too clean and regular,' said Jim, 'and besides look a bit closer.'

Nick leaned even further forward and Sarah zoomed in on the porthole.

'Now,' said Jim, 'does that, or does that not look like blood congealed on the inside of the glass?'

Nick fell silent for a moment as he looked intently at the screen.

'This isn't good,' he mumbled, 'this isn't good at all.'

Nick turned and faced the crew.

'This rather changes things,' he said seriously, 'because if that is what it looks like, we could now be looking at a murder scene. Sarah saved that footage and log it as... porthole damage, cause unknown.'

Jim turned to Duncan. 'I want you to contact RB and ask him to find out absolutely everything about the *Tricolor*. When she was built, where she was built, the nationality of the crew, the full inventory of the cargo, everything down to the contents of the safe, this is starting to develop a bad smell and I want to find out why.'

'Consider it done,' said Duncan and headed towards the radio room, closely followed by Ewan who volunteered to do a few searches of his own on his laptop.

'Right then Sarah, let's continue with our survey, but let's go slowly so we don't miss anything, it may take us the rest of the day to complete, but let's leave no stone unturned. Everyone else keep your eyes peeled.'

It was two thirty p.m. when Nick finally began to fly the ROV over the front of the ship.

The first sign of damage was to the huge hydraulically operated bow door section, which was well out of alignment with the rest of the hull.

'This doesn't look too good,' said Jim looking at the monitor above Nick's head.

'Could be caused by the collision with the seabed,' said Nick still trying to play the Devil's advocate.

'Yeah, right,' said Sarah. 'Let's drop down a bit and look at the bottom of the bow section and see what the hole looks like at close range.'

Nick spun the little robot around 180 degrees and dropped down below where the bow door section finished.

Everyone held their breath in the small control room wondering what the ROV would reveal with its pair of high-resolution cameras.

'There,' said Ewan, 'go to the right a little.'

Nick moved the tiny craft across and frame by frame the hole that they had spotted on the sonar a few days earlier began to materialise on the screen.

Everyone in the room fell silent as Nick circled around the hole, and then pulled away to give them a bird's eye view.

The damage was about ten feet in diameter and the torn metal was all disappearing into the hull of the *Tricolor*.

No one said a word for a moment or two as they tried to make sense of what they were witnessing.

Finally, Jim turned to Nick.

'Ever seen anything like that before?' he asked.

'Only once,' said Nick. 'We were looking for a fishing vessel off the Normandy coast about ten years ago, when we happened upon the wreck of a French warship sunk during the Second World War. She'd been struck by torpedoes, apparently and sank in a matter of minutes.'

'You think this is torpedo damage?' asked Duncan his voice trembling a little as he spoke.

'No,' said Nick, 'the damage is too localised, a torpedo would have torn half the ship apart. It was thought that the French warship was hit by two torpedoes and the hole we found that was similar to this one, was made by a misfiring device. The second hit was the one that did the real damage and sunk her.'

'So, if it's not torpedo damage, what do you think it is?' continued Duncan. 'It's far too regular to be collision damage.'

'There's only one thing it can be,' said Nick. 'A limpet mine.'

'A what?' said Sarah.

'A limpet mine; they were used to great effect during

World War Two to sink enemy ships while in port and cause the greatest amount of inconvenience possible. A team of specially trained divers would swim to the target vessel under the cover of darkness, plant the mines just below the waterline and then endeavour to escape before the timer hit zero. It was very dangerous work, but very effective. As you can imagine, if a ship could be sunk in the right place it could effectively trap other vessels in the port until the wreckage had been removed.'

'So how did they work?' asked Sarah.

'They worked like their mollusc namesakes, sticking to the hull of the target vessel with powerful magnets. The early versions would blow a hole up to three feet across in the hull of a battleship so the sort of damage we're seeing here on a merchant vessel would be about right.'

'And they're still in use today?' quizzed Sarah further.

'Oh yes, in the mid-eighties there was a Greenpeace ship called the *Rainbow Warrior* protesting against the French nuclear testing programme in the South Pacific. One night when moored in Auckland Harbour some members of the French Intelligence Service attached two mines to the ship and sank it.

'There was a huge row about it at the time and several French Ministers were implicated in the plot. If I remember correctly the French Government ended up compensating Greenpeace for their loss and the ship was temporarily re-floated and then scuttled in a nearby bay to serve as a dive wreck and artificial reef.'

Not for the first time the cabin fell silent.

'So, where do we go from here Jim?' asked Ewan, 'it's clear there's something very wrong here, how do you want to proceed?'

Nick manoeuvred the ROV away from the ship and let his hand relax on the joystick. As Jim opened his mouth to speak Nick turned to his crew.

'Ewan, Sarah, bring the ROV back on board. Jim, Duncan, you're with me, I need to know what we've got on the *Tricolor*. We'll all meet in the mess room in an hour.'

Nick got up from his chair and left the cabin, closely followed by Jim and Duncan.

'I've never seen him like this before,' said Sarah.

'No, me neither,' said Ewan, 'c'mon let's get the ROV back and see what the plan of action is.'

An hour later the crew were all in the mess room as instructed. In the middle of the table was a large saucepan of vegetable soup, with a ladle and a big plate of freshly baked bread that Roly had cooked that morning.

As he ladled the soup into six oversized enamel mugs Nick began to speak.

'As a crew we've worked together for some time now and on occasion we've had to deal with some very difficult and sometimes disturbing situations. This however, has blown all those previous operations out of the water and WE now have to make a decision as to how to proceed from here.

'I say "we" because there are two basic options available to us, but we need to be united in the direction we take.

'Thanks to RB and Duncan we now have a good deal of information to assimilate regarding the *Tricolor* and her crew, so I'll let Jim take you through what we have so far.'

Nick turned to his friend and colleague who took a quick gulp of his soup before picking up two pages of printed paperwork from the table in front of him.

'Right,' said Jim taking a bite of his bread. 'You will have to bear with me on this, as some of the information I have here you may already know, but here goes.

'The *Tricolor* was built in 1987 at the Tsuneishi shipyard in the Philippines for a Greek shipping company called Alcyone Ferries. Alcyone incidentally, was the Greek goddess of the sea, a fact that I doubt has any bearing on this investigation, but I'm a generous man and as long as we are together on this ship, I will continue to try to educate you numpties.'

'Why thank you, kind sir,' said Sarah smiling and tugging at a piece of hair on her forehead.

Jim smiled a put-on smile at her and continued.

'Originally named the *Aegean Princess*, she was one of a pair of vessels, commissioned to serve the larger of the Greek islands.

'Her and her sister ship the *Aegean Queen* are identical at 190 metres long and weighing in at 55,000 tons. They are a roll-on roll-off type of design with bow and stern doors and to help with the manoeuvring they were fitted with bow and stern thrusters, although these didn't prevent several very expensive and well-publicised collisions, the most costly, being with the *Saudi Prince*, a floating hotel ship moored in the entrance to Corfu harbour in 1992.

'Two years after this incident and with the ship's log full of scrapes and near misses both ships were sold and replaced with smaller but faster hydrofoils for passengers and smaller ferries for the freight.

The *Aegean Princess* was renamed the *Tricolor* when she passed into the hands of a Norwegian shipping company, who added an extra deck at the lower level where the lorry deck once was and another where the passengers, shops, bars and restaurants were housed before she started shipping BMWs Volvos and Saabs from Zeebrugge to Humberside. From here they would pick up a return cargo of Nissans, built in their new factory at Sunderland and take back to mainland Europe. This operation has been running smoothly since the mid-nineties and the shipping company, Norsklines, has built up an enviable safety record in that time with only a handful of damages reported despite the sometimes-hostile environment they have to work in.'

Jim paused for a moment as Roly ladled out some more soup into several outstretched mugs and then offered his own for a refill, taking advantage of the delay by taking another mouthful of bread before continuing.

'The *Tricolor* left Zeebrugge on the morning of December twenty-second with two thousand BMWs occupying her five decks. Total value, somewhere in the region of forty to fifty million pounds.'

'Bloody hell,' gasped Ewan. 'Fifty million pounds? Are they all gold plated or something?'

'I doubt it,' said Jim smiling, 'but the cars encompassed the whole of the BMW range with everything from 3 Series to the big X5 four-by-fours. When you consider the big BM saloons and four-by-fours cost fifty or sixty K each, well, it soon adds up.

'They left port without incident and no one has reported anything amiss with any aspect of the trip other than a change of crew, which I'll come to in a moment.

'The captain was a chap called Edward Collins who was forty-eight years old and lives in Hull.

'He has been in the merchant navy all his working life and was only promoted to captain at the beginning of last year. He has worked for Norsklines for nearly ten years and in a recent press conference was described by his employers as a solid, dependable and well-liked member of their team. He is recently divorced and has two grown-up daughters.

'The replacement crew were all from the Philippines and were hired for a couple of trips over the Christmas period while the regular crew enjoyed the festive break. The second officer and the rest of the senior crew were also from the Philippines originally, but have been working the North Sea and Channel ports for some years on various ships including ferries, so should have been well up to speed on how to handle the *Tricolor*.

'The total on board numbered twenty-three including Captain Collins and as you are already aware there has been no trace of any survivors to date.

'As far as we can ascertain she disappeared from the radar sometime on the night of the 22nd December and her transponder, which sends out a constant signal to help with searches like our own, also failed sometime after midnight on the same night. According to her owners a full health and safety audit was carried out on the 20th December and no major faults were highlighted in Captain Collins' report.

'As far as we know there was no other shipping in this part of the North Sea on that night partly due to the seasonal slowdown and partly due to the fact that where we are is not on a recognised shipping lane.

'Despite the depth of the Liberman Trench below us there are other areas of the seabed around us where the *Tricolor* would have surely grounded with her full cargo, so what she was doing here is a complete mystery. In fact, up until our recent discoveries with the ROV, Nick and I had felt sure that her sinking was something to do with hitting something in the shallower water around us, another wreck maybe?'

He paused once again for a mouthful of soup.

'So, what's the consensus on what we've found with the ROV?' asked Ewan as he reached forward and grabbed another chunk of the bread.

Jim looked at Nick who drew himself up to his full seated height before rising from his position at the head of the table.

He moved silently across to the fifty-inch plasma TV hung on the wall and tapped a few buttons on the keyboard on the table below it.

The screen sprang into life and a few seconds later an image taken by the ROV appeared on the screen showing the hole in the ship's bow.

'Okaaaay,' started Nick moving the mouse to open a second picture of a similar hole. He then split the screen to show the two images side by side and produced a small pen-sized object from his pocket. He held the top of the pen and pulled on the tip at the bottom and, like an old-style car aerial, the pen extended to a length of about eighteen inches.

'It doesn't take a genius to spot the similarity between these two holes,' he stated. 'The first one is what we saw this afternoon on the *Tricolor*, a symmetrical hole with all the damage thrust inwards into the hull of the ship. As I said at the time this looked to me like mine damage, possibly limpet.

'The second picture is one of many taken of the damage suffered by the *Rainbow Warrior* in Auckland Harbour. As you can see the damage is almost identical and, having studied both pictures in some detail, I've come to the uneasy conclusion that both ships were sunk by the same means; a limpet mine.

'As you can appreciate, we now have a huge number of unanswered questions, the biggest being why? Why sink a perfectly good ship full of expensive cars in the middle of the North Sea?'

'What about a vendetta of some sort?' asked Rory, 'against either the shipping company or BMW?'

'Possible,' said Nick, 'but this must have been a huge and well-planned operation and we have to assume at this point that none of the crew survived. That's an awful lot of death and destruction to hand out to innocent people just to get even with a large corporation.'

'Jim said the cargo was worth between forty and fifty million,' said Ewan, 'has anyone found out if it was all insured, even for a company like BMW that sort of loss is bound to make a dent in their coffers.'

'RB has checked it all out with Mark, our contact at Lloyds,' said Jim, 'and yes everything is fully covered.'

'What about an old Second World War mine?' asked Sarah. 'Fishing boats are still netting them from time to time, wouldn't that cause similar damage?'

'To an extent,' answered Nick, 'insomuch that all the damage to the hull would be inbound, but far less symmetrical, so for the moment I am ruling that out.'

The room fell silent for a moment with each member of the crew trying to reason why the ship should have been sunk so ruthlessly.

Ewan shifted in his seat. 'What about pirates?' he asked, 'was there something else on board that wasn't declared on the manifest, diamonds perhaps?'

'Yes, that's a possibility,' said Nick, 'but it would be very rare for diamonds to be transported like that. To my knowledge they are usually flown under high security.

'Pirates will attack long haul merchant vessels because they tend to hold large sums of cash on board to pay the crew, port fees etc. etc. The *Tricolor* was rarely away from her home port for more than four or five days at the most, so unless there was something extremely valuable on board, like diamonds, it would seem an unlikely target.'

'The only thing I can think of is the cars,' said Duncan placing his mug deliberately down on the tray in the middle of the table.

'In what way?' asked Nick.

'I'm not really sure,' answered Duncan, 'but nearly fifty million pounds' worth would seem like reward enough to me. I just can't figure out how anyone would be able to get nearly three thousand cars off one ship and onto another without being seen and in the timescale available. Then, if you did manage to pull it off, there is the problem of how to get rid of them; you can't exactly sell them down the pub.'

Everyone smiled at the thought of trying to pass off a forty-thousand-pound BMW down at their local.

'It would certainly piss off the guy trying to sell his pouches of rolling tobacco,' added Ewan.

For the first time in several hours everyone laughed.

'It's a nice thought Duncan,' said Jim, 'but I would imagine it takes a couple of days to load that number of cars, and that's on dry land! It would be impossible at sea anyway, never mind the timescale.'

'Well its certainly got me baffled,' said Rory speaking for the first time. 'We've got a ship which is well off its correct course and that looks like it's been sent to the bottom deliberately thanks to a mine. There's what looks like a bullet hole in one of the portholes, and as far as any of us can work out, no plausible motive of any kind for the sinking. The rest of the ship is unmarked; ruling out a collision, and the crew are all missing presumed drowned. The captain who is a well thought of and respected "company" man and none of us can come up with any scam or reason for such a diabolical crime. We must be missing something, but I'll be buggered if I can see what it is.'

Nick moved back to the table and retook his seat.

'Jim?'

Jim got up from his seat and moved across to the computer.

'There is one other piece of information that RB has come up with concerning the *Tricolor's* sister ship, but we're not sure if it has any relevance or not.

'As I mentioned earlier, she was named the *Aegean Queen*, and like her sister was sold off after several "incidents" in various Greek ports. Her buyer was a Russian millionaire called Sergei Petrov who operates out of the Russian exclave of Kaliningrad on the Baltic Sea.

'Now if you just bear with me a second, I'm going to let RB explain all this to you via our link with the office in Ipswich.'

A few seconds later a jerky image of RB appeared on the screen.

Jim moved back to his seat and asked RB if he could hear him okay?

'Yes, loud and clear,' came the reply although the synchronisation between sound and vision was far from perfect.

'Excellent,' replied Jim relieved that the link was working as it should.

'Can you explain about the *Aegean Queen* and Mr Petrov's business empire RB, and if you guys have any questions for RB just shout them out, as he is now an expert on the subject.'

RB could be seen settling in his chair and then picking up several sheets of paper from the desk in front of him.

'Okay,' he said, 'are we all sitting comfortably... Then I'll begin.

'Mr Petrov's background is very sketchy and to date I can find very little info on how he made his initial money, which suggests to me that it may not have been through entirely legitimate sources. He now resides in the Russian enclave of Kaliningrad.

'He bought the *Aegean Queen* in early 1997 and like her sister ship she was renamed when purchased and now goes by the name of the *Baltic Carrier*.

'Rather strangely she also works this part of the North Sea and is regularly seen in several Northern European ports, and this is where it starts to get interesting, but I'll give you a bit of background info first.

'When the former Soviet Union broke up in 1991, Kaliningrad found itself isolated from the main body of Russia by Poland and Lithuania. To help combat the problems this created, the country was designated a Special Economic Zone, with various hand-outs being made available to companies and investors who set up business in the region.

'One of those companies was a certain BMW, who took advantage of these handouts, the cheap labour, warehousing and excellent port facilities to set up a huge car plant.'

'You say Kaliningrad has a good port,' said Sarah, 'how come?'

'Good question,' replied RB.

'Kaliningrad is the only Russian Baltic port that doesn't freeze over during the winter months. Because of this the Russian Navy made its home there and, as we all know under the communist regime, if there was one thing the Soviets were never short of, it was cheap labour.

'Huge amounts of effort were spent making the port a shining example of Soviet efficiency, able to handle up to half the Soviet western fleet at a time if necessary.

'With the end of the Cold War and the subsequent break-up of the Soviet Union much of these facilities fell into disrepair and this was how it was until the mid-nineties.

'The first on the scene was Sergei Petrov who arrived seemingly out of nowhere and set up a car dismantling plant. This was one of the first of its kind in the whole of Europe and way ahead of the recycling boom that we all know today and it is thought that the project may have been partly sponsored by the Russian Government to recycle steel for the economy.

'Four years later BMW arrived on the scene and Sergei Petrov's business took off like a Saturn V rocket. Suddenly he had a manufacturer on his doorstep that needed huge quantities of steel. As you can imagine his business boomed and eighteen months later, he had become the "Mr BMW" of Kaliningrad, scrapping and dismantling BMWs only and then via a huge steel plant selling the steel straight back to BMW. It was mutually very good for both parties.'

'Does he only sell to BMW?' asked Roly from the galley where he was preparing the supper.

'BMW as you all know are regarded as a luxury car and

they are very strict on the quality of the materials they use. It's thought the main reason he has gone down this route, is so there is no call back on the quality of the materials he is supplying. If the steel, aluminium or whatever has already been passed and used by BMW on previous models it should be okay to use again on the next generation.

'There is also a second very good reason for him to only dismantle BMWs though and this came about with the arrival of the Internet. Alongside his main plant he has another company that specialises in supplying second-hand stroke reconditioned BMW parts.

'Like his other businesses this has become a monster, to the extent that if you now tap into your laptop "BMW spares" anywhere in the whole of Europe you almost certainly hit on a supplier who in turn is supplied by Sergei Petrov. Body panels, wheels, switches, or just a cover cap for a screw head, he can supply it either directly from the plant or via one of his satellite companies.'

'So, where does the *Baltic Carrier* fit into all this,' asked Ewan.

'The *Baltic Carrier* is the largest of three ship's owned by Mr Petrov and regularly turns up in Hamburg, Ostend and Dieppe to load up with damaged late model BMWs.

'My early enquiries suggest that Sergei Petrov has "agents" throughout Europe who are linked in with insurance assessors. When a BMW is written off, they get the first call and literally days later the vehicle is on its way to one of the three ports I mentioned a moment ago.'

'I had no idea there was so much money involved in scrap cars,' commented Ewan.

'Think about it,' countered RB. 'A second-hand low

mileage engine from say, a five series is worth several thousand pounds depending on the model. A set of wheels with tyres would be getting on for a grand, so that could be as much as five K for starters. Add to that heated seats, multi play CD units, satnav units, and all the other luxuries that go into a modern luxury car and you're talking big bucks.'

'And the components he can't sell on he sells back to BMW as raw materials,' mused Sarah out loud.

'Exactly,' added RB.

'You say he has two other ships?' said Ewan

'Yes,' replied RB. 'These are quite small in comparison and are used to distribute the spare parts throughout Europe. The first is called the *Anouska*, possibly named after Sergei's wife and the second is the *Martina*. Both are able to carry about 100 containers' worth of goods and make regular runs from Kaliningrad to Hamburg, Le Harve, Rotterdam and Felixstowe in the UK. From here the parts are distributed throughout Europe, via a huge distribution network.'

'So, are you saying there is a link between Mr Petrov and the sinking of the *Tricolor*?' asked Ewan.

'That's for you guys to work out,' said RB, 'but you have to admit it's a huge coincidence that both ships have relocated from the Med to the North Sea, and now earn their livings moving BM's around northern Europe.'

'Can you give us any more info on our friend Mr Petrov?' asked Sarah.

'Not really' answered RB, 'He seems to keep himself to himself and as far as I can tell only ventures away from home to go on holiday.

'To be fair to the man he seems to be entirely legit and if it weren't for the fact that he suddenly arrived in Kaliningrad out of nowhere, with a sizeable chunk of backing behind him, I would be telling you that he is just a very successful self-made millionaire who was in the right place at the right time.'

A hush fell over the galley interrupted only by Roly's knife cutting up some cheese for the bake on a chopping board.

'Right,' said Jim. 'Any more questions for RB?'

Nick cleared his throat, 'Yes, where was the *Baltic Carrier* on the night the *Tricolor* was lost?'

'According to the port records at Kaliningrad she was in port having some maintenance carried out on her, and before you ask her next voyage is scheduled for 14 January.'

'That's just over a week away,' pondered Duncan. 'Do you know where she's heading?'

'No afraid not,' answered RB. 'Probably one of her regular ports that I mentioned earlier.'

'So, when was her last voyage?' continued Duncan, hoping to find something unusual in the answers that would assist them in their investigation.

'Last trip was… hang on a minute.'

RB could be seen leaning forward over his desk his arm outstretched towards the mouse on his right.

'Last trip brought her back into the port on the 16 December,' he announced having scrolled further down the Kaliningrad Port Authority records.

Duncan scribbled the information in a small reporter's notepad and leant back in his seat.

'Anyone else?' asked Jim.

No one answered.

Jim turned to the TV.

'Thanks for the information RB, as usual you have excelled, we'll leave the comm. link open so you can hear our

151

deliberations and maybe help with any further questions.'

Nick stood up and faced his crew.

'I mentioned when we first convened that WE have a decision to make regarding what we do next. The facts that you have been given are all we have at the moment, but hopefully you now have a better view of the situation than you did an hour ago. The big decision we have to make is whether we turn all this over to the authorities now or continue until we have some hard evidence of what we all suspect, which at this stage points towards an act of piracy.'

Nick eyed each of the crew in turn, each one meeting his gaze without flinching.

Ewan was the first to respond.

'I say we have another look at the wreck. The stern door is slightly ajar and if we use Tiny the smaller ROV I think we should be able to get inside. It's risky, but I think we need to see what's in there before we hand it over to the red tape brigade.'

'I agree,' said Duncan. 'I've got a feeling that there's something dodgy here, aside from the hole in the hull and the possible bullet hole in the porthole.'

'And,' injected Sarah, 'I don't believe in coincidences and there are too many in this case that involve BMWs, and that's without a possible link between the *Tricolor* and the *Baltic Carrier*.'

'What do you think?' asked Nick.

'I have to agree with these guys,' he said looking at those assembled around the table. 'If we hand it over now it will probably take weeks to get the right people here with the right equipment. We are here and we have the right tools for the job, I say we take another look tomorrow and see if we can come up with some answers. If we don't then we turn it over to the Maritime Accident Investigation Branch and beat a dignified retreat.'

'Any comments Roly?' asked Nick.

Roly looked up from his cheese chopping.

'Nothing that hasn't already been said,' he replied flourishing his cooks' knife. 'It has to be worth a look to see if those Beamers are still on board.'

'Okay then,' said Nick, 'first thing tomorrow we drop Tiny onto the stern door and see if we can safely get him inside. Ewan? Can you run the full diagnostic and check the umbilical for any fraying? It's going to be tight in there and I don't want to get hung up on anything.'

'I'll get on it right away, what's for dinner Roly?'

'Potato, cheese and onion bake tonight, and before you ask it will be about an hour or so.'

'Thanks,' said Ewan and headed towards the door.

'Wait up,' said Duncan. 'I'll give you a hand.'

'Me too,' chimed Sarah, and seconds later they were all heading for the aft deck.

As the three crew members hustled their way out of the mess room, Jim thanked RB for his input and then turned to Nick.

'So, what do you think? Will we find anything?'

'I have absolutely no idea,' replied Nick, 'but I agree with everyone else that we have at least got to try and take a look inside the *Tricolor*. Let's just hope we find something tomorrow that we can hang our hat on, eh!'

'Indeed, so far this investigation has given us more questions than answers.'

11

The following morning dawned bright and sunny and a calm had once again returned to the North Sea. The storm had moved on and the sunrise was a rich red, which for a few minutes made the *Sandie Watson* and her surroundings look like they had been transported into the twilight world of H.G. Wells' *War of the Worlds*, with everything bathed in red.

The milder weather front had also brought with it a thin layer of fog that now blanketed the ocean like a huge duvet to a depth of about five feet. From the bridge of the *Sandie Watson* it was easy to imagine you were at thirty thousand feet looking down on the clouds, but on the exposed lower deck it held no duvet warmth and in a matter of minutes Ewan and Duncan, who were preparing Tiny for launch, were cold and wet.

In the control room Nick carried out his final checks and then issued the order to launch Tiny.

Duncan climbed onto the seat of the small crane and deftly lifted the small craft into the water. Once stable, Ewan leant over, unhooked the crane, and gave Tiny a push away from the ship's hull. At the same time Nick goosed the electric motors and blew the little craft's ballast tanks.

As it made its way down to the *Tricolor*, Roly appeared with a tray of steaming hot coffee and some home-made cookies, which Ewan and Duncan in particular, were very grateful for.

After a few minutes the control room fell silent, everyone peering at the monitor for the first glimpse of the stricken vessel.

'There she is,' said Nick, and with a deft touch brought Tiny to a gentle hover just above the rear door.

'Okay let's have a closer look at you, my beauty,' he said to himself and following an energetic rub of his hands he settled into his seat and once again took hold of the joystick, edging Tiny towards the opening.

The gap at the top of the door looked to be about six feet, which on land would have been plenty to get the two-foot-wide craft through. At the bottom of the sea however with currents to factor in, this was a small opening and Nick's only consolation was that once inside the ship it should be current free and Tiny would go exactly where he was pointed.

With the ship lying on her side Nick headed for the top of the opening looking for obstructions en route that may snag the umbilical.

'All looks clear enough,' said Sarah.

'Yeah, so far so good,' said Nick, 'here goes nothing.'

As Tiny entered the *Tricolor* the little ambient light that was available was snuffed out and the ship took on a darker and more menacing persona.

'Well, that went better than I thought,' said Jim, 'I thought you would get buffeted all over the place getting in there.'

'Yeah, me too,' replied Nick, 'I think I must have hit a bit of slack current there, maybe the gods are with us today.'

The visibility inside the ship was marginally better than it had been on the seabed, but even so Tiny's spotlights couldn't illuminate beyond three or four feet. Every so often they caught a brief glimpse of the local marine population that had already moved into the new real estate. Most took no more than a passing interest in their robotic cousin and shied away from the bright lights, but one or two were more curious and came in for a closer look, their faces eerily filling the screen in the control room, before turning away and leaving the scene in a flash of silver light.

As Nick began to move forward through the top deck of the carrier all he found was the bulkhead that separated the cargo deck from the rest of the ship.

With Ewan feeding out the umbilical to Tiny a few feet at a time they ventured deeper and deeper into the vessel.

'There's nothing here,' said Sarah. 'I thought you said there was two thousand cars on board, Jim?'

'That's was the manifest stated,' replied Jim, 'but don't forget she's on her side and the cars wouldn't be tethered for a calm crossing, so if they are here, they are probably below us in a big heap.'

'Okay,' said Nick, 'going down.'

Ten seconds later Tiny's lights found a red X5 four-by-four, which due to the revised orientation of the *Tricolor* was effectively lying on its side. As Tiny moved forward another X5 came into view followed by a 5 Series, both jammed up against the car next to them like giant automotive dominoes.

'I thought there would be more carnage than this,' said Sarah, 'but I guess there isn't much room in there for things to move too far.'

'The headroom between the floor and ceiling isn't much more than about eight feet,' offered Jim, 'so these big vehicles haven't got a lot of room to move even after plunging all this way to the seabed.'

'Let's look at the next level,' said Nick, reversing Tiny back towards the door.

With Ewan taking up the slack in the umbilical, Nick gently brought the little ROV out and then took it back into the ship twelve feet to the right, effectively onto a different deck.

Straight away it was apparent that the cars on this deck were much more damaged.

'Jesus,' exclaimed Duncan. 'Look at that!'

Nick moved Tiny up so that once again he was flying in the void where the cars would have been prior to the ship ending up on its side.

As he slowly flew along, the camera picked out car after car, smashed to pieces against its neighbour.

'These look like 3 Series to me,' said Jim. 'Smaller cars, means more room, and more room means more damage.'

Everyone stared at the screen and then quite unexpectedly there was a gap between the vehicles.

'That's odd,' said Nick, 'where have they gone?'

'Drop down a little and see what's there,' suggested Sarah.

Nick eased Tiny down about six feet into the void and then suddenly pulled him up into a hover.

'Oh my God!' said Ewan in a hushed tone, hardly believing what he was seeing on the screen in front of him.

'Now that's what I call a mess.'

Below them, lit up by Tiny's lights, was a scene more akin to a Hollywood movie.

Here the smaller cars had moved during the sinking and all they could see was dozens of vehicles piled up on one another as if in a salvage yard. Every now and then the light from the ROV would reflect off a rear light cluster or headlamp, producing a flash of brilliant red or a bright white light.

'Now that's more like it,' said Sarah.

Nick manoeuvred Tiny around the wreckage searching for anything unusual but found nothing other than tens of brand-new BMWs smashed to smithereens by the collision with the seabed.

'Just goes to prove the old saying about skydiving accidents,' said Duncan, 'it's not the fall that kills you, it's the sudden stop at the bottom that does the damage.'

'Okay I think we've seen enough,' said Nick, 'let's get Tiny out of there while we're still ahead, there's nothing more to see down here and we have at least confirmed that the cars are still on board.

'Ready with the umbilical Ewan?'

'Ready when you are,' confirmed Ewan.

Nick gently brought Tiny up above the wreckage and began to reverse the ROV out of the ship.

'Stop!' cried Sarah.

Everyone in the control room jumped at Sarah's sudden outburst.

'What's up?' asked Nick as he put Tiny into a hover.

'Go forward again and stop over that upturned 3 Series,' said Sarah excitedly.

Nick did as he was told and took Tiny back to the overturned wreck.

'Left a touch,' said Sarah.

'There do you see it?'

'I see a car upside down lying on the bonnet of the car next to it,' said Jim. 'What are you seeing that I'm not?'

'Focus in on the tyre Nick,' said Sarah her voice trembling

with excitement.

'Still ain't got it,' said Jim.

'It's worn,' said Duncan.

'Worn!' cried Sarah incredulously. 'It's completely flat spotted.'

The crew all stood silently for a moment or two looking at the badly scuffed tyre.

Nick lifted Tiny away from the tyre and moved him forward until they were looking at its opposite number on the other end of the axle.

'That one's not new either,' said Sarah triumphantly. 'Don't you guys think that's a little odd?'

'Very odd,' agreed Nick. 'Maybe it a crew member's car.'

'Possible, but not very probable,' said Jim. 'Let's see if we can find anymore upturned cars to have a closer look at.'

'We passed several on the way in,' said Ewan, 'before we came upon this void, let's take a look at those.'

Nick brought Tiny up out of the gap between the cars and started back towards the door.

'There's one!' cried Sarah, her voice even more excited than before.

Once again Nick took the ROV right up to the tyre on the upturned car.

'That's worn as well,' said Duncan.

Over the next ten minutes they examined a further five tyres, each one showing signs of wear.

'We need to get a good view of the markings on the side wall of the tyre,' said Jim.

'How's that going to help?' asked Nick.

'Do you remember that Subaru Impreza I bought second hand a couple of years ago?'

'Yep, what about it?'

'About six months after I bought it, I had to put some new rubber on it and at the time the car had done about 17,000 miles. When I was having the new tyres fitted, I got talking to the fitter and asked him if he thought this was the original set of tyres, or if I was now fitting it with its third set from new. He turned to one of the tyres he had just taken off and immediately told me the manufacture date of that tyre. It turned out that she'd done seventeen K on her first set, which I was quite pleased about considering it was a very high-performance car. It's a four-digit code, so I reckon if we can get a good view of the side wall we can see when it was made.'

'Sounds like a plan to me,' said Nick and spun Tiny around to face the wall of the tyre.

'We need to look at where the tyre meets the wheel rim,' said Jim, 'I'm sure that's where the date stamp is located.'

Nick focused Tiny in on the wheel rim and then expertly took the assembled crew on a circular tour of the wheel.

'There!' said Jim, 'that looks like it, can we zoom in with the camera and get a better view?'

Nick brought the ROV into a hover and then focused the lens on the four-digit code.

'Whoa that's not right,' said Jim as he looked at the number 2010 embossed on the tyre.

'Why?' asked Duncan.

'The four digits equal the week number and year in that order, which means that this tyre was manufactured in week twenty of the year 2010.'

'No wonder it's got some wear on it,' said Sarah

'Can we look at any other walls on this car?' asked Ewan. 'See if they are the same date?'

Nick reversed Tiny away from the wheel and followed the axle across the underside of the car. As he neared the wheel the front section of another vehicle impeded his progress.

'Okay,' he said calmly, 'we'll try the other end.'

Once again there was another car jammed up against the wheel, making any markings impossible to see. Undeterred Nick manoeuvred Tiny across to the fourth corner and this time was rewarded with a front wheel at full lock, giving him just enough room to fly into.

The date on this wheel was right at the top and following a few gentle tweaks on the joystick the numbers 4111 appeared clearly on the monitor.

'Week forty-one, 2011, right?' commented Duncan looking at Jim.

'This is making no sense whatsoever,' mused Jim 'I can't believe BMW ship their cars on old wheels and tyres, it just doesn't add up.'

'I think we've seen enough,' said Nick. 'Unless you guys can think of anything else that we need to look at?'

'I think we need to get one more date off a different vehicle,' said Sarah, 'just to corroborate what we found on this one.'

'Yes, that's probably not such a bad idea,' said Duncan. 'If we could get three sets of dates from three separate vehicles, that ought to be enough to keep HM Customs and Excise happy, or not, as is the case.'

Over the next half-hour Nick expertly manoeuvred Tiny around a final car on what they thought was deck two and then another two on the deck above. Each date stamp was from either 2010 or 2011 and on a couple of occasions they found damage to the rims that could only be as a result of hitting a kerb.

With Tiny clear of the ship, Nick handed over the controls to Sarah and then collapsed in the one decent chair in the control room. Flying a ROV was always hard work and the powers of concentration required were immense, but this mission had been one of the most challenging Nick had ever flown and as he sat quietly reflecting on what they had just found he had to concede that it was probably 30% skill and 70% luck that they hadn't got caught up on a piece of debris at some point or another.

With Tiny back on board the crew went back over the footage of the dive and printed photos of the date stamps on the tyres and the type of vehicle they were on.

Jim called RB and got him to check that the information he had regarding the configuration of the date was correct and that BMW transported all their new cars on brand new wheels and tyres.

Two hours later the crew were once again sat around the table in the mess room munching on Roly's celebrated bacon sandwiches. RB was once again in attendance to help with any computer-based information that they may need and opened his link by asking for a bacon sandwich to be somehow sent down the line to him.

Nick and Jim patiently waited for the crew to finish their chomping.

It was Roly who was last to finish and with his final mouthful in place, he wiped his lips with a piece of paper towel and then leant forward through the small hatchway that separated the galley from the mess room.

Nick quickly checked that RB's link was still good and

then stood up from his position at the head of the table and began.

'Right then,' he said very deliberately, to ensure he had everyone's full attention.

'As you guys are aware, we have moved forward a great deal in the last few hours and it appears our decision last night to go into the *Tricolor* was one of the best we have ever made. Unfortunately, as Jim has pointed out we now have even more unanswered questions than we did twenty-four hours ago, but by way of compensation we have answered the biggest question, in that it is now very clear that there is something very amiss with the sinking of this ship. Although we have no proof other than the photographic evidence that the two ROVs have provided us with, I think we should now provisionally assume that the porthole damage could well be due to a bullet and that the hull damage is down to a limpet mine.

'As you are all aware, we found some very unusual tyres on board the *Tricolor* and I would now like to invite RB into the meeting to explain what he has found since we brought Tiny back on board.

'RB.'

'Yes, thanks Nick, okay. Following Jim's communication with me a couple of hours ago, I've spoken at great length to a chap called Jeremy Rathbone who is head of Sales and Marketing for BMW in the UK. I sent him the photos from the dive and he has come up with a few points that you may find interesting.

'Firstly, surprise, surprise, all BMWs are sent out of their factories and transported on brand new wheels and tyres; in fact, his first words to me after the photos had arrived by email were, "Is this some sort of wind up?"

'I assured him that the pictures were genuine and asked him to look closely at them with his experienced eye and see if there was anything else there that we hadn't spotted. Half an hour later he called back with the following observations.

'The date stamps on the tyres were entirely correct and dated back to 2010/2011.

'BMW do not hold tyres on their shelves for more than a few weeks so these dates as Jim pointed out are very odd.

'The second point he made was that one of the tyres was actually a Goodyear product, a brand that BMW have never fitted to any of their European vehicles.

'The third thing he spotted was on this picture.' RB disappeared from the screen and in his place appeared a picture showing the top half of a wheel and tyre hanging from a front suspension.

'See anything odd?' asked RB from behind the picture, 'no? What about now?'

The picture changed on screen to an enhanced version of the original.

'This is one that Jeremy asked me to Photoshop; look closely at the suspension unit.'

'It's a bit grubby,' said Ewan speculatively.

'Exactly,' replied RB, 'these cars are never driven anywhere, they are always transported by truck, so that the purchaser gets a "new" car with only a handful of miles on. According to Jeremy that suspension unit should be gleaming like a new penny, not covered in several thousands of miles of grime.'

RB returned to the screen.

'There is one final observation that Jeremy made but he's not one hundred per cent sure on this one. The first shot you sent me, this one,' the screen temporarily flicked to another picture before returning to RB, 'Jeremy thinks this is a 3 Series, but can't be sure.'

'I think it was a 3 Series,' said Jim. 'It was one of the first cars we found on deck two.'

'Well, if it is a 3 Series,' continued RB, 'it's wearing the wrong size wheels, apparently that style of wheel was not manufactured to fit anything smaller than a 5 Series.'

'My word you have been busy,' teased Sarah.

'Not really,' retorted RB, 'all I did was make a couple of phone calls and send one email, easy really.'

'Only if you know who to call and send the emails to,' commented Jim. 'Good work RB.'

'Thanks,' replied RB and then sat back in his chair as if to signify the end of his presentation.

'Do you all remember what I said yesterday about *us* making a joint decision on the way forward?' asked Nick.

Everyone nodded in confirmation.

'Well, I think we are now at that point in time. We have a ship below us that doesn't belong there; it seems to have various wounds that we can't easily explain away and a cargo that doesn't, at least in part, belong there.

'Usually after several days of investigation we can start to answer a lot of questions about the loss of a vessel. With this one however we are now at a point where we still have more questions than answers and a plot that looks thicker than treacle.

'So, to keep this as simple as possible, I'm going to ask you each the same question. Do we hand this all over to the authorities or do *we* pursue this case beyond the seabed?

'Your answer will be either Authorities or Flatpack,

nothing else, does everyone understand?'

Once again, the crew nodded in the affirmative.

'Rory, Authorities or Flatpack?'

'Flatpack.'

'Sarah Authorities or Flatpack?'

'Flatpack.'

'Ewan?'

'Flatpack.'

'Duncan?'

'Flatpack.'

'Jim?'

'Flatpack and what about you Nick?'

Nick looked around the mess room with a serious face, and then broke into a huge smile, 'Flatpack of course.'

Jim and Nick swapped a knowing glance.

'Well, I think we can call that a unanimous decision,' said Nick still smiling, 'which is exactly as Jim and I predicted about half an hour ago before coming up with our plan.

RB, is Mark okay with what we are proposing, after all it's them that's picking up the tab?'

'Yes, they're fine with it,' confirmed RB. 'Lloyds want to get to the bottom of this sooner rather than later and they are also of the opinion that if we hand it all over to the authorities it will delay the investigation by several weeks at least. He also pointed out that as it stands at the moment there will be a minimum of three different departments wanting a piece of the action, one investigating what actually sunk the *Tricolor*, one investigating the possible homicide angle, and with all these suspicious cars on board, there is a good chance Customs and Excise will want to investigate a possible smuggling angle. Then you've got to consider the international perspective; it's a foreign-registered ship insured by a British Company with a Philippino crew and has sunk in International waters, it's gonna get very messy.'

'God help us,' muttered Duncan.

'That's good,'' said Nick, 'I thought Mark would see it our way. Okay everyone this is the plan of action, Jim?'

Jim stood up at the end of the table and made eye contact with each of the crew before proceeding.

'Sarah, Ewan, Duncan and Roly, your will remain with the *Sandie Watson* and carry out a detailed survey of as much of the *Tricolor* as you can, *without* re-entering the vessel. We may well have missed something important so keep your eyes peeled for anything unusual.'

'So where are you two going to be?' asked Duncan

'Nick and I are going to pay a visit to Kaliningrad and have a chat with a certain Sergei Petrov. As we have all noticed there are several coincidences that may link BMW and Mr Petrov, so that would seem like a good place to start, especially when he now owns an identical ship to the *Tricolor*, and besides I don't believe in coincidences.'

'Where exactly *is* Kaliningrad?' asked Sarah.

'The country or its capital city?' asked RB from his box on the wall.

'The country,' replied Sarah.

'It's between Poland and Lithuania, on a very similar latitude to Newcastle.

'Unlike Newcastle however it doesn't benefit from any warm air currents so this time of year it gets a bit nippy. Yesterday the top temperature was -10 degrees C and last night it dropped to -18, and they've closed the port today because of blizzard conditions.'

'Makes the middle of the North Sea seem positively tropical,' joked Roly from the serving hatch. 'Talking of which, how are you two going to get from here to Kaliningrad?'

'Good question,' answered Jim, 'how are we doing on this one RB?'

'Pretty good,' replied RB. 'Do you remember that helicopter pilot Russell Dean who we chartered to transport the black box from that plane crash in the Thames Estuary?'

'Yes, nice bloke as I remember, had that chopper with the pontoons so he could set down on water, bit crazy, but a nice bloke.'

'Well, he's booked for tomorrow providing the sea stays calm.'

'Have you got any timings on that?' asked Jim.

'Sure have. He will leave his base in Beccles at around eight. From there he will fly to Harwich where he will meet up with myself and Mark.'

'How's Helen?' asked Sarah.

'Making good progress by all accounts,' confirmed RB, 'apparently their two daughters have been fussing around their mother like a couple of old hens so Mark figured he might as well come back to work. Truth be told I got the impression that he was quite pleased when I called him to see how things were and ask if he knew of someone we could call to captain for the *Sandie Watson* while Nick and Jim were gallivanting around in Kaliningrad. Fairly jumped at the opportunity to re-join you lot, God knows why.'

'Anyway, by then I will have a large holdall of arctic clothing for our two intrepid explorers which Russell will bring out to you with Mark. He reckons the turn-around will take about half an hour with refuelling and the flight out to you about forty-five minutes, which will put him with you at around nine forty-five a.m.

'He will drop Mark at the *Sandie Watson* and then take you and Nick onto Copenhagen, from where you will be catching the three p.m. flight to Kaliningrad, I will send you all the details by email shortly.'

'Okay that's good,' said Nick. 'Thanks for sorting that RB; now isn't it time you went and did some shopping and don't forget, size XXXL.'

'Consider it done,' replied RB. 'Have a good trip.'

The screen went blank and the crew all looked expectantly at Nick.

'Right then, you have your orders, I want every inch of that ship checked over by the time we get back. Sarah, Ewan, you're flying, the rest of you stay focussed.

'Jim, I think you and I had better start packing, it sounds like were in for some stormy weather!'

12

The day had gone according to plan with Mark and Russell arriving at the *Sandie Watson* just before ten a.m. Once Nick had handed over the command of the vessel to Mark and outlined what he wanted them to do in his absence, he and Jim joined Russell in the Eurocopter AS 350 B3 for the hour flight to Copenhagen International Airport.

Visibility was good and they made excellent time, skimming along just above the water at what initially, at least, felt like supersonic speed. As they neared the Danish coast Russell started to climb a little, before contacting the radio tower at Copenhagen Airport for permission to land.

Once on the ground he had the chopper refuelled before taking off and heading back across the North Sea to his Suffolk farmhouse.

It was dark when Nick and Jim arrived at Kaliningrad Airport and the second they left the cosy confines of the Airbus A320, the drop in temperature hit them both like a brick wall travelling at sixty mph. Copenhagen had seemed a little colder but this was like walking out of the sauna and jumping into the plunge pool.

On the way from the airport to their hotel the taxi driver assured them in broken English that the weather was quite mild at the moment and that when it got really cold any exposed skin would freeze in less than a minute.

The irony of this statement was not lost on the two visitors, who both became mesmerised by the temperature display on the dashboard of his Mercedes, which didn't rise above minus fifteen for the entirety of the journey.

'I'm glad we didn't come when it's cold,' commented Jim as the gauge hit a low of minus eighteen degrees Celsius.

As they dropped down into the main town the dock area slipped into view. Floodlights brightly lit most of the quays and the dockers could clearly be seen rushing about their business in their bright yellow fluorescent coats.

At the far end of the complex covered in a heavy shroud of darkness they could just make out the *Baltic Carrier* standing in front of several massive warehouses.

'That *Baltic Carrier*,' said the taxi driver eyeing them up in the rear-view mirror. 'Belong to richest man in Kaliningrad; you see house lit up high on hill—' he pointed vaguely up and over his left shoulder, '—that his house.'

Jim and Nick peered up the hill at a huge grand house that was brightly lit by floodlights.

'What's his name?' asked Jim. 'Is he famous?'

'Sergei Petrov his name,' replied the driver, 'and he famous here.'

The driver laughed at his own joke and then added, 'He give lots of money to local kids home and help the poor.'

'So how does he make his money?' asked Nick keeping up the ruse.

'He breaks up old BMW cars and sell parts on Internet' replied the driver.

Before they could source any other information they already knew, the driver swung the cab up a short driveway and came to a halt under an ornate canopy that led into the foyer of the hotel. Without announcing their arrival, he leapt out of the car and proceeded to unload their two holdalls onto a small metal trolley.

'This way,' he requested swinging his arm forward to indicate the way.

Jim and Nick followed him into an imposing lobby with huge dark marble columns supporting a painted ceiling of clouds. The building judging by its grandness had obviously started out as an embassy or something and the huge, sweeping staircase that curved up to the floor above wouldn't have looked out of place in a royal palace never mind a hotel. In the centre of the lobby was a round reception desk, manned by a middle-aged blonde woman, who judging by her veiled smile, wasn't used to dealing with two scruffy, denim-clad, holdall-carrying foreigners.

The taxi driver was paid off and two minutes later they were climbing the stairs to their rooms.

'We'll have to do that again,' said Jim.

'What, turn up at a posh hotel dressed like tramps?' asked Nick.

'Well, you've got to admit it certainly got the front of house staff motivated.'

'Yeah, tell you what, let's check out in the same gear and see what happens,' chuckled Nick.

'All right, but how about a bet? I bet you five quid that we will be from reception desk to taxi in less than ninety seconds.'

'Not possible,' said Nick, 'I reckon two minutes minimum.'

The men shook on the bet at the top of the stairs and then found their rooms which were adjacent to each other.

'Restaurant at eight?' offered Jim

'Sounds good to me,' replied Nick as the two doors closed.

The restaurant was set in a wing off the main building and was equally opulent with a thirty-foot-high ceiling, and tall twelve-foot-wide full height windows dressed in heavy velvet curtain with huge swags hanging down from invisible pelmets.

At the centre of the room was a huge glass-domed ceiling, the weight of which was supported by a circle of eight marble columns.

With RB packing for them and a holdall their only option for helicopter travel, both men were resigned to wearing Chinos with a shirt and tie. Once again this seemed to galvanise the staff into action and barely a minute after entering the room the Head Waiter had found them an inconspicuous table for their meal in front of a pair of huge full-height curtains.

'So, what's the plan for tomorrow?' asked Jim, settling into his chair.

'Haven't really got a *plan*,' replied Nick emphasising the word "plan". 'But I think we need to have a wander round in the morning and see what makes this place tick before we go charging in like the proverbial bulls.'

'Good idea,' said Jim, 'did you notice when we came into the town that it is almost completely surrounded by hills? I reckon if we can get up high enough, we might be able to see right into the dock area and have a closer look at the *Baltic Carrier*.'

'It will also be interesting to see what sort of reputation our friend Sergei Petrov has around here as well,' continued Nick. 'Kaliningrad doesn't seem like a huge place so someone of his wealth living here must be the talk of the town.'

'Only problem is Nick, we don't talk the talk.'

'Already thought of that,' said Nick with a knowing smile on his face, 'before we left the *Sandie Watson* I asked RB if he could find us a translator here. He sent me a text message about an hour ago with three names and numbers and before you ask, I haven't got a clue how he managed to come up with that information!'

Jim looked up to see a waitress heading their way. 'We may need that translator sooner than you think,' he said nodding towards the tall Russian woman heading their way.

'Good evening gentlemen, my name is Anastasia, but you may address me as Anna,' she paused briefly and handed them each a menu and wine list. 'Would you like any drinks from the bar while you make your selection?'

Jim opened the leather-bound folder and took a quick glance at the menu.

'Unfortunately, your English is 100% better than our Russian; I think we may need to start with a translation of the menu please Anna.'

'I know it's a bit of a long shot,' interjected Nick, 'but would your surname happen to be Eltsina?'

Anna looked a little surprised by the question, but quickly regained her composure.

'Yes, but how did you know that?'

Nick smiled his best Cheshire cat smile, 'I'm sorry, let me explain. My name is Nick Edwards and this is Jim Jackson and we are here on business, but as Jim explained our grasp of the Russian language is zero.

'Before leaving on this trip I asked our colleague for the names of interpreters in Kaliningrad whose services we could call on, yours was one of those names, it's just sheer chance that we should be staying in the same hotel in which you work.'

Anna looked positively relieved at the explanation.

'I would be happy to help, but we will have to talk about this later, my boss doesn't like us to engage too much with the customers, according to him we are here to take orders and serve food, anything else is not permitted, I'm sorry.'

Jim and Nick looked past her to where the head waiter was standing glaring back at them.

'We understand,' said Nick, 'would you like to translate the menu for us now, we can talk later.'

Anna took back Jim's menu and began to run through the courses. The head waiter gave her an approving glance and then disappeared into the kitchen.

The following morning produced a complete whiteout the likes of which neither Nick nor Jim had ever seen before. From their table in the restaurant, they could now see out into the gardens of the hotel, but with the heavy snowfall the visibility was limited to about six feet, which didn't take them much beyond a patio area outside the French doors.

Breakfast consisted of an omelette with a choice of toppings followed by crepe-style Russian blini pancakes rolled in honey and butter, all served with copious amounts of tea or coffee.

'Doesn't look like we will be able to meet up with Anna today after all,' said Nick tucking into his third helping of pancakes.

'I don't know,' replied Jim. 'I woke quite early this morning and when I looked out of the window the weather was just fine, this lot has only moved in over the last hour or so.

Could be that it will move away just as quickly.'

'We'll just have to wait and see,' mumbled Nick through his pancake, 'but sure as eggs are eggs, I'm not going out in that, you'd be pushed to see your hand in front of your face at the moment.'

Jim sat quietly surveying the restaurant's slightly faded grandeur. The room was semi-circular in shape, with a small dwarf wall circling its perimeter, on which stood full-height arched window's. There were four sets of huge French doors positioned between each of the windows, each mimicking the windows arched shape. Either side of the doors were more marble columns similar to those supporting the domed glass ceiling in the middle of the room, and from these columns the ceiling vaulted its way across to the nearest main column to form a series of graceful arches that fanned their way around the room. The ceiling was exquisitely plastered with leaves and vines and then finished with either bright vibrant paint or gold leaf. Stretching out from the central dome were four cherubs, pointing towards four gold globes with N, S, E and W painted on them in a rich guardsman red colour.

The heavy burgundy velvet curtains that had obscured the windows, doors and garden the evening before, were now tied back to the columns and despite the grey weather outside, the glass walls bathed the room in light.

Jim dropped his gaze back to Nick and found him also studying the surroundings.

'Interesting place, eh?'

'Yeah, my guess is that it used to be some sort of embassy building, it's grand enough to have once been a private residence but somehow too formal as well, maybe Anna will be able to tell us more.'

'That's if we manage to get out to see her,' said Jim letting his eyes wander upwards towards the dome in the centre of the room. Nick followed his gaze and for a moment or two they both watched as the snowflakes slid down the steep glass to add to the giant white doughnut that was forming around its base.

'Nothing else to do but wait it out,' commented Nick waiving his empty coffee cup at one of the attendant waiters.

An hour and three more cups of coffee later the snow started to ease a little and, as Jim and Nick walked through the reception area to get back to their rooms, they found it abuzz with fellow guests who had also decided that now would be a good time to venture outside.

Ten minutes later Jim and Nick were standing under the canopy at the front of the hotel looking at a hastily drawn napkin map that Anna had provided for them the previous evening.

The snowstorm had now subsided to a lazy squall and both men were thankful that RB had supplied them with decent boots, thick ski trousers and gaiters with which to wade through the fresh snow. After ten minutes Nick turned into a side street and once again pulled out the map.

'Can't see a street name,' he said looking at the walls of the buildings that surrounded them, 'but I think this must be the correct street, we've only passed one other street, right?'

Jim just nodded his head, keeping up with Nick's six-foot six-inch frame was hard enough work at the best of times, but in deep snow it was very nearly impossible.

Without further comment Nick turned and began ploughing his way along the footpath. If this were the correct street there would be a small alleyway halfway along it on the left that would lead into a small courtyard, where Anna's house was located.

'Looks like the alleyway coming up,' said Nick over his shoulder.

The alleyway turned out to be a tall archway that spanned the gap between the adjacent buildings. Once through there was a large courtyard with space to park upwards of four or five small cars and beyond that a selection of four three-storey dwellings. The front of the houses were protected from the weather by a kind of cloister that ran around the three sides of the quadrangle, at the front of which was a small wall to stop the snow from driving up to the front door. A small gate allowed access to the front doors and, with the virgin snow lying thickly on the courtyard and the roof of the cloistering, it all looked very picturesque.

As Nick pulled out the napkin from his pocket to check the address, a front door opened immediately ahead of them and Anna waved them forward.

'Come, come,' she shouted and moved forward to open her gate.

The two men quickly made for the opening and, once beyond, quickly stripped off their boots and gaiters before entering the house.

Although Nick had wrapped a scarf around his face, the bottom fringes of his beard were heavily frozen, a consequence that Anna had obviously catered for before.

'Here,' she said, presenting Nick with a warm towel. 'Wrap your beard in this and it will be as good as new in minutes.'

'Thank you,' said Nick patting his beard.

'I didn't know if you would come or not,' said Anna, 'we

178

are used to weather like this, but I know your winters are quite mild in England.'

'Have you ever been to England?' asked Jim

'Yes, I lived there for three and a half years, Cambridge, that is where I studied English.'

'You didn't want to stay in the UK?' asked Jim.

'Work brought me back here, there are more Russians needing things translated into English than there are English needing things translated into Russian.

'Please come this way.'

Anna led the way along a short hallway, and then turned right up a flight of stairs.

'My house is upside down,' she commented as she climbed the stairs, 'you will see why in a moment.'

Jim dutifully followed the shapely pair of calf muscles that protruded from beneath Anna's knee-length skirt and was less than disappointed when she turned and continued up a second flight.

'My ground floor has a dayroom, small kitchen area and bedroom with en suite,' she continued climbing the second flight, 'my first floor has two further bedrooms and a main bathroom and then the top floor has my main living area.'

As they neared the top of the stairs the aromatic smell of fresh coffee began to waft from the floor above. The stairs led straight into a lounge area and to one end of the room that encompassed the whole of top floor was a small kitchenette. To their left was a huge picture window and the reason for the upside-down nature of the house now became very apparent.

'So, what do you think?' asked Anna as she moved towards a large percolator full of fresh coffee.

'Wow,' said Jim. 'That's quite a view.'

'That's amazing,' agreed Nick.

Not being familiar with the geography of Kaliningrad both men were unaware that both their hotel and Anna's house were in fact located towards the top of a hill overlooking the city. From their lofty position they could now look down on the snow-covered rooftops of the houses below and beyond that into the harbour area. Jim estimated that they must have been about 400 feet above the sea level.

'I had no idea we were so high up,' commented Jim as he turned to face Anna, 'what a fantastic house.'

'Yes, it is, isn't it? Please take a seat, would you like some coffee?'

Both men confirmed the offer of a hot drink and then settled themselves in a pair of wing-backed leather chairs that sat either side of the window.

The room was furnished with the usual Western accompaniments, a hi-fi system, TV and DVD player and in front of the window there was a low coffee table with some framed photographs of a middle-aged couple cuddled up on a swing seat, surrounded by pink bougainvillea.

'That's my mother and father on holiday in Greece about ten years ago,' said Anna noticing Jim looking at the pictures.

'I can see where you get your good looks from,' he said, picking up one of the photos for a closer look, 'they make a good-looking couple.'

'Thank you,' came Anna's voice from over his shoulder as she placed a tray with mugs of coffee and a plate of cookie-style biscuits on the table in front of the two men.

'Here, these should warm you both up,' she said as she offered the steaming hot mugs to them, 'help yourselves to the cookies, they're home-made.' Nick gave his beard a final rub with the towel and then took the mug.

'Thank you, that feels a lot better,' he said whilst running his fingers through his drying whiskers and reaching forward to take one of the cookies.

Anna leant forward to take her mug from the far side of the tray and as she did so her blouse parted slightly to give Jim an eyeful of her right breast, straining to escape the confines of her bra. As she stood and moved across to the sofa between them, she shot Jim a glance and smiled, leaving him in little doubt that this had not been entirely accidental.

'So how can I be of help to you gentlemen?'

Nick took a sip from his mug and leaned forward slightly in his chair.

'Jim and I both work for an investment bank in the UK and have been sent here on a fact-finding mission to learn as much as we can about Kaliningrad, its people and more important its local business. The bank has a huge portfolio of international clients, one of which is interested in taking advantage of the tax breaks and incentives being offered to set up business here.

'We would like to look at some of the larger local businesses and if possible, talk to those at the top. We know BMW has a large plant here and have already spoken to their headquarters in Munich and they have agreed to let us talk with their Operations Manager here.

'Then there's a local businessman called Sergei Petrov who seems to be doing very well working alongside BMW and we would be interested in his viewpoint too.

'We would also like to look at the company accounts of any business that has set up here during the last few years and if possible, get some figures for the port. We also need some maps of the port area with the depths of the main shipping channels in and out of Kaliningrad.

'If there are any newspaper cuttings about local businesses, we would like to look at those, and also study any census information, so we can try and ascertain the social demographics and skills of the people who live here.

'Our biggest problem with all this is obviously the language and if you agree to help us translate the information we glean, you will be paid handsomely for your efforts.'

'How long are you planning to be here?' asked Anna putting down her coffee and picking up a notepad from a small table beside her.

'We usually work on about three to five days,' replied Nick, 'but with snowfall that is measured in feet rather than inches and the language problem we have extended this to a week.'

'May I ask the nature of the business that is interested in setting up here in Kaliningrad?'

'You can ask,' replied Jim with a smile, 'but even we don't know that. We have been sent here at very short notice. Our colleague who usually deals with this part of the world was seriously injured in a car accident on New Year's Day and Nick and I were drafted in to take his place.

'Our usual remit is central Europe and between us we are fluent in Italian, German French and Spanish, but Russian is not one of our specialist subjects, hence your involvement.'

Anna sat quietly for a moment looking closely at the two men and Nick tried to work out if she had taken the bait or was about to send them packing.

Jim took a sip of his coffee, whilst pondering similar thoughts.

'You two don't look like bankers,' she said after a few moments' thought.

'That's because were not,' replied Jim smiling, 'in fact I don't think either of us have ever spent more than three consecutive days in an office during our whole careers. We are just gofers, we travel around Europe, living out of suitcases, getting information for our bosses, it's not much of a life, but we enjoy it.'

Anna fell silent again and Jim could tell she wasn't convinced by their story and decided to try a closing gambit.

'Look,' he said, 'I can tell this is not your usual translation assignment and that maybe you're uncomfortable digging around for information in old archives and public libraries, so maybe it's better if we just leave, we've got two other names on our list that we can contact.'

Jim rose from his chair and Nick shuffled forward in his seat to do the same.

'Wait,' she said moving forward in her chair and effectively blocking any attempt Nick could make at standing up.

'You're right, this is not my normal remit of sitting in my day room downstairs with my computer and a cup of coffee, translating some boring document, but it doesn't mean I'm not interested. In fact, it all sounds quite appealing, so when do we start and where?'

Jim smiled at Anna and gave her a wink. 'You won't regret it,' he said, 'in fact we will even pay you up front for the first couple of days, if you want to pull out after that, it's your choice okay?'

He reached into his coat pocket and pulled out a bundle of notes. 'Here, this should help,' he said, peeling off several of the Russian banknotes and handing them to Anna.

'This is just for two days' work?' asked Anna looking at the notes.

'Yes, I told you we pay well, *but* we do need access to you 24/7, so if we have to arrange a meeting in the evening, we may need to call upon your services, is that okay?'

'Yes, that's fine, I'm a single girl and I have few commitments and for this sort of money I can take a break from the waitressing for a few days. So, what do you want to do first?'

'Right,' said Jim, 'I have a meeting this afternoon with the chairman of BMW and as I understand it he speaks excellent English, but even if he doesn't I have a good grasp of German so I should be okay there. Nick?'

Nick repositioned himself in his chair and pulled a small reporter's notebook from his pocket.

'Does Kaliningrad have a decent library?'

'Of course,' replied Anna. 'It's quite close to your hotel and because we were once the home to the Russian navy's Baltic Fleet it is one of the largest and best-equipped libraries in the whole country. What is it you are after, in particular?'

'Just general information on the port,' said Nick. 'In particular the depth of the channels at low water, the amount of warehousing available, and the wharfing companies available on the dock. I also need to know the maximum tonnage of vessel that can safely get in and out of the port.'

Nick wasn't at all comfortable spinning a web of lies to the pretty young Russian lady and looked across at Jim for some help.

Jim continued:

'We have already done a little research on the port using

the Internet but have found in the past that this information is not always completely trustworthy, especially where shipping channels are concerned. River estuaries like the Pregola are notorious for shifting sand banks, so any up-to-date information would be most useful.

'It may be useful if we could talk to the port authority and local pilot. Do you know of any large vessels that regularly use the port or are based here? If so, maybe we could talk to their officers about any potential problems that don't show up on the charts, unusual currents for example?'

Anna sat and thought for a moment. 'I can only think of only one large ship that uses the port regularly. She's called the *Baltic Carrier* and is owned and run by Sergei Petrov who you mentioned earlier, he owns a big car dismantling plant at the far end of the dock.'

'That could be interesting,' said Jim turning to Nick, 'see if you can find out her weight and draught, if she's more than 40,000 tonnes we could be in business.'

Nick scribbled forty thousand tonnes in his notebook for Anna's benefit, even though he already knew the *Baltic Carrier* tipped the scales at fifty thousand tonnes.

Jim looked at his watch. 'I think we had better get moving,' he announced, 'my meeting is at two thirty p.m. which doesn't leave much time. Can you meet us at the hotel at two p.m. or will your boss there make a fuss?'

'No, he will be okay, he knows what I do to supplement my income, he just doesn't like me doing business in his time, which is okay.'

Nick rose from his chair and tucked the notebook and pen back in his pocket. As he turned towards the stairs Anna picked up the roubles Jim had given her, folded them once and, with her eyes fixed on Jim's, tucked the notes in her bra. Jim stood spellbound for a couple of seconds as Anna returned his earlier wink and then followed Nick down the stairs.

'Well, that went well,' said Jim five minutes later as they trudged their way back to the hotel.

Nick gave him a shake of the head. 'I've just seen a completely different side to you, where did you learn to lie like that? You even had me convinced there for a while.'

'It comes from working in the insurance industry. I've spent years working with liars trying to defraud their insurance. I guess when you watch people lie for a living some of it rubs off. Are you going to be okay this afternoon with Anna?'

'Yes, no problem, you've set it all up so well, all I'm doing later is going on a fact-finding mission, admittedly ninety-nine per cent of the information is going to be of no use to us whatsoever, but I guess we need to make our visit look genuine.'

'Exactly,' said Jim, 'we are in a foreign country where we don't speak the lingo, looking for clues as to why a ship was seemingly deliberately sunk in the North Sea. We don't know who we can trust and *IF* the *Baltic Carrier* is somehow involved it could get a bit nasty, so let's make our bringing new business to Kaliningrad mission look as legitimate as we can.'

Nick paused for a moment as they reached the corner of the street. 'So, what are you going to be up to while I'm trawling through the best library in the whole country?'

'Shopping for some clothing that doesn't make us stand out like bloody tourists. This high efficiency thermal wear is great, but we don't exactly pass for locals and if we are going to get a close look at the *Baltic Carrier* we need to look a little bit more down-to-earth.'

'Down there could be a good place to start,' suggested Nick pointing down the road to their left where there seemed to be some sort of shopping precinct.

'Looks like an option. I'll meet you back at the hotel later, have a good afternoon with Anna.

Jim set off down the street before Nick could make any further comment.

'Don't forget minimum XXXL for me!' Nick shouted after him and Jim raised a thumb as an acknowledgement as he half walked and half slid down towards the slight incline on the street.

It was five thirty p.m. when Nick arrived back at the hotel and, as he walked through the foyer, he spotted Jim, sitting in a large wing-backed chair in the bar area.

'Looks like you've been here some time,' he said looking at the array of beer bottles littering the table next to him.

'About an hour,' he replied looking at his watch. 'The service is okay but the beer is crap, wanna try some?'

'Don't mind if I do, I'm parched.'

Jim caught the waiter's eye and ordered three more beers.

'So how did you do with the clothing?' asked Nick as he removed his coat and flopped down in the chair opposite Jim.

'Not too well I'm afraid, a combination of my non-existent Russian and being in the wrong part of town, from what I could make out. That complex we spotted was just a sort of local food market and from what I could understand from one of the traders the main town centre is about a mile inland.'

'No local gear then?' confirmed Nick.

'No, we'll just have to stick to the tourist trails for the moment.'

At that moment the waiter appeared with three bottles of beer on a silver tray.

Nick picked up two of the bottles in one of his bear-like hands and to the astonishment of the waiter proceeded to pour them simultaneously down his throat. Ten seconds later he put the empties back on the tray and signalled to the waiter that he would like two more.

For a split second the waiter just stood beside Nick with a weird look on his face, seemingly unable to take in what he just witnessed, before turning and heading back to the bar for the refills.

Jim looked at Nick and shook his head. 'We're supposed to be keeping a low profile,' he remarked. 'Remember?'

'Sorry,' said Nick. 'I couldn't resist it.'

Jim shook his head again. 'So how did you get on with Anna this afternoon?'

'Very well, we started by looking up the details of any new companies to the area. Apparently, they are granted tax and custom duty breaks on any goods they send back to Russia and one in three Russian televisions are made here in Kaliningrad.

'Hummer have also got a plant here making those huge off-road four-by-fours and small companies making amber products, jewellery and the like, are also quite plentiful. One of the more unusual businesses we found makes electric motors for vacuum cleaners, nothing else, just the motors and we also came across a company that makes specialised road haulage trailers for transporting oversized cargos.'

'So, it's quite a thriving industrial centre, then?' said Jim pausing as the waiter returned with two more bottles of beer. The waiter hovered for a few seconds beside Nick with the beers still on the tray as if waiting for a repeat performance, but on realising that was not going to happen quickly placed the bottles on the table and retreated.

Jim waited until the waiter was out of earshot and continued.

'So, did you get as far as Mr Petrov?'

'Of course we did and I don't think I would be overstating the case if I said he's the key to this whole economy.'

'How come?' said Jim with a slightly puzzled look on his face.

'Think about what I've just told you,' replied Nick pausing for a moment.

Jim closed his eyes and mentally scanned through the businesses Nick had just told him about.

'No sorry, I can't see any connection between TVs, amber jewellery, electric motors and oversized truck trailers.'

'Metal,' smiled Nick, happy to have got one over his pal. 'Once I sussed this small, but very important fact, I sent Anna on a wild goose chase researching the port, biggest ships, high water, the sort of things we outlined this morning.

'While she was doing this, I jumped on one of the computers and started doing some research of my own.

'As we know Sergei Petrov operates one of the largest car dismantling plants in the world, right here in Kaliningrad and because labour is so cheap here, he can afford to strip these vehicles bare of anything of any value.

'Cars contain a varied assortment of metals and plastics and if you cross-reference those metals with what is required to make amber jewellery, electric motors, televisions and even specialised truck trailers, you get an exact match.

'Whereas in other parts of the world it would not be cost effective to remove the small amounts of gold and platinum from circuit boards, here it is and with an abundance of amber in the region the local jewellers are crying out for something to mount the amber in.

'Television sets and electric motors both need an abundance of copper wiring to make them work, and it goes without saying that the truck trailers need a suitable supply of steel.

These companies have all set up shop here because of one man, Sergei Petrov, and although he's a local hero in these parts, no one seems to know where he came from and how he made enough money to become the spider sitting in the middle of a huge web of satellite businesses that feed off his dismantling plant.'

Jim sat back and digested what Nick had just told him.

'We don't know if the *Tricolor* sinking has anything to do with Mr Petrov or not, but it seems a bit more than a coincidence that so far everything seems to be pointing in his direction.'

'Ah, but I saved the best bit until last, look at this.'

Nick unfolded a piece of paper from his pocket and handed it to Jim. It was a photocopied picture taken from a local newspaper. The picture showed a couple standing in front of three men and behind them was what looked like the *Baltic Carrier*.

Below the picture was a brief explanation in Russian along with the names of the people in the photo, Viktor Demidov, Mikhail Duggan, and Alexei Nikitin, at the back and Sergei and Anouska Petrov in the foreground.

The picture was dated May 2012.

'So at least we know what he looks like,' mused Jim. 'His wife is a good-looking lady. Who are the other three and what's with the chap Duggan, doesn't sound very Russian to me!'

'I found this quite by chance,' confessed Nick, 'and then texted the email address to RB requesting he researched the three characters at the back as thoroughly as possible, I'm still waiting to hear back from him.'

Both men fell silent for a moment and watched as a good-looking young couple arrived at reception.

It struck Jim that it didn't matter where you were in world you can always spot the well-heeled. You can put a lottery winner in an Armani suit and a Ferrari, but he will still look like a lottery winner, these two however had class and you can't buy class.

As they watched a porter arrived with six tan leather cases, all beautifully monogrammed and then led the way to an ordinary-looking panelled oak door beside the main lifts. On opening the door, a small lobby revealed itself and from their position Nick and Jim could see a small private elevator car which the porter and his guests now entered. A second porter arrived and as the lift doors closed began to unload the cases from the trolley against the wall of the lobby. Seconds later the elevator doors opened to reveal an empty car. Monogrammed suitcases were now placed inside the elevator and, with the button pressed, he then moved back into the main foyer and closed the panelled door.

Neither Jim or Nick passed comment on the couple, they just sat quietly and people watched for the next few minutes, mulling over the *Tricolor* and Sergei Petrov who seemed to be somehow linked, but how?

It was Nick who was the first to break the silence.

'I think we need to get a closer look at the *Baltic Carrier*,' he announced seemingly out of nowhere.

'Not to mention the dismantling plant,' added Jim.

'The problem is how do we get close enough to either without raising suspicion?'

Nick smiled a knowing smile at Jim and tapped the side of his nose.

'Don't worry it's all sorted.'

'How?'

'We're here researching out a new business venture, right? So, what does a business need most of all?'

Jim thought for a moment.

'Premises.'

'Correct.

'When I left Anna, I asked her to start researching sites around the port area exceeding 20,000 Square metres. She said that she would get back to us mid-morning tomorrow. Now I figure if that doesn't get us near the *Baltic Carrier* or car plant tomorrow afternoon, a tourist trip up into the hills for a bit of panoramic sight-seeing, should do the job.'

'I like your thinking,' said Jim.

At that moment Nick's mobile began to ring.

He answered it and mouthed RB to Jim. After several minutes of conversation punctuated with *ums, reallys* and *you're kiddings*, he hung up and looked triumphantly at his partner.

'Bingo.'

'What have you got?' asked Jim excitedly.

'Still nothing on Mr Petrov,' answered Nick, 'and Viktor

Demidov seems to be equally difficult to trace, however the other two are a different story.' Nick lent forward in his chair and carried on in a hushed tone.

'Alexei Nikitin is a home-grown Russian mafia boss based in Moscow. With his two sons Vasyl and Vladimir they control a good part of the Russian capital and have their fingers in many different pies many of which are of an international nature. He is thought to have links with mafia groups in both America and China and is suspected at being involved in international fine art smuggling, not the sort of man we want to meet in a dark alley late at night.

'Mind you neither is Mikhail, real name Michael Duggan. Born in Southern Ireland to English parents he was seconded from the SAS in the early eighties to go deep undercover and infiltrate the IRA. Did a good job by all accounts, but then went AWOL and has been on the top of the British government's most wanted list ever since. Reports are that he has been fighting all over the world as a mercenary, but every time anyone gets close to him, he vanishes.'

'Bloody hell,' whispered Jim, 'sounds like a pretty resourceful kind of guy.'

'A pretty dangerous one as well,' quipped Nick.

'Yeah right. I think we need to have a very public look around tomorrow under our guise of investment bankers and then make moves to head for home. Once back in the UK we can hand this all over to the authorities and let them run with it.'

'You're not going to get any arguments from me on that score,' said Nick rising from his seat, 'I'm off to get a shower.'

Jim rose as well.

'Think I'll come up with you, all of a sudden this place doesn't feel so comfortable.'

13

The following morning dawned bright and sunny, with the snow that had fallen the previous day still laying heavy on the ground.

After a leisurely breakfast the two men retired back to Nick's room and waited for Anna to call.

The call came at just after eleven o'clock and half an hour later Anna arrived at the hotel suitably dressed in knee-high leather boots and a long light-coloured fur coat. She quickly spoke to the receptionist and ten minutes later they were in a taxi heading down to the dock area with an excited Anna, who was confident she had found a plot of land suitable for their needs.

The land turned out to be exactly what they were looking for; well, it would have been had their story been genuine. Situated on the far side of the port it was accessed through an entrance guarded by two, armed, security men. Just after the sentry post was an access road on the left that led into a small compound, at the back of which was a large warehouse in need of some considerable renovation work to make it suitable for anything other than storage of all but the most basic of cargos.

The front of the warehouse was made of concrete blocks and there was a row of windows just under the shallow-pitched roof.

Nick and Jim were inwardly kicking themselves as the

driver turned into the compound. For the last ten minutes they had been on a target course with the *Baltic Carrier* moored further up the dock and the left turn had now blocked off any view of the ship.

Anna explained that the land was owned by Sergei Petrov and the high security was there because further down the road was the main entrance to the car dismantling plant.

The inability to check out the *Baltic Carrier* was a bit of a blow, but the fact that the land was owned by Sergei Petrov gave them an ideal opportunity to ask more questions about the entrepreneur without raising Anna's suspicions and, from the way she could almost instantly answer any questions posed, it became clear that in his home town at least, he was very well known.

Two minutes after they arrived a black Mercedes drew up alongside their taxi and a man in a big heavy black fur coat got out and approached them with his hand outstretched.

Anna shook his hand and then introduced Nick and Jim to Mr Tarasov. After several exchanges she then explained that he was taking care of the sale on behalf of Mr Petrov and if they had any questions, he would try to answer them. She also explained that she had told him about their role with an investment bank, something that to Nick and Jim's relief Mr Tarasov had had dealings with before when setting up the deal with Hummer.

Mr Tarasov went to the boot of his car and pulled out a large snow shovel and began digging a path through the eighteen inches of snow towards a small Judas gate in the main warehouse door. After a couple of minutes of digging he took a breather and turned to Anna, pointing at a huge house clinging to the side of the mountainside above them.

'That's Mr Petrov's house,' she explained, 'and every New Year's Eve he has a huge firework display in his garden which can be enjoyed by all the townsfolk.'

'Sounds like quite a guy,' said Jim.

'Yes, he is,' replied Anna, 'he gives so much back to the local community, sponsoring building projects and giving money to local charities.'

She turned and paused for a moment to get her bearings.

'There, over there, you see that new building with the glass frontage?'

Nick and Jim followed her pointing finger.

'The three-storey one with the steeply pitched roof?' asked Jim

'Yes, that's a new medical centre he built a couple of years ago. We share a hospital with the next town Bagrationovsk, which is thirty kilometres away. About five years ago there was a nasty accident on the dock, several men were badly injured and one died on the way to hospital. The locals were, how you say, up in arms about it and Mr Petrov promised to build them a new medical centre to deal with emergencies within the community. Anything really serious still has to go to the hospital but almost everything else can be dealt with there.'

'He must be very popular with the local people,' said Jim.

Anna paused for a moment and checked that Mr Tarasov was out of earshot before continuing in a hushed tone.

'Not all of them,' she replied. 'He also has a very dark side. A few weeks ago, a friend's husband was caught stealing from the plant. He was thrown into the icy dock and then just before passing out with the cold he was pulled out with a, what's the word?' She made a large J shape in the air.

'Fishermen use them to get fish onto the deck,'

'Gaff?' said Nick.

'Yes gaff,' agreed Anna. 'While he was in hospital, he told a nurse friend of mine about the incident and then he disappeared, hasn't been seen since. And he's not the first person to vanish either, if you are going to deal with Mr Petrov my advice to you is not to cross him.'

Jim and Nick exchanged glances, their suspicions about Sergei Petrov's more sinister side having been confirmed.

Behind them a loud creaking sound emanated from the Judas gate, and Anna led the two men between the banks of snow into the deserted warehouse. As they reached the door a muffled thump was heard followed by the tinkling of fluorescent tubes coming to life.

The warehouse was like a million other warehouses around the world, the only difference being the huge amount of superstructure holding up the roof. Mr Tarasov noticed Nick looking up at the steelwork and said something to Anna.

'The snow can be as much as two metres deep during a harsh winter so the roof is heavily reinforced to take the worst of the weather.'

'That makes sense,' said Nick and started to walk down the centre line of the warehouse taking great care to look like he was taking in every tiny detail.

Jim pulled a camera from his coat pocket and gesticulated to Mr Tarasov that he would like to take some pictures.

The Russian shrugged his shoulders and held out his arms as an invitation for Jim to proceed.

There wasn't really much to look at, but Jim and Nick continued to examine the warehouse and take photographs of every last detail to keep their pretence alive.

As they returned to the front of the building, Jim spotted a staircase rising up in one corner.

'What's up there?' he asked Anna, who immediately referred the question to their Russian guide.

After a short conversation she explained that it led to a suite of offices.

'Okay to have a look?' he asked Anna, but before she could answer Mr Tarasov was climbing the staircase and encouraging the others to follow.

At the top of the stairs was a long corridor to the right of which was a series of half-glazed open plan offices.

To the left was a solid-looking door and on entering the room they came across an executive office with windows looking out across the port.

'Wow that's quite a view,' commented Jim as he moved towards the window with his camera still in hand.

Moments later he was joined by the others and they all stood silently for a second or two taking in the view of the port.

Jim had already noticed the massive hulk of the *Baltic Carrier* now visible to his left but decided to make a play of looking in the opposite direction to where a huge breakwater protected the port from the Baltic Sea.

Opposite their vantage point was the main port with two vessels tied up at the quay discharging their goods onto the dockside. Beyond that was the town of Kaliningrad scattered across the hillside in a mad jumble of different-shaped houses, shops and public buildings.

Jim checked his camera was still in standby mode and started taking pictures of the offices.

Meanwhile Nick kept the ruse rolling by making notes and asking questions about the cost of the building and details of any other charges that would be levied against their "clients" should they choose to take up the option.

True to his word Mr Tarasov proved very helpful and said that once he got back to his office, he would prepare a full dossier on the warehouse for Nick and Jim's bosses to examine.

Jim by now was back at the window and starting from the breakwater end of the port started to take a set of panoramic pictures of the port. With the camera clicking away in auto wind mode, he lazily swung the camera in a 180-degree arc. At the end of the arc, he slowed down to ensure he got as many pictures of the *Baltic Carrier* as possible without raising any suspicions, and then turned back to face the others.

As he did so Anna moved back to the window and then turned and spoke to Mr Tarasov in a questioning sort of voice.

Mr Tarasov shrugged his shoulders again and turned towards the stairs.

'What's up?' asked Jim, seeing the puzzled look in Anna's eyes.

'That,' she said pointing out of the window at a large motor yacht heading for the open sea. 'I've never ever seen that leave the harbour before April when it gets sailed down to the Med for the summer, most unusual.'

'Maybe it's in need of some maintenance or something,' offered Jim.

'Yes, maybe.'

She turned and followed the Russian down the stairs.

Once outside Jim took some more pictures of the warehouse before thanking Mr Tarasov and heading to their waiting cab.

'Is there anywhere we can get a view of the whole port

from high up?' asked Jim in a matter-of-fact sort of way.

'There is a viewing point up on the main road,' replied Anna pointing up the mountainside above them.

'Sounds great,' said Jim. 'Might as well do the sight-seeing bit while we are here.'

Anna spoke a few sentences to the taxi driver who nodded enthusiastically at the thought of the extra fare. Business must be slow, thought Jim.

It took them half an hour to navigate through the town and onto the main road that linked Kaliningrad with Znamensk. The road climbed steeply at first but then levelled out, following the contours of the mountain. Although covered in snow the taxi with snow chains on it tyres coped well with the hostile conditions. As they rounded a left-hand bend the driver swung into a large lay-by on the right and came to a halt.

In front of them was a three-foot-high stone wall, and as they walked towards it a breathtaking view of the river Pregola with Kaliningrad and the Baltic Sea beyond unfolded before them.

'Bloody hell,' muttered Nick in a hushed tone. 'Now that's what I call a view.'

'I thought you'd be impressed,' smiled Anna, 'it's probably one of the best views in the whole country.'

Jim looked down into the valley, the river Pregola meandering its way down towards the sea, a small ribbon of water laying at the bottom of a four- or five-mile-wide glacial canyon that was now home to a colossal industrial monster.

He started to study the dismantling plant which seemed to stretch on for miles. Closest to them and running alongside the river was a huge pound stacked high with BMWs and he estimated that there were several thousand cars there, waiting to be processed. Beyond that was a massive building covering several acres which he guessed to be the recycling plant and, to the far side of that, were two chimneys belching out thick grey smoke. Two huge furnaces could be seen through the smog, their bulbous shape reaching up into the sky, their blackness a stark contrast to the snow that covered everything else. The whole site was linked by miles of railway tracks on which diesel locomotives busied themselves shunting huge skip-like wagons of stripped car parts to the furnaces.

Nearer the dock front where the *Baltic Carrier* was moored, there were more huge sheds outside which were tall stacks of coiled steel waiting to be transported to the various factories strung out along the far side of the valley.

The BMW plant was the nearest and its shiny new offices were a stark contrast to black grime that surrounded it. A huge neon sign on its roof let everyone know that BMW were in town, but even from this distance Jim noted that there seemed to be very few shinny BMWs in the car park next to their prestigious offices.

Behind the offices was the manufacturing plant and like the dismantling plant it covered several acres. In the far distance a huge car park of brand-new BMWs stood glinting in the snow, their bright colours lighting up the landscape like a massive field of mixed tulips.

For Jim though the centre point was the *Baltic Carrier*, her red and white paintwork standing out sharply in the lunchtime sunshine. This was the first clear view he had got of the vessel and, once again, Jim nonchalantly pulled the camera from his pocket and started snapping away trying to look like a tourist and not a spy.

Realising what Jim was doing Nick took Anna to one side and asked her about the mountains in the far distance from which the river Pregola seemed to begin its course to sea.

To her credit Anna explained in some detail where the Pregola rose and how at the end of the winter when the snow started to thaw the river took on a completely different course, scything down the valley like an avalanche. She pointed out where the river changed course when swollen by the thaw and explained that that was why the dismantling plant had huge ten-metre-high walls around its perimeter.

By now Jim had finished taking pictures, and they agreed that it would be a good idea to return to the warmth of their taxi before as Nick put it, 'bits started to drop off!'

An hour later they were back at the hotel sitting in the bar just off the main reception, hugging huge mugs of strong Russian coffee that Anna had ordered from one of the kitchen staff.

Nick sat in one of the big winged-back chairs, while Jim and Anna sat opposite him on a similarly high-backed settee.

'I have two other sites that may be of some interest to you.'

'Tell us more,' replied Jim over the rim of his mug.

'Well, the first one is a lot smaller than the warehouse we looked at this morning and it's further along the quay towards the dismantling plant. The only way we can look at that is with special permission from Mr Petrov and accordingly it comes with a much higher level of security.

'Our friend Mr Petrov seems to guard his plant very thoroughly', said Nick, finally deciding to ask the question that had been preying on his mind for some time. 'Is there something dodgy going on behind those closed doors or is he just a bit paranoid?'

Anna shot him a "if looks could kill" look, followed by a miniscule shake of the head and continued.

'The third site is more towards the town centre and is government owned, which shouldn't be a problem. Our government is very welcoming to foreign investment at the moment as you can see. It was formerly a storage warehouse for Russian Navy but has been empty for some years now and could really do with knocking down and rebuilding. Once again, I think the local officials would be most helpful as long as your company used local labour and materials.'

Nick noisily took a last slurp for his mug and then announced that he was going to his room for a nap.

'Want me to take your coat up?'

'Yes, might as well thanks,' replied Jim giving Nick a wink.

Nick got the message straight away and, having thanked Anna for the tour, headed for his room where he could download Jim's photographs onto his laptop.

Anna moved across the settee and now faced him, their faces only inches apart.

'Have I upset him?' she whispered.

'No, he'll get over it,' he replied in an equally hushed tone.

'You can't ask questions like that around here,' she continued. 'Sergei Petrov is like a god to most of our people. He has brought so much to Kaliningrad, jobs, community projects and to some considerable wealth. But he has a very dark dangerous side and the people who worship him let him know of any dissenting voices.'

Jim sat looking into Anna's dark eyes.

'Did you hear what I just said?' she asked.

'Mmm,' he replied still not breaking eye contact, then he kissed her.

14

It was four thirty p.m. when Nick was awoken from a shallow doze by a knock on the door.

When he opened it, Jim was standing there with a smile from ear to ear on his face.

'Had a good time?' he muttered grumpily.

'Yes, thanks,' replied Jim, 'she's quite a lady.'

'I know, I've had to listen to you two for the last hour and a half.'

Jim gave him a strange look.

'Oh, come on,' continued Nick, 'think about it. We've stayed in hotels all over Europe and never once have we failed to be kept awake by the amorous goings-on in the adjacent rooms. What I couldn't work out though, is why she orgasmed in English.'

He gave Jim a quick grin and headed towards the laptop.

'Where is Anna now?'

'Gone home to freshen up a bit, I said we would treat her to dinner tonight, so she'll meet us in the lobby at about seven thirty. Is that okay?'

'Yeah, that's fine, now look at this.'

He poked the mouse pad and the screen leapt back into life.

'These are the pictures you took of the *Baltic Carrier* today. I've cleaned them up a bit and then compared them with the picture RB sent us of the *Tricolor*.'

He pressed the next frame icon and an enhanced version of one of Jim's pictures filled the screen.

'Okay now look at this.' He clicked the next frame icon again and an almost identically sized picture appeared showing the *Tricolor*.

'Notice any difference?'

Jim sat down at the table and scrolled backwards and forwards between the two pictures. After a couple of minutes of silence, he turned to Nick.

'They are identical in every way.'

'Exactly,' agreed Nick.

'So, I phoned RB and got him to get us up-to-date pictures as possible of both vessels and then call me back if he could see any differences between the two ships. Now we know they were built at roughly the same time in the same shipyard in the Philippines, but that was fifteen years ago! They've spent the last ten years or more under different ownership they can't still be absolutely identical after all these years.

'Then I got to thinking about the photograph I found in the local rag, the one with Sergei and his wife on and the heavy guys stood behind. I also asked RB to translate the article to see if there were any clues there.'

'So, have you heard back from RB?'

'About half an hour ago, he confirmed that there are some subtle differences between the two ships, positioning of life rafts and radio antenna etc, etc, nothing major but if the two ships were sat side by side you might notice some small discrepancies.

'He said the article in the paper, related to the *Baltic Carrier* arriving back in port having undergone a new paint job. So, he then contacted the Norwegian owners of the *Tricolor*, West Coast Shipping, and guess what? She was also repainted at the beginning of last year.'

'Another bloody coincidence?' stated Jim leaning back in his chair and tenting his fingers under his chin.

Nick let him think for a moment or two before throwing in his bombshell.

'I've got a theory about what's going on here, care to hear it?'

Jim nodded.

Nick rose to his feet and walked across to the window that overlooked part of the port.

'Think about what we've got so far. We've got a ship doing regular runs backwards and forwards across the North Sea which suddenly goes missing rather conveniently at the only time of the year when there is a slight lull in shipping traffic, with next to no wreckage, and no survivors.

'As we've discovered, it looks suspiciously like it's been deliberately sunk and the crew on board were not her regular crew. Added to this are the facts that she is found miles away from her designated course, a course that her captain should know like the back of his hand and that when we finally find her, she's in a trench that forms the deepest part of the whole North Sea, strange or what?

'The cars on board are all BMWs as far as we can tell, BUT they are not "right". They have the wrong wheels and part-worn tyres on them and that's just for starters.'

'Fine so far,' said Jim not seeing where the conversation was heading.

'Okay, now add what we found out on the *Sandie Watson* to what we've discovered since we've been here.'

Nick turned from the window and paced around the bed to the minibar.

'Want anything?'

'No thanks.'

He took a bottle of beer from the fridge and opened it before continuing.

'I think our friend Mr Petrov has been planning this for years, possibly even before he managed to buy the *Baltic Carrier*, in fact it may have been the reason he bought the ship in the first place. The ships were to all intents identical and I think this is critical to his plan.'

Jim looked up at Nick. 'What plan?'

'Hear me out.

'I think in order to pull this off he had to keep the *Baltic Carrier* looking identical to her sister ship, so when the *Tricolor* was repainted early last year he had to have the *Baltic Carrier* done as well so that they remained in the same state of repair.'

Nick took a heavy swallow of his beer, allowing him time to formulate his thoughts.

'I can't really decide whether the *Tricolor*'s captain Ed Collins was in on this or not. I suspect he was, because it seems a little strange that the crew was changed for that sailing. So, either he's sitting on the bottom of the North Sea or he's on a Caribbean island sipping cocktails.

'Hang on a minute, you've completely lost me now,' said Jim getting slightly exasperated by Nick's obtuse explanation.

'Okay,' said Nick taking another gulp of beer and taking a deep breath.

'What if the ship down there in the harbour,' he waved his near empty bottle at the window, 'is actually the *Tricolor?*'

'The *Tricolor?*' stuttered Jim.

'Yes, the *Tricolor*, now renamed the *Baltic Carrier.*'

Jim sat motionless in his chair.

'I think you'd better explain some more of your theory,' he said, intrigued by what Nick was saying.

'I think the original *Baltic Carrier* is now masquerading as the *Tricolor* in the Liberman Trench. As you know we are one of only a handful of organisations in this part of the world that have ROVs at our disposal, but in order to try and cover their tracks they sank her in the deepest part of the North Sea. They had no way of knowing we would arrive looking for her with some of the most high-tech equipment this side of the Atlantic. And if my theory holds water, excuse the pun, then the *Tricolor* is now moored up over there as the *Baltic Carrier.*

'Remember the lack of wreckage? If I'm right and this had been planned for some time, I reckon the *Baltic Carrier* would have been stripped of anything of any value, or any item that could be identified as coming from that vessel. That's why no one found any wreckage. I'd put money on it, that if we could go inside the ship in the Trench, we would find just a bare shell, nothing but an engine, a few bridge controls and a cargo of second-hand BMWs.'

'That would certainly explain the lack of wreckage,' Jim agreed.

'Remember that huge pound of old Beamer's we looked down on this morning from the mountain? Well, I think Mr Petrov has been stockpiling the newer models for the last few months.

'It wouldn't have mattered how damaged they were if they're on a one-way trip to the bottom of the North Sea, because as we saw, they've all ended up in a big heap anyway.

We didn't even consider the damaged at all, it was the worn tyres and subsequently the wrong wheels that caught our attention. One other thing that may be of interest to you is that BMW are about to launch a new set of models right across its whole range, so the timing would be perfect.'

Jim was beginning to warm to the theory.

'Okay that's good so far, but how do you commandeer a ship in the middle of the North Sea? It's not like hijacking a car, you can't just pull alongside and threaten the driver with a gun if he doesn't pull over, these are large vessels and, more to the point, how come nobody saw anything?'

'That's another reason why I think Ed Collins *was* involved,' continued Nick. 'Sure, ships get raided by pirates all the time, although admittedly not in the North Sea, so we know it's possible to take over a ship quite quickly with the right personnel. But they couldn't do that on a main shipping lane. Two identical ships sitting side by side with the possible crack of gunfire was bound to have caught someone's attention; too risky.

'My theory is that the two ships met up over the Liberman Trench. If you look at the map, the position we found the wreck is more than fifteen miles from any shipping lane. That, rather conveniently as you know, puts them beyond the horizon of any passing vessels.'

Jim got up and took a bottle of spring water and a packet of dry roasted peanuts from the minibar.

'Thought you didn't want anything.'

'Your theory is making me hungry,' quipped Jim.

Nick continued:

'We know the sea was flat calm that night, which must have made the whole operation very easy. I suspect knowing what we know now, that the boarding was commanded by Michael Duggan and with a new Pilipino crew who were unfamiliar with the ship's layout and procedures, I'm guessing he probably had the whole ship sealed up in about fifteen minutes flat.

'I'm guessing that the crew were then transferred to the original *Baltic Carrier*, locked up somewhere secure and went to the bottom with the vessel when it was mined, hence no one found any survivors.'

Jim took a swig of his water and emptied some peanuts into his mouth. In between munches he threw Nick another question.

'Would this be possible? To completely change the identity of two ships like you're suggesting?'

'I don't see why not, I reckon all the necessary work had already been done on the original ship, name changed and so on, so all they had to do was change the name of the *Tricolor* to the *Baltic Carrier*, swap any key give-aways, like life rafts, ship's bell, transponders, you know the sort of items that are unique to each ship and then head back here to Kaliningrad. Allowing for the odd "incident" I'm guessing the whole operation probably only took about five or six hours and all under the cover of a long winter's night, piece of cake!

'Mr Petrov still has his 50,000-ton ship, except the value of the cargo has increased from a few hundred thousand pounds to about £50 million, not a bad return for a dodgy night's work in the North Sea.'

Jim sat quietly for a moment or two, still munching on his peanuts.

'It certainly fits very snugly with what we have so far,' he said after some thought.

'How long did it take you to come up with that?'

'This whole case has been puzzling the hell out of me since we found the ship so far away from her plotted course. I've been doing this job for many years now and usually by now there's at least a couple of facts that tie together the two ends of the rope, the cause and effect.

'Absolutely nothing we've discovered so far adds up, so while you were entertaining Anna next door, I started to bounce some ideas about in this empty old head of mine and that's the culmination of my thought processes so far.'

'Not bad for a beaten-up old wrestler I have to admit,' said Jim.

'Yes, I'm pretty pleased with it myself,' grinned Nick. 'All we've got to do is get some facts that support my theory.'

'So, what's next?'

'Well, I also made a call to the *Sandie Watson* and asked Ewan to dive onto the ships bow and see if he could spot any tinkering with the ship's name. He said he was in the middle of a dive looking at the bridge area, and that he would divert the ROV to the bow and get back to me. Haven't heard anything yet.'

'Your theory would certainly explain why the guards down there are all walking around with machine guns slung over their shoulders,' said Jim gesticulating in the general direction of the window.

'But how do you get rid of nearly two thousand shiny new BMWs?'

'Ah, I've got a hypothesis on that as well.'

'We learnt from the photograph that Mr Petrov has contacts with the Russian mafia in the shape of Alexei Nikitin. What's the betting that when the *Baltic Carrier* sails out of here on the fourteenth which is the day after tomorrow incidentally, she's heading for a small secluded port somewhere around the world to offload those BMWs into mafia hands?'

'We know it can't be any further north of here because the sea will be frozen solid, but they could have made arrangements with any number of powerful mafia groups from the Americas to China, who knows?'

Right on cue Nick's mobile began to ring.

'Hi Ewan, what have you found?'

Jim could hear Ewan's voice talking excitedly on the other end of the line.

'You sure? Excellent well done. I'll explain it all to you later, thanks.'

Nick hung up and looked triumphantly at Jim.

'Confirmed; the nameplate on the ship in the trench is freshly welded into place. Apparently, it looks like they have tried to paint over the weld but the paint has started to flake off revealing shiny new metal.'

Jim sat down on the edge of the bed, flicked a peanut high into the air and then caught it in his mouth. He repeated the trick several more times before turning to Nick.

'This has taken rather a serious turn now, so I think I had better call Mark at Lloyds and see what he thinks we should do next.

'Originally, we were recruited to simply find a sunken ship, now we are looking at the possible murder of up to twenty-three men and, if you include the cost of the *Tricolor/Baltic Carrier*, a fraud that adds up to many millions of pounds sterling.'

'Yes, it has taken a rather serious turn,' agreed Nick, 'well while you're doing that, I'm going to have a shower.'

Nick took some clean underwear from the chest of drawers and headed for the en suite.

When he re-entered the room fifteen minutes later, he found a note on the bed which simply read 'looks like we're heading home tomorrow morning, see you in the bar at 7.15.'

When Nick reached the bar, he found Jim sitting in one corner with two glasses of beer on the table before him.

'Been here long?' he queried.

'About an inch,' replied Jim holding up his beer which was only missing its head.

'So, what did Mark say then?'

'The gist of the conversation was that we have done a good job, but that this is now beyond our remit as we neither have the knowledge, skills, authority or resources to take our investigation any further without putting ourselves in danger. I then called RB and he has booked us a flight out of here tomorrow morning at eleven a.m. It's going to be a reversal of the trip in, with another chopper ride back out to the *Sandie Watson* with Russell from Copenhagen International Airport.'

Nick took a gulp of his beer and both men sat silently watching the comings and goings in the foyer.

Suddenly from behind them appeared Anna who bent over and kissed Jim very firmly on the mouth.

'Where did you come from?' Jim asked, sure he would have spotted her enter through the front door of the hotel.

'I sneaked in the back door,' she smiled, seemingly very pleased with her unexpected entry.

'So, would you like a drink first or shall we go straight through to the restaurant?'

'I am rather hungry,' she confessed. 'I seem to have built

up quite an appetite.'

'I wonder what caused that!' said Nick getting up from his chair and giving Jim a wink, 'must be all that research you're doing.'

Anna gave Nick a coy look before standing, grabbing Jim by the hand and linking arms with the two men and steering them towards the restaurant.

The restaurant seemed unusually quiet, although given the early hour it was hardly surprising. There were two other tables occupied, one by a middle-aged couple who sat silently eating their food and another by a group of four businessmen talking in hushed tones.

The waiter showed them to a table in front of the French doors and then proceeded to close the full-height curtains to stop any draughts.

Anna introduced the waiter as Yuri and then in an avalanche of Russian ordered for the three of them.

'I've ordered a traditional Russian meal. We will start with Borsht, which is beet soup with added meat and vegetables, it has a lot of different flavours, I think you will like it. When I was in England, I used to like your shepherd's pie, but everyone seemed to make it slightly differently. Our Borsht is like that, but the chef here makes a very good version.'

'Moussaka in Greece is a bit like that too,' said Nick. 'I've eaten that all over the country and it always tastes slightly different according to the local traditions.'

'Exactly,' smiled Anna. 'Here, because of the climate, we don't have access to much fruit and vegetables, so at this time of year especially we use lot of bread, potatoes, curd, sour cream, eggs and of course meat. It makes good filling food and gives us the warmth and energy we need to get through the winter months.'

'Lots of carbohydrates, eh?' added Jim.

'Yes, when I was studying English, I found it helpful to read books and magazines in your language. It didn't really matter what they were about, it was just useful to help me understand how your language is constructed.

'One of the articles I read was about the problems the Western world has with obesity, particularly in children, and the author made a very valid point which is still relevant here today. I think it was written by a Cambridge professor and his argument for why there are so many overweight people, was that it is down to our Neolithic ancestors.'

'What's Neolithic man got to do with kids eating too many burgers and fries?' asked Nick a little perplexed.

'Genetics,' replied Anna. 'Over many thousands of years our ancestors learnt which foods were the best to eat, i.e., those high in carbohydrates, fats and proteins. They worked out that eating grass or wood bark for example didn't give them the energy levels that they needed, but by trial and error they found the leaves, roots, fruits, herbs, berries and meats that were good for them.

'The professor's argument was that we are all genetically programmed to eat high fat, starch, protein and carbohydrate foods because in the past these were the best way of staying healthy and being able to survive in the sometimes-harsh climate. The professor reasoned that now, as in the past, we still seek those same qualities in the food we eat.

The problem is that in the past our ancestors would have possibly spent days hunting down their next meal or collecting the herbs and roots that they needed to survive. Nowadays there is a fast-food restaurant on every corner, no need to hunt very hard for those!

'If you apply the professor's theory to what we eat here in Russia, it does make sense, but here as in the past, we burn off all those carbohydrates etc, just getting on with life.'

'The man's got a point,' said Jim, 'think about it, Nick, say you were sitting in The Cherry Tree in Woodbridge right now what would you order?'

Nick thought for a moment or two.

'Well, I'd probably start with those deep-fried local mushrooms in the beer batter. Followed by a nice piece of fillet steak with some chunky chips... and then finish with their home-made treacle tart and custard.'

Jim looked triumphantly at Nick and gave Anna's arm a squeeze.

'I think you've just covered all the bases in the professor's argument. A fatty first course followed by a second course full of protein and starch and a sweet dessert full of carbohydrates.'

Jim put on his best professorial voice and looked at Nick:

'I'm glad to report sir, that your genetic preferences are still alive and working well.'

Anna and Jim burst into laughter, and Nick smiled widely under his beard as he quickly realised the irony of his menu selection.

'Ah here comes the wine,' said Anna spotting Yuri heading their way with a bottle in the crook of his arm.

As Yuri approached the table, the heavy curtains next to them suddenly sucked themselves inwards and a cold blast of air entered the room. A split second later the curtains parted and four men in black combat gear holding sub-machine guns surrounded the table. One of the men shouted 'Move!' and pointed towards the open French doors with the barrel of his gun.

When none of the shocked dinners made any movement towards the doors he shouted 'Now!' and swung at Jim with the butt of his gun. Jim ducked under the flailing gun and managed to catch himself before he tried to retaliate.

Moments later they were outside being frisked for any weapons, the unfortunate Yuri seemingly trying to explain by pointing at his clothes that he was only the waiter and didn't know these people. This time the ringleader spoke in Russian and Yuri fell silent.

The night was clear and cold, with a half-moon high in the sky. Jim suddenly realised that four more men had joined their comrades and, as they were frogmarched down an alley to the side of the hotel, he managed to briefly meet Nick's eyes. The big man gave Jim a slight shake of the head and he immediately dispelled any thoughts of escape from his mind.

At the end of the alley were two small vehicles and they were split into two groups, Anna and Yuri in the first and Jim and Nick in the other. As he entered the back of the second vehicle Jim noted that the trucks looked more like armoured personnel carriers than ordinary commercial vehicles, with a bench seat down each side and a very heavy looking bulkhead between them and the driver. One of the kidnappers threw some blankets at them and seconds later the whine of the heavyweight transmission told them they were underway.

Both men were flanked by two kidnappers and a third man sat on Jim's side of the truck with his gun trained on Nick who sat opposite.

Jim looked at the man facing him. 'I don't understand,' he said, 'What have we done, where are you taking us?'

The man continued to stare straight ahead, either not understanding the question or choosing to ignore it.

Despite the blankets it was still freezing in the back of the APC and for the next few minutes both men tried to adjust the blankets they had been given to best insulate themselves against the freezing conditions. To try and take his mind off the cold, Jim closed his eyes and tried to map out the route they were taking in his head, but after ten minutes or so, all he could be sure of was that they were heading downhill rather than uphill.

He opened his eyes and looked across at Nick, who also had his eyes closed, his head leant back against the side of the vehicle. Jim had seen Nick do this many times before between rounds in his wrestling bouts and recognised the fact that he was planning to make some sort of move on the Russians.

After a few more minutes the vehicle came to a halt and following a few words of Russian from outside they then proceeded at a much slower pace. Jim deduced they had just gone through some sort of checkpoint, and sure enough after another minute they came to a halt.

The guard nearest the door got out and the guard to Jim's left followed him out of the vehicle. The guard on Nick's right was next to get out and then it was Jim and Nick's turn to step outside.

They were inside a large dimly lit warehouse which apart from their two vehicles appeared to be completely empty. Two huge doors had been partially closed behind them when they entered, but through the gap between the doors they could just make out a huge red and white hull in the moonlight outside.

As Nick left the back of the vehicle, he made a brief eye contact with Jim and darted his eyes to the guard behind him.

In a swift move, Nick grabbed the door at the back of the APC and swung it closed with all his strength. There was a loud crack as the door impacted on the fourth guard's leg, trapping it between the back of the vehicle and the bulkhead and in one fluid movement Nick then swung his clenched fist round and caught the guard behind him squarely under the jaw with the back of his hand. There was another crack as the guard's jaw parted company from the rest of his skull and the force of the blow sent him flying backwards through the air, the subsequent landing on the concrete floor knocking him unconscious.

At the same moment Jim mule-kicked the guard behind him in the groin and the Russian hit the ground with a smack, fighting to catch his next breath.

As Nick turned to tackle the third guard, he felt cold steel against his neck and heard the loud click of a pistol being cocked. He instantly raised his hands in the air and seconds later six more men brandishing submachine guns appeared from out of the darkness.

The men surrounded them and proceeded to cuff their hands behind their backs with cable ties before marching them towards the far corner of the warehouse where a set of steel stairs rose up towards a mezzanine floor.

Behind them they could hear Anna sobbing quietly and Yuri seemingly still pleading his innocence in a garble of incomprehensible Russian.

As they mounted the staircase a door at the top opened and a large heavily built man stood waiting for them, an automatic pistol in his right hand.

|Once at the top of the stairs they were roughly pushed through a large heavy oak door and to their surprise landed on

the luxuriously carpeted floor with a dull thump.

The room they now found themselves in was like a museum exhibit with the walls lined with display cases full of samurai swords, shields and suits of armour.

Apart from the display cases the only other light came from a banker's desk lamp sitting on a large partner's desk at the far end of the room. The green glass shade gave the room an almost spooky ambiance and as they fought their way back onto their feet a figure rose from a big leather captain's chair behind the desk and moved forward towards them.

'Mr Edwards, Mr Jackson, I have obviously underestimated your abilities, where a good old-fashioned fight is concerned. Please, take a seat.'

Two of the guards that rushed them in the warehouse appeared behind them with leather office armchairs and Jim and Nick were simultaneously forced to sit down, both men inadvertently leaning forward to take the pressure off their cuffed hands.

'Remove the ties,' said the man from the shadows.

The ties were immediately cut and both men now sat back rubbing their wrists, all too aware that the two guards still had semi-automatic machine guns trained on them

'Mr Petrov, I presume?' said Nick looking straight into the eyes of the figure moving towards them.

'Very good Mr Edwards. I see we have no need for introductions.'

Sergei Petrov was just as Nick expected him to be, middle aged, average height with dark hair and a glint in his eye that left you feeling slightly uncomfortable.

'You could have just invited us for dinner,' continued Nick, trying hard to appear confident and somehow in control of the situation even though he knew the odds were very much stacked against them.

'Ah, but that wouldn't have been any fun, would it?'

Behind them the door opened and a third man dressed in black entered the room. Jim and Nick instantly recognised him from the photograph as Michael Duggan and the temperature in the room seemed to instantly fall by a couple of degrees. There was nothing remarkable about his stature, being of average height and build, but he oozed a confidence that only comes from a man who knows how to handle himself, a man who knows how to kill.

Sergei moved back into the shadows behind his desk and had a brief exchange with Duggan.

'Um, not bad for a couple of amateurs,' said Sergei out loud as he and Duggan moved back round to the front of the desk. 'One badly broken leg, a smashed jaw and one of my best men is still out there looking for his balls, that was quite a show you put on there.'

'I take offence at being kidnapped before dinner,' said Nick, starting to warm to the duel of words.

'I admire your confidence,' countered Sergei, 'but you must realise, how do you say, you are way out of your depth.'

Jim looked Sergei in the eyes.

'Maybe you had better explain to us how that is the case. All we've done is come to your country on behalf of our clients to explore the possibility of setting up a business here and up until tonight things were going very well, now I'm not so sure.'

Sergei moved back to the shadows behind his desk and pushed a button. From outside the office a low buzz could be heard and seconds later the door opened and Anna was escorted in. Another chair was set beside Jim and as she sat down, she reached for Jim's hand.

'How touching,' said Sergei, as Anna, visibly shaking, clutched his hand in a vice-like grip.

'There's no need for Anna to be here,' said Jim. 'We have simply employed her services as an interpreter, she knows nothing of our business dealings.'

'On the contrary I think she needs to hear what is said,' continued Sergei and sat back down in his leather chair.

He took a small bunch of keys from his pocket and unlocked the top drawer of his desk. He pushed a small button on a console within the drawer and seconds later the surround sound system installed within the office came alive with Nick's voice.

'Think about what we've got so far. We've got a ship doing regular runs backwards and forwards across the North Sea which suddenly goes missing rather conveniently at the only time of the year when there is a slight lull in shipping traffic, with next to no wreckage, and no survivors.

'As we've discovered, it looks suspiciously like it's been deliberately sunk and the crew on board were not her regular crew. Added to this are the facts that she is found miles away from her designated course, a course that her captain should know like the back of his hand and that when we finally find her, she's in a trench that forms the deepest part of the whole North Sea, strange or what?

'The cars on board are all BMWs as far as we can tell, BUT they are not "right". They have the wrong wheels and part-worn tyres on them and that's just for starters.'

'Fine so far,' interjected Jim's voice.

'Okay, now add what we found out on the *Sandie Watson* to what we've discovered since we've been here.

'I think our friend Mr Petrov has been planning this for years, possibly even before he managed to buy the *Baltic Carrier*, in fact it may have been the reason he bought the ship in the first place. The ships were to all intents identical and I think this is critical to his plan.'

'What plan?' came Jim's voice again

'Hear me out.

'I think in order to pull this off he had to keep the *Baltic Carrier* looking identical to her sister ship, so when the *Tricolor* was repainted early last year he had to have the *Baltic Carrier* done as well so that they remained in the same state of repair.'

There was a slight pause in the recording before Nick's voice continued.

'I think the original *Baltic Carrier* is now masquerading as the *Tricolor* in the Liberman Trench. As you know we are one of only a handful of organisations in this part of the world that have ROVs at our disposal, but in order to try and cover their tracks they sunk her in the deepest part of the North Sea, they had no way of knowing we would arrive looking for her with some of the most high-tech equipment this side of the Atlantic. And if my theory holds water, excuse the pun, then the *Tricolor* is now moored up over there as the *Baltic Carrier*.'

Sergei pushed the stop button and the room feel into a deathly silence.

Jim fought the urge to look at Nick, could feel Anna's grip of his hand slacken, and could sense her eyes boring into the side of his head.

'You bugged our hotel rooms,' he said indignantly.

'Oh yes, and very entertaining it was too. You should have

considered a job in the porn industry judging by what I heard this afternoon.'

Anna started to sob lightly and swung a half-hearted clenched fist at Jim, which he caught by the wrist and then placed gently back in her lap.

He tried to give Sergei a hard stare but the Russian was still barely visible in the shadows behind the desk and he failed to make eye contact.

'I have had you under surveillance since you anchored up over the *Tricolor*. In fact, had you not decided to come to Kaliningrad, you would now be at the bottom of the Liberman Trench with the rest of your crew.'

This time Jim did shoot a look at Nick and the look he got back confirmed his thoughts that they were now in way over their heads.

Sergei continued:

'My organisation has had you two locked down since you started your investigation.

'I know who you work for and what you are doing here, I know who you've spoken to, and what about, I know about your past careers, I know all your personal details, what cars you drive and where you live, your likes and dislikes, who your friends are, and what you like to eat. I even know about the loss of your respective partners, in fact if you need to know anything about yourselves just ask me and I will tell you.'

The final reference to Sandie and Catherine and Sergei's attempt at humour was too much for Nick and with a roar of defiance he leapt out of his chair and headed for Sergei, still sat behind his desk some twenty feet away. The guards at the back of the room could do nothing but watch, unable to open fire in case they hit their boss. Duggan on the other hand had it covered and met Nick halfway with a sliding karate move that took Nick's legs from under him. Nick hit the floor hard, face down and was immediately smothered by Duggan who in a split second was sitting on Nick's flailing legs and had both of his arms tight against his shoulder blades. The guards returned Nick to his seat and proceeded to cable tie his wrists to the chair.

Sergei moved back round to the front of the desk and perched his backside on its edge, with a totally unflustered Duggan beside him.

'That's not very friendly,' mocked Sergei, a comment that did little to quell Nick's rage.

'Now, where was I? Oh, yes.'

Sergei looked Nick square in the eyes and continued in his business-like tone.

'Your appraisal of the situation this afternoon was very good and as you suspected Captain Collins is indeed at the bottom of the North Sea with his ship and not sunning himself in the Caribbean, and the cars will shortly be on their way to China.

'The Chinese economy is booming and the call for upmarket luxury cars is at an all-time high. My organisation has spent the last few days re-mapping the onboard computers and given each vehicle a completely new identity, even BMW engineers would find it difficult to tell them from the genuine article.'

'Why are you telling us all this?' asked Jim, even though he was pretty sure what the answer would be.

'Why not?' answered Sergei with a cold glint in his eye. 'My organisation has invested huge amounts of money on this operation, the paint job on the ship alone cost nearly $100,000

US dollars, never mind sourcing all those nearly new BMWs from all over Europe.

'In two days' time the "*Baltic Carrier*" will leave here for the trip to the Far East with three extra pieces of cargo not mentioned on its manifest.'

He pointed a finger in turn at Anna, Jim and Nick.

'By the time we leave the Baltic Sea the team on board my private yacht will have dealt with the *Sandie Watson* and there will be a full-scale search and rescue operation going on north of our course, looking for your ship that has suddenly disappeared without a trace. Once nightfall comes you two will be jettisoned overboard to join your colleagues.'

Nick was by now incandescent with rage and was desperately trying to break the straps around his wrists so he could have another attempt at Sergei and his men. The straps were cutting into his tissue and blood was dripping onto the floor. Duggan signalled the two guards to circle round to his end of the office so that they had a free shot should anyone try to make a move.

Anna was by now sobbing uncontrollably and shrugged off the comforting arm of Jim when he tried to put his arm around her shoulder.

Sergei stood up and went to a row of full-height bookcases behind his desk. He pulled out a large volume on samurai swordsmanship and out of view of everyone in the room dialled in a safe combination. There was a soft clunk and the centre section of the bookcase swung silently open to reveal a walk-in vault.

Duggan spoke to the guards in Russian and they moved forward to get their three hostages. He then went to the door and called in two more guards from the corridor outside and then took hold of Anna by the arm. The two guards from the corridor brought Jim to his feet and, with a small pistol pressed to his neck, moved him towards the vault.

Sergei moved forward to where Nick was still strapped to his chair.

'My men are going to release you from the ties now,' he said in an even voice, 'if you make any attempt to escape my men have orders to shoot your friends, do you understand?'

Nick nodded his head, and the remaining guards moved forward and cut the ties on his wrists. Nick rose from his chair and an AK-47 assault rifle was pushed into the small of his back. They escorted Nick into the safe first and then Jim and Anna followed, the door closed behind them with a dull thud and there was a soft whirring sound as the combination was reset.

The vault was about eight feet by ten feet and two of the four walls were lined with long drawers from floor to ceiling. The third wall had what looked to be high security sports lockers across it and Jim deduced that this was where Sergei kept his samurai collection when he was not in Kaliningrad.

There was a single light bulb in the middle of the ceiling and the quiet murmur of a ventilation system which obviously kept Sergei's collection at the right humidity.

'Well at least were not going to suffocate,' commented Jim.

Nick gave Jim a strange look and then placed his finger across his lips. He moved close to Jim and whispered very softly in his ear.

'Judging by how thoroughly we've been bugged since we've been here, best to assume that this is also wired.'

Jim nodded his head and then moved across to Anna and

gave her the same message.

Anna nodded her head, wiped her eyes on a tissue and then whispered into Jim's ear in a defiant tone.

'Right, so how are we going to get out of here then?'

Jim reeled back in amazement as the sentence lodged in his brain.

'What did you just say?' he whispered.

'I said, how are we going to get out of here?' she replied

Jim stood back and gave Nick a puzzled look.

Anna beckoned Jim back to her side.

'There's something you need to know about me,' she continued. 'Everyone in this part of Russia has to do national service and I was no exception. The thing was I really enjoyed it and while I made my mind up as to what career path to follow, I signed up for an extra two years. If Nick hadn't put them all on high alert, I could have taken those guards out single handed.' She paused momentarily, and then conceded, 'Duggan might have been a different story though.'

'But?'

'It was all an act, they now think I am just a sobbing wreck of a woman, which means they won't pay me much attention. You and more especially Nick will be the ones they watch closely, that puts us at a definite advantage.'

Jim stepped back and Nick immediately moved forward to find out what was so astounding about the conversation he had just had with Anna.

He explained the conversation to Nick and when he finished Nick winked at Anna before whispering in Jim's ear, 'I have an idea.'

It was at about ten o'clock the following morning after a fitful night's sleep on the safe floor that they were aware of the quiet turning of cogs within the vault door and the door swinging open.

'Good morning my friends,' said Sergei menacingly as he entered the vault closely followed by two guards armed with their semi-automatic rifles.

'I hope you slept well, I've brought you some breakfast, you must be hungry?'

A third guard squeezed between his comrades with a small tray on which was some bread, jam and small bottles of orange juice.

The guard put the tray down just inside the threshold and retreated out followed by Sergei and his two accomplices.

'Enjoy,' said Sergei before swinging the door closed and resetting the combination.

'I don't wish to be picky,' said Jim out loud, 'but how are we supposed to get the jam from the jar to the bread without any knives.'

Nick fudged through his pockets and pulled out their room key-card from the hotel.

'Guess we won't be needing this anymore,' he said and stuffed the card into the plastic pot of jam, transferring a dollop onto the bread.

Jim and Anna followed Nick's lead and the three of them sat on the floor quietly with their makeshift picnic waiting for Sergei's next move.

It was half an hour later that the whirring of the vault's lock alerted them to Sergei's return. The door swung open and from outside came Sergei's voice telling them to come out with their hands on their heads where he could see them. They all exchanged glances and Anna moved forward with her hands on her head as instructed.

She was met by two guards who pushed her roughly towards the rear of the office. She noted with some satisfaction that Duggan wasn't present, just five guards all heavily armed with AK-47s and Sergei who sat in his large leather chair behind the desk. Jim was next out and he was marched to a point mid office, before one of Anna's guards obviously feeling under no threat from the weak woman, moved forward to greet Nick.

When Nick didn't appear straight away there was a series of sideways glances from the guards who seemed unsure as to what to do next.

Anna's timing was perfection personified, and at the moment the guards were most distracted by Nick's no show, she swung a low elbow at the guard just to her left. It caught him mid stomach and winded him so badly that he hit the floor before the other guards realised, they were under attack.

A split second later, Jim took out the guard furthest away from Anna with a mule kick to the midriff, and as his accomplice tried to react Anna karate-kicked his knee from the side smashing the joint and leaving him screaming in pain on the floor. The two guards waiting for Nick to appear from the safe turned to see what was going on and as they did so the big man rushed them and with a sickening crunch of bone smashed their heads together. They both fell to the floor, unconscious before they even met the carpet.

Sergei had by now brought up a small pistol from his desk drawer and as he took aim at Nick, who was his closest opponent, a short burst of automatic fire came from the back of the office. The gun spun out of his hand and the bookcase behind him was instantly splattered in blood as his right hand blew apart. Sergei screamed out in pain, a horrified look crossing his face as he realised what little was left of his right hand. He turned to Anna with a look of awe on his face, and then a thin smile crossed his lips as he realised how he had underestimated his fellow Russian.

'They taught you well,' he grimaced as the pain started to kick in.

Anna lowered the machine gun to her hip and covered the door in case there were other sentries outside, while Jim quickly moved all the weapons out of the guard's reach.

Hearing no response from outside the door Jim started to move the guards into the vault stripping them of ammunition as he did so, while Nick wheeled Sergei into the centre of the office where he could be covered by Anna.

Two minutes later they swung the door of the vault shut and Jim spun the dial on the lock.

With the two men now back at her side Anna moved across to one of the large display cases housing a collection of daggers. She smashed the lock with the butt of the gun and reached inside taking first the collection of daggers and then the purple velvet lining from inside the case. 'These might be handy,' she said tucking two of the elaborately decorated knives into the waistband of her skirt and passing two each to Nick and Jim. She threw the lining at Sergei, who, now in considerable pain, proceeded to wrap it tightly around his what was left of his heavily bleeding hand. Jim pulled the phone cable out of the wall and then secured Sergei to his chair with it, making doubly sure all the knots were securely tied. Anna tore another piece of velvet from the cabinet and gagged the pain-stricken entrepreneur.

'Okay,' said Nick, 'so far so good, now let's get out of

here. I don't know about you guys but I've had quite enough of Mr Petrov's hospitality.'

Nick spotted a coat stand in the corner and pulled three heavy coats from it.

'We may just need these once we get outside,' he said struggling into the biggest of those on offer.

They moved to the door and Anna killed the lights in the office before gently opening it far enough to peer out. She beckoned Jim and Nick forward and slipped through the opening onto the landing. The warehouse below looked completely empty apart from the two trucks that had brought them there the previous night but, with the doors to the dock front now only ajar, there was very little light with which to make a totally accurate assessment. Anna put her finger to her lips and moved quietly down the flight of stairs, with the two men closely behind. Once at floor level the three of them took another sweep around the warehouse, it was deserted.

They moved swiftly around the walls of the building until they reached the point where the two huge doors almost met. The gap between the doors was just enough for a man to pass through and as they peered outside, the bright sunlight blinded them for a few seconds.

While in the vault the previous night they had quickly come to the conclusion that Sergei Petrov's influence within Kaliningrad meant that escape by road, rail, or air was going to be at best risky, if not totally impossible, which left them with one option: a boat.

They were now within forty feet of the dock front but a good half a mile from anything they could hijack to make their escape, things were not looking good. With the *Tricolor* in front of them being prepared to sail, the dock front was awash with personnel, loading on supplies and filling her tanks with fresh water and fuel oil.

As they peered out at the busy dock front a now familiar face came striding towards the gap in the warehouse doors.

'It's Duggan,' whispered Anna, 'the corner.'

The three of them quickly made for the corner of the warehouse and pressed themselves tight into the shadows just as Duggan came through the doors. He strolled purposefully across to the stairs and then bounded up them two at a time before lightly knocking on the door and entering Sergei's office.

Anna moved back towards the doors, knowing they now had a very small window of opportunity in which to escape. From upstairs came the sound of Sergei's voice and it was clear from the tone that he was less than pleased with Duggan's security procedures. The conversation seemed to be very one sided and, just as they reached the gap in the doors, there was a dull-cough sound of a heavily silenced pistol followed by quiet.

Moments later Duggan appeared at the top of the stairs where he paused momentarily before heading back down into the warehouse.

Anna, Jim and Nick were now completely trapped, unable to move from their position, their only hope being that the bright light from the gap in the doors would create enough shadow to disguise their position.

As Duggan reached the bottom of the staircase he paused once again, before strolling at a very leisurely pace across to the opening. Ten feet away from the gap he stopped and turned slightly so he was directly facing them.

'So, what's the plan then?' he asked. There was a slight

pause. You have got a plan?'

The three of them stood fixed to the spot not quite knowing what to make of this change of events.

'You don't trust me, eh?'

He took a step forward and pulled a silenced Glock pistol from the small of his back.

Anna instinctively gripped the butt of her AK-47 a little tighter and took up the slack in her trigger finger.

Duggan held the pistol between his thumb and forefinger and gently put it on the ground near his feet, before standing back up and kicking the weapon toward her.

Nobody moved.

'Okay let me explain,' said Duggan taking a deep breath. 'Sergei Petrov did not do failure, he did not do incompetence, in his world there was no place for such luxuries. He was without doubt one of the most ruthless men I have ever met in my whole life. Oh, sure he came across as very friendly, he gave loads of money to local causes and built new hospitals to help look after the locals, but underneath he was a complete psychopath. My predecessor as head of security ended up as shark bait on a fishing trip, following a small boy finding his way into the grounds of his villa in Portugal.

'You guys have just taken out some of my top men and shot Sergei's right hand to pieces, so let's just say even before I put a bullet through his head, I wouldn't have been anywhere near the top of his Christmas card list.

'That leaves me with very limited options, no, let me rephrase that, that leaves me with one option, which coincidentally is exactly the same as yours: a way out of here.'

The warehouse fell silent and suddenly they all became aware of the hubbub going on outside.

Jim stepped forward slightly out of the shadows and picked up the pistol from the floor.

'Would we be right in thinking that even with your help escape by road, rail, or air would be, err, "difficult"?'

'The only thing we have in our favour is that Sergei's right-hand man Viktor is currently making his way out to sink the *Sandie Watson*. However, Sergei was very hands on and I don't think it will be very long before someone ventures up to his office and finds the body. When that happens, the whole town will be locked down in a matter of minutes, so in answer to your question, none of those are really an option.'

Duggan thought for a while before continuing.

'Which only leaves one option, a boat.'

'That's the same thought process we went through last night,' said Nick, 'but they are all up the other end of the dock, can you help us reach there?'

Duggan thought for a moment.

'There is another option, wait here, I'll be back in five minutes max.'

Before anyone could speak Duggan walked through the opening on to the dock front and started shouting out orders to the dockers.

'What's he saying?' Jim asked Anna.

'He's telling them to take a break and go and warm themselves up with a cup of coffee.'

As the dock began to clear they could hear him shouting at someone on the *Tricolor*.

Anna translated.

'Now he's telling the guys on the ship to go and have a break as well.'

Three minutes later Duggan casually walked back into the

warehouse before turning sharply into the shadows.

'Okay that's the ship and dock front cleared, but now you're really going to have to trust me.'

'Given the circumstances I don't see we have much choice,' said Jim turning to get the approval of Anna and Nick.

'I need the pistol back,' he said.

Jim looked at Anna who was staring intently at Duggan.

'Wait,' she said and took the gun from Jim and removed the magazine from it.

'At this stage I'll do any shooting,' she said and handed the empty weapon back to Duggan, who shrugged an acceptance and quickly explained what he was going to do.

When he had finished Nick looked at him like he was completely mad.

'You want us to commandeer the *Tricolor*?'

'Why not? It's the closest escape route we have and by far the best. Once we get under way there is nothing that can stop us and besides, there is only a skeleton crew on board at the moment. If I give the orders and they are kept unaware of what has happened to Sergei they will not question my instructions.'

'But who's going to sail her?' continued Nick somehow knowing what the answer would be.

'You are.'

'But—'

'Look, we researched your ship a few days ago and fundamentally it's exactly the same as the *Sandie Watson*, she's got port and bow thrusters same as your ship, it's just a little bigger.'

'A little bigger! It's at least ten times the size.'

Despite the gravity of the situation Jim smiled at Nick's quandary.

'Come on big man you can do it. She moored up facing the open water, so once we're clear of the quay it's straight ahead and besides, imagine the welcome we'll get when we sail her into an English port with all those brand-new Beamer's on board.'

Nick nodded his head in agreement.

'Okay, okay I'll give it a go, but only because we don't have any other options.'

Anna patted him on the back.

'Let's get moving,' she said, 'before the dockers come back from their break.'

Nick led the way out of the warehouse his hand clasped behind his back as if cuffed. The reality of the situation was that his hands were holding the assault rifle, tucked in the back of his trousers. Jim followed in a similar manner followed by Anna who had her hands across her chest cradling the AK-47 under her coat. Duggan brought up the rear of the crocodile procession, the pistol placed on the back of Anna's neck.

It was only forty or fifty feet from the warehouse to the gangplank of the *Tricolor*, but to all of them it felt like miles. Nick, Jim and Anna looked straight ahead but at the rear Duggan took a sideways glance up and down the quay to try to monitor any potential problems. A hundred yards to his right there were three men smoking cigarettes and as they neared the gangplank another appeared from the ship and started to move towards them. Duggan shouted an instruction at him and he turned and re-entered the doorway.

Things seemed to be going well until they at the top of the gangplank, when out of nowhere a loud female scream was heard coming from the warehouse that contained Sergei's office.

'Shit!' he muttered into Anna's ear, 'looks like someone's found Sergei, keep your wits about you this could all go a bit tits-up.'

'Tits-up?' questioned Anna from behind pursed lips.

'Bad,' offered Duggan by way of an explanation.

He took a quick glance down at the dock front and noted that the three smokers were now heading into the warehouse from where they had just come. On hearing the scream Nick lengthened his stride slightly and ten seconds later they reached the relative safety of the doorway that led into the ship.

Once in the service corridor Duggan told Nick to halt and then ordered the two men at station by the door to go and investigate what the commotion was about. As they ran down towards the dock Nick stood ready by the electric winch button that raised the gangplank into its seagoing position.

Duggan waited a couple of seconds as the men raced into the dark warehouse and then instructed Nick to hit the button. Seconds later the two men reappeared with the three smokers and, on seeing the gangplank heading skywards, first questioned Duggan what was going on and then, on not receiving an answer, opened up a volley of automatic gunfire on the still open doorway.

Duggan ducked inside the doorway before the gunfire hit the ship and then pushing Nick out of the way of any errant gunfire, continued to raise the gangplank until it was a good twenty feet clear of the dock. He thought briefly about trying to close the door, but the bulkhead behind the opening was acting like a mirror does to light, sending bullets and small pieces of metal shrapnel flying in all directions.

'You guys go to the bridge!' he shouted over the gunfire,

'I'm going down to the engine room, I'll contact you from there.'

'Here!' shouted Anna holding up the magazine of bullets she had relieved him of a few minutes earlier and one of Sergei's samurai daggers. 'You might need these.'

Duggan smiled at her, caught the magazine and dagger and then bent over and pulled up his right trouser leg from the knee. Strapped to his ankles was a custom-made holster in which there was some clips of ammunition and a small handgun.

'Thanks,' he said and winked at Anna.

He quickly reloaded the magazine and then fired off a couple of silenced rounds into the control mechanism for the gangplank before turning and running off down the corridor towards the rear of the ship.

Nick, Jim and Anna quickly recovered their weapons and then, with the schematics of the ship still fresh in his head from the earlier dives, Nick led them along the corridor towards the main staircase that would bring them up just behind the bridge section of the ship. They got to the staircase without incident and began to climb the six flights that would take them to bridge level. As they neared the deck level, they began to hear shouting and Anna brought them to a halt so she could try and decipher what was going on.

'I can only hear one side of the conversation,' she said after a minute or so, 'but from what I can make out they seem to think we have somehow kidnapped Duggan, killed Sergei and are now hiding on the ship.'

'Great,' said Jim. 'Well at least we know where we stand, can we get up to the next level?'

Nick furtively looked around the corner of the stairwell.

'Can't see anyone.'

They moved slowly up the next flight and Nick once again peered around the next corner.

'All clear,' he whispered and they silently made their way up the next flight.

Bit by bit they rose up through the ship until finally arriving at the bridge level. As they crept towards the bridge itself, they could hear a voice in the radio room.

This time Nick and Jim didn't need a translator, as it was clear from the incredulous tone of the radio operator that the ship to shore conversation was not going their way. The three of them moved slowly along the corridor until they were alongside the sliding door of the radio room.

Nick peered into the room and found a single operator sat at a desk on the far wall. In front of him was an array of individual components all neatly housed in a console that stretched from wall to wall and to his left was a computer keyboard and a monitor. Luckily it was all very familiar to Nick and as the operator finished his conversation with the shore and reached across to the ship's intercom to give his crewmates the latest news on their situation Nick made his move. Pulling him clean out of his chair by the neck, Nick dropped him to the floor, his left arm still tight around his neck and then from his kneeling position behind the shocked crewman, he brought his right elbow down on top of the man's head, rendering him instantly unconscious.

'That was close,' he said to Jim as they dragged the man back to a storage cupboard they had passed and locked him inside. 'Ten seconds later and we would have been headline news all over the ship.'

They returned to the radio room and Nick moved to the

desk and quickly flicked a few switches before hailing the *Sandie Watson.*

'*Sandie Watson, Sandie Watson,* this is the Caveman are you reading me? Over.'

The air was filled with a static hiss for a few seconds.

Nick clicked open the channel once again.

'*Sandie Watson, Sandie Watson,* this is the Caveman are you reading me? Over.'

Anna looked over her shoulder at Jim.

'Who is the Caveman?'

'I'll explain la...'

'Caveman this is the *Sandie Watson,* good to hear from you guys, how's it going? Over.'

'It's Ewan,' said Jim recognising the Scotsman's voice.

'Ewan, listen carefully, we have upset the locals here big time and I mean BIG TIME. We have been led to believe there is a Ferretti cruiser heading your way. This vessel must be considered to be very, very, hostile, so I need you to up anchor and head back to port immediately, I repeat this vessel is hostile do not engage, over.'

'Okay Nick, do you require any assistance? Over.'

'Nothing you can help with Ewan, just get the hell out of there and don't spare the horses, over.'

'Roger that, over and out.'

From the radio room they quickly moved up to the bridge taking care to check all the adjacent cabins and cupboards en route. They found no one and when they entered the bridge itself, they were relieved to find that this too was completely empty.

The bridge was almost the full width of the ship if you included the small flying bridges on either side which helped with visibility when docking in port. Each wing bridge was about six feet wide and fifteen feet long and there was a door on each end leading out onto a gantry that ran right around the whole of the bridge superstructure.

Anna now came to the fore and started issuing instructions.

'We are very vulnerable up here,' she said looking around at the mass of glass that surrounded them and pointing to the doors at either end.

'Jim? You and I will move along to the wings but keep low and stay in a position whereby you can cover the main entrance to the bridge that we have just come in through. Nick you start to make yourself familiar with the controls, the minute we get some power from the engine room we need to be under way.'

'There is one problem that we haven't thought about yet,' said Nick almost absent-mindedly as he began to study the controls.

'What's that?' asked Jim.

'We're still tied to the dock, even a ship this size won't pull itself loose, we have got to get rid of those mooring lines.'

'You leave that to me,' answered Anna confidently and started towards the starboard wing.

As she got to the end she peered over the lip of the superstructure and out of the window onto the dock front. Below her there was a scene of complete pandemonium with upwards of fifty dockworkers and security men seemingly arguing over the best way to retake the vessel. From further down the quay more men were jogging towards the throng, curious to find out what all the commotion was about. As Anna watched on, Sergei's wife appeared from between the warehouse doors wearing a full-length fur coat with matching hat and dabbing her eyes with a handkerchief.

The crowd of men suddenly fell silent and as Anouska walked forward from the gap between the doors, the men parted leaving her way clear to view the *Tricolor*. She paused for a moment looking at the ship and then called a big brutish looking man forward.

Anatoly Sidcrov was head of dockside security and along with Duggan and Viktor was one of the three men that Sergei had trusted the most with looking after his "interests". With Viktor away taking care of the *Sandie Watson* and Duggan apparently kidnapped and now held hostage aboard the *Tricolor*, it now fell to Anatoly to bring the situation back under control. After a couple of sentences with Anouska he moved towards some wooden pallets stacked on the quayside.

Climbing up onto the stack he then began to shout out his instructions to his security detail and selected a few of the dockers who he knew he could trust to carry out their tasks without question.

Although unable to hear what was being said, Anna could see him pointing towards a large dock crane, mounted on huge wheels that sat on heavy rails let into the quayside. Three men started to sprint towards the crane that was several hundred yards away while Anatoly carried on briefing the rest of the men at his feet.

Anna turned to Nick.

'How are you getting on over there?' she asked.

'It's starting to make sense,' he replied, 'but we aren't going anywhere unless Duggan can get those engines turning.'

Unbeknown to Anna, Jim and Nick, Duggan was in exactly the

same position as Nick, studying a huge control panel that was quite unfamiliar to him as an infrequent visitor to the engine room.

His trip down to the engine room had been far from uneventful, crossing paths with several of the crew en route. It quickly became apparent to him that he was supposed to be a hostage and because of this the first two crewmen he came across gave him the few seconds he needed to take them while they decided what to do next.

The only safe lockable area belowdecks was the food storage area adjacent to the main galley. This comprised two rooms, one refrigerated and the other an unheated pantry where fresh fruit and vegetables were stored. As he frogmarched the two crewmen to the galley, they ran straight into one of the ship's engineers, walking back from the galley with a steaming mug of coffee in his right hand. Seeing his two shipmates coming towards him his initial reaction was to greet them with a raised coffee cup and a cheery hi, but halfway through this process he saw Duggan's pistol pointed at the neck of the second crewman. Unlike the two crewmen he had already captured, the engineer seemed to understand what was going on in a split second and threw the contents of the mug in Duggan's general direction before turning and starting to run down the corridor. Duggan used the crewman in front of him as a shield and, as the man cried out in pain at being hit by the hot liquid, the silenced pistol coughed once and the back of the engineer's skull exploded, plastering the light-coloured walls with blood, bone and brain tissue.

The first of the two crewmen shouted out in fright as he watched his shipmate hit the floor before projectile vomiting down the wall of the corridor. Duggan ordered him to stand up and, as he returned the pistol to the neck of the crewman in front of him, the man's bladder let go and deposited his morning's liquid intake down his right leg.

'Great,' muttered Duggan under his breath in English, before ordering the men to keep moving into the galley area.

Duggan was surprised to find the galley area completely empty as this was usually where most of the men would congregate when part of a skeleton crew. He quickly marched the men through to the pantry and was shocked to find the key in the lock.

The key was usually under the custody of the head chef who was held responsible for all the stores within the two rooms and it wasn't until Duggan roughly pushed the men into the pantry that he realised why the key was in the lock. The head chef turned to see who was interrupting his inventory just as the door slammed closed and proceeded to beat wildly on the inside of the heavy metal door, screaming wildly at Duggan in a mixture of his native Norwegian, English and broken Russian.

From the galley Duggan moved quickly back into the corridor and dragged the engineer out of sight, although even he had to concede that the blood-splattered walls and carpet painted a pretty graphic picture of what had happened there.

He dropped down a couple of decks and headed towards the engine room passing a cleaner hoovering the corridor. Duggan didn't recognise her at all and with time a major consideration took the unprecedented step of assuming she didn't know him either. He knew it was a risky decision and was against every piece of training he had ever had, but he also knew the men on the quayside and in particular Anatoly Siderov would be moving quickly to retake the ship so trying to subdue and then secure a scared cleaner was going to use up valuable time that he didn't have. He would have to deal with her later.

As he entered the engine room, he could hear someone working far below him. The engine room was split over three levels and, on peering over one of the parapets, he could see one of the junior engineers wiping over one of the two huge red painted engine blocks with a rag. Thinking quickly, he went back to the bulkhead door and slammed it shut with a loud clang. He then ran across the walkway making as much noise as he could on the metal gangway before sitting down at the control panel that monitored every aspect of the two massive engines. As expected, he was quickly joined by the junior engineer who, on seeing Duggan seated at the control panel, paused slightly before joining him.

'What's going on?' he asked.

'Number three warehouse is on fire,' Duggan answered urgently, 'we've got to move the ship and fast, do you know how to power up the engines?'

'Er, um...'

'Look it's down to you and me kid, Captain Anderson is on the bridge, but we aren't going anywhere without your help, now do you know how to do this or not?'

Without further prompting he moved forward and started flicking switches and turning various control knobs watching closely as the dials started to flicker into life. From far below them Duggan could hear the two engines come to life and reached forward to take two pairs of ear defenders from the top of the control console. He handed a set to the young engineer and then asked him how long before the engines could be brought on line.

'It will take about three minutes,' he replied

Okay, is there anyone else on board that knows this control panel?' asked Duggan knowing full well what the answer would be.

'Only Vladamir, he went up to the galley for a cup of coffee.'

'I'll go and find him, you stay here and do what you can until he gets back, I'm sure Sergei will reward you well if we save his ship.'

The young engineer smiled.

'What's your name?'

'Leonard.'

'Okay Leonard, remember don't move from here until Vladamir returns, okay?'

'Okay,' he replied, 'you can rely on me.'

'Good man,' said Duggan reassured by the fact that Leonard knew who he was.

'Are there any walkie-talkies down here so we can keep in touch?'

'Over there,' replied Leonard pointing to a large glass-fronted locker with several handsets sitting in a charging rack. 'There's a set down here and a set on the bridge in case the internal comms system fails.'

Duggan swiftly moved across to the cabinet and deliberately picked up a single handset before running back to the bulkhead door before Leonard could make any comment.

He gave Leonard a quick wave and went through the door.

After the noise of the engine room the rest of the ship seemed amazingly quiet and Duggan quickly made for the stairs that would lead him up to deck level. As he neared the hatch that would take him out onto the stern of the vessel, he suddenly became aware of the hubbub below him on the quayside.

He peered gingerly over the gunwale and saw a group of dockers and security men getting themselves organised on the quay. To his right was a large crane being manoeuvred along the quay to a position near the bow of the *Tricolor*, and he could see several heavily armed men standing on a makeshift platform cobbled together out of pallets and strops for an assault on the ship.

He reached for the radio and called to the bridge. Luckily for them all Nick had spotted the charging rack on entering the bridge and had one of the radios set beside him on the helm.

'Duggan calling bridge, Duggan calling bridge.'

'Duggan! Where the hell have you been?' shouted Nick. 'World War Three is about to break out up here.'

'I know, I know, I'm sorry, but it all got a bit complicated down here. Look I'm on the stern now and I can see the natives are getting restless, so this is what we are going to do.' He quickly outlined his plan to Nick, before crawling along the deck to the stern mooring line.

Aiming the silenced pistol at the mooring rope he fired several rounds at close range. The shots did most of the work but the rope refused to fully break and he reached for the Samurai dagger located in the small of his back that Anna had given him earlier. He rubbed his thumb across the blade to check its sharpness and then, satisfied, started to saw at the remaining plats of hemp that formed the rope. Suddenly the fibres came alive and started to break apart. Duggan was momentarily mesmerised by the rope's demise and watched with some amusement as, one by one, the strands gave up the fight. The ropes final act reminded him of a firecracker going off with tens of mini explosions all happening in quick succession. The separated rope then sped off through the hawsehole as gravity took hold and a few seconds later Duggan heard a loud splash as it hit the water.

The security detail was the first to react and as Duggan reloaded the Glock with an extended magazine of thirty-one armour piercing bullets a burst of automatic fire ricocheted off the superstructure around him.

Because of the slab-sided construction of the ship there was a small deck area at the bow and stern and the only way of getting from one end to the other was along an internal corridor that ran adjacent to the car decks. Getting up on all fours he scuttled along the short length of gunwale and headed for the bulkhead door that led into the corridor and the bow of the *Tricolor*. At the halfway point he reached the large cargo opening where the four of them had boarded the ship half an hour earlier. Taking a furtive look down at the dockside Duggan was relieved to see that for the most part the dockers and security detail were focusing almost all of their attention on the bow and stern sections of the ship. He quietly picked up all the spent shells that had been fired earlier and then, with no obstructions to get in the way, gently started to close the doors.

As the doors came together, he took one last glance down at the dockside and noted that the crane was now close enough to reach the ship. Anatoly and three of his men wearing body armour were stood on a makeshift platform hanging precariously by four heavy duty strops from the hook on the crane and, as the crane began to lift, it was clear from the looks on their faces that neither the men nor the crane operator were entirely convinced that this wasn't going to end in disaster.

Although heavily armed with spare automatics over their

shoulders and hand grenades hanging off their belts, they were having to hold on so tightly to the strops that any form of engagement whilst in the air would have been disastrous and Duggan knew that if they were going to escape with the *Tricolor* he had to act now.

Easing the two doors open slightly so that he had a small crack to fire through he took aim at the four men being lifted towards the bow of the ship.

One of the things Duggan had always liked about the 9mm Glock was its accuracy over longer distances, but even with the armour-piercing bullets this was still a big ask for such a small weapon. The first round missed its intended target but with the silencer still in place the only giveaway Duggan noticed was a small puff of concrete dust that shot up well behind his target when the bullet hit the quayside.

The boarding party were about thirty feet off the ground by now and despite their perilous position the crane driver was wasting no time in getting them onto the ship.

Duggan took aim again, but before he finished squeezing the trigger, a volley of automatic gunfire was heard from the bow and moments later, he caught a glimpse of the forward mooring line arcing through the air before slamming into the water below.

'Good girl Anna,' Duggan whispered to himself realising that she had taken it upon herself to severe the mooring rope rather than wait for him to get there.

At the same moment he could feel the ship start to move away from the quay slightly as Nick threw some power into the side thrusters. The four men on the platform also noticed that the ship was moving away from them and started shouting at the crane operator to get them closer to their quarry.

Duggan looked at his Glock and decided that maybe trying to aim the pistol was not such a good idea. Steadying himself against the closed half of the two doors he let rip with a quick-fire burst of six or seven rounds.

This time he hit two of the four men and both fell to a kneeling position on the small platform clutching at their stomachs. Duggan knew that at this range the bullets would not have penetrated the armour but even so their impact would have been like someone hitting you in the ribs with a well-aimed golf ball. Anatoly screamed at the crane operator to get them back down to the quay, realising that he was in no position to be able to return multiple fire, let alone make it onto a ship that was inching further away from him by the second.

Duggan closed the door and made sure it was locked before sprinting towards the bridge to join Jim, Nick and Anna.

He quickly scaled the stairs and was just about to run out onto the bridge when the world exploded in front of him.

From his position back on the quay Anatoly's only option now was to take the bridge out and a total of ten men now stood on the quayside emptying their AK-47s into the bridge of the *Tricolor*.

Because of the trajectory from the quay to the bridge the initial burst only took out the windows on the port side but with these now removed, the whole of the bridge turned into a shooting gallery with bullets ricocheting off the steel in all directions.

Next to go were the starboard-side windows which exploded over Jim, who by now was prostrate on the floor. As the glass shards settled, he gingerly raised his head and looked across to where Nick had been standing at the helm. He too was on the floor and their eyes met as he looked across.

The firing relented for a moment as the men on the quay moved into a better position and reloaded their weapons and Jim and Nick both decided it was time to evacuate the bridge. As they made their move the AK-47s opened up again this time taking out the massive array of bow windows.

The noise was deafening as glass and bullets rained down on Nick and Jim and, as Duggan rushed forward to try and offer some help, he was knocked flat by Nick and Jim throwing themselves off the bridge.

'So much for Russian hospitality!' shouted Jim pulling a four-inch splinter of wood from his right arm.

Superficially both men looked in a bad way with hundreds of small nicks from the flying glass oozing little rivulets of blood.

As the onslaught continued Jim and Nick sat opposite each other removing the larger shards from each other like a couple of chimpanzees having a grooming session.

'Where's Anna?' shouted Duggan.

'She went down to the bow to get rid of the mooring rope,' said Jim as the gunfire ebbed for a moment. 'I'm guessing she's still down there.'

At that moment the multiple gunfire from the quay was replaced by a single burst from closer to home.

'She's taking them on single handed,' said Duggan. 'Quick, now's your chance Nick, let's get some forward motion going here and see if we can move out of range of those bloody guns.'

Nick leapt to his feet and ran back onto the bridge the glass crunching under his feet. As he skidded to a halt on a sea of broken glass, he saw Duggan move across to the port side of the bridge. Leaping up from under what was the window

Duggan fired off a quick volley of five shots before ducking back down for cover.

With the sudden return of automatic fire, the men on the quayside sprinted for cover and within twenty seconds the whole of the dock front was devoid of human life.

'She's forced them all back into the sheds,' he reported back. 'All we need to do now is keep them there.'

Duggan moved several feet along the bridge and then stood and fired several more rounds.

Below them Anna was running low on ammunition and was limited to two or three round bursts of fire.

Duggan had also noted the reduced fire rate and decided now would be a good time to re-arm himself and Anna. He ran across the bridge to the large chart table at its rear. Below the teak top were ten shallow drawers that contained a complete set of nautical maps covering the world's oceans. He reached down to the plinth area of the cabinet and pushed a small invisible button and the plinth fell forward to reveal a long metal drawer filled with clips of ammunition and several handguns.

'They only finished installing this yesterday,' he grinned at Jim and Nick. 'Always pays to have a spare or two lying around, wouldn't you say?'

Nick turned his attention back to the bridge controls and noting that there were several craft between him and the open sea gave a long blast on the ships horn to warn them he was on the move.

'I'm bloody glad he's on our side,' quipped Jim.

Duggan meanwhile was heading out of the starboard wing bridge door and down a steep flight of steps to the bow.

There was still sporadic gunfire coming up from the quay

but Anna's two or three round bursts seemed to have kept Sergei's men pretty well pinned down with only the occasional return of fire.

As he reached the bottom of the steps, he looked across the deck to where Anna was hiding behind one of the large steel capstans. With the ship now developing a small amount of forward movement she was having to constantly shift her position in order to be able to fire through the forward hawsehole.

Duggan walked part of the way towards Anna before ducking down and then dropping onto his hands and knees for the final ten feet or so.

Anna was so engrained in what she was doing that she only noticed Duggan when he began scuttling across the deck on his hands and knees. As he flopped down beside her, he passed her three more clips for the AK-47.

'Thought you might need some help,' he grinned.

'Better late than never,' she retorted before rolling onto her back and pushing home a fresh clip of bullets.

As she rolled back into position, she let out a cry.

'Duggan they've got an RPG aimed at us!'

He didn't need telling twice realising that if the rocket propelled grenade hit the bridge it would kill Nick and Jim and their ticket out of Kaliningrad.

He grabbed the AK-47 from Anna and stood up to see Anatoly swinging the RPG up to his shoulder. With the gun on fully automatic he let loose with the complete magazine of thirty rounds before ducking back down behind the gunwale. At precisely the same moment Anatoly pulled the trigger on the RPG.

The force of the bullets slamming into his chest just as the grenade left the launcher was all it took to send it off course and, as Duggan and Anna cowered on the deck waiting for the explosion, the grenade flew high over their heads and seconds later smashed into the hillside on the opposite site of the harbour.

Nick and Jim were blissfully unaware of the RPG until they saw the grenade whistle past the shattered windows. They watched transfixed as it arced over their heads before blowing a sizeable crater in the hillside and dislodging several large boulders that then crashed down onto the buildings below.

'Bloody hell, now they're firing missiles at us!' shouted Jim, 'for Christ sake Nick give this old girl some beans, I think we've outstayed our welcome here.'

Nick pushed the throttles forward another notch and slowly the ship started to gain momentum.

From his second-floor office near the entrance to the port, Mikhail Todorov, the chief of police had been watching the events unfold with total disbelief. He and Sergei were friends and he was quite prepared to look the other way from time to time and, as the new BMW touring motorcycle in his garage testified, his efforts did not go unnoticed. This however was way beyond turning a blind eye, and as the grenade flew over the ship and exploded, he started to issue orders to his officers.

Duggan and Anna's work was now complete down on the deck. The AK-47 had an effective range of little more than 400 yards and as the *Tricolor* continued to gain speed they were now beyond its limit.

'C'mon,' said Duggan, 'better see if we can be of any assistance up there.'

He turned and pointed up towards the bridge and then promptly sat back down with his back against the gunwale.

'Jesus! I know we took some fire up there but that is incredible.'

He sat for a moment surveying the damage. Apart from the complete lack of glass, the whole of the bridge superstructure was a mass of little dents and puncture holes where the bullets had hit home. The steel roof of the bridge that extended out to provide some shade now looked like a piece of Swiss cheese and the white paint was now pockmarked with hundreds of little red dots where the topcoat of paint had given way to the reveal the red anti-rust protection underneath.

Anna flopped down beside him.

'Now you know why I had to take them all on single handed,' she said looking up at the devastation above. 'I figured I needed to divert some of the fire before they either killed you all or shot the bridge up so bad that it could no longer operate.'

Duggan shook his head and then raised his palm into the air. Anna smiled and high fived him, before crawling towards the starboard stairs that led back up to the bridge.

Up on the bridge things were very tense as Nick worked out how to handle a ship of the *Tricolor*'s size. His saving grace was that like the *Sandie Watson* she had bow and stern thrusters which made manoeuvring much easier and more instantaneous than the steering gear alone.

They were now halfway along the dock and from below they could hear the sound of police sirens moving towards them. When Duggan and Anna arrived back on the bridge, they found Jim peering out of the port wing bridge at the quayside below.

'What's going on?' asked Duggan.

'The police have arrived en force and seem to be rounding up all of Sergei's men on the quay.'

'That's good, at least they won't be giving us any more trouble,' commented Nick as he concentrated on keeping a straight course.

No sooner had the words left his lips and the ship to shore radio crackled into life. To Nick and Jim, it was all undecipherable but after a minute or so the voice stopped and Anna offered an explanation.

'That was chief of police Todorov ordering us to heave to. He says he has some questions about what has just happened down on Sergei's quay. He also pointed out that the ship's port dues are currently unpaid and unless we settle them the harbour master will reject our clearance to leave the port.'

Everyone looked at Nick for an explanation.

'Whenever a ship enters a port and berths there are fees to be paid to that port,' he explained. 'Could be anything from berthing and pilot fees to the topping up of the freshwater tanks. What our friend is politely saying is that if we don't pay our dues, we will not be granted permission to leave the port by the harbour master and will effectively become fugitives. Under the circumstances I think we can ignore the radio message, and I don't know about you guys but I ain't about to stop for no one. Theoretically he could contact the Russian Navy and effectively have us arrested, but unless we are extremely unlucky and there is a naval frigate hanging around just outside the port entrance, we should make it to International waters with ease.'

'How far out are the International waters?' asked Anna.

'Twelve miles,' replied Nick.

'Is there anything else they can do to stop us?' asked

Duggan.

'Not in a vessel of this size,' Nick replied. 'They could try blocking our path with a tugboat or something but I think that is extremely unlikely.'

A few moments passed and the radio came alive once more. Anna translated.

'He says that if we don't cut power, he will have no alternative but use force to stop us. He also says that we won't be able to proceed much further anyway because the canal is closed.'

Nick defiantly pushed the throttles up another notch.

'What does he mean by "the canal is closed"?' asked Anna. 'I didn't even know we had a canal?'

'I guess its confession time,' said Nick with a slight frown. 'Kaliningrad is one of only a handful of ports around the world where we have to navigate a length of canal before entering open water. I'm guessing it is due to the tidal currents in the Baltic Sea silting up the river. If the currents are really bad, the only way to keep a navigable passage open without constant 24/7 dredging is to build a canal, I'm amazed you didn't know about it.'

'So am I,' agreed Anna, 'but in my defence unless you are connected with the port in some way or another, why would you? How long is this canal then and what does Todorov mean by "its closed"?'

'It's twenty-four miles long, that's nearly forty of your kilometres and when Todorov says it's closed he means it's closed to traffic from the port. Because of the cost of constructing a canal like this, they are usually single carriageway and there are set times during the day when traffic can enter and leave a port. Unfortunately, I wasn't aware of the canal until about twenty minutes ago when I first examined the charts and to be honest at that time it was the least of our problems. So basically, we are about to sail the wrong way up a one-way street.'

'Sorry guys,' offered Duggan, 'I should have thought of that before we made a play for the ship.'

'We didn't have much choice as far as an escape route went,' conceded Jim. 'How busy is this port Duggan? What are our chances of escaping through the canal without colliding with something coming the other way?'

'It's a very busy port, but if you look around us at the moment most of the berths are full, that's got to be a good omen.'

They were now nearly two thirds of the way out of the main port complex and the river was bearing left slightly before it swept round to the right and entered the canal. The canal had been built without lock gates and was completely tidal and it was only on extreme ebb tides that vessels had to check with the port authority's that there was enough draft for their safe passage.

The radio squawked into life once again and the now familiar but increasingly animated voice of Todorov spoke once again, Anna translated.

'Todorov says this is our final warning and if we don't come to a full halt immediately, he cannot be held responsible for the repercussions.'

As Nick tried to figure out in his head what the repercussions might be, a large tugboat began to inch its way out from a jetty further along the dock front.

'Looks like we've got company,' said Nick pointing at the emerging tug.

'Can he stop a ship this size?' asked Anna watching the comparatively small tug pull away from its mooring.

'No not really,' replied Nick, 'but those things are built like tanks and could certainly do us a fair bit of damage if it hit us in the right place. Let's call his bluff and see what happens.'

Nick pushed the throttles up a couple more notches and sounded the ship's horn to warn the tugboat of his approach. The water at the rear of the *Tricolor* turned to froth as the propellers bit hard into the water.

Up ahead, the tugboat turned out into the river and turned to face the them head on.

'Bloody hell,' said Jim. 'This is like a wild west duel.'

'Better brace yourselves,' said Nick keeping the *Tricolor* in the central channel of the river. 'Looks like he is going to take us on.'

The tug held its position and with less than a hundred yards between them disappeared from view under their bow. Nick gave a final defiant blast on the ship's horn and then braced himself against the helm for the impact.

The impact was a lot lighter than everyone was expecting, consisting only of a light rumbling sound.

'She chickened out,' said Nick, the relief obvious in his voice. 'Didn't hit us head on just a glancing blow. With all the padding around a tugboat I doubt if she even took the paint off.'

Jim and Duggan ran across to the wing bridges to see which side of the ship the tug went down.

'She's over here!' shouted Jim from the starboard side.

'Keep an eye on her engines!' shouted Nick. 'Let me know if they try and push us off course, I've got to throttle back a little to make the turn in the river so we may not be out of the woods yet.'

The pressure on Nick was beginning to show and despite the fact that a cold wind was blowing onto the bridge through the shattered windows, small beads of sweat were now clearly visible on his brow.

As he reduced the speed slightly, he felt a slight nudge from the rear of the vessel.

Jim shouted from the wing bridge, 'She's turned onto us and is pushing us to port.'

Nick activated the bow port thrusters and pushed back against the tugboat. At the same moment Duggan rushed across the bridge with his AK-47 and roughly pushed Jim out of the way on the starboard wing bridge.

'This will give them something to think about,' he said pushing home a new clip of ammunition. Within the confines of the bridge the automatic fire was deafening and, as the final shells left the rifle, Nick shouted at Jim:

'Let me know the second they look like they're backing off.'

Jim pulled Duggan out of the way as he reloaded another clip for a second assault.

As he looked down the froth at the rear of the tugboat began to subside.

'Now!' he shouted to Nick.

Nick shut down the bow thruster and felt the boat come back under his full control once more.

'Okay,' he said, 'now let's see what our luck is like in the canal.'

The river was now a good quarter mile wide and the shipping channel was on the opposite side of the river to the main port. As they passed the Police Headquarters a few rounds rang out from the quay but at that range their weapons were about as much use as bows and arrows.

As the *Tricolor* neared the end of the river section, the hills that they had climbed the previous day to look down on the port began to diminish in size. A few moments later Nick was able to see around the headland and along the canal, and to his relief it was void of all shipping.

Behind them the tug was following in their wake obviously looking for an opportunity to maybe run the *Tricolor* aground or force her off course.

With the bend in the river successfully negotiated Nick once more kicked the throttles up a couple of notches.

'You're starting to lose the tug,' said Jim from his position on the wing bridge.

'Good, thought as much,' replied Nick, 'those guys are built for torque rather than speed; I don't think he will give us any further problems. Anna, I need you to monitor the radio and listen out for any ships that ask the port authority for permission to enter the canal. Jim gets a message to RB explaining the story so far.'

'No problem, consider it done,' he said moving across to where Anna sat beside the helm watching the depth gauge.

They quickly got up and taking no chances, Anna reached forward and grabbed her AK-47 before heading for the radio room. Once inside Anna quickly tuned into the port frequency while Jim tapped away on the computer keyboard filling in RB with the events so far and outlining what they were planning to do next.

On the bridge Duggan stood beside Nick and monitored his progress through the canal.

'When you get to the other end don't turn too early,' he offered. 'There is a shallow sandbank on your port side which you need to pass before turning.'

'Where are you off to then?' asked Nick as Duggan began to pick up weapons and ammunition from around the bridge.

'I have to go a see a young man called Leonard who is looking after the engines. I told him we needed power because there was a fire in one of the sheds and we needed to get the *Baltic Carrier* out of harm's way. To be honest I'm surprised he hasn't cut the engines by now, although it is pretty noisy in the engine room, he probably hasn't heard World War Three going on up here.'

'So what you going to tell him?'

'No idea at the moment, I think of something,' said Duggan patting Nick on the back as he left the bridge.

Dugan made it down to the engine room in less than five minutes. On his way he had made a precautionary sweep of the medical centre and the galley where he had locked up the crew. The medical centre was deserted and on entering the galley he deliberately knocked a large saucepan onto the floor. It hit the floor with a loud clang and as he hoped the men locked inside the fresh food pantry started banging on the door and shouting for help, which confirmed to Duggan that they were still safe and secure.

On entering the engine room, he found Leonard in a very anxious state pacing up and down in front of the huge control panel. The relief on Leonard's face when he saw Duggan walking towards him was enormous and Duggan knew straight away that he was going to have to come up with a good story for the young engineer.

'Where's Vladimir?' shouted Duggan over the noise from

the engines.

'I was going to ask you the same question,' replied Leonard. 'I thought you were going to send him down here to help me.'

'I was, but when I didn't see him on my journey up to the bridge, I assumed we must have passed each other somewhere en route.'

'I haven't seen a soul since you left me.'

'Oh, that's strange, maybe he saw the fire early on when he was getting his coffee and went back onto the dock to try and help.'

'Yes maybe,' shrugged Leonard.

Leonard didn't seem convinced so Duggan tried to shift the conversation in a different direction.

'How's it looking?' he asked with a nod towards the control panel.

'Everything is good, one of the thrusters got a little warm earlier when we were manoeuvring but it's fine now.'

'Excellent, well done, now let me bring you up to speed on what's going on.'

Leonard leaned forward slightly; keen to catch up with what was happening.

'The fire in the shed was very fierce and began to get out of control very quickly, setting fire to the shed next door where all the gas bottles are stored for the dismantling plant. As Sergei gave the order for us to leave port several of the acetylene bottles exploded and one of them launched itself into the bridge almost completely destroying it in the process. Luckily no one was hurt but it made a bit of a mess and most of the comms are down, hence why we haven't been in contact with you.'

Duggan studied Leonard's face to try and ascertain how much of his story was being believed and how much was being dismissed for the bullshit it actually was. Sensing that it was so far so good, he drew on his SAS training and threw in a sentence of truths that Leonard couldn't argue with and a compliment which would take care of most doubters.

'As you probably know once we get beyond a certain point within the port we can't moor up or turn because we are too big, so Captain Andersson is taking us out into the open waters of the Baltic Sea. He plans to simply circle around for a few hours and then return to port once the fire is out and it is safe to go back. I think he will be most impressed when I tell him that you are down here on your own and I'm guessing that there may be a large bonus in your wage packet this month from Sergei for the fine work you've done.'

Leonard took it all in hook, line and sinker and Duggan could tell from the grin on his face that his job was done with the young seaman.

'Now are you going to be okay on your own for a while, or do you need some help?'

'I'll be fine, this thing practically runs itself, but I could do with something to eat and drink. Can I go up to the galley and get a sandwich and a cup of coffee?'

'No better you stay here and monitor this lot,' replied Duggan nodding once again at the bank of gauges and dials.

'I'll go get you something, here take this,' he handed Leonard one of the radios and tested it. 'There, that's working okay; it's the only way to keep in touch at the moment, if you need anything just shout. I'll be back in a few minutes with some food and drink for the hero of the moment.'

He gave Leonard a wink and a pat on the back before heading back to the bulkhead door.

It took him a further fifteen minutes to sort Leonard out a hot mug of coffee and a large cheese sandwich from the galley. As he re-entered the engine room, he was pleased to find the young engineer sitting back in his chair with his feet up on the control desk looking very relaxed and very pleased with himself.

Duggan chastised him for his unprofessional attitude, gave him the sandwich and coffee and then left him to it with strict instructions that if he needed anything, he must call him on the radio.

Leonard gave him the thumbs up as he glanced back from the bulkhead door; Duggan gave him an okay sign by touching his forefinger and thumb together and then exited through the door and headed back to the bridge.

15

To the outside world the brief radio conversation between the *Tricolor* and the *Sandie Watson* must have seemed strangely stunted, although at the time neither party gave it a second thought.

As Ewan listened intently to the orders from Nick to evacuate the area and avoid all contact with the Ferretti motor yacht, he could see out of the small porthole in the radio room a very similar vessel heading their way.

Moving quickly onto the bridge he was relieved to find Mark standing at the helm with a pair of binoculars trained on the approaching vessel.

'Strange that she should be out here as well, we're well off any charted shipping lanes out here!' he commented before Ewan could fill him in on his brief radio conversation.

With the ship stationed in the same position for the last few days, Mark had dropped the anchor and as Ewan quickly explained the message from Nick Mark's hand was on the control for the anchor winch.

With the anchor making its way back to the surface, he dialled up the engine room and a few seconds later a low rumbling could just be made out from deep within the bowels of the ship.

'Which way are we heading?' Mark asked Ewan as the anchor smacked the side of the bow and the winch came to a halt.

'The way Nick described that ship,' said Ewan pointing at the Ferretti, 'the opposite direction to her might not be a bad idea.'

'We won't be able to outrun her,' commented Mark, 'but we should be able to make a heavy wake if she wants to pull alongside and board us.'

The Ferretti was now about a mile away but with her big twin engines pounding at the sea and her quarry in sight she was closing quickly on the *Sandie Watson*.

With the anchor now back on board, Mark gunned the engines and took a heading away from the chasing cruiser.

'I know with our upgraded engines we have a maximum speed of about fifteen knots,' said Ewan, 'any idea what they may be capable of?'

'At least double what we can achieve,' replied Mark. 'If it's the model I think it is they've got a pair of 1350HP engines hidden under that rear deck that will happily push her up to over thirty knots.'

'Shit, I think we'd better come up with a plan B then, 'cause with that sort of speed she will be on us in minutes.'

'Don't panic. The one advantage we do have is bulk. The *Sandie* may be slow but they won't dare get to close in case I ram them. Those Ferretti's are made for speed, one heavy contact from us and she'll sink like a stone.'

Despite her considerable bulk Mark quickly brought the *Sandie Watson* up to her maximum speed, but the gap was now down to only a few hundred yards.

Ewan was standing looking out of the starboard side bridge window with a pair of high-powered binoculars and his usual calm demeanour suddenly changed to one of complete panic.

'Oh my God! They've got some sort of rocket launcher trained on us!' he shouted at Mark, despite him being only five feet away.

Not needing to be told twice Mark spun the wheel to port just in the nick of time and seconds later a small projectile whizzed past the ship and exploded off their starboard bow kicking up a thirty-foot-high wall of water. Mark straightened up the bow and pushed the throttle to its stops.

'Jeeesus these guys really mean business,' said Ewan just as Sarah, Duncan and Roly arrived on the bridge.

'Keep your eye on them Ewan, let him put the launcher to his shoulder, count to two and then shout NOW!'

'What the hell's going on?' asked Duncan, oblivious to the fact that they had just cheated death by seconds.

'We're under attack,' spat back Mark, 'it appears Jim and Nick uncovered more about the *Tricolor* than we have and those guys out there aren't too happy about it.'

Duncan and Sarah followed Mark's pointed finger and looked at the cruiser still closing the gap on the *Sandie Watson*.

He took the short lull to shout across the bridge to Duncan:

'Duncan? Get on the radio and issue an SOS giving our position and stating that we are under attack by an unknown vessel carrying rocket launchers.'

'Aye, aye, Captain,' replied Duncan, seemingly still not grasping the gravity of the situation.

'One, two NOW,' shouted Ewan.

Mark spun the wheel to starboard, sending everyone staggering across the bridge.

Moments later a second missile shot up a huge plume of

water in front of them.

Duncan watched wide eyed as the plume of water fell back to the surface in a hissing froth, before snapping into action and running for the radio room.

Despite their dire situation Mark and Ewan swapped a quick smile as Duncan raced past them.

'I think he's got the picture,' said Ewan, bringing the binoculars back up to his eyes.

Mark once again straightened up the ship so they didn't lose any more distance than was necessary between the two vessels.

The Ferretti was still closing on the *Sandie Watson* and Mark and Ewan both knew that the closer they got the better their chance of a direct hit.

'I've got an idea,' said Ewan, 'it's risky but it might just work.'

'We're running out of time fast!' shouted Mark. 'So let's hear it.'

Ewan quickly explained his plan whilst keeping the binoculars trained on the cruiser.

'One, two, NOW,' he shouted again.

This time Mark went to starboard once again, and the missile landed several hundred yards to their port.

'Go for it!' he shouted at Ewan. 'Russian roulette is not a game where your luck lasts forever.'

Ewan gave the binoculars to Roly and explained the technique that had worked so well for them so far and then he and Sarah rushed down to the stern of the ship.

As they passed the radio room Ewan shouted to Duncan to meet him on the stern once he had finished sending his SOS.

Duncan didn't reply but gave Ewan a thumbs up to

acknowledge he had understood the request, feverishly sending out the SOS, unaware that the Ferretti was blocking the communications.

When he and Sarah reached the stern of the vessel they ducked inside the small cabin where the ROVs were housed and got to work.

'We'll use Tiny,' said Ewan as he tied three empty plastic Coke bottles to a length of rope.

'Okay,' acknowledged Sarah, starting to give the little ROV a quick once-over.

As Ewan quickly tied the other end of the rope to the small ROV he felt the ship lean to starboard once again.

Yet again the missile missed, although how much of this was down to luck, good seamanship, or just the problem of firing a powerful rocket from a base that was bouncing up and down at thirty knots was open to debate.

He and Sarah pushed Tiny onto the rear deck keeping low so they would not be seen from the still closing cruiser, before Sarah headed down to the control room.

Another missile came inbound and this time it was within a matter of feet of finding its target, the explosion rocking the ship violently and spraying the stern of the vessel in a big, frothy wave of icy water.

'Shit!' shouted Ewan, realising that they were now in serious danger of being hit.

Sarah meanwhile was in the control room powering up the systems for what was likely to be Tiny's final voyage.

'It's all go down here,' she shouted up to Ewan.

'Me too, let's do it.'

Sarah made the call to the bridge and as she did so Ewan ran to the front of the ship with a white T-shirt on a pole.

As he ran along the deck, he felt the *Sandie Watson* sink into the water as the power was cut to her engine. Then she gently turned to face the Ferretti that was still closing at full speed.

Ewan waved the T-shirt as a sign of surrender from the bow, and to his huge relief saw the man with the rocket launcher de-shoulder the device. The Ferretti roared past the *Sandie Watson* at full speed and then as if to emphasise her greater speed and manoeuvrability turned sharply in a wide 180-degree arc, before sinking back into the water some 400 yards off the *Sandie's* stern.

This was not what they wanted so Mark quickly turned them around with the side thrusters so they once again faced their foe head on.

As he did so Ewan propped the white T-shirt up against the bow so it was still visible and then rushed back to the stern of the ship to where Tiny and Duncan were now waiting.

With little in the way of pomp or circumstance, Duncan and Ewan picked up the tiny ROV and, with a final check that they couldn't be seen, dropped it into the water behind the ship.

Down in the control room, Sarah sent the little robot into a full-on dive and thirty seconds later with Duncan and Ewan feeding out the umbilical cord for all they were worth, the rope and Coke bottles that Ewan had tied to the craft disappeared below the surface of the water.

Up on the bridge things were a getting tense with the two boats now standing in a face-off position, each captain waiting to see what their adversary was planning next.

On board Sergei's boat Viktor was letting the Ferretti drift on the wind and was a little surprised by the *Sandie Watsons* insistence of staying perfectly stationed on her bow.

An hour earlier he had been made aware of Sergei's demise and the loss of the *Tricolor* and was already formulating a plan to recapture the ship when she came out into the North Sea.

His first priority however was to take care of the *Sandie Watson* and, although his passions were still running high at hearing the news from Kaliningrad, his cold mercenary side was now quite happy that he didn't have to waste any more of his limited armaments on the survey ship.

'Bring us alongside,' he told his helmsman, 'I need to remove any evidence they have against us first and then we'll do what we did with the *Baltic Carrier* and send them to the bottom with their ship.'

His helmsman gave him knowing sort of nod and then applied some power to the twin engines to bring the Ferretti onto the *Sadie Watsons* port beam.

Mark had spotted the slight movement in the Ferretti's bow and seconds later a heavily accented voice came over radio stating his intentions to pull onto their port side and warning of the consequences of any resistance.

Duncan who had now returned from helping Ewan launch Tiny, replied an affirmative to the message, before relaying down to the control room the news that Sergei's cruiser was heading for their port beam.

Sarah had kept Tiny stationed directly below their hull and with the news from Duncan she took him off to the port side.

As the Ferretti approached the *Sandie Watson* the crew of five came out onto the deck heavily armed with AK-47s, each crewman emphasising their superiority by wearing a bulletproof vest around which was slung a belt with extra magazines tucked into its pockets.

To the uninitiated on board, the survey ship these guys looked ready for action and Mark was starting to have doubts as to whether their plan would work.

Turning towards the radio room he shouted at Duncan to let Sarah and Ewan know that they had some serious opposition and to be prepared to take cover.

With Mark monitoring the helm and Sarah flying the ROV it was down to Duncan and Ewan to keep both parties abreast of the others situation.

With Sergei's boat now less than a hundred feet away Sarah started to bring the little ROV gently up beneath its hull, everyone on the *Sandie Watson* aware that the timing of this manoeuvre was critical if they were to make it home in one piece.

To give Sarah as much time as possible to get the little craft in the correct position, Mark kept feathering the side-thrusters so that the distance between the two boats was kept almost at a constant. Slowly he let the gap diminish whilst listening intently to the conversation that Ewan was having with Duncan.

Between the two vessels the empty Coke bottle suddenly broke the surface to the obvious amusement of the machine gun wielding crew, who were all egging one another on to blast them out of the water, none of them seemingly interested in asking themselves where an empty Coke bottle attached to a piece of rope would come from in the middle of the North Sea.

Below decks Sarah could begin to see the daylight through the green water on Tiny's camera. Ewan could also see the change and told Duncan to make Mark aware that their plan was about to come to fruition.

'Okay Duncan, ask Mark to bring us forward a little.'

With the boats now feet apart in a bow to stern formation Mark again feathered the throttles to bring the *Sandie Watson* forwards a couple of feet.

As he did so, Tiny came to the surface unseen on the far side of the Ferretti in line with the propellers.

Sarah quickly swung Tiny around so she could see the cruiser and, as the helmsman added a little throttle to his twin engines to match the manoeuvre Mark had instigated, Sarah and Ewan saw Tiny get pulled down sharply into the water.

'NOW!' shouted Ewan loud enough to be heard on the bridge without the need for the radio and then he and Sarah threw themselves onto the floor of the control room.

Up on the bridge Mark gunned the engines throwing the throttles to their stops before he Duncan and Roly hurtled headfirst into the corridor behind the bridge.

For a split second their adversaries were caught off guard, but then all hell broke loose as the *Sandie Watson* was peppered with sub-machine gun fire.

Unaware that Tiny, the Coke bottles and several feet of rope were about to wrap themselves securely around the Ferretti's twin screws the helmsman also gunned his throttles, and for a split second the boat made some forward progress before the driveshafts screamed in protest and the engines came to a shuddering halt. Up on deck the crew were thrown off balance and two of them fell overboard into the sea, whilst the other three ended up sitting on the deck with a look of complete shock on their faces. Viktor raced forward out of the protected bridge area with a pistol and fired indiscriminately at the fleeing vessel.

The bullets thudded innocently into the woodwork and

seconds later there was a loud crack as Tiny's umbilical cord was severed from the rear of the boat. Sarah looked up at the control panel and the large monitor screen and sucked in a sharp intake of breath as she watched everything go blank. Tiny had always been her favourite of the ROVs on board, he was much nippier and manoeuvrable than the slightly larger units and had a sort of terrier personality, always seemingly getting into mischief but equally, he always managed to get out of a tight squeeze, he was her little baby and now he was gone.

Ewan gave Sarah a prod back into reality and taking their cue from the lack of incoming fire, they burst out onto the rear deck and fired two distress flares at the cruiser. Both managed to find their target, with Sarah's doing the most damage by smashing through the glass into the bridge area, adding still further to the confusion of Viktor and his helmsman.

Seconds later a second burst of machine-gun fire was heard but with the survey ship now putting distance between itself and the cruiser; it was all but completely ineffectual.

Realising he was all but dead in the water Viktor shouted at his men to re-launch the rocket attack, but his orders fell on deaf ears as the three men still on board tried to haul their heavily clad comrades from the freezing water.

Jumping down onto the stern deck of the Ferretti Viktor picked up the launcher himself and quickly loaded it before slinging it up onto his shoulder.

At the range he was now firing from, the chances of hitting the target were at best slim, but with the added burden of rushing the whole procedure the missile landed a good fifty yards behind and to the port side of its target.

He reloaded and tried again to hold the launcher steady enough to hit the target, but once again the missile was way off. With a maximum range of little more than 500 metres the rocket launcher was now useless and, realising this, Viktor threw the weapon to one side and headed down into the cabin to fetch his scuba gear.

Back on board the *Sandie Watson* they were celebrating their escape with loud shouts and cheers.

'Boy that was too close for comfort,' commented Ewan as he and Sarah returned to the bridge.

'You can say that again,' said Duncan who was standing beside Mark at the helm.

'What's the damage look like?' Mark asked Ewan.

'Mostly superficial, don't think we took anything below the waterline, but I think we are going to have our hands full answering some very difficult questions when we get back to port.'

'Mmm, you're not wrong there,' said Mark thoughtfully, before snapping back into command mode.

'Ewan go check the engines and make doubly sure we didn't take any low hits. I'm not easing up on these throttles until we re-enter harbour and we can't be sure how much time Tiny's sacrifice bought us, so keep an eye on the gauges for the next couple of hours.

'Duncan, what's going on with the radio? Why haven't we had any replies to our SOS message? We are near one of the busiest pieces of ocean on the whole planet; I can't believe no one heard us.'

Duncan and Ewan quickly left the bridge and Mark turned to Sarah who was standing gazing out at the sea ahead of them.

'You okay?' he asked noting that she was not making any effort to get involved with the conversation.

'No,' she replied turning to look at Mark her eyes full of

tears.

'Hey, hey, hey, come here.'

Sarah moved across to Mark and threw her arms around his shoulders.

'I'm sorry,' she sobbed.

'Hey no problem, it's probably just the shock coming out, you're now in a pretty exclusive club, you know.'

Sarah gave a loud snuffle. 'What do you mean?'

'Well, there can't be too many ex-Southampton University students who join a research vessel and end up in the middle of the North Sea being shot at with AK-47s and rocket launchers.'

Sarah gave another little sob.

'It's not so much that, it's what you said about Tiny making a sacrifice. I know it sounds stupid but I was very fond of that little robot.'

She gave another sob and then pulled herself away from Mark's comforting shoulder.

He tutted. 'And there was I thinking it was the bullets and rockets that had got to you.'

He pulled her back towards him and gave her a peck on the forehead. 'We can replace Tiny, replacing this ship and her crew is much more difficult. Now how about going to see what Roly's up to and fetching us a cup of coffee?'

Sarah wiped her eyes with the cuff of her sweatshirt.

'Aye, aye, Captain,' she said throwing a mock salute before kissing him on the cheek and heading for the galley.

'You're going soft in your old age,' came Duncan's voice from behind Mark.

'Maybe,' he replied thoughtfully before looking over his shoulder at Duncan's grinning face.

'So what have you got for me you old hard-nosed bastard?'

Duncan continued to grin at Mark knowing that he had touched a nerve.

'Well, it appears that our mayday message never reached anyone due to "localised interference",' said Duncan holding up the first two digits on both hands to emphasise the air quotes. 'I managed to get an email through to RB telling him what's been going on and he in turn filled me in on the situation with Jim and Nick. He says that there are jamming devices available that will block radio signals and knowing what he knows now it seems very likely that that's the reason why no mayday message was ever heard from the *Tricolor*.'

Duncan waved two pages of A4 in front of Mark.

'Wanna hear what the two amigos have been up to and why we are being shot at?'

'You make them sound like bandits.'

'After you've read this you may well think calling them bandits is a little tame.'

'You read it to me. I've got my hands full here at the moment.'

Duncan began to read the two pages and was almost immediately interrupted by a radio message from RB.

As Duncan patched it through to the bridge, Roly and Sarah appeared with a tray of bacon sandwiches and mugs of coffee. Everyone immediately took advantage of the offerings as RB filled them in on developments.

'Following your earlier email, I thought I had better contact the coastguard and warn them of a heavily armed vessel in the middle of the North Sea with a jamming device preventing any vessel in the vicinity sending out a distress call.

They have just called back to say that a Danish submarine that was on exercise in the area is now being sent to the co-ordinates you gave me to investigate a possible act of piracy.

'They have also told me that the Royal Navy warship HMS *Quorn* which is currently on a four-day visit to its home port of Ipswich is being scrambled to rendezvous with you and escort you back into port before heading back out to take the *Tricolor* back into Hull.'

Mark, Sarah and Roly looked at one another with questioning looks, but before anyone could ask what was going on Duncan was replying to RB.

'Christ that all sounds a bit heavy... over,' he commented.

RB came back on the radio.

'Unbeknown to most people following the multiple hijacking of ships off Somalia, all European governments have put in place a contingency plan in the event that anything like that ever happens in European waters. Apparently when I informed the Coastguard Service what happened to you guys, the balloon went up and here we are, half an hour later, with two navy vessels from different countries heading your way. Over.'

'Thanks RB.' Mark over and out.'

As everyone took in the gravity of the situation, Ewan appeared back on the bridge.

'She's running sweet as a nut down there,' he said looking at Mark. 'No holes no issues.'

Ewan could sense something was up and looked around enquiringly at his crewmates.

Duncan broke in by waving his two sheets of A4.

'I think I had better read this,' he said perching his bottom on the edge of the map table, I think it may well answer some of the questions I sense you guys are about to fire at me.'

When he had finished relaying what Jim and Nick had been up to, the bridge fell into a stunned silence.

'No wonder those Ruskies or whoever they were on board the Ferretti were so pissed off,' said Ewan. 'But how the hell did Nick and Jim manage to steal, let alone manoeuvre a ship of that size out of a foreign port in one piece? Unbelievable!'

'So, it wasn't the *Tricolor* we were looking at in the Liberman Trench after all,' mussed Sarah, 'it was the *Baltic Carrier* and all those cars were from Sergei's dismantling plant and were damaged before they went to the bottom.'

'And I would bet good money that anything of any value had also been stripped off them,' said Ewan. 'Catalytic converters for example contain platinum, which is very valuable, especially in the sort of quantities you can salvage off a couple of thousand cars. It all starts to make sense,' he said thoughtfully.

'Oh, and you were right Duncan,' Ewan continued, 'it *was* a big fraud, but they didn't have to get the cars off the ship to sell them down the local boozer, the ones that held the value were on a different ship altogether.'

Everyone smiled at the memory of Duncan's comment several days earlier about selling fifty million pounds' worth of BMWs down the local.

'So, the ships really were totally identical,' pondered Roly looking at Duncan.

'It appears so,' said Duncan. 'Certainly, a close enough match not to attract the attention of the authorities at Kaliningrad port when she arrived there after the switch. We know Sergei Petrov had his ship repainted soon after the *Tricolor* and to the casual observer at the time this was nothing more than a coincidence, but as we now know it was to keep the ships looking identical.'

'Has RB mentioned anything about the crew in any of your conversations?' asked Sarah with a certain amount of trepidation.

'No afraid not, but judging by the crew they sent out after us this morning I think it's fairly safe to assume they went down with the *Baltic Carrier*. These guys are big time professionals. I'm guessing they don't take prisoners, in fact, if we hadn't managed to escape this morning, we would probably have joined them.'

'Has Mark at Lloyds been informed of what's happened?' Ewan asked Duncan.

'Yes, RB has sent him a copy of what I've got here, so he's probably a very happy man at the moment. Thanks to us and providing Nick and Jim can bring the *Tricolor* home safe and sound he's now fifty million pounds' better off than he was twenty-four hours ago.'

'Do we know where they are at the moment?' continued Ewan.

Duncan shuffled through a couple more sheets of A4 before finding the page he was looking for. He then began to mumble his way down the page before stating.

'Ah here it is. According to Jim when he wrote this, they were heading up the eastern coast of Denmark and expected to be back in the North Sea at about,' Duncan looked at his watch, 'well anytime now actually.'

'In normal circumstances their route would have taken them through the Keil Canal,' said Mark, 'but with their experience, a skeleton crew and who knows what after them, I guess they felt safer in open water.'

'So how far is it from northern Denmark to Hull?' asked Sarah.

'Top of my head? Probably between 400 and 500 miles,' answered Mark, 'but they have taken some damage and if the ship wasn't due to leave port for a few days or even a week or so they may not even have enough fuel on board to make it back to Hull. Like us they're not home and dry, just yet.'

16

Back on board the *Tricolor* things had settled down considerably with a sense of calm beginning to prevail following the fire fight in Kaliningrad Harbour.

Jim had taken the opportunity to fill Anna in on what they knew so far and what they had found when they sent Tiny down to the *Baltic Carrier*. He also explained fully what they really did for a living and all about the *Sandie Watson* and her eclectic crew.

'I knew there was something not quite right about your working for a bank story,' she said giving Jim a punch on the arm.

'Why what was wrong with it?'

'I'm not sure, but usually when a new company wants to invest somewhere, they let it be public knowledge quite early on and visit the local business leaders and town officials. They also come fully prepared with their own interpreters and arrange drivers and appointments before they arrive. You and Nick just arrived out of the blue and did everything, how do you say, off the scruff.'

'Cuff.'

'Sorry?'

'It's off the cuff.'

'Oh right.'

'Had you going though didn't it?' said Jim leaning

forward and giving her hand a squeeze.

'Little bit,' she conceded, 'but in Kaliningrad when an offer of a job comes up that pays good money you would be a fool to turn it down.'

'Money talks eh?'

Anna gave him a strange look.

'It's a phrase we have, which means that if you have money you can get things done quicker than if you don't have money.'

She nodded her understanding, before pulling a pistol from her pocket checking the chamber and making sure the safety was locked in place.

'Going somewhere?'

'Yes, I think it's about time I checked out the crews' quarters and make sure there is no one else on board who could cause any trouble.'

'Good idea, but be careful.'

'You bet; I've got an exciting opportunity of a new life ahead of me, of course I'll be careful.'

She leaned towards Jim and gave him a full kiss on the lips.

'See you in a bit.'

Five minutes later Jim rejoined Nick up on the bridge, both men now wrapped up in multiple layers of clothing to protect them from the chilling January winds blasting through what was left of the smashed glass all around them. Their top layer was a bright orange survival suit borrowed from one of the life rafts, fully zipped up with only their faces showing. It wasn't pretty or very practical, but under the circumstances nothing less would do.

They were now in the Baltic Sea and Nick was trying to make sense of the instrumentation, but with some smashed and some seemingly not working at all, the information gleaned was, at best, hazy.

One of the few dials that did seem to be working okay was the fuel gauge which showed quarter-full tanks. Even with a large chunk of guesstimation Nick was sure that would see them home okay, so assuming the reading was correct, that was one thing less to worry about.

His biggest issue however was going to be navigation. Whilst in the Baltic he was fine, with several hundred feet of water permanently under his hull, but when he entered the North Sea that was going to change quite drastically.

During the fight several bullets had hit the main navigation binnacle rendering it totally useless, so it was now up to Jim and Nick to pull out the maps and plot a course back to Hull the old-fashioned way with compasses, pencils and rulers.

Duggan was now back in the engine room pacifying Leonard who, despite his limited time at sea, had sussed from his young sea legs that they were not going around in circles as Duggan had earlier indicated.

'Apparently the fire has got out of control and is spreading further along the quayside,' he lied. 'Sergei has decided we may as well head for Rotterdam and pick up some more cargo before trying to return home. The rest of the crew will meet us there.'

Leonard seemed to trust Duggan and this latest update appeared on the surface at least to satisfy the fledgling engineer. Just to make sure however Duggan decided it would be best to keep his charge company for the next few hours, as after all the earlier fighting breaking out of Kaliningrad the last thing they needed now, was some sort of renegade act from within.

Anna meanwhile was sweeping the crew quarters and living accommodation for any unexpected signs of life. The accommodation block was not huge because of the size of the ship and even moving quite slowly through the area it only took her ten minutes to check out every cabin. As she moved towards the end of the corridor, she was suddenly aware of a prefabricated door that had been welded over an existing opening. It was totally out of keeping with all the other doors and looked very out of place in the well-decorated and pristine corridor. As she approached, she could hear voices from within. She grabbed the handle to open the door and it gave out a squeak of protest but refused to open and almost instantly the conversation from within ceased. Looking more closely at the handle she realised there was a substantial-looking lock on the door as well, plus two equally heavy-duty padlocks at the top and bottom.

'Hello, is there anybody in there?'

There was silence for a moment before a voice with a slight oriental accent answered.

'Hello? Who you?' Came back the reply.

'My name is Anna, who are you?'

From behind the door Anna could hear several different voices talking in a language that she didn't recognise. The conversation lulled and the man addressed her once again.

'Help us; we been locked in here for nearly one week.'

Anna's heart skipped a beat.

'How many of you are there?'

'Twenty-two,' came back the reply.

Anna stood dumbstruck for a moment before there was a commotion from within the room and banging on the door.

'Hello, this is Chief Officer Phillip Crane, who am I speaking to?'

Anna introduced herself again and explained what she knew about what had been going on, assuring the chief officer that they were all safe and no harm would come to them.

In return the Chief Officer explained what had happened during the raid on the ship and over the next few minutes they each managed to fill in some of the blanks and form a better understanding of what had been going on.

'How are you all holding up in there?' asked Anna, 'do you have enough water?'

'We are fine on that front,' answered the Chief Officer. 'This room has three large vending machines in it, so as well as the food our captors supplied us with, we have been able to snack on crisps, chocolate bars and there is a small kitchen area where we have access to water and hot drinks.'

'Okay Phillip, that's good. Now I have some good news and some bad news for you.'

'Ooookkay give me the good news first.'

'The good news,' said Anna, 'is that we are on course for the Hull and should make port in the next few hours.'

'And the bad news?'

'The door I'm facing looks very substantial and has a large lock and two big padlocks fastening it. To be honest with you Phillip unless we can locate the keys, I think it is unlikely we will be able to release you without some heavy-duty cutting equipment, so you need to be prepared to stay where you are until we dock in the UK. I'm really sorry.'

The chief officer went quiet for a moment before replying.

'Okay, not a problem, to be honest after what we've been through over the last week another few hours, won't make too much difference, besides which with one toilet between us and no chance to wash or change our clothes, you probably wouldn't want to open the door even if you could.'

Anna felt a twinge of remorse that she probably wouldn't be able to get the men out, but was also pleased that the chief officer had still got a sense of humour.

'I'll come back every hour and give you an update,' she replied, 'hang in there.'

Anna could hardly contain her excitement and raced back to find Nick and Jim.

'Guys, I've found the crew,' she blurted out, as she entered and came to a halt beside the two men.

'What all of them?'

'Yes, all except the captain, they are locked behind a make-shift door in the recreation room.'

'How many men are there?' asked Jim, wanting to confirm numbers.

'Twenty-two, they don't know what happened to their captain but the rest of them are all accounted for, isn't that great?'

Nick and Jim looked at each other the relief clearly etched on each other faces.

'That's brilliant news Anna,' the three of them coming together for a congratulatory three-way hug. 'How are they doing for food and water?' asked Nick, as he pulled away.

'They're fine,' replied Anna, still clinging onto Jim, 'they have plenty of drinks in the room and are snacking on crisps and chocolate bars from some vending machines.'

'So what are the chances of getting them out?' continued

Nick.

'That's the problem bit,' replied Anna. 'There are two industrial sized padlocks and a third built in lock on a very heavy looking steel door. Without some sort of cutting equipment or a set of keys I don't think we will be able to release them. I've been talking to the chief officer, Phillip Crane and he understands that they maybe there until we dock, not ideal but I don't see to many other options at the moment.'

'Can't you shoot the padlock off?' asked Nick.

'Shooting at a padlock at close quarters is probably not a good idea in a steel lined corridor,' replied Anna. 'A bullet could ricochet like a pinball in a pinball machine.'

'Yes, I see your point,' conceded the big man.

The conversation went quiet for a moment as they all thought about how to release the men from the reception room. The silence was broken by Jim.

'Duggan!'

'Duggan?' queried Anna.

'Yes Duggan,' replied Jim, 'he must have been at least partly responsible for putting them in there in the first place, he may even have a set of keys in his pocket.'

'Bloody hell,' said Nick, 'why didn't we think of that earlier?'

'Probably because we haven't had any meaningful sleep in the last thirty-six hours,' commented Jim.

'Anna, you go back to the recreation room, and I will contact Duggan and get him to come up to meet you there. Even if he hasn't got any keys, he may have something in the engine room that we can use to cut the locks or something.'

Anna was starting to feel the cold standing out on the open bridge and didn't need asking twice to head back down to the lower decks where the warmth was and disappeared.

It was a full ten minutes before Duggan came strolling down the corridor towards Anna looking very sheepish.

'I'm sorry Anna, with everything else that's been going on, I'm afraid I just clean forgot about them,' said Duggan keeping his voice down so as not to alert the crew to his presence.

Anna shot him a look.

'How could you forget about them Duggan?' she hissed.

She pointed to the doors to the right and left of the room the crew were in and did a quick guesstimation as to its size.

'You've got twenty-two men in there, in a room no more than ten metres by four metres and you just forgot about them?'

'Well, it wasn't so much forgot about them as just put them to the back of my mind while everything else was kicking off.'

'Duggan!'

'Look I've said I'm sorry,' he hissed grabbing Anna by the arm and leading her down the corridor to a point where they could converse in normal tones.

Anna was still not happy and now turned and looked him straight in the eye, her hands firmly on her hips in a take no prisoners sort of pose.

'So have you got a set of keys to those locks?'

For a split second he thought about trying to come up with some sort of excuse to try and break the news gently to his new friend, but then thought better of it.

'No, I'm afraid not, my ex-comrade Viktor was in charge of keeping them fed and watered while we were in port and he has the only set of keys to those locks.'

'So what about cutting them out or something?'

'It might be possible but I doubt it, not without some pretty specialised cutting equipment.'

Duggan pointed back down the corridor.

'As you can see Sergei was never a man to do things by halves, why only put one lock on a door when you can add two huge padlocks as well? That is just so typical of the way he worked and, on that principle, you can bet your last dollar that those padlocks are the best money can buy.

'Then we have the problem of me going into the engineering storeroom and helping myself to a load of tools to try and cut these guys out. Our young engineer friend is probably at this moment in time, the most important person on the ship, and I don't think any of us should risk doing anything that may cause him to doubt all the bullshit I've been feeding him and shut down the engines.'

Anna was still standing with her hands on her hips looking directly at Duggan. After ten seconds of silent thought, she threw her arms down by her side and took a kick at the nearby door.

'Shit! Shit! Shit!'

'Sorry Anna, hopefully we are only a few hours from the UK now, so they won't be in there much longer. C'mon let's go to the galley and make the guys upstairs some coffee and something to eat.'

Duggan set off back along the corridor and then turned left into the galley. Anna watched him disappear and then followed.

As she walked in through the door there was a loud banging sound from the rear of the galley, followed by Duggan's voice shouting in Russian to shut the fuck up.

The banging stopped and Anna found Duggan looking through a small pane of glass at a man and a woman locked in a cupboard.

'Now what?' she asked in a slightly exasperated voice.

Duggan turned.

'Let me introduce you. This is the ships Chef Vladamir Siknin and Serafina Antonova who is one of the cleaners who keeps the ship spick and span.'

Anna gave him a look. 'Spik and spam?'

'No, it's spick and span; it means clean and tidy.'

'So what are they doing in there?'

'Keeping out of trouble basically. I found them both while I was searching the ship earlier and because they are both fiercely loyal to Sergei, I thought it might be an idea to lock them in the pantry. Unfortunately, they will definitely have to stay put because I don't think we will ever convince them that what we have done is for the better good.'

Anna nodded and looking around spotted a large refrigerator on the far wall. Inside she found some bacon, sausages and eggs and putting a large frying pan on the hob she lit the gas and started to lay the bacon and sausages in the pan.

Duggan meanwhile started making a small and large jug of coffee and fifteen minutes later they had a tray of coffee and breakfast rolls ready to go.

'I'm going back down to Leonard,' he said helping himself to two rolls and the small jug. I'll see you later.'

'I'd forgotten how shallow this area is,' commented Jim, several cups of coffee and two breakfast rolls later, looking down with Nick at the huge chart laid out on the map table at the rear of the bridge.

'Yes, but you've got to remember twenty thousand years ago when the last Ice Age had the world in its icy grip, you could walk across here.'

Nick waved his arm in the general direction of the sea outside before returning his gaze to the map.

Nick tapped the map with his forefinger at an area in the middle of the North Sea east of Scarborough and directly on their course to Hull.

'Look here, this is the Dogger Bank, a huge sandbank in the middle of the sea which at best offers a depth of only fifteen metres. We've got to go around this in order to get back home. It's lucky I'm heading to Hull and not further south cause that is where it gets really dodgy.'

'What, shallower than fifteen metres?' asked Jim, keen to build on his knowledge of the North Sea.

'Oh yes, in fact this area just off the Netherlands has to be regularly dredged to allow the larger vessels passage.

'Our first set of obstacles are here, though.'

Nick pointed at the area of the chart to the south of where they were going to rejoin the North Sea.

'These are the Little Fisher Bank and the Jutland Bank and a ship this size will easily run aground on them if we swing south too soon. So, for now we will keep heading directly due West.'

Jim peered out of the shattered bridge windows.

'I hope you haven't lost your touch with the charts,' he said looking back at Nick. 'It's going to be dark pretty soon and without any GPS we could be in trouble.'

'Don't you worry I was reading charts before you were out of short trousers, it's like riding a bike, somehow you never forget. Besides it would be very foolhardy to set sail and not be able to navigate with the charts, you never know what might happen.'

'Yeah, you might get your bridge shot out by a group of crazy Russians and then where would you be?'

Jim laughed at his own joke, and for the first time that day Nick cracked a smile at his friend.

'I can't believe we got away,' mused Nick as he walked back to what was left of the helm.

'No, me neither, and I wish I had had a camera handy when Duggan told you his escape plan. You should have seen your face when he told you it involved you sailing this beauty out of Kaliningrad, it was priceless.'

'Pah, piece of cake,' scoffed Nick with a huge grin on his face.

For the next hour they sailed quietly out of the Baltic Sea and back into the North Sea keeping the dangerous sandbanks to their south. It was now three thirty in the afternoon and the winter sun was quickly heading for the protection of the horizon. Anna kept flitting in and out, monitoring the radio and popping down to give the crew their hourly updates.

By four p.m. they were clothed in a blanket of darkness and, with very little lighting left working on the bridge, Nick and Jim were starting to rely on instinct as much as anything else.

At four fifteen p.m. Anna arrived with some huge mugs of tomato soup that she had discovered in the mess. She continued to talk excitedly about her tour of the ship and finding the crew members and seemed to the two men to be perfectly at home in the situation she now found herself in. Jim made a mental note to himself that if their relationship continued, as he hoped it would, never to underestimate her abilities.

Nick in the meantime was barking out his instructions from the chart table carefully calculating where and when the course changes needed to take place, while Jim stood stoically at the helm making the course changes with the help of a cobbled-together binnacle, housing a spare compass they had found in a locker underneath the chart table. Anna, who was now also dressed in a fetching orange survival suit which was at least four sizes too big for her, kept watch with a pair of powerful night vision binoculars.

It was at about five thirty that Anna first spotted another ship on their port side. She was a good size although not as big as the *Tricolor* and seemed to be on a heading very similar to their own.

'Better keep an eye on her,' said Nick who had also spotted the vessel. 'I know the bridge is pretty beaten up but the rest of the ship is well lit so she should be aware we are here.'

Over the next few minutes, they all watched as the ship got closer and closer. Nick moved across to the map table and looked for any shipping lanes that ran close to where they were currently positioned, but with no GPS to help him his exact position was, by modern shipping standards, a little vague.

Nick turned to Jim.

'Go and see if you can raise them on the radio and make them aware of our situation, we don't want any accidents after what we've been through.'

'Aye Aye, Captain,' he replied, mostly for the benefit of Anna who was now pushing all the broken glass into a corner with a large shovel she had found in the cleaning cupboard.

'You two work well together,' she commented as she

paused to catch her breath.

'I put it down to life experience and respect. I believe that as you go through life there are things that happen to you that shape your life and make you follow one course or another. It's all down to timing in the end. Jim's been through what he's been through, I've been through what I've been through and those two life cycles came together about five years ago. Either of us could have taken a different course at any time during the previous thirty years that would have not matched us up, but we didn't and consequently here we are, getting on like a house on fire, due in part at least to our life journey so far.'

'That's an interesting take on it,' said Anna.

'Think about it,' continued Nick. 'How many times have you heard stories about couples meeting up many years after their initial meeting or friendship only to fall head over heels in love with the same person they didn't give a second glance all those years earlier? The only thing that has changed over the years is their life journey; everything else is the same, they still come from the same family, their background and upbringing hasn't suddenly altered. It's like their lives have run parallel courses and then something just brings them together and boom, its wedding bells!'

Anna stood silently deep in thought for a few moments.

'Not convinced eh?'

'No to the contrary, I was just thinking of where we would be right now had you, Jim, me and Duggan not converged together over the last two days. In fact, I don't think we would be standing here now had those life's journeys not brought us all together in that huge apocalyptic moment in Kaliningrad.'

Now it was Nick's turn to stand and think.

In the radio room Jim had been unable to raise the mystery ship on any of the recognised frequencies. He was just about to report back to Nick when he heard Duncan calling him from the *Sandie Watson*.

'*Sandie Watson* this is *Tricolor* over.'

'Jim, its Duncan over.'

'Hi Duncan, boy am I glad to hear your voice, how are you doing? Over.'

'It's a long story, but let's just say if you hadn't warned us about Sergei's gin palace, we wouldn't be having this conversation now. Sandie's a bit shot up and we had to sacrifice Tiny, but no one was hurt in the skirmish and we are now en route back to Harwich. How are you guys doing? Over.'

Jim went on to fill Duncan in with the missing pieces that he hadn't relayed to RB about what had happened in Kaliningrad and how they had hooked up with Anna and Duggan.

'So, let me recap,' said Duncan. 'You are now on board the *Tricolor* proper with its original cargo of BMWs worth about fifty million pounds. You've hooked up with an ex-SAS assassin and a crazy Russian woman who both know how to handle themselves and, having blasted your way out of Kaliningrad, the *Tricolor* now looks like a piece of Gouda. You're now making for Hull with a captain who, excuse the pun is way out of his depth, you have no navigation, no instrumentation, and a working crew of five, one of which is completely oblivious to what's been going on around him, how am I doing? Over.'

'That pretty much sums it up, glad you were paying attention, over,' concurred Jim.

'Never a dull moment, hey! Listen I may be able to offer you guys some comfort. I've just come off the line with RB and the authorities are treating what's been going on as Acts off Piracy.

Apparently, *The Times* ran a story this morning about what happened in Kaliningrad following a post on the Internet showing a huge gun battle in the port. Somehow, they have put two and two together and most of Fleet Street are now metaphorically banging on RB's door requesting more information on the *Tricolor* and your involvement. Not only that, Whitehall have also got involved and it has just transpired that the PM is now asking for the Royal Navy to come and escort you back into British Territorial Waters. We don't have any details yet but we have been asked to ask you to keep an ear open for a message from Her Majesty's Navy so they can arrange a rendezvous point, over.'

'That might be easier said than done, as I've already explained we haven't got any navigational aids other than a botched-up compass and a set of nautical charts.'

As Jim was finishing the sentence Anna appeared in the door of the radio room.

'Looks like I'm needed back on the bridge Duncan, I'll radio you again in an hour and give you an update, over.'

'Okay, understood. Take care of yourselves, over and out.'

'Will do, out.'

Jim looked up at Anna, her eyes twinkling in the half-light of the radio room.

'The unidentified ship is keeping station on our port side, but Nick thinks we are approaching another sandbar which will force her away from us for a few miles. Any luck raising her on the radio?'

'No nothing, either they are not manning the radio which is highly unlikely considering the close proximity of the two vessels, or they are choosing to ignore me which is probably far more worrying.

'I'd better head back to the bridge. Do you know how to operate the radio?'

'I'm ex-army, of course I know how to operate a radio.' Anna replied indignantly.

Jim quickly filled her in on the Royal Navy situation before zipping up his survival suit and heading for the door. As he left, he gave her a smack on the bum.

'How wude!' she exclaimed mimicking Jar Jar Binks from the *Star War* movies.

Jim laughed before heading back down the short corridor to the darkness of the ship's bridge.

'She looks further away,' said Jim nodding to the shadow on their port side.

Nick followed his gaze out through the smashed windows.

'They have got to avoid a large sandbar out there, so we should be fine for the next half-hour or so. Any luck raising them on the radio?'

Jim quickly explained how he had tried unsuccessfully to raise their neighbours and the radio message he had had from Duncan, taking care to leave out the bit about the *Sandie Watson* being shot up by the crew of Sergei's motor yacht and the loss of Tiny.

'So, we have got Her Majesty's Navy coming to help us out. Hope they arrive pretty damn quick 'cause I'm not entirely sure those guys' intentions are very honourable.' Nick waved at the port side of the ship before continuing.

'Besides which it goes against just about every rule in the

maritime handbook to ignore another vessel's radio calls, especially when the two ships are this close together.'

'Maybe their radio is down?' offered Jim.

'Very unlikely, besides they will have a backup, failing that they could always use a signalling lamp, or at this range a good megaphone. Can you remember what our friend Mr Petrov's other ships were called? It could just be one of those!'

'They were the *Martina* and *Anouska*, both small-sized container carriers which, if I remember RB correctly, plied their trade between several European ports dropping off container loads of reconditioned BMW parts for Sergei's network of spares suppliers.'

Nick thought about this for a moment and then turned and looked at the faint lights of ship running a parallel course their own.

'Size and shape fits.'

Nick fudged the radio Duggan had given him out of his survival suit pocket and putting on his best Norwegian accent hailed the ex-SAS man.

Duggan's initial reply was almost drowned out by the din from the engines but, after a few seconds and with a bulkhead door between him and the engine room, he could be more clearly heard.

'How's it going down there?' asked Nick still maintaining the accent until he knew for sure that Leonard was not within earshot.

'All clear,' stated Duggan before going on to explain the story he had given his young charge about having to now sail to Rotterdam where they would be reunited with the rest of the crew.

'Sounds like there's a new career in estate agency

awaiting you when we get back to the UK, I haven't heard that much bullshit since I sold my last house.'

'Now there's a thought,' he quipped, 'what's up?'

'We need you up on the bridge, there's another ship tracking us on an identical course and speed and it's starting to give me the willies. We know that Sergei has a couple of small container vessels in his fleet ferrying parts around Europe, have you seen these ships? And if so, would you be able to identify them in the dark?'

'Yes, I've seen both of these ships and yes I'm fairly confident I should be able to recognise if it's the *Martina* or *Anouska*. Give me a couple of more minutes to further hone my "estate agency" skills on Leonard and I'll be right up.'

The radio went dead and Jim looked at Nick

'Time for another plan B, I think.'

17

It took five minutes for Duggan to reach the bridge and he was still zipping up his survival suit when he peered out of the shattered port side windows at the mystery ship.

They were now coming to the end of the sandbar and his job was made that much easier by their nemesis starting to converge on their course once again.

'So, what do you think?' asked Jim.

'It's the *Anouska,*' replied Duggan confidently. 'I recognise the configuration of the bridge windows, the position of the life raft and the general profile of the whole ship, no doubt about it.'

Nick moved back across to the chart table and Jim retook the helm.

'From the charts it looks like we are in open water now for a while, so I think if she is going to make a move it will be quite soon. Duggan, can you see if you can find a signal lamp? I want to try one more attempt at contacting them before we consider her totally hostile.'

'Okay, but I tell you it's definitely the *Anouska.*'

Duggan headed off the bridge passing Anna on his way out.

'What's the latest then?' asked Jim as she sidled up to the helm.

'Good news at last,' she replied with a smile, 'the Navy

vessel RB was talking about has been in touch. She's called the HMS *Quorn* and depending on *our* course and speed which I was unable to accurately give, the first officer reckons she should be with us inside the hour. I told them about our neighbours and he said to keep them informed of developments. Apparently, they have scrambled a helicopter from RAF Wattisham to locate our exact position. What's RAF Wattisham?'

'It's a Royal Air Force base in Suffolk. That's good, we need all the help we can get right now.'

At that moment Duggan reappeared clutching a signal lamp.

'What do you want me to say to them?' he asked Nick.

'Simply ask them to identify themselves.'

Duggan went to the end of the wing bridge and started to signal his message before the lamp suddenly exploded in his hands.

'Shit!' he cried before throwing himself to the floor, closely followed by Jim, Nick and Anna.

A split second later the bridge was once again rifled with small arms fire.

'For fuck's sake!' shouted out Nick, 'do all Sergei's ships carry a full arsenal Duggan?'

'So it would fucking seem!' he shouted back clearly angry with himself for not factoring that into the equation.

'Duggan, you okay?' asked Jim, as another salvo pinged in above them.

'Okay,' came the reply.

'Nick? Anna?'

'Okay', 'okay.'

A third round of bullets rattled it way around the already

devastated bridge.

'Time for Plan B methinks!' shouted Jim at Nick as the ricochets subsided once more.

Nick took a quick peek at the *Anouska* before another burst of gunfire erupted into the bridge of the *Tricolor*.

'Have we got anything to fight back with Duggan?'

Duggan was already halfway across the bridge floor, his hands and knees picking up small glass shards that Anna's shovel had failed to catch with every movement. He had propped the semi-automatic rifle up against the wall at the back of the bridge thinking it was done with and for the second time in a minute he was cursing his lack of forethought. What had happened to that killing machine that went to Northern Ireland, he thought, as he painfully made his way across what seemed to be the longest twenty feet he had ever had to cover?

'I'm on it,' he grimaced as he reached the weapon.

'Anna gets back to the radio room and let the Navy know we are under attack. Jim you're with me, Duggan hold your fire for a moment or two.'

Anna was down on her hands and knees tucking her hands up into her survival suit sleeves to try and avoid the glass. As she neared the entrance to the corridor where the radio room was located another burst of fire came in, a stray bullet grazing her rear on its pinball excursion around the steel walls.

She let out a small scream before dropping to her stomach and continuing the final part of her journey commando style.

'You okay?' shouted Jim.

'Just a graze!' she shouted back as she reached the safety of the corridor.

Nick was now positioned at the helm with Jim beside him. Nick killed the engines for ten seconds before pushing them forward to their stops. The ship lazily started to slow and then equally slowly started to gain momentum again. By now the *Anouska* had gained half a ship's length on them and the two men gave each other a nod before taking turns to pull down on the ship's wheel. They felt the *Tricolor* swing to the port under them and then, as they straightened their course, they ducked down to floor level waiting for the next blast of incoming fire.

Duggan worked out what they were doing and immediately let out a burst of automatic fire at the *Anouska*. The fire was immediately returned and he dived for cover, landing with a groan as a slightly larger shard of glass punctured his survival suit and buried itself in his stomach.

Unbeknown to those on the *Tricolor*, on realising that their quarry had now turned aggressor, the captain of the *Anouska* had steered hard to starboard to try and lessen the impact from the slightly larger vessel.

'Brace yourselves!' shouted Nick as loud as he could to try and ensure Anna heard the warning. Seconds later there was an almighty crash as the two ships met and their forward momentum was temporarily stalled. This was quickly followed by an ear-shattering graunching noise as the twisted remains of the *Anouska's* stern scraped along the hull of the *Tricolor*.

Unable to see what was happening, Nick now gunned the engines in what he thought was an effort to push the *Anouska* out of their path, but instead of more graunching and wrenching of metal against metal, all they heard and felt was the sound of the massive engines below thumping them forward, unabated.

Giving Jim a puzzled look he peered forward out of the

glass-less frames and just saw darkness.

Leaping to his feet he ran to the starboard wing bridge and watched as the fully lit *Anouska* wafted past the stern of the *Tricolor*, her own stern in tatters and obviously taking on water fast.

'She must have turned into us to try and lessen the impact,' said a puzzled Nick still watching as the lights of the stricken vessel disappeared behind them.

'Looks like she didn't turn quick enough though, we caught her stern with our bow, not much of a competition really when you consider how much metal there is at the front of one of these babies.'

The three men stood in shocked silence for a moment realising how lucky they had been before Nick brought them back to reality.

'Right Jim, I need you to take one of the radios and go down to the lower decks and see if we have sustained any damage ourselves. Duggan go and give your new friend in the engine room some more *Jackanory* time, and one of you see if Anna is okay.'

'On my way,' said Jim the relief of yet another averted disaster written all over his face.

Duggan removed his survival suit and thought about how the hell he was going to explain this latest incident to Leonard, surely there was only so much baloney the young engineer could digest? The truth he decided was the way forward, so with the machine gun still firmly grasped in his hand he headed off to tell Leonard what was going to seem like the most far-fetched story he had ever heard. He decided that it would depend on how aware Leonard was of Sergei's nefarious operations as to whether he would need the machine gun or not.

On his way down through the ship he stopped to remove the glass from his hands, knees and stomach and was pleased to note that it looked a lot worse than it was and, although very sore, none of his wounds were, in army terms at least anything more than superficial. It also meant that trying to bullshit Leonard whilst standing in front of him with heavily bloodstained clothing and hands was definitely not going to work. Smiling to himself he concluded that even estate agents had to tell the truth, sometimes.

Now once again alone on the freezing bridge, Nick steadied the throttles before thinking about the poor souls he had just left behind on the *Anouska*. It went against every bone in his seafaring body to not turn back and try to save some of the crew, but it had become very clear to him over the last few days that these guys did not play by the rules, at least not any rules that he was familiar with.

He settled his conscience in the knowledge that they would all be able to abandon ship with the help of lifeboats and rafts and a cold night on the North Sea would be a holiday camp compared to what the legal system would throw at them when they got picked up later by some heavily armed naval vessel.

He checked their heading once again and was cross referencing this against the charts when Anna appeared beside him.

'Hey how is it in radio room land?'

'It was fine until you decided to go from about ten knots to standstill in a second. What happened?'

Nick explained that he and Jim had decided that the best form of defence was going to be attack when the time came and how lucky they were when the signal lamp got shot out of Duggan's hand.

'That was the tipping point, we then knew for sure that it was the *Anouska* and that their intentions were hostile, they played straight into our hands. What we didn't bet on was the captain swinging her hard to starboard rather than port. We took a huge chunk out of her stern, I just hope we haven't damaged the *Tricolor* too badly, Jim is down there now checking for leaks. You okay?'

'Bit bruised and I've got a groove across my bottom, but apart from that I'm fine. I was talking with the *Quorn* when you hit the *Anouska,* they said the helicopter should be with us in about ten minutes.' She looked down at her watch. 'Anytime now in fact.'

Nick grabbed a pair of binoculars from a rack at the rear of the bridge and checked them for damage.

'How the hell did they survive?' he muttered to himself before raising them to his eyes and scanning the sky ahead.

'Nick? This is Jim over.'

Nick fumbled around in the survival suit pockets and pulled out the radio.

'Hi Jim, how's it looking down there? Over.'

'Surprisingly good all things considered, the bow doors are damaged and leaking what seems to be a lot of water, but I've been watching the water levels down here for five minutes or so and it appears the pumps are coping well 'cause the level is holding steady. Looks like we have got Lady Luck riding with us on this trip, over.'

'We have Jim and she's standing beside me; she says she's going to need a bit of patching up on her keel but apart from that, she's fine.'

'Keep an eye on that water level for a few more minutes, do the bow doors look like they could collapse? Over?'

'No, on the contrary they have been pushed slightly into the ship, I'm no engineer but I don't think they are going to be going anywhere soon, I just hope we don't get the bill for putting this right, it's a bit of a mess, over.'

Nick chuckled. 'I tell you what, if we get this cargo back to Hull, I don't think they will be worrying about a few hundred thousands of repair bills. Radio me back in fifteen minutes with an update, over.'

'Roger that, over and out.'

As he stuffed the radio back in his pocket, Nick spotted a bright light coming towards them at some speed.

'Here come the cavalry.'

Anna gave him a strange look.

'It means here come the good guys.'

They both watched as the lights got closer and closer. Although the bridge had been through a war zone the rest of the ship was still well lit and it didn't take the Sea King long to home in on the *Tricolor*.

'You had better get back to the radio Anna, they are probably trying to raise us.'

'You okay up here on your own?' she asked.

'You bet, I've done quite a few graveyard shifts in my time, this is just one more to add to the history books.

As she disappeared, Nick watched the helicopter approach, slowing as it reached the *Tricolor*. It then disappeared from view before reappearing over the bow.

'They are going to land someone on the bow,' shouted Anna from the corridor, 'the pilot has asked that you maintain course and speed until he is down.'

'Understood.'

The Sea King moved into position and a bright spotlight lit up the deck in front of them.

With the overspill from the spotlight Nick took a look around him.

'Oh my God,' he muttered to himself as he surveyed the carnage. There was barely a square foot anywhere that had not got a bullet hole in it or a dent where the bullet hadn't had enough energy left in it to fully penetrate.

All that was left of the windows were jagged edges like rows of small piranha teeth ready to inflict some serious damage to anyone who ventured near. As he looked into the corner of the bridge where Anna had shovelled the glass, he realised why every footstep taken earlier had been accompanied by a loud crunch, the large heap containing not only glass, but wood, chunks of metal and seemingly hundreds of spent rounds of ammunition, it was going to take a cleaning crew hours to get the bridge clean and free of debris. Even the ceiling, which had started out life as a minor masterpiece to the carpenter who had built it, was raked with bullets and here and there large chunks of beautifully finished pine were hanging down ready to stab the unwary. Nick took the opportunity to pull loose the bits around him before turning and brushing out the captain's chair of debris. As he did so he noticed how bloodied his hands were and held each one up to the light in turn to check for any major lacerations. There was nothing obvious but the tiny stabs of pain that accompanied every grip told him that he had inherited some foreign bodies somewhere along the way.

He was suddenly aware of the downdraft of the Sea King above him and put his forearm across his face to shield his eyes as an assortment of debris started to blow around the bridge. From behind his raised arm, he caught sight of a bright orange body descending to the fore deck of the *Tricolor*. Seconds later he was down and shining a torch towards the bridge. Above him the Sea King moved away slightly taking its downdraft with it and Nick lowered his arm to find the orange-suited winchman had disappeared.

It took less than a minute for him to find his way to the bridge and he came towards Nick, hand outstretched.

'Sergeant Andy Wilkins at your service, please, call me Andy, wow! It must have been one hell of a party you had here,' he said sweeping his flashlight around what was left of the bridge.

'Nick Edwards, yes it got a bit out of hand I'm afraid! Still all the best ones do, don't they?'

'Mmmm,' came the reply. 'Look, I think you had better fill me in on the story here, we have only got a very sketchy description of what you guys have been through, hence they have asked me to come aboard and get some more details. The guys upstairs,' he pointed his finger skywards, 'will want know I'm okay down here, so firstly are there any hostiles on board?'

Nick started by telling Andy who was on board including the good news about the crew and the bad news that they were going to have to stay there and why. He then went on explain the story so far focusing mainly on the events following their arrival in Kaliningrad. As he finished Jim hailed him on the radio, leaving Andy Wilkins to radio his colleagues hovering above.

'Jim to Nick, over.'

'Hi Jim, this is Nick, how's it looking down there? Over.'

'Good news, if anything the water level has actually subsided, over'

'Thank god for that, might as well head back up here then, I'm gonna need all the help I can get as we get nearer our destination, over.'

'No problem, I'm on my way, over and out.'

Five minutes later Jim had been introduced to Andy, as had Anna who had now abandoned the radio room.

Andy explained that the Sea King would hold station for another twenty minutes, by which time the *Quorn* would be within sight, and they would swap over responsibility for the *Tricolor*.

Anna beckoned Jim towards her and whispered something in his ear.

'Just got to attend to something in the radio room,' he announced before following Anna off the bridge.

Once in the radio room Anna closed the door and struggled out of her survival suit before dropping her jeans, pointing Jim to a first aid kit on the desk beside her. Jim stood shocked, momentarily looking at Anna's white knickers that were now mostly red. On her left cheek there was a tear of about four inches long across her knickers and beneath the torn material he could see a groove of about the same length through the flesh.

'Oh sweetheart,' he said and Anna turned around to face him, a smile on her face.

'What?'

'You've never called me that before.'

Jim's face started to redden.

'Sorry,' he blurted out trying to recover the situation.

'Don't be sorry, I know in your language it is a term of

313

affection. Thank you.'

Before he could react, she continued:

'Now I am going to remove my panties and bend over the desk so you can clean me up and apply a dressing to the wound. And no funny business, okay? This is not the time or the place.'

She kissed him lightly on the lips before turning and removing her knickers and bending over. For the smallest of moments Jim stood looking at the pert little bum in front of him, lustful thoughts racing through his head.

'Jim.'

'Okay, I'm on it.'

He picked up the bottle of saline solution and a wad of cotton wool and cleaned her up. The blood had run down her leg and, without asking, Anna parted her legs slightly to allow him to clean her inside leg. The temptation was far too much for Jim to take and he lightly ran his wad of cotton wool up to the top of her leg and lightly touched her pussy with the top of his hand. Much to his surprise she was quite moist but, when he moved up again, she reached down and slapped his hand.

'Jiiimm.'

Chastised he refocused and took a look at the wound itself that was about the size and depth of a drinking straw and had already stopped bleeding. As gently as he could he applied some antiseptic cream to the wound and then gently taped a large gauze pad to it, patting her other cheek as he finished.

Anna reached for her jeans and pulled them back on before stepping back into her survival suit.

'Thank you,' she said, 'I have to admit that was very strangely quite erotic.'

'Mmmm, you too,' he replied glancing down at the bulge

in his trousers.

They kissed long and hard, before Anna pulled away and opened the door.

'About time I went and serviced the other men up here,' she said winking at him before heading towards the galley to make some coffee and sandwiches.

A few minutes later Jim returned to the bridge and took over the helm as Nick re-calculated their course.

'We will get you a pilot on board when we arrive at the mouth of the Humber,' Andy informed them. 'He will know the terrain and currents and bring you safely into port, I believe a special pier has been reserved for the *Tricolor*, slightly away from the main port. It will give you a bit of privacy for a few hours while HM Customs and the police carry out their respective investigations.'

'Do they know we have several foreign nationals on board with no documentation?' asked Jim, very aware that Anna was in a very precarious position as far as immigration was concerned, and that Duggan was officially still wanted by the army for going AWOL.

'By the time you reach port I will have written my report, so yes they should be aware of the situation, but, off the record, I think you guys need to get together and work out what you are going to tell the authorities.'

Nick looked at Jim and Anna.

'This whole escapade has been so far-fetched I don't think we have much choice other than tell them the truth,' he commented. 'They probably won't believe it anyway, Christ, when I think of what we've been through in the last few days, even I don't believe it!'

Anna and Jim nodded in agreement.

Down in the engine room Duggan was facing a very bewildered-looking junior engineer. His decision to tell Leonard the full story of what was going on had been an easy one to make, but in practice trying to convince him that Sergei had International Mafia connections and was as bad as any man he had ever met was proving a hard story to tell. Leonard was finding this very difficult to take in, quite understandably, and was more than a little concerned about what would happen to him once they had docked in the UK.

Unbeknown to Leonard, Duggan was also wondering what the future held and although he wouldn't have too many issues on the immigration front, once the authorities found out that he was back on UK soil there was no telling where he would end up.

18

As predicted, it took twenty minutes for the *Quorn* to arrive over the horizon and make contact with the *Tricolor*. Nick held his speed and heading and the *Quorn* performed a large loop which brought the grey minesweeper up on their starboard side.

From her station the Sea King now moved in once again and took up position over the bow.

Finishing a conversation on his radio Andy made his way over to Nick on the helm.

'I'm just going to lower the gangplank down so the Navy can get a small crew aboard to assist and then I'll be off. It's been an honour to meet you guys, I can't believe what you've been through over the last few days! Best of luck.'

'Funny you should say that,' chuckled Nick 'thanks for your help and look after yourself.'

The two men shook hands and Andy disappeared down the corridor at the back of the bridge.

Jim and Anna reappeared from the radio room and relayed to Nick that the *Quorn* was going to send an inflatable across with four crew members to join them and act as a communication link between themselves and the minesweeper.

'Looks like we are home and dry,' commented Jim looking across at the grey silhouette of the *Quorn* beside them.

Although a lot smaller than the *Tricolor* and by naval ship standards quite lightly armed, it was clear, even to the untrained eye, that she would be a formidable adversary, should any more of Sergei's fleet approach them on the final leg of their voyage.

Nick looked at his orange-suited friend and gave him a weary smile.

'Yes, now just remind me what your job description was when you joined Flatpack.'

Jim thought for a moment.

'Mmmm, I think it went something like helping out Nick and his crew to investigate possible fraudulent marine claims.'

'So no mention of kidnap, criminal damage, gunfights, hijacking of ships, or any number of other maritime misdemeanours then?'

'Err no, I guess Nigel forgot to add those in, he didn't mention any danger money either.'

'If we were going to get danger money, I think you and I are staring retirement in the face right now,' smiled Nick.'

'A nice new BMW would be good,' offered Jim. 'what about you Anna?'

'I don't know much about cars, but when I was growing up my father's big dream was to one day own a Lada; can you get them in the UK?'

Jim looked at Anna with a mixture of surprise and amusement on his face, turned to Nick and both men burst into laughter.

'I think we can do better than that,' said Jim

'I know you can get better cars but I still want one, if only to remind me of my father.'

Jim looked hard at Anna and from the determined look on

her face suddenly realised that she was actually quite serious about her request.

'Okay, okay, I'll tell you what, when we get home, I will buy you the best Lada we can find, how does that sound?'

Anna gave out a little squeal of delight, threw her arms around Jim's neck and kissed him several times in quick succession.

'Thank you, thank you, thank you,' she squeaked between kisses like an excited teenager who had just got her first late night pass from her father.

Jim turned to Nick and both men shrugged to each other.

The Navy personnel sent over from the *Quorn* included a medical officer and over the next hour he slowly and meticulously removed all the shards of glass and wood that had embedded themselves in the makeshift crew. Once discharged they took turns to shower in the captain's cabin and put on some fresh clothes.

They re-convened in the galley where they sat quietly drinking coffee and eating some chocolate digestive biscuits Nick found in the pantry. They then took the opportunity to go onto the car decks and look at what all the fuss had been about.

Before them were hundreds of bright shiny new BMWs all tightly packed in with the keys in them ready to be off-loaded at Hull. Nick walked down a thin cordon on the right-hand side of the bay which was the only place there was access to the cars. Spotting a dark blue X5 he opened the door and climbed into the driver's seat, the smell of new leather engulfing him.

'Not bad,' he commented to Jim who stood beside him, 'wouldn't mind one of these.'

'You might have to raid your piggy bank.'

'How much are we looking at for one of these then?' asked Nick knowing Jim was into his cars.

'Depending on the spec I guess you're looking at 50k upwards.'

'Bloody hell, it's nice, but it's not *that* nice.'

Next stop was the radio room where they made contact with the *Sandie Watson* which was now safely back in port. Ewan filled them in on the full events of the last few days which included the news that during one of the dives on the *Baltic Carrier* they had taken a closer look at the bullet hole in the porthole. While close in they witnessed the grizzly sight of a body floating around in the cabin, and with the rest of the crew now accounted for, they could only conclude that this was the body of Captain Collins.

Ewan also told Nick about the attack on his vessel and the loss of Tiny and seemed a little surprised by his boss's lack of concern. It was only as Nick and Jim explained in full what they had been through, that Ewan began to realise that the loss of the little submersible and a few bullet holes was nothing compared with what they had encountered.

On their return to the bridge the *Quorn's* Commander, a lieutenant, warned them that they may have to face some media attention after they had been debriefed by BMW and the owners of the *Tricolor* who were desperately trying to play down the events of the previous few weeks that had resulted in the death of the captain on one of their vessels.

It was seven o'clock in the morning when they first caught sight of the UK once again. Behind them the sea and sky were turning crimson as the sun began to climb its way over the horizon. Ahead was a twinkling patchwork of lights that

320

initially got stronger with each nautical mile covered before dimming once again as the ambient light from the sun's reappearance dulled their effect.

Duggan had been relieved of babysitting Leonard in the engine room and as they neared the port all four of them stood shoulder to shoulder on the bridge watching as Grimsby and Cleethorpes loomed up before them.

About a mile out they noticed a small vessel heading their way with the pilot on board. The boat arced around them and from the wing bridge Jim saw another orange suit jump expertly from the boat to the still-lowered gangplank. The pilot boat turned away back into open water before speeding back to the port. The pilot made his way up to the bridge and greeted the waiting team.

'Good morning gentlemen,' he greeted before noticing that one of the orange suits was a woman, 'and lady' he added in an official sort of way.

Surprisingly he made no comment on the state of his office for the next hour or so, his only action being to gently kick some debris to one side before planting his feet on the newly uncovered carpet and wriggling his boots from side to side to ensure he had a good firm stance.

He then began to advise the Navy helmsman on speed and heading seemingly oblivious to the fact he was standing in what was nothing more than a shell of a ship's bridge.

As they entered the mouth of the Humber, they felt the ship start to get pulled about by the tidal surge heading out to sea.

'That's why the big boys have a pilot,' commented Nick to Jim, 'very easy to get caught up in a current and end up stuck on a sandbank without the right knowledge on board.'

As the pilot pointed out various markers for the helmsman to follow, Nick's eye spied three figures standing at the end of Spurn Point, a long spit of land that stretches out from the northern shore of the estuary.

The desolated position struck him as a strange point to be standing, especially at this early hour and his confusion was added to when he realised that the figures were all female, wearing long dark coats and shared the same long blonde hair.

As he watched the centre figure stepped forward and produced a wreath from behind her back. With the *Tricolor* now at it closest point to the shore she stepped up to the shoreline and threw the wreath with all her might into the sea.

Stepping back, she linked arms with the other two figures and all three bowed their heads.

It took them a further half-hour to navigate their way up the Humber. As they neared Kingston upon Hull, they started a starboard turn into the inner dock.

As they broke water in the dock Nick and Jim were joined on the bridge by Anna and Duggan who had been on another coffee run. The Navy helmsman under direction of the pilot once again swung the ship to starboard towards a large dockside shed. It was only then that they spotted the reception committee.

'Bloody hell,' mumbled Jim.

'What the?' added Nick.

In front of them was a dockside, crowded six-deep with film crews, photographers and seemingly thousands of assorted onlookers, some smartly dressed in suits, some in jeans and fleeces. Further down the quay there were six large TV outside broadcast vehicles with huge satellite disks on their roofs all pointing skywards, streaming their feeds out to the World.

Towards the front of the crowd was a selection of uniforms, police, army, customs and excise personnel and, slightly less formally attired, what Jim guessed were immigration officers.

Duggan looked at Anna and puffed out his cheeks.

'I've seen some reception committees in my time but this certainly takes the biscuit, looks like we might have a few questions to answer.'

Anna moved over to Jim and cuddled up beside him.

'I don't want to go back to Kaliningrad, I want to stay with you in the UK.'

'Don't worry I'm sure we can do some sort of deal, especially after you've just helped bring home fifty million pounds' worth of BMWs. As they say money talks.'

Jim glanced at Duggan as Anna snuggled closer.

'How the hell did they know to turn up?'

Duggan was staring out at the military police clearly wondering what the next few hours were going to hold for him.

'Sergei had a lot of "contacts",' he replied putting the *contacts* in air quotes for emphasis. 'Once it was clear that we were home and dry Anouska must have been straight on the phone to someone high up over here who is now going to be dining out on my name for the next few weeks.'

'We'll do what we can,' offered Jim.

'Thanks, but I'm not sure you are going to be able to save me from my past, I've crossed too many people in high places over the years.'

'We'll just have to wait and see,' said Jim, hoping to calm the thoughts racing around in Duggan's head.

It took another fifteen minutes to bring the vessel to a halt alongside the quay and for the mooring to be deemed secure. The pilot thanked everyone for their help before heading back down the gangplank to be verbally assaulted by the world's press, keen to be the first to get the story. His somewhat stoic demeanour was reflected in his only comment to a reporter following a question as to the state of the bridge on the *Tricolor*.

'I am a ship's pilot, employed to oversee the safe passage of ships large and small in and out of this wonderful port. It is not part of my remit to comment on the tidiness or cleanliness of the ships I board or their crew, I thank you.'

With that he strode out along the quay doing a very passable impression of a ship's bow wave, the twenty or so reporters and cameramen fanning out in his wake before slowly dissipating behind him as they realised, he had made his one and only comment.

The rest of the day was spent in a state of organised chaos with the various enforcement bodies initially holding discussions on the dockside as to who should be the first to board the *Tricolor*. It didn't take long for them to work out that airing their requirements in front of the world's press was maybe not such a wise move and an agreement was quickly made to post a dual guard of military police and local police at the gangplank to secure the area, before continuing their discussions behind closed doors.

By ten am the situation had been made considerably worse when the CEO of BMW Europe, Gerard Muller arrived with a posse of legal experts, who seemed in no mood to compromise with anyone. As far as he was concerned it was his cargo and he should have access to it and be the first to thank the men and woman who brought it back home safely!

A few seconds later, after a very upright no-nonsense British army colonel had pointed out that the ship could still be hiding some gun-toting Russians, his keenness to board the ship had waned slightly and he then agreed with the consensus that the first move should be to send an army team on board to make sure the ship was fully secure and to safely remove any weaponry.

On board the *Tricolor* the mood was sombre. Nick and Jim were both deeply concerned about how things were going to pan out for their two newfound friends. It was now four nights since they had slept soundly in a bed and the acute tiredness was starting to affect their reasoning.

Strong black coffee seemed to be the only thing keeping them going and the initial fractious discussions between the various parties who wanted a slice of their pie had done little to persuade them that now would be a good time to grab a few hours' kip.

It was ten thirty when Nick was told to meet the army colonel at the top of the gangplank.

At his request Nick led him up to the bridge and introduced him to Jim, Anna and Duggan. As he shook Duggan's hand Nick noticed a slight adjustment in the colonel's stance which told him very clearly that the authorities were very aware of his history and that this particular officer was leaving nothing to chance.

'Good morning Lady and Gentlemen,' he said in a strong welsh accent. My name is Colonel Williams and I will be in charge here for the next few hours while we secure the ship. Firstly, can I ask you all to surrender any weapons you may have on your persons?'

Anna moved forward and put her handgun on the chart table along with three clips of ammunition.

Duggan responded by slowly turning around and lifting his jacket by the fingertips to reveal the handgun tucked down the waistband of his trousers. The sergeant who had accompanied the colonel onto the bridge gently removed the gun and emptied the chamber before adding it to Anna's on the table. Still without uttering a word Duggan now gently lifted his right trouser leg to reveal a second weapon strapped to his ankle. With this also removed, the sergeant gave him an enquiring look.

'Try the left ankle,' he stated matter of factly, 'and you may wish to remove my jacket?'

The sergeant bent down once again and removed a flick knife from Duggan's left boot before unzipping his jacket and handing it to another colleague.

Nick, Jim and Anna stood and watched in awe as the jacket gave up its contents. Two stun grenades, four clips of ammunition, a throwing knife and another Glock handgun were laid out on the chart table.

'Anything else?' The colonel asked Duggan in a resigned voice.

'Yes, you've missed two craft knife blades in the collar of the jacket.'

The colonel cursed under his breath before smiling at Duggan and nodding at his colleague, who was now feeling his way around the collar of the jacket. With the blades now removed the jacket was handed back and all four were then given a full pat down for any other concealed weapons.

'Okay this is how it's gonna work. We are here to make

this vessel safe and to remove all weaponry from the ship along with any hostiles. The crew who I am led to believe are secured in the recreation room, will be released and then taken to a local Territorial Army base where they can get cleaned up, give some statements and prepare to be sent home. Apparently, BMW have already offered to fly home any of the crew who wish to return to the Philippines, which I think is a very nice gesture. Anyway, moving on, I and a couple of senior police officers will now hold a debrief with you guys and then Nick and Jim will be taken to a local hotel where you will have a further debrief with the ship owners and BMW UK. They will also prepare a press statement for that lot down there,' he pointed at the quayside.

'What about Duggan and Anna?' asked Jim clearly concerned for their new friends' well-being.'

'Duggan, as you may be aware, is wanted by the military police and on leaving this ship will be arrested and taken to Credenhill base on the outskirts of Hereford where he will be asked some more "in depth" questions.'

Duggan shrugged his shoulders and gave his friends a resigned look.

'Credenhill is the home of the SAS and to be honest I expected nothing less,' he commented.

'And Anna?' said Jim looking the colonel square in the eyes.

'You, young lady, will need to be interviewed by immigration officials,' he replied looking at Anna. 'They will then decide if you can remain in the UK. Under the circumstances and with the information I have so far, I don't believe that will be a problem and once these guys have given their statements, which will hopefully corroborate what we already know, you should be free to join your friends again if that's what you wish?'

Anna just nodded her head.

'Any other questions?'

Duggan was the only one to speak.

'Down in the engine room you will find a young engineer called Leonard who will probably be scared shitless when several of your men enter the area. He has co-operated fully with us and as far as I am aware, he is the only crew member that is currently "loose" as it were, on the ship. The rest of the crew are locked in the recreation room behind a steel door for which I'm afraid I don't have a key.'

'Anything else?' asked Colonel Williams.

'Well, um, there are two crewmen, the Head Chef and a cleaner locked in the pantry in the galley and these guys will be pretty pissed, so may need handling with a little care.'

'Okay thank you, right let's get…'

Duggan cleared his throat noisily.

'Yes?' said the Colonel, turning back to Duggan.

On the same corridor you will also find a cupboard with the ship's Chief Engineer Vladimir Ruskov in it.'

'Okay, and is he likely to cause us any problems?'

Not wanting to shock Jim, Nick and Anna further, he moved forward and spoke quietly in the colonel's ear.

'Unlikely sir, he's got half of his head missing.'

The next two hours were spent relaying the story of what had happened, from Jim and Nick's first email from Lloyds with the details of the missing ship, to the point where they teamed up with Anna and Duggan and escaped Kaliningrad. At one p.m. they broke for lunch and it took them a further hour to relay the rest of the journey home including the encounter with the *Anouska* and the escort from HMS *Quorn*. By the time they had finished the men interviewing them sat back with completely stunned looks on their faces.

'Unbelievable, completely unbelievable,' was all the colonel could say, as he pondered the events and the odds that the four people in front of him had overcome.

It was three thirty p.m. by the time they left the ship and the four of them had a group hug at the bottom of the gangplank before heading their separate ways, much to the delight of the world's press who had been stood in the cold for most of the day. Cameras flashed in the fading light and reporters shouted questions at them from afar.

As Nick and Jim were ushered towards a black Range Rover they watched as Duggan was put into a cage in the back of a Military Police Transit van. Anna was escorted to a Silver Mondeo and soon disappeared from sight with seemingly half the world's press on her tail.

'What is it about the press in this country?' asked Jim a little perplexed by the way she had become the media's main interest.

Nick looked at his friend.

'A young pretty woman like Anna or a couple of grizzled old dogs like us, which one would you follow?'

Jim just nodded and settled down into the plush leather seats of the Range Rover.

The trip to the hotel was quite short and as they arrived in the foyer, they saw Nigel and RB heading towards them from the hotel bar accompanied by two men in suits, and a small entourage.

Nigel did the introductions.

'This is Gerard Muller, CEO of BMW Europe and this is Benjamin Goldsmith whose company owns the *Tricolor*.'

The four men shook hands before being taken to a small meeting room just off the main reception area.

Once seated with fresh cups of coffee, both of the company executives took it in turns to thank Nick and Jim for bringing the vessel and its cargo home safely.

Although they had been told to keep most of their story under wraps, it still took the rest of the afternoon for Jim and Nick to explain how they had managed to uncover the truth about the *Tricolor* and the fake cargo they had discovered on its sister vessel.

By the time they had finished answering questions and preparing a statement for the press it was nearly six p.m. and after saying goodbye to their two new best friends, and apologised for not being able to attend the press conference they flopped into the back of Nigel's E-Class Mercedes for the trip home.

It was eleven p.m. when Jim and Nick finally pulled up alongside the *Poacher* at Woodbridge. RB and Nigel had shared the driving from Hull on what turned out to be a clear and frost-free night, but now after nearly five days without any meaningful sleep Jim and Nick were literally the walking dead.

Woodbridge is a quiet place at the best of times, but at this time on a weekday night at the end of January, quiet took on a whole new meaning. Jim got out of the car first and slowly pushed on the door until the latch clicked it shut. Looking further up the quayside he noticed in the moonlight the tide was out. He was suddenly reminded of Catherine as he looked at the thousands of tiny footprints glistening in the muddy foreshore where the local bird life had been searching for a meal, but at this time even they had now turned in for the night.

Nick came up beside him and they stood and watched as RB and Nigel headed back to Ipswich ten miles away and the comfort of their own beds.

Both men stood silently, just breathing in the silence like a connoisseur sampling a good wine. Their lives had been a tortuous cacophony of noise over the last couple of days and the silence was now quite overwhelming.

It was a full five minutes before either man took a step towards the gangplank of the *Poacher* and then dropped onto the deck, their shoed feet seemingly making huge amounts of noise on the wooden deck.

As they opened the hatch to what was now the main cabin, the waft of over a hundred years of cargo hauling came up to meet them. They each rolled out their sleeping bags on the bunks, zipped themselves up fully clothed and wished each other good night and, seconds, later sleep overcame them both like a Hawaiian surf wave.

19

The next few weeks were spent dealing with the aftermath of the previous month with everyone and his dog wanting a piece of the action.

The press, were the biggest problem. They knew they had a big story and were determined to mine out every last seam of information about what had actually happened.

It didn't take them long to find the *Poacher*, which made that out of bounds for Nick and Jim, so they ended up once again lodging with Nigel and his family in Ipswich where the local constabulary managed to supply some help.

The MFI office was also staked out as was the BMW headquarters and Lloyds, the reporters all looking for a way into this biggest of scoops.

It had taken two days for Anna to be released from the custody of the immigration department following her request for asylum in the UK on the grounds that it would be dangerous for her to return to her homeland. As a very tired and frustrated Jim put it to the immigration official at the time 'no shit Sherlock!' which seemed to pretty much sum up the options available to her.

'That'll be another lodger for Nigel, then,' concluded Nick dryly as the judge gave his verdict.

While this was all taking place Jim and Nick were also

required to write a report of their findings and a full description of how the events unfolded. This report was to be given to the Military Police, Lloyds, the Home and Foreign Offices and BMW, and after two days of considerable work for Jim and Nick and a lot of help from RB, the report was sent out.

The next week was then spent answering further questions of a more detailed nature at various offices around London as each recipient's legal department did its best to cross the Ts and dot the Is and cover their backsides should it all escalate into some sort of international incident, which under the circumstances seemed quite plausible.

The Russians however were keeping very quiet about what, at least for the people of Kaliningrad, was a monumental event that touched the lives of a large proportion of the local population. Despite several requests from the Foreign Office the Russians were either unable, or unwilling, to shed any light on the incident, a stance that was both puzzling but also somehow quite reassuring for all the parties involved.

Duggan meanwhile was being held under heavy security at the Hereford base of the SAS and had chosen that his case should be heard as a court martial, which would hopefully help his case overall and keep the proceedings to a minimum. Nearly all court martials in the UK are held at either Aldergrove, Bulford, Catterick, Colchester or Portsmouth, but due to the highly sensitive nature of Duggan's case this one was to be especially convened with the Judge Advocate and the officers on the board coming to him rather than the other way around. Nigel had spoken to his bosses at Moore's & Thackery and got permission for a top military legal expert to be hired to help Duggan with his defence and, although nobody could be sure how the hearing would go on March 1st after what Duggan had been through prior to his going AWOL, the help he had given to the recovery of the *Tricolor* and the breaking up of what appeared to be one of Russia's largest mafia group's income stream, it seemed likely that his case would be looked on very favourably. Added to this was that in the years since he had left Northern Ireland the troubles had now pretty much come to an end, with peace at last ruling the streets of the province.

Anna meanwhile had quickly settled back into the English way of life and threw herself into helping out with Hannah and Georgia who seemed to love having someone else to make their sandwiches each day and Karen seemed happy to have some help with cooking a meal for them when they returned from school in the afternoon. After dinner each night she would then sit down with them and help with the homework assignments, although their English History homework was as much of an education for her as it was for the girls. After putting the girls to bed the five adults would either sit around and talk for a while or play gin rummy with Anna showing a skill at cards that left the others in her wake. 'Is there nothing this woman can't turn her hand to?' thought Jim as he was beaten once again by the beautiful Russian lady sitting opposite him at the table.

Although Nigel's invitation of refuge had been open ended, it was clearly not a long-term solution. The house was large with three en suite bathrooms, but there were still times when they all got under another's feet, so when Nigel called a meeting at the end of the third week Jim, Nick and Anna thought they could see the writing on the wall.

That evening they all sat down at the eight-foot-long oak

refectory table in the kitchen and Nigel began to talk through where they were at.

'I have decided to have this meeting here at home because there are some big decisions that I am going to require one or two of you to think about and I wanted to make sure you are all relaxed and in full listening mode rather than at work where, to be perfectly frank, it is complete chaos at the moment.'

'Sounds serious,' commented Jim.

'Serious yes! But hopefully in a good way. Now as you know this has been the biggest coup in the history of Moore's & Thackery and while you guys have been dealing with various meetings, writing reports and escaping the press on a regular basis, I have been involved in some talks with the directors about the fees that are applicable to this particular case and other aspects of the fallout from what happened in Kaliningrad.

'Nick, your fees will remain the same as usual, but obviously we will see you right for the damage sustained to the *Sandie Watson*, the loss of Tiny and also pay you and the crew out for the downtime you have had to put in place following your much publicised homecoming. The Board also want to discuss with you the possibility of getting either another vessel or updating the *Sandie Watson* still further at our expense. The enquiries we have had following your return have been off the scale and we are currently having to pull people from other parts of the business to cover off what's going on in Flatpack and we think this could be the start of a new era for the company.'

Nick cleared his throat as if to say something but Nigel held up his hand and asked him to let him finish.

'Anna, as I said since you guys arrived home, the phone hasn't stopped ringing with enquires from around the world and our website has crashed several times due to the level of interest being shown in our business. We now urgently need someone to help handle this business and with your language skills you would be very well suited to working alongside RB, although having read the reports, if it looks like it's going to erupt into a firefight I would just as soon have you beside me than anyone else sitting at this table.'

Nick and Jim smiled at the memory and before Anna could say anything Nigel once again held up his hand.

'Later.

'Okay now for the big news. As you are aware, we usually work for a set fee with Lloyds, they pay our expenses, your wages and then a percentage figure on top to keep everyone in business and make it all worthwhile. It's all very transparent and clear for everyone to see and no one gets ripped off.

'What you guys don't know, is that when our recently retired director, Rachel McIntyre, negotiated the deal she also had included a percentage of any monies raised from the sale of recovered goods. Nick, do you remember that catamaran we recovered from the Solent about five years ago?'

'Sure do, quite a big vessel as I recall.'

'Yes, it was and despite the nasty-looking damage to the hull it was actually quite repairable. It was later put up for auction and Lloyds got just over £80k for it of which we got somewhere around £6k, not a fortune but a few of those each year helps to keep our offices painted and well furnished.

'Now I can see you all doing the sums in your heads and although the final figures have yet to be confirmed the preliminaries are looking very good. We know the cargo was worth about fifty million but there is also the value of the *Tricolor* to be considered which is estimated to be about thirty million pounds, which under normal circumstances would give us a sizeable bonus pay-out.'

'Bloody hell!' interjected Jim 'that could run into millions.'

'Yes, but before you guys start running away with wild figures in your heads you have to know that there has been a huge amount of negotiation and legal arguments about whether the recovery of the *Tricolor* falls under the term "salvage".

'As you are all aware the word salvage is defined as "the rescue of a wrecked or disabled ship or its cargo from loss at sea". Technically what happened with the *Tricolor* did not strictly fall into that category. However, over the last few weeks a deal has now been done with Lloyds, BMW and West Coast Shipping all of which are extremely keen to be seen as being very grateful for the return of the *Tricolor*, its cargo and more especially its crew. Subsequently a substantial pay-out has been agreed, the amount of which I am not at liberty to divulge, but let's just say it runs well into six figures.'

'That's good,' said Nick, 'although I have to say I did secretly harbour some doubts as to what we as a company might receive re the salvage aspect.'

'Yes, not bad for a couple of weeks' work, but that's very easy for me to say, I wasn't the one getting kidnapped, shot at, or nearly ending up at the bottom of the North Sea like the Captain of the *Tricolor*.'

The kitchen fell silent for a moment as the memories came flooding back.

'The directors have therefore decided that due to the

extremely unusual circumstances that surrounded this case they would like to offer you guys a bonus from that fund.

'Nick, you will receive seventy-five K yourself and a bonus for each of the crew of £7500.

'Jim, you will also receive seventy-five K and Anna although you are not officially part of the company YET, we would like to give you twenty-five K as a thank you and to help you with your new life over here in the UK, which as a company we feel we are more than a little responsible for.

'Duggan will receive the same *if* he is freed after his court martial hearing and as you know we are putting every effort into trying to ensure that is the case.

'RB will get a payment of five thousand pounds for his excellent work behind the scenes.

'So, congratulations and thank you to you all, any questions?'

'I will need some time to think about your offer of a new ship,' Nick said thoughtfully. 'There are many pros and cons to consider, yes a larger vessel would be better in so many ways, but with that comes much higher running costs... so?'

'Give it some thought over the next few days, put some ideas for and against down on paper and we can look at the options.'

Anna stood up and walked round to where Nigel was sitting at the head of the table with a very serious look on her face. Putting on a thick Russian accent she leaned down to within a foot of his face.

'You are a very clever man Mr Nigel, I suppose I won't get zee bonus unless I join your company, yes?'

Nigel looked up at her, clearly surprised by how his offer had been taken.

'We would not be able to pay you the money, no, the

company accountants are going to have enough issues paying out Duggan, if he gets off, so paying out two large sums would leave us with some major explaining to do.'

'In vitch case I vood like to accept your offer,' she said still maintaining her accent.

Nigel looked up at her once more, but before he could say anything Anna launched herself at him and kissed him all over his face.

'Ven do I start?'

Nick and Jim erupted into laughter and clapped a round of applause, closely followed by a very relieved Nigel.

As Anna retook her seat Nigel went across to the huge American fridge-freezer and pulled out a bottle of champagne.

'There is one more piece of news that I have that you may be interested in,' he said as he took the foil and cage off the top of the bottle. BMW have asked me to offer you two,' he pointed at Jim and Nick, 'a car each as a thank you for bringing back the cars on the *Tricolor* in one piece and crippling Sergei Petrov's network of second-hand parts outlets. Apparently, they never really liked the arrangement and would obviously prefer to sell their own parts when they are required. Apparently, they are now looking into setting up their own franchised second-hand parts network using Sergei's existing contacts. This they think has several key win points, firstly they have control over the quality of the parts supplied, secondly it puts money back into their coffers and thirdly it will keep the environmentalists happy and give them some good PR.'

'Sounds good to me, so what are they offering?' asked Jim.

'Anything you like, small runabout to large four-by-four take your pick!'

20

The following day Nick, Jim and Anna went into the office together for the first time since their return.

The press had finally given up camping outside and moved onto the next big story, involving the infidelity of a premiership footballer, so at last things were returning to normal on the quayside.

As they entered the office a huge cheer went up, everyone standing to give them a huge ovation.

Jim did an impromptu thank you before introducing Anna to RB and other key staff members with whom she would shortly be working.

Ten minutes later RB took the three of them to one side and gave Jim an envelope in which was a neatly handwritten letter. He unfolded the letter, read it once before reading it again out loud.

To whom it may concern,

I understand that it is your company that has been investigating the strange goings on around the loss and then rediscovery of the Tricolor, my late husband's ship. I have now been officially informed of his loss and although I'm sure there is still plenty to learn of this incident, I just wanted to take this opportunity to thank you all for uncovering what you have and allowing my daughters and I to grieve the loss of a wonderful man.

From what I have been told so far, it looks as if the history books will paint my husband as a corrupt greedy captain who cared little for anyone else but himself.

This could not be further from the truth; he was a good man who toiled hard for his family and treated his co-workers with respect and compassion. This incident was completely out of Ed's character and carried out whilst under a considerable amount of personal pressure for which I have to shoulder much responsibility.

Thank you once again and I wish you continued success in your investigations. God bless.

Yours,

Margaret Collins.

Jim placed the letter back in the envelope and passed it back to RB. Without a word the three men then turned and left the office with a very puzzled Anna in their wake. Down the stairs, through the foyer and along the quayside they went, arriving at the bar of the Malt kiln two minutes later, still with Anna respectfully in tow. The barman recognised the routine and immediately prepared four shots of his finest Irish whiskey and placed them on the bar. Each man and a still confused Anna picked up a glass.

'To Edward Collins,' toasted RB before each man downed the golden liquid and then stood silently for a minute as a mark of respect. Anna followed suit, realising that this was a ritual that needed to be observed and respected and that there would be plenty of time for all the questions she had later on.

March the first came around all too soon and Duggan's court

martial appearance was the last major piece of "tidying up" that affected the Flatpack team. Jim, Anna and Nick had all travelled to Hereford the day before but due to the secrecy around Duggan's past all they could do was wait outside for the verdict. They arrived early and were escorted to an anteroom to what appeared to be a gymnasium and twenty minutes later witnessed the arrival of the Judge Advocate and six serving officers who between them would issue the verdict on the case. Ten minutes after their arrival Duggan and his solicitor were escorted into the court by two military police officers. He was smartly dressed in a charcoal-coloured suit, the only giveaway to his military background being his dark cropped hair. He seemed genuinely surprised to see his newfound friends waiting for him and gave them a guarded smile as he was led past.

'So, what's the procedure then?' asked Nick aware that Jim had been doing some homework on the workings of the British system.

'Well according to my research this is now looking particularly serious. The Judge Advocate can be joined by anywhere between three and seven officers who effectively act as a jury. They are known as The Board and unlike a civil court the judge will consult with The Board to decide if the charges are to be upheld and then ask for a majority verdict. Once this has happened, he will then also consult with them as to the punishment.'

'So what's worrying you then?' asked Nick.

'Well, the number of officers present seems to be dependent on the magnitude of the case. We just witnessed six officers with the Judge Advocate, that means it's being viewed as very serious.'

'Maybe,' said Nick, 'but I like to look at it from a different perspective. The more people on a jury the more chance there is of a split decision and if it's tight that could clearly work in Duggan's favour.'

'Let's hope you're right,' said Jim clasping Anna's hand for moral support.

'In my experience with the military, it is rare for a case such as this to go the wrong way,' offered Anna. 'There has been no real crime committed, Duggan didn't steal anything, didn't do someone some harm, or even bring the army into disrepute, all he did was go AWOL due to the pressures he was under whilst serving undercover. There are only a handful of people that know this and, unless he has been keeping something from us, there has been no real damage done to your Queen and Country.'

'Fingers crossed, eh,' offered Nick holding up both hands with his first two fingers crossed over each other.

Forty minutes later they heard the sound of several chairs being pushed back across the wooden floor as their occupants rose.

The double doors opened and the Judge Advocate and his board marched forth from the room. A few moments later Duggan and his solicitor appeared at the door flanked by the two military police officers. The two policemen paused for a moment before marching off down the corridor.

Duggan turned and thanked his solicitor before turning to his friends.

'Well, I don't know about you guys, but I need a bloody drink.'

This book was inspired by actual events involving a ship called the *Tricolor* which following a collision with another vessel in December 2002, sank in just 30 metres of water with its cargo of Volvos, Saabs and BMWs seventeen nautical miles off Dunkirk in the English Channel. Over the following weeks and despite the deployment of marker buoys and patrol vessels to keep shipping away from the wreck, three more vessels managed to hit the sunken ship which was lying on her side just below the surface. Because of its location, where two shipping lanes merged, a decision was made to salvage the ship and between July 2003 and October 2004 she was cut up using a carbide-encrusted cutting cable that sliced the wreck into nine sections of 3,000 tonnes each.

It was as I was reading about this on Wikipedia that my curiosity was spurned on to investigate the losses involved. In 2002 it was estimated that the cargo was worth about thirty million pounds, although at the time industry experts said the retail value would be almost twice that much. Then there was the value of the ship itself and its salvage value which again rose into the millions of pounds, seemingly huge sums to the everyday man on the street.

Clearly my version of events in no way correlates with the facts surrounding this accident, but the large sums involved got me thinking…

I hope you have enjoyed the experiences of the *Sandie Watson*'s crew in a corrupt and broken world and if you would like to continue to follow their adventures look out for *The Castle in the Hill* which will follow, shortly.